Rage in Silence

A NOVEL BASED ON THE LIFE OF GOYA

Rage in Silence

A NOVEL BASED ON THE LIFE OF GOYA

by DONALD BRAIDER

G. P. PUTNAM'S SONS   NEW YORK

For Lucia and Malcolm Reiss, with affection and gratitude. And for the doctors and nurses of St. Patrick's Hospital, Dublin.

—*Compadre, quiero cambiar*
mi caballo por su casa,
mi montura por su espejo,
mi cuchillo por su manta.
Compadre, vengo sangrando,
desde los puertos de Cabra.
—*Si yo pudiera, mocito,*
este trato se cerraba.
Pero yo ya no soy yo,
ni mi casa es ya mi casa.

FEDERICO GARCÍA LORCA

PART I

María

one

HE WAS SQUAT AND STRONGLY MADE, like a blacksmith, inclining to fleshiness, with a puffy, clean-shaven face, a high, clear forehead, and bright black eyes. He was, on this afternoon in February, 1795, incongruously dandified in a well-tailored cloak of fine gray serge and a tall beaver hat of the same shade; a man of his conformation should be of more subdued a taste.

He appeared to be annoyed as he stumped from the door of his house in the fashionable Alcalá section of the city. He nodded curtly to a footman who opened the door of his admirable carriage and made no perceptible acknowledgment of the man's assistance as he settled himself within. The footman closed the door and joined the coachman on the box. A pair of handsome, brightly caparisoned horses responded eagerly to the driver's whip. The carriage jerked forward, beginning its brief journey to the Palacio de Liria on the outskirts of Madrid, where its single passenger, Don Francisco Goya y Lucientes, was to discuss with the Duchess of Alba the possibility of his painting portraits of herself and her husband.

Goya was nearly fifty. Second only to his dying brother-in-law, Francisco Bayeu, he was the most respected painter of Spain; he was certainly the richest, and without peer among portraitists. He was a director of the Academia de Bellas Artes de San Fernando. He had received every honor and accolade his country could bestow on an artist except two posts still officially tenanted by Bayeu, who was fourteen years older.

Goya possessed great influence, the reward of a consuming ambition harnessed to consummate skill and a genius for giving pleasure to his patrons. Close friends occupied many of the highest posts of government. (It troubled him profoundly that others, having similarly served the previous regime, now languished in exile or even in prison.) Among those who had supported him substantially during his long, agonizingly gradual rise from impoverished nonentity to his present position were numerous aristocrats. Even royalty had figured significantly in his career; a dozen years before, he had spent six weeks at the extensive country estate of Don Luis de Borbón, dead brother to the previous king, Carlos III. There he had painted portraits of this prince, his children, and his beautiful morganatic wife. He had been privileged to ride with his host across the blasted countryside of Ávila in pursuit of game. This royal patronage had been of crucial importance for Goya.

He was a great figure, and this was what he had resolutely intended to be since childhood. He had every reason to be proud of what he had achieved. But at the end of each stage of his climb, his satisfaction had been mitigated by grimness; he must go higher still. He couldn't be content until he had reached the very top. Now, for all practical purposes, he was there. But the game no longer seemed worth the candle. For Goya was embittered—not by the degree of success he already knew, but by the galling appreciation that there was so little true pleasure to be derived from a success whose sweetest fruits he was incapable of tasting.

Two years earlier, Goya had been struck down, while on a visit to Cádiz, by an illness that had nearly finished him. For weeks after this sudden seizure, his doctor and attending friends believed him to be on the point of succumbing. It even appeared to them that this death would be providential; he was blind, the worst conceivable fate to befall an artist. He was deaf as well. Though much impaired, his sight was restored to him. He had thereafter to wear spectacles for reading and for work.

But he remained stone-deaf, and every physician he consulted was in accord with the original prognosis: He would never hear again. To a man who enjoyed music much more than art, this loss was devastating. No longer could he sing in his rumbling baritone the songs of his native Aragón to his own guitar accompaniment. Nor was there more than nostalgic joy in the *seguidillas* which, since boyhood, had been among his favorite diversions. The dances without the music were caricatures, abortive and maddening; to try to imagine the accommodating sound was merely frustrating.

When his recovery was as complete as it seemed likely ever to be, Goya sought refuge in adultery. These were not his first extramarital excursions; in a capital scarcely less renowned than Paris for such dalliance, his reputation as a womanizer was particularly distinguished. Now, however, he discovered that sound was intimately related with sexual delight. The moans, the giggles, the laments and cries of the moment's mistress, as well as his own bellowed responses, were an integral part of the whole. The feverish silence of his new contacts was disconcerting, in much the same way as he was upset by the mimes of the *seguidillas*. After several depressing experiences with women who had, theretofore, afforded him great pleasure, Goya declared to his friends that he was renouncing their company forever—an oath which they received with incredulity. It was, they said, improbably radical; he might as reliably assure them that he was about to take holy vows.

Goya's reaction to their derision was less than gracious, and he avoided them for a time. To one who had been gregarious since infancy, for whom more than an hour by himself was almost insupportable, this experiment with solitude was doomed from the start. Deafness augmented the horror. When he was alone now, the silences were not silent, but filled with the shrieks and shrills and howls that had, again and again since earliest recollection, echoed harrowingly through his nightmares—the most dismaying features of his occasional illnesses and periodic depressions. These were more fearful now, because they were the only sounds of his life.

In despair of his efforts to teach others more than the rudiments of a sign language that would make their thoughts intel-

ligible to him, Goya learned to read lips, which made at least
basic communication possible—though he often complained
that Spaniards spoke without opening their mouths. There was
a single compensation for the loss of hearing: His other senses
had become more acute, especially those of touch and smell. Yet
the chief result of this increased sensitivity was to render him
more than usually nervous.

The isolation imposed on him by his deafness was the most
terrible aspect of this new and terrible existence. Sacrificed at
greatest loss was the wonderfully easy conviviality of the hours
spent at the *taberna* where, since his arrival in Madrid as a
youth more than thirty years ago, he had made and gathered
with most of his closest friends. On the arm of his ancient scribe,
Pedro Gómez, or his main assistant, the younger Ascensio Julio,
he still made the familiar journey almost every evening—but
the happiness was out of it. He was easily confused by a conversation involving more than one other person, and when the talk
became animated and general, he gave up any attempt to follow
its direction. Instead, he bibulated even more than was his
generous custom, and grumbled.

His friends called him Paco, and they loved him; though
when he wasn't with them they agreed reluctantly that the
changes wrought by his illness were disquieting. Gone were his
garrulous gaiety and his resonant gusts of country laughter
which seemed to shake the walls of the smoky room. No more
roisterous or melancholy songs about love or death or the
corrida. No more ringing affirmations: "I am Spain." "The
garrote for all Jesuits." "My piss tastes better than this manzanilla."

In vain were their attempts to persuade him to retell the
details of some of his more celebrated escapades such as the
seduction of a group of pretty nuns in Rome, where he had
been a student. The numbers of deflorations thus accomplished
varied from version to version; as did the size of the gang, also
in the Eternal City, that had attacked him, attempted to rob
him ("though I had nothing in my purse but dust") , and been
driven off in astonished confusion by the vigor of his bare-
handed defense. "A Spaniard is worth ten Italians," this ac-

count usually concluded. But now Goya sullenly brushed aside
their blandishments. "I tell fairy tales only when I'm happy."

Paco Goya's disposition had never been equable. But in an
endearing way, there had been in the past a reasonable measure
of raucous good humor to counterbalance the outbursts of
temper. His notorious querulousness had been more than offset
by expressions of great generosity, mawkish sentimentality, and
occasional bucolic wit. Now he seemed to live in a perpetual
condition of self-pitying anger, the rage different and somehow
more menacing than before—black, surly, profound. It took
almost nothing to infuriate him—an overturned glass, a garbled
phrase, a glance whose meaning he mistook. His friends continued to love Paco for the man he had been, and they pitied
him lovingly for the man he had become.

They weren't alone in having to suffer his rages. Josefa
Bayeu, his meek, sickly wife of more than twenty years, would
not have imagined it possible to regret a change in Paco. Any
alteration, she thought, could be only for the better. Nevertheless, the conduct that had so distressed her throughout most of
the years of their marriage seemed, in contrast to his present
blackness, mere naughtiness—artist's license. Rarely had he
rubbed her nose in the squalor of his miscreant behavior, and
then only when provoked by what he considered her prurience.
Today, deprived of so many of the pleasures to which she had
objected, Paco turned to her a face she had never seen before.
He terrified her. When she was alone with him, Josefa felt the
urge to withdraw, to run away, to hide from him, from all
existence—since, for her, Paco *was* almost all existence.

Yet she braved as best she could the whirlwind that was her
altered husband. She was sadder and more wistful. She was more
silent—and appreciated the irony of *that* where he was concerned. Her great brown eyes widened with alarm as they were
held by his baleful glance. He wasn't the boy of sixteen she had
beheld in her brother's salon for the first time—the gawky, ill-
dressed fellow whose peasant awkwardness she had found so
amusing, his beautiful voice so beguiling. Nor was he the man
of twenty-six whom she had married, nor was he the father who
had sobbed helplessly over the death of each child she had

borne him. He was unrecognizable. His face was gutted by the illness and by dissipation, the never-smiling eyes red with drink, the voice slurred, uncertain of its volume or timbre, the mouth no longer voluptuous but flabby, the manner tense. It was as if he were motivated by some inchoate fury.

However much she feared for her own safety, Josefa had greater misgivings for that of little Javier, their only child. She had recently taken to placing herself between Paco and the boy. He was only eleven and must be protected against a distracted father who might, without evident provocation, lash out even at the sole mortal in whom he had, until his illness, always vested a perfect, blind affection. She couldn't prevent herself from making this impulsive gesture, though she well understood that it signified a good deal more than maternal solicitude. For Javier as well as for Paco, it signified separation.

The boy cynically relished the exacerbation of a division between parents of which he had long been conscious. He found security and comfort in his mother's shadow. So it had always been. Papa was to be feared, to be avoided, to be scorned—save, of course, as Mama indulgently pointed out, that it was *he* who provided the necessities and the luxuries. And for Javier, this was a vital exception. He learned to play Paco off against Josefa in the higher interest of his exceeding greed. For in things, Javier had early discerned a quite adequate substitute for love.

The man who rode in the splendid carriage through the broad, tree-lined streets of Madrid considered himself precisely as much a physical and moral shambles as did his sorrowful wife and friends. It was pitiable. No one knew better than he how he had suffered, how he suffered now; and no one gave the matter greater attention. Broken in health and spirit, he soldiered on, like an old overladen mule; he continued to live. He was mindlessly propelled onward if not upward. It was easier to follow the patterns established in the past than to try to create new ones whose delights, he doubted not, would be no prettier.

Curiously, there was a single drive left to him, the passion to go on accumulating gold. Not that Goya had any cause to fear for his financial well-being. His oldest friend, the Zaragozan merchant Martín Zapater, had advised him from the onset of his success to invest his savings in property. Another intimate, Ceán Bermúdez, a banker and historian of Spanish art, had counseled him in these acquisitions. So Goya's wealth was as solid as the soil of Spain. But the very thought that it might *not* be, the very thought of poverty could stiffen him with terror. As vivid as the most brilliant sunset were memories of the penury that had been so poignant and bitter a part of childhood; thin soup, stale bread, sour wine, poor clothes, and the terrible, biting cold of the winter wind coursing down the valley of the Ebro, rattling the windows of his father's house in Zaragoza. So he continued to paint. Besides, it helped to relieve the monotony, the boredom of life as it had become since his illness, and to shut out the hallucinations of imagined sounds that inhabited the awful loneliness of his deafness.

The summons to make an appearance at the Palacio de Liria had been completely unexpected. He had assented automatically; she was a duchess. A woman of lesser rank would have had to come to his studio. There had been many years when this opportunity would have evoked tremors of excitement, when he would have been as thrilled as a schoolboy at the prospect of a first formal encounter with the person so often characterized as the greatest lady of Spain.

He had seen her often, of course, but at a distance: in the Plaza de Toros of Madrid, in a palace ballroom, at a party given by the Duchess of Osuna, who had been for more than a decade Goya's mistress and his most faithful patron. Once, he had been casually introduced to the great lady. She had accepted his greeting with a small, indifferent smile and returned her gaze to the man she had been talking with—a *torero,* an actor, a dancer, a poet, perhaps; her current lover, or the lover to be. The greatest painter in Spain had made no impression on her. He detested her in that instant as one could detest only what was most desired and most surely unattainable.

From his first sight of her at relatively close range, at a royal ball ten years before, the Duchess of Alba had seemed to Goya the most completely desirable woman he had ever seen. Her grandeur was definitive; she was more regal by leagues than the slatternly Princess of the Asturias (who was now, alas, Spain's queen). La Alba carried herself like a goddess, certain of her beauty and elegance to such a point that all the obvious considerations of self seemed to have been disdained. There she was. That was all anyone needed to know.

"I'd paint *her* portrait for nothing," Paco had said to Josefa, who was beside him as the duchess passed on the arm of her frail-looking husband. Josefa had understood, and confessed to her pillow that night that since her husband must sleep in arms other than her own, she would prefer to be betrayed by the Duchess of Alba than by any other woman she had ever beheld. From an utterly faithful wife, there could not possibly be a higher compliment. Yet Doña María de Alba was the only great lady of Spain who had not earnestly solicited Goya's services as portraitist—until now.

And now it was palpably too late. Not even a genuine goddess could arouse his interest. Paco reckoned himself a dead man—not like Francho Bayeu, who was literally dying, but as a shell that persisted in living because the tissues of his body were more obstinate than the will. He didn't want the time his doctors had so cleverly managed to borrow for him. He was sure that his days were numbered (if any, in fact, were left to him), that he was dying, like his beloved Spain, and of the identical malady—decay.

But had this call come to him only three years sooner . . . Goya removed his hand and leaned his head against the blue velvet upholstery of his carriage, trying to drive the tantalizing reflection from his gloomy, tormented mind. It was too fraught with rue to be bearable, even to a man who had renounced the world of pleasure, who knew too well that all his capacity for passion had been expended, that he had been shriven of every goad but greed and rage.

Her full name was Doña María del Pilár Teresa Cayetana de Silva y Álvarez de Toledo, thirteenth Duchess of Alba. Her husband of nearly twenty years was Don José Álvarez de Toledo Osorio Pérez de Guzmán el Bueno, eleventh Marqués de Villafranca. He was thirty-nine, six years older than his wife, and he had long suffered from imperfect health. The duke's consuming interest was the chamber music of Bach, Haydn, and Mozart; the duchess' predilection for the more passionate compositions and improvisations of Spain he thought deplorable.

Their different tastes in music characterized the whole of their relationship. He required order and tranquillity; she demanded and thoroughly relished a regime of benign anarchy. He was in all things temperate, even in his occasional pederasty; she was in most things profligate. The couple was childless, a condition that was particularly sad for the duchess, for she was an only child and therefore the last of the direct line of the Alba family. More upsetting was her realization, based on more than one very good reason, that the failing of impotence was hers. Perversely, however, she blamed *him*, and treated him now and then to extravagant vilification. Mostly, she pitied him for the neat, circumscribed, painful little existence he preferred—and went her own promiscuous, generous, sentimental way, the way of the classic romantic that she was.

The duchess wholly deserved her reputation for capriciousness and eccentricity. She had inherited these propensities from her paternal grandfather and her mother, the dominant figures of her childhood. Her father had died when she was eight, so that the Alba title had passed to her on the death of the old duke—an apostle of the French Enlightenment who had nevertheless remained a staunch absolutist. Her mother had been an indefatigable patron of every art, a worshiper of men, a lover and protectress of children. Traits of these quite different progenitors blended without conflict in the temperament of the duchess. She was not a whit less haughty than her grandfather in practical and social dealings. She hadn't the least uncertainty about her unassailable position in Spanish society; she was, in her own right, one of the richest women in Europe, and she readily understood the security this vast wealth afforded her. She could be totally indifferent to the opinion of others. She did as she pleased, and no one, not even the king, stood in her path.

Doña María possessed her late mother's buoyancy and enthusiasm for life, but only a modicum of her all-encompassing affection for the arts. In the theater, she enjoyed especially the frothy, stylish, witty plays of manners and morals that were imported from France—that country which was the fountainhead of aristocratic culture in Madrid. But she was unable to understand her ancestors' or her husband's admiration for painting and sculpture; the pictures and statues that had been part of her immense inheritance bored her. They were dull and static, lifeless. Intellectual discussion invited her immediate scorn, particularly if the subject turned to theology. On the other hand, she was passionately interested in politics and the gossip involving royalty and politicians. She was devoted to her country and she despised the queen.

She loved fine clothes and would pay any price to obtain them. She loved to dance. She loved games. She loved to ride or drive through the countryside of her many estates. She loved the *corrida,* in part for its pageantry, in part because she loved to watch the movements of the lithe young *toreros,* and she rejoiced without malice in her usually successful rivalry for their attentions with the older Duchess of Osuna, the only woman she deigned to call friend. Unlike La Osuna or the queen, however, Doña María never permitted herself to become the slave of any man's body. If it seemed that a lover was demanding too much of her time or patience, too greedy for her gifts, she would rid herself of him with neither ceremony nor regret. There were plenty of others where he had come from.

Outrageously arrogant and self-willed in the company of her peers, she felt no need to be pretentious with her inferiors—and she had no doubt that they *were* inferior. She took delight in circulating incognito at popular fiestas, whether in Madrid or in the provinces, dressed in the gowns of her maidservants. Of those who criticized this practice, she asked coolly, "How else shall I find out just what my people think of the life I give them? I'm responsible for the happiness of fifty thousand souls." And she was speaking the truth.

She took a detailed interest in the operation of her domains all over Spain. Her concern was as much humane as financial. She never forgot her grandfather's apothegm: "A happy peasant can double your harvests. An unhappy one can ruin *you* as well as himself." If she learned that an overseer had been excessively zealous in the exercise of his duties, he was flogged and dismissed. Sometimes she administered the punishment in person if the offense was particularly heinous—and wept for days afterward.

She loved practical jokes and would go to great lengths to bring them off. When the queen appeared at an important gathering dressed in a magnificent gown she had just received from Paris, Doña María had a dozen copies made and commanded her servants to wear them at a reception she herself gave the following week. This gesture did nothing to improve relations between the two great ladies which, in any case, had never been cordial.

The duchess detested the queen for her ugliness, for her ignorance, for the authority she exerted over her vain, stupid, sluggish husband; but mainly for her abject dependence on the flesh of Don Manuel Godoy, her young lover, who was in practice now the ruler of Spain. The queen hated the duchess for her wealth, her youth, her beauty, and her complete disdain for royal sensibilities. "The Albas were conquering Europe when *her* people were minding sheep in the Abruzzi," said Doña María of Doña María Luisa de Parma. Whether wounded by the tone or the accuracy of such observations, the queen promised herself revenge.

The duchess adored children and followed her mother's example by adopting a pair—María de la Luz, the mulatto daughter of a servant who had been importuned by a black sailor in Cádiz; and Luis de Berganza, the orphaned son of friends. Undoubtedly her fondness for these waifs was due partially to her inability to bear children of her own. But she felt sure that there was more to her affection than this. Children were to be cherished, and she lavished upon them gifts and attention and embraces, treated them as pets, and sternly supervised the conduct of her old *dueña,* the toothless La Beata, under whose care she placed them.

She was quixotic. Much as she loved the presence of the well-made young men who frequented her salon and her bedchamber, she reserved a different but comparable hospitality for outcasts, the pathetic creatures broken by life who found their easy way to her side. Nothing was more typical of this quality of her personality than the moving tenderness she evinced for Brother Basil, an aged friar who was crippled by arthritis and suffered an impediment of speech so severe that he was incomprehensible to all but her. Why did she shelter him? effete friends inquired. "What would happen to him if I didn't? Should I consign him to one of those charnel houses that the church calls a hospital?" she replied. Brother Basil served no purpose in the household except that whenever she called for him, he was near. "You see," she said, "he's just for me. What more do you think he should be?"

It was Doña María's charity and compassion for those in distress, the wretched and the crushed, that inspired the Duchess of Osuna, who had already done her own inadequate best to help Goya out of his despondency, to speak to her of the painter's plight.

"Here's a whipped cur for you, María. But if anyone can bring him back to life, it's you. You have all the joy and fervor he needs."

The younger woman was surprised. *"You* offer *me* a man?"

"What's left of him."

"But *Goya?* After making me swear to leave him to you?"

"I release you from that oath."

"But I have nothing to say to him."

"Ask him to paint your portrait."

"You know how I feel about painting."

The Duchess of Osuna laughed. "I know how you feel about Brother Basil."

Until the majordomo announced Goya's arrival, Doña María had forgotten her summons to him. After her conversation with the Duchess of Osuna, she had composed the note casually, re-flexively, as if writing a draft against her bank—nothing more significant than that. However, she quite enjoyed the unex-pected and watched with sympathetic amusement the painter's awkward progress across the exquisite carpet of her brilliantly decorated reception room to the chair she occupied.

But how he had changed since her last sight of him. It was tragic. La Osuna's gift was chaff. His meaty hand grasped hers gingerly and barely brushed it to his lips, as if he feared he might do her harm—she, who had so often cheerfully accepted the brutal attentions of the most lascivious young men of Spain. Was he, then, so ill at ease, so apprehensive, so deferential? Or was it that he didn't care?

Her black eyes, smiling, rose to meet his and at once became grave. His face was old and ravaged. Obviously, he ate too much and probably drank too much as well. But what intensity she saw, what force, what fury . . . what promise of passion. She was repelled. She was attracted. She was torn. She shuddered and withdrew her hand, placing it almost demurely in her lap, and looked away.

"I'm so happy you've come, Don Francisco. Do sit down." When her guest made no motion to comply with the request, she returned her eyes to his, mildly surprised.

He was shaking his shag of graying hair and pointing to an ear, his expression apologetic but not abjectly so. "I hear nothing, Doña María. You must speak slowly and distinctly, and look at me when you do. Then I'll be able to understand most of what you say."

"I forgot," she said. "Forgive me." She indicated a chair be-side her and shifted her position as he sat down so that she faced him. "You're very welcome," she added, enunciating as clearly as she could.

"That's right," he responded. "If you do it that way, I'll know what you're saying. You wanted to see me about two portraits."

"Not simply that, Don Francisco. The pleasure of seeing you . . ."

"Don't lie, Doña María. Everyone knows that it's no pleasure to see Goya these days."

She overlooked the interruption. "Portraits of myself and Don José."

Goya grimaced. "Very expensive. You can have them much cheaper from another fellow."

"As good as Goya's?" She lifted her black brows.

"No."

"You prefer not to paint us, then?"

"I have much work."

"Then why did you come?"

"You sent for me. One doesn't decline a duchess' summons."

The reply amused her. "That's not the way it is at all. You want me to implore you, don't you? Goya paints a portrait only when the subject begs him. Well, I'll not beg. I've never done that. I shan't start now."

"I *have* begged, Doña María, but I no longer have to. So you see, no matter how different we are, we're equals."

"What a suggestion."

"But precise, isn't it? You have more than you need. So do I. You want something I can give you. And I don't particularly care whether you get it or not."

His audacity surprised her. No one had ever so treated her before. She kept her temper and asked him evenly, "Do I understand that we're bargaining over the price?"

It was Goya's turn to laugh. "I haven't even agreed to your proposal. How can it be a question of money?"

"Well, what is it? You're worried perhaps that Doña María Teresa de Osuna might object?"

"That is a thing of the past," he answered coldly.

"But you know there was a time when she would have objected, when in fact she *did* object."

"She never owned me." Goya's eyes flashed angrily.

"Yet I always understood . . ."

"Incorrectly, then. Oh, I'm not denying that she and the duke have been kind to me, but you need never have thought me her chattel. I belong to no one."

"How lonely for you."

Paco studied her lovely features, trying to fathom the implications of that phrase. "I am *not* lonely," he finally pronounced, but his tone betrayed him. He shrugged. "My life is no more secret than—" He broke off the sentence and flushed.

"Than *mine?*" Her smile was wry. "Say it, Don Paco. You may be correct, but I think you're boasting. *I'm* more notorious than you."

"If that's so, your beauty is responsible. *My* notoriety comes from my talent."

She grimaced. "Stalemate. Let's begin again. Do you make every potential subject go through such a performance?"

"No. It's just that I wonder at your choosing this moment to ask me, *now*, when I'm past my prime."

"What do you imagine my motive?"

"I imagine nothing. I'm perplexed."

"Where's all that self-assurance of a moment ago?"

"That I know myself to be a fine painter still doesn't mean that you necessarily *think* me so. But then, how would you know? Do you know anything about painting?"

"Nothing."

"So you could have other reasons to send for me. I think you do. But I don't know what they might be."

"You may suspect me, Don Paco, but I have the impression that I displease you in some other way too. You don't admire my face?"

"You know better."

"How could I?" she asked, but her eyes disclosed her comprehension.

"You're playing games with me."

"And you don't enjoy that?"

"It makes me want to strangle you."

She considered the sullen, worn features and was torn between mirth and vague apprehension. "How dare you say such a thing to me?"

"I dare anything. I'd easily dare to strangle you."

"You dare to refuse to paint my portrait?"

His mood seemed to shift. "But I've *not* refused, Doña María. I've simply suggested you choose another painter."

"You don't care to please patrons as others do?"

"I used to care about nothing so much. No more."

"You don't even care to paint?"

He reflected for a moment. Did she want to hear the truth? The devil with it. "I never *have* liked it very much."

His candor astonished her. "Then why in God's name did you become a painter?"

"There was no choice, Doña María. We were very poor. My father was a gilder in Zaragoza. Tomás, my older brother, became his apprentice. The shop couldn't support *me* as well. So I entered the studio of José de Luzán and learned painting." As he spoke, Goya's voice softened, his expression warmed, his heavy hands relaxed. "I would have preferred to be a *torero* or a mason or a cabinetmaker, almost anything but an artist. It didn't seem like manly work to me."

"And here you are."

"My mother would permit nothing else. She was of the Lucientes. Her family connections meant everything to her. When I was sixteen, I came to Madrid to study with Francisco Bayeu."

"Your brother-in-law? I didn't know that. He's very ill, I'm told."

"It's only a question of time."

"You don't sound regretful. Because you'll probably take his posts?"

"I *used* to be ambitious, Doña María, but I was never so ambitious that I'd wish the death of a man, even of Francho, whom I don't like very much."

"Yet he was good to you. You worked with him. You married his sister."

"But after that, there were things—it's of no interest."

The duchess sat back and clasped her slender, jeweled fingers. "What a pity you didn't get your wish. I've known some splendid masons and carpenters."

"And some *toreros*."

She was uncertain of her reaction to this addition. Should she be angered or amused? "I don't expect reproaches from my craftsmen."

"*Was* I reproachful, Doña María? Forgive me if I gave that impression. Should I care how you find your pleasure?"

"Certainly not." She made it plain that the subject was closed. "So you became a painter."

"And I arrived by climbing, Doña María, by scrambling. But I've not lost my memory of servitude. People like you don't permit that."

"There are no people like me, Don Paco."

"As your craftsman, I shall try to remember that."

"So, you *will* do the portraits?"

"If you insist."

"Goya, I *demand* a more affirmative answer. You must *want* to paint me. Can you make a good picture when, as it appears, the humor isn't on you?"

"The humor is never on me, Doña María. If I'd had to wait for that, there'd be no pictures by Goya. But whether I want to or not, I can paint the Virgen del Pilár with my eyes closed."

"I'm not a virgin," she said, but the softness of her voice was lost on him.

"Do you expect me to care?"

"A definite answer, Don Paco. Will you paint my portrait or not?"

"Until my illness, it was my greatest hope to have the privilege of painting you. Since our first meeting . . ."

"So? I'm afraid I don't remember that."

Goya's recollection, however, was so vivid that he was seduced by it once again, by her. He winced. "I suppose it's natural that you should forget. It was very brief."

Her smile was compassionate. "I shan't forget you a second time."

"I'll try not to let you."

The duchess discovered that her hands were trembling. She clasped them again. It wasn't the painter's words, but his tone, that moved her. She made her manner brisk and businesslike, but she was unnerved. "It's agreed, then. You'll make portraits of Don José and me?"

He bowed. "At your convenience, Doña María."

"No, Don Paco, at *your* convenience. You've told me how very occupied you are."

He lowered his head. "I occupy myself these days to keep from going mad. Some say I'm mad already."

"Ridiculous. They say the same of me. It doesn't matter. What monstrous self-pity."

"I don't think it really concerns you, Doña María."

"Then why say it to me?"

He stared at her, surprised. "I don't *know*. I honestly don't know." What was happening to him? He smiled deprecatingly. "What I should have said was that I could never be so occupied that your concern would be secondary."

"How gallant. No one told me you were gallant."

"Before I was ill, I used to be quite gallant now and again, as gallant as a country boy *could* be. But recently . . . the spirit hasn't moved me. You bring out the best in me."

She raised a forfending hand. "Oh, no, Don Paco, no, no. I'm not going to allow such flagrant flattery. Must you say the same thing to every woman you paint?" She paused, her expression guileful. "I'm told . . ."

His gesture was the same as hers, his stubby right hand pushing her words away from him. "Lies. I assume you were going to repeat the rumor that Goya makes his best portraits of women only after making love to them."

"Lies?" Her expression was owlish.

"You want a confession?" He amazed himself again. What was this woman doing to him?

"Why not? You've already confessed so much."

"It *has* happened, but not very often. It's not a custom."

"And no great lady has ever refused you?"

He reddened. "Not many, but as I say, it didn't happen very often."

"What a man you must be."

He sighed. "What a man I *was*."

"Poor Goya. And *were* the portraits better for the lovemaking?"

"I'm no judge."

"*Modesty,* Don Paco? You stagger me. I'd understood that
you considered yourself the *only* competent judge of your
work."

"You enjoy mocking me. Why?"

The beautiful duchess stirred uneasily in her elegant French
armchair. This ruin of a man was disturbing, but not in any
way she could have logically foreseen. Her response to him was
not the pity or compassion she felt for Brother Basil or La Beata
or the two children in her care. Her emotions, rather, resembled those she had enjoyed when first meeting the superb
young *torero* Costillares, or Isidoro Maiquez, the actor who was
now captivating all Madrid.

Indeed, she recognized that her feelings were even more profound, more shattering. She failed to understand them, or perhaps she declined to. It didn't matter which, did it? *Love?* For
this hot-eyed old wreck, gross in spite of his fancy clothing,
rude, self-pitying, self-seeking, egocentric? The Duchess of Alba,
who could have any man she chose, selecting Goya, an upstart
from Aragón, a disagreeable, bitter, revolting old hulk of a
bumpkin who might, except for chance, as easily have been
one of her peasants? Her mind boggled at the absurdity of the
idea. *Love?* Impossible. Yet certainly she was feeling for him
more than the familiar, simple, straightforward animality that
governed her relations with other men, the ones she was able to
reject with an arrogant toss of the head. She tried to avert her
eyes from his, and failed. She flushed and blinked rapidly,
trying to compose herself.

The silence was prolonged. His blazing eyes continued to
hold hers. What was he thinking? she wondered. What was *she*
thinking? How ludicrous? How miraculous? How strange? How
ironic? How frightening? How beautiful? She had never before
been shaken to the core—and that such a man should be the
occasion . . . How terrible and wonderful and ridiculous. She
felt, at once, lost and found. She laughed as she began to speak;

then, recalling his deafness, she tapped his wrist, for he had looked away. "The point is that I don't care about the portrait either, Don Paco. I care about *you*."

Goya was stunned. *Had* she said that? *Could* she? Did she mean it? Did she mean it as he interpreted it? Out of the question. His face must be registering his transfiguration. She was smiling. Mocking him again? No, the expression was gentle. What to say?

Before he could find the words, the Duke of Alba came into the room—tall, immaculately groomed, emaciated. "Ah, Goya, I'm happy you've come," he said to the painter's back and was annoyed that his warm welcome prompted no response.

"He's deaf," said the duchess, irritated by the interruption and assuming now her perfunctory social demeanor. "You'll have to speak to his face."

The duke moved hastily forward. Goya sprang to his feet and made a stiff little bow as he took the man's fragile hand. "I'm honored, Don José, that you and Doña María desire my services."

"We should have asked you long before this if I'd had my way. Some silliness on my wife's part, an agreement with Doña María Teresa de Osuna."

"I understand."

Don José appeared startled, and not happily so, by the artist's easy answer. "That's more than *I* can say. Just women's pettiness, if you ask me."

"No one did ask you," said the duchess icily. "As a matter of fact, María Teresa *suggested* that I ask Don Paco."

Apprehensive that the painter might grasp the tenor of the dispute, Don José twiddled his fingers and stepped adroitly to an inlaid harpsichord at the end of the salon. He placed his left hand on the polished surface of the lid and whirled gracefully to confront Goya and his wife, striking a pose that was intended to be heroic. It was merely comical. "I think I'd like you to paint me this way. The musical association, you understand."

Goya had not caught all the words, but the meaning was plain. He approached, shaking his head regretfully. "Another

pose would serve you better, Don José, something a little more
natural, preserving the musical association, of course. If you
don't mind my saying so, the way you're standing now makes
you look like a Roman senator or a general."

The duchess giggled. The duke blanched. "If you mean to
paint me, Goya, you'll paint me in the way I choose. Is that
clear?"

"Perfectly, Don José. But if you want a portrait by Goya,
you'll have to accept my suggestion."

The great aristocrat was incredulous. "You have the
temerity—"

"It's not a question of temerity, Don José. I know about
painting as you, I'm sure, know about music. Even in the days
when I could hear, I'd never presume to tell you how a piece
should be performed. Do *you* presume to tell *me* how to paint a
portrait?"

The ruffled duke pointed to a large canvas suspended on the
wall near the instrument. "That's the sort of thing I have in
mind."

Goya chortled. "Good God. Do you really want to appear as
wooden as that poor old codger?"

"That poor old codger," he said with acerbity, "happens to
be the duchess' grandfather. And it was painted by Mengs."

"Then, *señor*, as I've just been saying to Doña María, you
should engage another painter. I'm not Mengs."

The duke was scandalized. "You don't admire Mengs?"

"I admired him. I even liked him personally. He was very
good to me. He gave me the first commissions I ever received in
Madrid. But his work"—the painter sought a suitable phrase—
"was too polite, completely on the surface of things. He had no
depth, no feeling, no understanding. As I say, too polite, too
timid."

The Duke of Alba breathed deeply several times, as if he
were trying to gather courage to say what was on his mind.
"You needn't imagine, Goya, that the fact that you're probably
going to make love to my wife gives you the right to presume
with me." The man was panting, exhausted by his daring.

Goya trembled with indignation. "What a hideous thing to say."

"What a hideous thing to *contemplate*. I trust I don't have to mention your reputation."

The artist's laugh was wholehearted. "Do I have to mention *yours,* Don José? At least *I* don't have small boys smuggled in through my back door in the dead of night."

The duke gasped and fled, teetering precariously in his embarrassment and offense. Goya turned to Doña María. "I'm sorry. As usual when I get angry, I said more than I intended."

She was unmoved. "No more than the truth."

"You don't object?"

"We go our own ways."

"But what could have made him say such a thing to me. At *my* age, I've learned discretion."

"Oh, Don Paco, if that was an example of your discretion, I shudder to think what you were like when you were younger."

"I mean, I've tried to avoid scandal. There was no cause for him to say that. It was a gratuitous insult to you as well as me."

"You're more provocative than you seem to think. Are you so direct and brutal with all your subjects?"

"Only with the ones who think they know better than I. But what he said—"

The duchess grinned. "Poor José believes he knows my nature."

"And does he?"

"Who can say?"

"*You,* I should think."

"Does that mean you expect me to seduce you?"

"You know very well that you've seduced me already."

Her smile was small and resigned but not at all sad. "Then, Don Paco, the seduction has been mutual."

"I know." He tried to keep a note of calm in his voice, but he trembled.

"Will you give *me* value?" She smiled.

"I don't know, Doña María. We require a time and a place for that to be determined."

"The time is now, *amigo*, and the place is here." She grasped his powerful biceps and propelled him from the room.

Goya smiled, then shivered with alarm as he recalled the damned silence that had doomed him before to such frustration. Would this occasion be different?

Dramatic. Her body was dramatic, all tensions and contrasts; cream of white tinged with pink, nipples of madder, the lamp-black of her thickets. Her flesh was completely under her control, plentiful without superfluity. It was firm and springy as his hand pressed its journey from ankle to breast, to the strong chin. He turned her face to his and kissed her. She smiled, half in pleasure, half in anxiety. She didn't know him. He would be gentle, yet he sensed the ferocity and precocity of her desire as she collected the energy of her muscles to greet his entry. They trembled. He knew that this first sweet thrusting would be over too quickly, and he feared to disappoint her. He looked for a sign and was relieved to see a tranquil smile of glad exhaustion. He loved her. For God's sake, he *loved* her. She had brought him back from the dead. It was a miracle. The silence hadn't mattered. He was alive again.

"I love you," he murmured.

She shook her head. "You don't have to say that."

"If I hadn't felt the need, I wouldn't have said it."

"You seemed to say it so easily. Do you say it often?"

"Only once before in my life."

"I don't believe you."

"Would I lie?"

"To please me, to flatter me."

"No."

"Whom did you say it to?"

"To Josefa, my wife."

"You love her still?"

"I *loved* her, or I thought I loved her. *You* make me ask myself whether it was real love or not."

"Do you make love to her still?"

"No."

"Why not?"

"Because, when I came back from Cádiz, after I was ill, I tried to, and she wouldn't let me. I swore to her I'd never touch her again. Besides, she's never liked it much . . . woman's weal, that kind of thing. But I have a deep affection for her. She's the mother of my son." He toyed with a nipple and was pleased to see it contract beneath the gentle pressure of his fingers. "But not love. Or no longer love."

"And La Osuna? You never loved her?"

"You want me to say I love no one but you. I've already said it. Do you forget everything so quickly?"

"I want to be sure of my position, Paco."

"You're supine."

"My *permanent* position."

"Permanence? How can you possibly think of permanence in the afternoon?"

She pouted unconvincingly. "I don't care about the security of my lovers, but I care about my own."

"All right, María Teresa and I were useful to each other for a time. She took advantage of my body and I took advantage of her influence. It was over even before my illness. I'd become too old for her. As one ages, one prefers to love the young."

"Ah?" The fine dark brows were lifted.

"Yes," he said. "I *wonder* about you."

"So do I. Do *I* love well."

"I don't want to talk about it."

"I disappointed you."

"I'd rather not discuss it."

"Yet you'll talk about me with your friends at the *taberna*."

"You know a lot about me."

"You thought I'd let myself be seduced by just anyone? And you *will* tell them about me, won't you?"

"I think not."

"Because I was so easy a conquest?"

"Because you're a *love,* not a conquest. I could tell them about a woman, but not about a love."

"Tell *me.* I'm a good mistress?"

"Will there be other men?"

"Perhaps. You don't want me to pretend with you, do you?"

"Please God, no."

"And there'll be other women for *you.*"

"I doubt it." He caressed her rich belly and rejoiced in her responsive shudder. "I'm too weary to keep even *one* woman for very long. You'll see."

She snorted. "I'll not believe that and I don't think you believe it either. You're a mighty man and you know it."

"You could make me think so again."

"You'll be climbing over another woman soon."

"No. I told you. I love you, María. There's a total difference."

"And you've enthralled *me,* Paco. It's preposterous, but it's true."

"You love me, then?"

She was touched by the apprehensive note, but replied honestly. "I love you *now.* It's the first time I've said that to anyone. Ask me no more."

two

⚛ IT *was* LOVE, and of comparable measure, though of somewhat different quality, for each of them. They contrived to meet nearly every day, at first at the Palacio de Liria ("the Palace of Delirium," Goya described it), where there was the excuse of the portraits. For all his initial remonstrances with Goya, the duke was delighted by the master's achievements, though he felt it necessary to observe that the portrait of the duchess was superior to his own, an opinion in which both Paco and María could only concur. The lovers also met occasionally in the painter's studio; but in the early days of their affair, they resorted primarily to a secluded apartment made available to them by the amiable and discreet Duchess of Osuna, who had brought them together.

Inevitably, passion came first, and it was daily more gratifying. Great as were its joys, however, these were gradually, but never completely, eclipsed by those of companionship. After their first violent collisions, when all that seemed to matter was the hot union of their flesh, came the more tranquil pleasures of simply being together in a room by themselves. So satisfying were these hours for Goya that even after they had parted for the day, he no longer dreaded the silence, for it was filled not with the sinister figures of dream and imagination, but with images of his beloved María. And in *his* absence, the beautiful young duchess contemplated with diminishing astonishment the marvel of discovering herself to be content to be the mistress of a man who was nearly old enough to be her father. Was it, she speculated dimly, as simple as that: Was she transferring to Paco the adoration she had felt for her grandfather? It was a thought she spared her lover.

They showered each other with small and large attentions, tokens and phrases to be treasured in secret, amulets to ward off the possibility of a rupture—for both recognized this menace as distinct just because they were the kind of beings they were, mercurially emotional, willful, stubborn, difficult, capricious. Love illuminated their lives, a sun neither had previously known, and in this unexpected radiance, changes occurred in their behavior and dispositions which took all their acquaintances by surprise.

Superficially, it was Paco who seemed the more spectacularly altered. In the months following their first meeting, the lines of his face became less pronounced, his eyes were clearer, his hands steadier, his bearing less ponderous and sluggish. His social manner softened. Indeed, friends of the *taberna* wonderingly acknowledged to one another that never in their long experience of him had Goya appeared serene—yet this was the only adjective applicable to him now. It was a miracle.

After recovering from the shock of finding herself in love, María became aware that her passion for Paco made her care for more than his purely physical well-being; she was concerned about his soul—though she wouldn't try to define more precisely than that just what she meant. *He* mattered; therefore, everything about him mattered. Her life, her being, belonged to him; therefore, her happiness utterly depended on his. And his happiness was incomplete; so, therefore, was hers.

No one was long in the dark about the reason for Goya's transformation. Though he and María had made every reasonable effort to keep their affair a secret, both were aware that in gossipy Madrid the probability was slim. It required the tongue of only one traitorous servant to spread the word; then followed fantastic embellishments on the simple fact. Reactions varied. Many were skeptical. "Beauty and the Beast" was a description much in vogue. Paco's friends were as relieved as they were astounded—but they maintained their equanimity. They understood well enough what Goya saw in the duchess, but what could she see in him? The queen was said to be delighted by the news; there had been a period when the painter had attracted *her*, but since his illness his appeal had dwindled to a nullity. "He's just good enough for La Alba," she was purported to have remarked. "At last she's found the right gutter to wallow in."

Josefa counted her blessings and kept her peace. If the reality of Paco's adultery with the duchess was less edifying than had been her earlier contemplations of it, she could accept with unflawed gratitude its spectacular amelioration of his temperament. Life at home was more tranquil than she had ever known it, in part because he no longer paid much attention to her or even to Javier. For the time being, that had to be enough. Nevertheless, she wept ruefully in the darkened loneliness of her bedchamber, recalling the night in the summer of 1793, shortly after Paco's return from Cádiz, where he had nearly died. Her brother Francho was the only dinner guest. Paco was being nice to him because Bayeu had paid him a long visit during his recuperation in the south. Josefa hoped that the prolonged enmity between husband and brother was finally at an end. But to her, Paco had been beastly throughout the meal, a display for which she compensated by being inordinately gay; it was, after all, the first time they had entertained since his homecoming, and Francho's being their guest appeared a happy augury. And in itself, the beastliness was no surprise; since his return, Paco had been more than usually surly, a development she attributed to his deafness and his continuing frailty.

The moment he drained the last drop of *coñac* from his glass, Paco rose and bowed to his brother-in-law. "Forgive me, Francho. I'm exhausted. I have to go to bed."

He merely glanced at Josefa, but there was no mistaking the hostility, and he left the room without a word to her. Bayeu, embarrassed, hastily excused himself. Vaguely disturbed, Josefa followed her husband to his room only to find him apparently locked in a drunken slumber. She kissed him lightly on the

forehead and retired to her own chamber. With the aid of
Alfonsa, her personal maid, she prepared herself for the night.

Out of a custom so firmly established that it no longer was,
even to her, more than cursory evidence of her intense devotion, she knelt at her bedside and offered to the Virgen del Pilár
of Zaragoza, to Christ, to God, and to the Holy Spirit her
prayers for the protection through the night of herself and those
she loved. When her prayers were ended, she slipped between
the deliciously cool sheets and blew out the candle. Sleep failed
to overtake her with its habitual speed. She thought of Paco's
new darkness, his strangeness. She knew it was wrong of her to
treat him with such circumspection, yet she was helpless. It was
wrong too of Javier, though more understandable, to look on
his father with distaste, to respond so glacially to his offers of
affection. It wasn't Christian; there could be, for Josefa, no
greater sin.

She tried to induce repose by praying for a greater store of
compassion, and as she murmured the appropriate formula, her
door opened softly. There was the sound of footsteps shuffling
hesitantly across the carpet, drawing inexorably closer. Oh, dear
Jesus, Mary, and Joseph, she should have better understood the
reason for Paco's ugly mood at dinner. She should have locked
her door. Josefa closed her eyes and feigned sleep, but her body
stiffened.

He was now at the foot of her bed. His hand grasped the
mattress for support and moved uncertainly upward. His breath
was rasping, drunken, redolent of the wine and brandy he had
imbibed throughout the day. He paused and sat down heavily,
sighing. He bent over her, a hand discovering her right shoulder, his face only inches above hers. "*Amada,*" he whispered
noisily.

She knew she should say something, but what? She remained
silent.

"I couldn't go back to sleep after you kissed me just now.
That was a sweet thing to do. I was thinking about you, and I
suddenly realized that you wanted me."

Josefa uttered a silent prayer but still found no words. He
must feel her shivering beneath his heavy touch. His lips were
on her brow, and she visualized his face.

"Was I mistaken?"

Still no reply, no responsive motion.

"Well, damn it, *I* need *you*." His tone was more peremptory.
She turned away.

"Josefa." This was a command.

"Yes," she mumbled.

"*Querida?*" Now he was plaintive. He laid a coarse palm on
her cheek and caressed it gently, as one might stroke the head of
a dog.

"Yes," she repeated dully. Then it came to her that he
couldn't hear her. She felt herself grow tenser under the increasing passion of his hand.

Goya growled and threw off the covers that sheltered her
from the cool air of the June night. How could she make him
appreciate her feeling of revulsion? She rocked her head fran-
tically from side to side and placed her small hands on his
shoulders, attempting to force him away. But even in his weakened condition he was too strong for her; her frail elbows
buckled as he pressed down on her. He stretched out at full
length beside her, slipping an arm beneath her back, the other
across her chest, and buried his reeking, perspiring head in her
throat.

"No, Paco, no, please," she whimpered, shaking her head.

Why was she resisting him? However repellent, he *was* her
husband. Was she afraid that he might injure her? Not since
their wedding night had he so frightened her. But he had a
perfect right. She must compel herself to yield to him; it was the
will of God. The marriage vows were clear. This injunction,
however, had no effect. She was unable to give herself up to his
pleasure. A force more powerful than either reason or faith
opposed it. He was a stranger to her, or this, at any rate, was
what her body sensed. She could only resist; she had no choice.
Her flesh demanded that its honor be defended against this
intrusion.

Paco persisted. He grew rougher in his handling of her. He raised her nightgown and forced her legs apart, penetrating her with a finger, impatient. This she found exciting. How surprising. Was this what women felt when they were being raped? A pleasure in spite of oneself? The thrill of taking part in something criminal, sinful? The odd thing was that the excitement seemed to be enhanced by her continuing resistance. She went on rebuffing him in the only way left to her; she remained absolutely passive, uttering not a sound, and resolutely repressed every impulse to respond, though her eagerness grew with his growing fever of desire. She permitted herself not so much as a quiver of belly or thighs.

Paco was groaning. He was wailing. He pressed his aroused sex against her leg and continued to prepare her; and still she pretended disinterest. "God damn you, Josefa, be *human.*"

She shook her head again and tried to displace his exciting hand.

"What's *wrong* with me? What's the matter with *you?* What are you thinking of?"

These were reasonable questions. But in the darkness there were to be no answers for the deaf man. He was a stranger. His breath came more rapidly. His hand became more forceful. Tenderly at first, he nibbled at the soft skin of her shoulder. Then, as his passion mounted, so did the ferocity of his bite. She cried out in pain and ecstasy. Though she was certain he felt the vibrations of her larynx against his cheek, he refused to relent.

It was more and more exciting, more and more hideous, more and more corrupt, more and more confusing. She must try to keep her head. It was in this instant that she understood the accuracy of something Paco had said to her years before: "It's practically impossible to rape a woman who doesn't want to be raped." She felt her muscles react involuntarily despite her revulsion. Her flesh was at war with her flesh, her instincts with her instincts, her mind with her mind, her conscience with her conscience.

Suddenly, and before she had time for further reflection, he was inside her, his strong hands clutching at her pathetic little buttocks, their pelvises colliding. This, it struck her, was more rage than love, more fury than desire. He was trying to murder her. He was testifying not to his body's need for hers, but to its hatred. There had been many times when she had wished that Paco would visit her instead of lying with some dancer or actress in a hidden corner of Madrid. Why was there no such wish tonight? She was cursed. "You're a damned Jansenist," he had said to her more than once. She tried to will her body to join with his in this supreme expression of nature's genius. Her flesh refused.

She was perverted. There was no doubt of it. When she had thought it rather attractive to be the wife betrayed (albeit by a duchess), she had in fact been enjoying the role of martyr. Martyrdom by design was, in the happiest light, a perversion; in the most unfortunate view, it was heresy. She could be considered fodder for the Inquisition. She was a ruined woman. Her body was proof. For in spite of her will, the pleasure of this moment could be only Paco's. No, not quite so—and this was the most dannable of all; *her* pleasure derived from the idea that she was being ravished by a stranger. It was too horrible.

Just as she sensed that he was reaching his climax, Josefa screamed and wrenched herself from his grip.

"You silly, selfish bitch," he roared, and struggled clumsily to his feet. She could hear, over the pounding of her anguished heart, the rustle of his nightshirt as he adjusted it. "Never again, do you hear me? Never again. That's the last ride you'll get from me as long as you live. You *liked* it. You *wanted* it, just as much as I did. I could tell that. But you wanted more to spoil it for me. I'll never forgive you for that. You wanted to spit on me the same way that you've been spitting on me since I came home, so smug and proper. But it's over. Everything is over between us except marriage itself. I'll *keep* you. But I'll have nothing more to do with you. Do you understand?"

All too bitterly well did Josefa understand—and all too bitterly did she sympathize. Then there was a timid knock at the door. A candle appeared, a single amber star in the gloom. It illuminated the anxious, sleep-folded features of Alfonsa. Her

eyes were wide with bewilderment and wonder. The light drew
Paco's attention. He turned toward her and raised an arm
threateningly. "Get out, get out, for the love of God. What do
you think you're doing here?"

The girl trembled but held her ground in the doorway. "I
heard," she began fretfully, then stopped and simply pointed to
her ear.

Goya nodded curtly. "All right, all right. You can look after
Doña Josefa now that you're here." In the wavering candlelight
he stormed from the room, slamming the door behind him.

Alfonsa approached Josefa gingerly, her face filled with concern. "You're safe, *señora?*"

Josefa gave the girl a wan smile which, she hoped, was
endowed with at least a tinge of reassurance. "I'm perfectly safe.
I was just having a bad dream. It was nothing of importance.
Go to bed."

Alfonsa departed, leaving with her mistress the remembrance
of her little grin of peasant comprehension. Josefa wept.

And she wept again, in recollection of that terrible night
nearly two years before. But the tears came less copiously and
less frequently with the passing months. For the loss had to be
set off against the gain. Paco was kinder and more considerate
than he had ever been. He appeared willing to leave the day-to-
day care of Javier entirely in her hands. Even to Francho, with
whom he had managed easily to quarrel again after their recon-
ciliation at Cádiz, he was showing a generosity of feeling; he
visited him on the few afternoons when her ailing brother was
well enough to see anyone. Indeed, one of the few portraits that
Paco painted in the months immediately following his conjunc-
tion with María was of his dying brother-in-law. Though honest
to the man as only a Goya portrait could be, this picture was
imbued with a tenderness that was remarkable, given the
stormy nature of their prolonged relationship.

And after making his portrait of María, Goya painted one of
himself at her request—a canvas that disclosed the gentleness
and openness that marked their love. He also painted a scene
typical of the Madrid he loved—a pair of young *majas* seated on

a balcony, one of them the image of María as he thought she must have appeared when she was a girl. She was pleased and touched by this imaginative evocation of the past, much more so than by the formal portrait. "If that's how you see me, Paco, I'd rather be a *maja* than a duchess."

Important though she was in his life, not all of Goya's new ebullience could be attributed to the advent of María de Alba. As he had felt himself emotionally identified with Spain during what he chose to regard as their simultaneous decline, so did he imagine that they were similarly linked in fortune as they appeared to rise from their respective despair. Or this, at any rate, was what he said to his friends. He was cheered by the news that Spain and France were nearly in agreement over terms to end the war that had been fitfully waged between them for several years.

The only obstacle to settlement was the personal safety of the young Capet, as the French revolutionaries insisted on calling the son of the dead Louis XVI. The Spanish king's first minister, the vainglorious, greedy satyr Manuel Godoy, let it be known in Paris that if offered a choice between the life of Louis XVII, as he was known to the émigré Royalists, and an entire Spanish province, Carlos IV would unhesitatingly opt for the former.

Goya's friends who met regularly at the Taberna de la Corrida, which was near his house, included a number who belonged to an informal group called the *acalofilos,* the lovers of ugliness—a sardonic reference to their affection for Spain in spite of the abuses that pervaded every level of society. Fearing that he might jeopardize his position, Goya had resolutely refused to admit that he was more than remotely sympathetic; he loved Spain, he said, but he declined to involve himself in anything resembling a movement whose design was to undermine the authority of the crown. This caution did not, however, prevent him from associating with men he well knew to be inimical to the present regime. Prudence, after all, could be exaggerated.

Membership in the *acalofilos* had increased significantly since the onset of actual fighting with France. Godoy's egregious assertion of the king's anxiety for the life of his little Bourbon cousin prompted the remark "Perhaps Don Carlos prefers a French Louis to his own moronic Fernando as heir to our throne." Close to the truth was the rumor that Godoy himself harbored hopes of the little royal bastard Francisco de Paula's becoming Spain's next king. This infante, the offspring of Godoy's liaison with the queen, was treasured by Doña María Luisa de Parma above all her other children, to the detriment of her eldest son, Don Fernando, Prince of the Asturias and logical heir to the throne.

Whatever lay behind the minister's pronouncement, its import was rendered irrelevant by the ostensibly natural death of the French pretender in June, 1795. A peace treaty was signed the following month. Jubilation was universal. Even the detested Godoy was allowed to bask for a brief period in unwonted popularity, of which he made predictable use to distribute titles and emoluments to relatives and useful friends. He himself acceded to a dukedom and was named Prince of the Peace. His worth, at the age of twenty-eight, was reliably estimated at 180 million reales. It was a fair showing for ten years of conscientious rutting with the porcine queen.

Godoy's only wholly commendable action was the granting of amnesty to his two immediate predecessors, the counts of Floridablanca and Aranda, both of whom had been imprisoned for the crime of setting their patriotic intelligence against his treasonous cupidity. Himself a former guards officer, Godoy had known as well as Floridablanca and Aranda that the Spanish army was no match for the French. Yet he had pressed for war because of his mistress' purely sentimental whim. The cost was vast.

Less than a fortnight after the announcement of the peace, Francisco Bayeu died in his sleep. Paco was startled by the degree of his sorrow and remorse. Relieved that their old antagonisms had been tacitly patched up, he nevertheless felt guilty that they should have gone on for so long. After the funeral, he attempted to communicate these feelings to Josefa, who appeared unwilling to hear him. Francho had been of her flesh, not Paco's; his grief, therefore, could be nothing when compared to hers. She clung to Javier and turned her back on her husband.

María was more hospitable to his confession. "He was the dullest man I ever knew, but I don't think he ever did anything in his life that he thought incorrect or cruel," he told her.

"I can't imagine anyone less likely to be attracted to you."

"I've wondered about that too. But he *was* attracted to me, you know. I wouldn't be here, wouldn't be *anything*, if it hadn't been for Francho." Maudlin tears filled the painter's eyes. "And what did I give him in return? The back of my hand."

"Stop puling, for God's sake. Why don't you simply admit that you're just not a very nice man a good deal of the time?"

"But I've never been cold-blooded, *amada*."

"Never?"

"I can't recall an incident."

"Bravo, Goya. Still, I suppose you must have been pleasant enough to Bayeu at the beginning."

"We got along very well for a long time, until about fifteen years ago."

"What happened then?"

"There was a commission to make frescoes for the cathedral of Nuestra Señora del Pilár in Zaragoza. Francho was nominally in charge of the work, but in fact *I* was to do most of it myself. I was supposed to follow the studies he made, but I didn't like them, so I painted them to my own designs." Goya laughed. "I painted what it pleased me to paint."

"Bravo again."

"Wait till you hear. Francho was furious. Why hadn't I followed his instructions? I was getting too full of myself, he said. He'd teach me a lesson. So he told the canons of the cathedral chapter that he disapproved of what I'd done. They ordered me to repaint the whole thing. God, I was angry. I can still feel that rage. I could have killed him."

"You were humiliated."

"He'd beaten me, and I'm a very poor loser. I always have been. Even when I was a boy, playing games, I hated defeat. If I was on the losing side, I'd accuse the winners of cheating."

"So of course you quarreled with Bayeu, on whom you were dependent. How did you live?"

"Fortunately it was at that moment that Jovellanos introduced me to Floridablanca. I painted his portrait, for nothing."

"Extraordinary."

"I had to find a new beginning on my own. I didn't know at first that he wasn't planning to pay me. But he did much more than a few thousand reales could have done for me. He introduced me to Don Luis de Borbón, and after I spent that time at the Arenas de San Pedro with Don Luis and his family, I was presented to the Osunas—"

"And María Teresa recommended you to *me*," said María with a wry little smile.

"After ten years of waiting."

"For *me?* No, for Bayeu's directorship of the Academia."

"Don't be coy."

"But you'll take his place, won't you?"

Goya nodded. "I ran against him seven years ago, and he beat me. I'd have mortgaged my soul for it then. Now I don't give much of a damn."

"But you'll allow your name to be put forward."

"Oh, yes, *amigita de mi alma*. I owe it to myself. In a backward sort of way, I owe it to Francho's memory. He denied me the honor while he lived. Only his death can make it possible. There's a neat bit of justice for both of us in that. Besides, it will bring me more money. I can always use that."

"I'll listen to no more talk about money. What a fool you are, Paco. You spend practically nothing. All you do is invest and invest and invest. So hold your tongue about the money. It would be a great honor, and one you deserve, as you're the first to say. If you're elected, I'll commission your friend Merchi to make a bust of you and present it to the Academia."

"To be placed on a shelf? Is that where you'd like to see me, María?"

"In a niche, like the head of a Roman emperor."

"Which emperor do you have in mind as my prototype?"

"Caligula, I think—mad, passionate, and possessed by black visions."

Goya was more eager to become director of painting of the Academia than he had confessed to María. He might be less ambitious than he had been before his illness, but this particular mark of official recognition was desirable if only because it had been denied him. In 1788, when Bayeu had been elected, Goya had run a poor third.

He was unlikely to be named by acclamation. Members took much less enthusiastically to his work than did his own clientele. They often complained that the tapestry cartoons and portraits of his earlier years were too realistic, by which they meant too unflattering. And of his more recent paintings, in which he depicted scenes of public celebrations and penitence, of madhouses and witchcraft, they offered even more violent objections; they were too fantastic, too shocking, too "advanced"—though to Goya himself these works appeared a perfectly logical extension of tendencies he had demonstrated since his arrival in Madrid. The majority of Spanish academicians preferred the classical idealism of Mengs or the pretty fluffiness of the Tiepolos, foreigners whose influences still reigned in the capital two decades after their departure. Moreover, Goya had long displeased his colleagues for other reasons: He refused to meet with them socially and expressed openly his scorn for their timidity and their passive acceptance of alien tastes.

He was convinced that until some artist of different inspiration and of great personal authority attained the highest academic post this unhappy state of affairs would continue to obstruct progress toward the emergence of a truly Spanish art. Thus, as he saw it, he owed it to his countrymen as well as to himself to seek election by any means so that Spain could hold her head high, as she had not been able to do for more than a century, since the accession of the French Bourbons to the throne. For Goya had no doubt that of all his contemporaries, he was the most Spanish, the most truly indigenous and individual.

There was to be only one other candidate for the Academia office, Gregorio Ferro, whose technique resembled that of the dead Bayeu. Paco thought this circumstance both gratifying and unfortunate. It would afford the electors a clear-cut choice, which was probably helpful to his cause. But it seemed a possible hazard too, because it might well be that they would prefer an apostle of the familiar to an advocate of fairly radical change. Ferro certainly would never propose to disturb the patterns in which his fellows were most comfortable.

Goya's oldest friend in Madrid was Gaspar Melchor de Jovellanos, Spain's chief justice and an adviser to the former first minister, Floridablanca. He was sympathetic with the artist's motives, but he thought it an error for him to seek the post. "You're not a leader, Paco. You're a renegade. And you're stone-deaf, which is scarcely an advantage for anyone who has to preside at meetings. Not only that, you're no administrator. You say you want to establish a new trend, but you couldn't propound a theory of art if your life depended on it. So it's idle to rant as you do about changing public tastes and bringing Spanish art out of the wilderness. The job simply isn't for you. If you *were* elected, all the real work would have to be done by someone else. Just the same, if you'll admit that all you're really concerned about is the *honor,* for its own sake, I'll help you, because I think it's time for you to have that. I can't stomach the hypocrisy of the rest of it."

"You'd be surprised how efficient I can be when the need arises," said Goya defensively, "and how well I can express my ideas."

"In painting, I agree," said his friend, the connoisseur Ceán Bermúdez, who was seated with them in the *taberna,* "but in talk, you'd be hopeless."

"You may be right, Ceán," said the painter, somewhat humbled, "but wouldn't it be a good thing for me to have that post?"

"I don't suppose it would do any harm so long as you don't involve yourself in the kind of quarrel you're so liable to when you get together with other painters, and provided too that you have nothing to do with the day-to-day functioning of the Academia."

Jovellanos then added to Goya's anxiety by alluding to a possible complication that hadn't occurred to him—the opinion of the queen and of Godoy. "It's a bit of patronage he's not had control over so far, but you can't tell. He has agents everywhere else. Why not in the Academia? And if you'll forgive my saying so, your friendship with Doña María de Alba isn't likely to improve your outlook. And there's the question of your association with the *acalofilos* . . ."

"I've never been associated with them."

"You're seen among us often enough. As far as Godoy is concerned, that would seem the same thing. *We* don't elect our members, you know."

"Why should my knowing men like you be unhealthy for me? It's not prevented you from becoming chief justice. Moratín and Ceán have government offices."

"I can speak only for myself, Paco," said Jovellanos. "And I'm certain that if it weren't that I'm an *acalofilo,* I'd be minister of justice."

Ceán Bermúdez noted unhappily that he was morally certain that his present minor post in the ministry of finance was the highest he would attain in any government led by Godoy. He added that Leandro Moratín, another of the painter's intimates, was merely royal librarian, hardly a sensitive political position in a country of almost universal illiteracy. Ceán agreed with Jovellanos that the Prince of the Peace must be reached in Goya's behalf by someone the first minister trusted.

The name of the Franco-Spanish banker Francisco de Cabarrús was raised. In Paris, where he was now Godoy's personal emissary, this extraordinary man had a dual renown; in his own right he was recognized to be a master of intrigue. He was also the father of Thérèse Cabarrús, mistress of Jean Lambert Tallien, whose arrest and condemnation to death by the French

Comité de Salut Public had provoked (or so many Parisians believed) the *coup d'état* of July 27, which was called in the Revolutionary calendar 9 Thermidor. Goya had painted a portrait of Cabarrús a decade earlier and through his good offices had secured other commissions. But Jovellanos' suggestion dismayed him. "Godoy may trust him, but *I* don't. I'm sure he's playing a double game, pretending to be an *acalofilo* and acting purely for Godoy."

The justice was puzzled. "I thought you were more sophisticated than that, Paco. You don't understand what he's up to. He finds it more useful to work from the inside than to stand outside thrashing his arms about helplessly. So do I, for that matter, *and* Ceán and Moratín. It was Cabarrús, *amigo,* who really negotiated the peace with France, the best thing that's happened to Spain since Godoy became our master, you'll concede. And you can't accuse him of getting much of a reward for it. No one calls *him* Prince of the Peace, or even duke. No one gave *him* the Order of the Golden Fleece."

"He was made a count," said Goya sulkily.

"In Godoy's dictionary of public gratitude, that's like throwing a bare bone to a dog."

"I'll never understand," said the doleful artist, "the nuances of our politics. That's why I've always tried to avoid them."

"And don't forget Francisco's daughter. They say she'll lie only with republicans. Would a fellow be loyal to a child like that and be unsympathetic to our activities here?"

The painter eyed Jovellanos curiously. "*Are* there activities here, Gaspar? I've seen no sign."

The justice chuckled darkly and refilled their glasses with manzanilla. "You've not been looking very hard these past few months. Your eyes have been for other things. There are plans."

"*Republican* plans?"

"Plans to bring down Godoy."

"But *not* Don Carlos," said Goya anxiously. "I'm still the king's man, Gaspar. I know he's a fool, but I promise you it would be a fatal error in any plan if the king's position were threatened. The people would never stand for it."

Jovellanos sighed. "That's hardly the point right now, is it? The point is that you want this post and Godoy can easily prevent it. Cabarrús *is* friendly to you. He can be helpful and I'm sure he would be. You need have no compunction about asking him. It makes sense from his point of view, just as a simple business proposition. Don't you have a good deal of your money invested in Cabarrús' bank?"

Goya grinned sheepishly and nodded. "I'd not even thought of that."

"And now that you *have* thought of it, do you find it unpatriotic, king's man or not?"

Paco followed his friends' advice and wrote to Cabarrús, who immediately agreed to intercede for him with Godoy. Though he never learned whether or not this aid had been effective, he was named director of painting of the Academia the next October—by a margin of only two votes. And as he had predicted to María, the feeling of triumph was hollow. Once elected, he ignored the obligations of office but cheerfully banked its benefices.

Immediately after his investiture, the duchess kept her promise to commission Gaetano Merchi to make a bust of the painter. The Italian was a perfectly competent sculptor, a year Goya's junior, whose career had taken him far from his native Brescia. He had spent some years in St. Petersburg, a period of which he recounted several amusing anecdotes. Eventually, he had left for Paris to join his musician brother. At the outbreak of the French Revolution, the Merchis had emigrated to Madrid.

"You find the Spaniards more to your taste than the French or Russians?" Goya inquired.

"I like your people, but they take everything so seriously," said the sculptor with regret. "Even your amusements are serious. Some of them are even deadly. You don't seem to know how to *enjoy,* if you follow me. I speak, of course, of the *people,* not of the nobility. Your nobility is strictly French. But the *people* have no laughter."

"What do you think our people have to laugh about, for God's sake? You imagine the peasant's life is a joke?"

Merchi gave an elaborate, purely Italian shrug. "You mustn't be angry with me, Don Paco. The peasants of Italy have nothing to laugh about either, as you mean it. But tell me the truth. Does crying make anything easier?"

"It makes you feel better to empty your soul of sorrow."

"Oh, I'll agree that you Spanish know how to cry superbly. But in Italy, we laugh and sing. Yet if you look at the conditions there, the problems are even worse than in Spain. We're the pawns of Europe's chess games. There's nothing we can do to change that. Certainly, crying won't help. But right now in Spain, you *do* have something to laugh about. Your war is over. And still you cry."

"With reason. Godoy is proposing to involve us in another war, against Britain, as soon as he can arrange the terms with France."

Merchi grimaced broadly. "And can you do anything to stop him?"

"Probably not."

The Italian flung wide his arms and bobbed his head vigorously. "So there you are. You might as well laugh, Don Paco. It's good for the lungs, and it purifies the soul even more than tears."

three

▲ HIS WORST ENEMIES were reluctantly willing to agree
that Manuel Godoy, Prince of the Peace, was probably not all
bad. Some of the projects he had initiated during his three years
as first minister were of positive merit—cultural, social, and
economic. The trouble was that because of the vast sums demanded by the inane war with France and his own insatiable
avarice, little was left for their realization.

Nor was he altogether the monster he was so generally proclaimed. His sharpest critics, among them Goya's closest friends,
had to concede that the very fact that they could continue to
express their relatively radical views was a tribute to Godoy's
restraint in the exercise of what amounted to limitless powers of
political repression. Unlike Floridablanca, he preferred the
opposition, however vociferous, to operate in the open so that,
if the need arose, it could be the more readily contained.

This was as near to genuine cleverness as the prince ever
came, and his policy was vindicated early in 1796 with the exposure of a conspiracy to overthrow him; its leadership was
provided by no less a figure than the conservative Cardinal-
Archbishop of Toledo, the Spanish primate. Godoy was able to
deal with the plot summarily, but its extent shook him, as well
it might.

Aside from his superhuman greed, there were other and more
fateful defects in the prince's character, one of which was a

passion for political intrigue and secret diplomacy—arts of which he regarded himself as without peer in Europe. In the view of Francisco de Cabarrús, who had had to negotiate with the redoubtable former Bishop of Autun, Charles Maurice de Talleyrand-Périgord, this boast was worse than idle; but the banker kept this knowledge to himself, knowing better than to disabuse the proud but stupid Spaniard.

Godoy sent personal representatives like Cabarrús to every major European capital and was more inclined to give credence to their reports (most of them tailored to his well-known tastes) than to those that reached him through official channels. These secret assessments pandered to his taste for duplicity. He was constitutionally incapable of accepting an obvious truth, even one that was favorable to his country's interests.

Although delighted with his elevation to the rank of prince, he was galled to have to acknowledge to himself that the occasion for this honor, the peace of July, 1795, had been a defeat. Since it appeared impossible to beat the French in battle, he now proposed to join them in their war against Spain's quondam ally, Britain. France was icily agreeable to this turn of events. For a year, she had been considering an invasion of the British Isles. To succeed, the assistance of the Spanish fleet would be advantageous—though the French were as aware as Godoy of the quality of his navy, three hundred decaying vessels, manned by incompetents, commanded by cowards and knaves, the prince's friends and relations. On the whole, however, it was preferable to have a friend rather than an enemy on the long frontier of the Pyrenees.

The idea of Spain's involvement in yet another war didn't dismay the *acalofilos* nearly so much as Goya had anticipated. Godoy's negotiations were much less secret than he imagined. The prospect of an alliance with France appealed to the liberals because, they hoped, it would have the effect of rendering Spain more accessible to the French concept of government by constitution, either republican or monarchical. The forward-thinking Spanish intellectuals looked wistfully to France as one of the two possibilities of relief from Godoy's virtual dictatorship. The other hope lay with the queen; she might withdraw from him her favor and protection. Of the two, the former seemed more likely.

The latter eventuality had appeared remote until an occurrence in the first months of 1796, which led Godoy's enemies to dare dream of such a breach. The incident disclosed as never before, in public, another of his shortcomings—his passion for womanizing, a tendency he was both unable and unwilling to suppress, nor even attempt to conceal. The queen had abided his lechery with a forbearance that even a patient wife would have thought exemplary, such apparently was his capacity to satisfy *her* exotic demands. She took solace from the fact that Godoy never tolerated the presence of a second woman for more than a week at a time, leading Doña María Luisa to presume that she remained his favorite. Of this presumption, he now disillusioned her.

One day among the countless supplicants who filed through the reception rooms of Godoy's palace in Madrid were Doña Catalina Tudo and her three daughters, all of them comely. Like other petitioners, Doña Catalina was perfectly willing to exchange, for services rendered, the charms of any of her progeny. The prince's choice fell on the youngest, a languid, voluptuous child of nineteen, Josefina.

At first, there seemed to the queen no reason to pay more attention to Josefina than to any other of the army of young women who had passed between Godoy's sheets. Like her predecessors, she would emerge from the palace one morning soon and be heard of no more; this was the custom. But as her stay in his custody lengthened, it became evident that Josefina, or Pepa, as the prince called her, must possess for him attractions not discernible to the naked eye. And when she was installed as what seemed a more or less permanent fixture of Godoy's ménage, his proliferating opposition had reason to hope that at last he had gone too far. Doña María Luisa, however indulgent in the past, couldn't possibly countenance so flagrant a flouting of her position as his *maîtresse en titre*. If Pepa were not dismissed, the queen would certainly use her influence with the king (if she could distract him from his obsession of the chase) to effect the dismissal of Godoy.

His foes called Godoy the "sausage merchant" for the obvious reason and because he was a native of the Estremadura town of Badajoz, renowned for its pork products. The prince's enemies rejoiced in vain. "The queen rages," Jovellanos reported to his friends at the *taberna*, "but neither she nor the king can muster the courage to throw Godoy out, and *he* can't bring himself to throw La Pepa out."

This was precisely the situation. Doña María Luisa grudgingly accepted her rival as a member of her official household and consoled herself as best she could with a selection of handsome young guardsmen, from whose recruits she had previously chosen Godoy himself a decade before. She hoped to arouse her defecting lover's jealousy in this way, and was mistaken. Within months, she named Pepa Tudo to the post of lady of honor; the girl's mother and sisters received gifts and annuities which, however gratifying to the beneficiaries, added substantially to the popular grief about the cost of government by Godoy out of the queen.

Goya's bookish friend Moratín took the blow more philosophically than did the other *acalofilos*. "If Doña María Luisa *can't* get rid of La Pepa," he mused, "and *won't* get rid of Godoy, I suppose she feels that the next best thing is to make the whore a part of her establishment and trust that the sausage merchant will be content with a diet of two mistresses instead of one."

"And we," responded Ceán Bermúdez, "must be content to be governed now by *two* whores instead of one?"

While Madrid seethed with anecdotes of Godoy's complicated personal life and rumors about the projected alliance with France, Goya continued to rejoice in *his* complicated relationship with María de Alba. As their appreciation of each other increased, he recognized that his was the more powerful emotion—probably because his was the more vulnerable position; he was older, he was poorer, he was ugly and deaf.

However, his acceptance of the inferior role didn't come to

him easily. A crisis was reached about a year after their meeting. He arrived unexpectedly at the Palacio de Liria. He had been driving through the Florida district of the city, which adjoined her property, and decided, on the spur of the moment, to call on his mistress. As was his habit, he entered by a side door and made his familiar way to her apartment—there to discover her in bed with a young man whom he recognized as a promising *torero*.

María looked up from her lover as Paco came into the room, her expression one of only mildest surprise. He might have been one of her servants, or La Beata or Brother Basil, so careless was she of keeping her life a secret. "Oh," she said blandly, "it's you."

Her nonchalance was so deflating that the rage of indignation he had always imagined he would be overwhelmed by in such a circumstance failed to materialize. This, she was wordlessly saying to him, was the way she was; he could take her or leave her, but he couldn't change her. "I love you *now*," she had told him a year ago. "Ask me no more." She made no effort to conceal her nakedness. And the young man simply turned his head away. Goya, feeling not so much jealousy as affront, was sure he was smiling.

"You might have told me," he murmured.

"If I'd known you were coming . . ."

He pointed to the figure beside her. "I mean about him."

"So did I."

"You'd have kept him a secret from me?"

"He's not the first, Paco."

"You're no longer interested in me. I've become a habit."

"Nonsense. You're just feeling sorry for yourself again. How else can I measure you if I let myself forget what other men are like?"

This guilelessness was its own best defense. She would do as she pleased, but never with malice, never with an eye to hurting him or keeping him on edge. She showed him an amused tenderness which, while wholly sincere, was just light enough to leave him a little anxious. She satisfied him, he came to realize, by not satisfying him too much.

Thereafter, she made a point of showing him the gifts she chose for his rivals, and at precisely the moment when she believed he might explode or at least reproach her for her cruelty, she would present him with something far more intimate and considerate—a small object he had admired, brushes especially imported from France, a set of engraving tools, a block of sketching paper of the sort he had complained he was unable to obtain. In response to his rueful gratitude, María said, "If gold could keep you with me, Paco, I'd buy you the earth. But I know you better than that." Thus did she constantly disarm him.

In the earliest days of the bright spring, María proposed that Goya accompany her and the duke to pass the summer months on her estate at Sanlúcar in Andalucía. He thought the idea repellent, not only because he and Don José were on no friendlier terms than they had been on first meeting, but because there remained in the painter's character a trace of respectability, a remnant of his Aragonese upbringing. A *maison à trois*, however acceptable to the duke and duchess, was not for him. He offered as excuse the obligations of work that bound him to Madrid. "Why don't you stay here with me? Let Don José go alone this time."

He had advanced this suggestion with little conviction. María loved the provinces and frequently referred to the necessity of her making an appearance at least once a year in Sanlúcar, to let her people know that she was still in control. So he was certain that she would turn him down. Her reply, therefore, confounded him. "You're right, Paco. I should have thought of it myself. I'm told it's much cooler, if not so unbuttoned, in Madrid. I've never spent a summer here, and I think it would please José to play the great duke by himself."

"You're actually going to do something I ask?"

"Just to be perverse."

"To keep me off balance."

"That's not fair, Paco. We keep each other off balance."

"Perhaps we keep each other *in* balance," he replied.

"A balance of apprehension and happiness? Yes, it's possible."

During the next two months, María and Paco diverted themselves by making plans for a summer in the capital which would, she insisted, be interrupted by brief trips elsewhere—to the Escorial, which she hadn't visited since childhood, to her husband's ancestral castle near Toledo, to Ávila and Segovia, and to Aranjuez. It would, they excitedly agreed, be a season always to remember with joy.

María's judgment was correct. Don José was delighted with the opportunity of passing a few months by himself at Sanlúcar. He departed from the capital in early June and reached Seville a few days later. There he was stricken by a fever to which, in his habitually frail condition, he succumbed almost at once.

María reacted coldly to her husband's untimely death. "The best I can say for him," she told Paco, "is that he never tried to interfere with my life. I'll neither miss him nor mourn him." Nevertheless, she insisted on leaving at once for Seville so that she might accompany the duke's remains on the trip to Toledo, where his burial was to take place.

On the day of her return to Madrid, Paco was received in the Palacio de Liria by a very angry duchess. She handed him a message from the royal palace which had been delivered during her absence. "Their Most Gracious Majesties wish to convey to Doña María del Pilár their most profound condolences on learning of the death of Don José. Although they will find intensely painful her absence from receptions at court, Their Gracious Majesties will think it proper if Doña María del Pilár passes a period of mourning on her estates at Sanlúcar, and would therefore not take it amiss if such a period were to last one year." The letter bore the signature of Manuel Godoy, Prince of the Peace.

"How dare they?" she asked Goya when he had finished his perusal. "How *dare* they?"

"Obviously, at this moment, they dare anything. What are you planning to do?"

"What would *you* do?"

"I don't know. It's a command, of course. I had no idea they hated you so much."

"Well, now you understand. That bitch of a María Luisa swore she'd have revenge against me. Now she's found a way of killing two birds with one stone. She can get rid of me and she can separate *us*, because she knows that will cause me pain. Any plausible excuse would have served her purpose. What will *you* do?"

"What's safest for you."

She snorted. "I'm in no danger, Paco."

"They could make things uncomfortable for you."

"Not really. They could hurt *you* much more, and they *would* if they were sure it would hurt me too."

"I don't care," he said stonily.

Her expression softened. "Do you mean that Goya is willing to take a chance?"

"You don't have to put it that way. You know there's nothing I wouldn't do for you."

"I know," she responded gently.

"But you have to go, María. You can't oppose the queen."

"You said you'd do anything for me, Paco. Will you forget everything else that's important to you, your money, your career, Javier, everything, and come with me?"

Goya sat down and let his heavy arms drop to either side of his chair. "A holiday in Sanlúcar? Well, it's not exactly a summer in Madrid, is it? But why not? A whole year? You know, *amigita*, I've never had a real holiday in my life."

"And the company reassures you," she said complacently.

It took a little time for Goya to make arrangements for his departure with María. However elated by the prospect of a year away from work, he was at pains to instruct his assistant, Ascensio Julio, to maintain the routine of the studio, which consisted of copying the artist's more popular pictures, notably royal portraits, for which there was a steady demand. To old Pedro Gómez, who took care of his correspondence and his household and professional accounts, he confided the more

delicate responsibility of watching over Josefa and Javier.
Though discretion moved them to express dismay, both wife
and son rejoiced over his leaving. Goya was not deceived, nor
was he embittered. He had no right to complain of their resent-
ment; he had earned it.

They reached the duchess' sprawling Andalucian hacienda in
August, just before Assumption Day. News of María's arrival
had preceded her, and though preparations to celebrate the
Virgin's rise were in full swing, the people of Sanlúcar greeted
her with an improvised ceremony, their enthusiasm convincing
Goya that she had been amply justified in her repeated assertion
of her peasants' love and respect. *"Here,"* she told him tri-
umphantly, *"I* am Spain."

They rode in her open carriage into the village on the
morning of Assumption Day, where María would, as had her
great ancestors, preside over the festivities. These were to begin
with a *corrida* in the main square. Her parasol afforded little
protection from the fearful sun as they traversed the verdant
countryside that bounded the estuary of the Guadalquivir, and
before the coach passed through the gates, it seemed to Goya
that Sanlúcar would prove just another provincial hamlet, flatter
and less interesting architecturally than those of Aragón or
Castile. In its plan it certainly adhered to the classic pattern:
narrow alleys, dusty despite a thunderstorm that had broken
over the valley the previous night, led them past houses which
were brilliant in their fresh coats of whitewash. The central
plaza was flanked, inevitably, by the church, some shops, an inn,
a number of *tabernas,* and the *ayuntamiento.* There was one
remarkable difference from other villages he had known—an
atmosphere of prosperity, shown not only in the tidiness of the
buildings but in the cleanliness and obvious contentment of the
inhabitants.

As they proceeded grandly through the streets, everyone in
the path of María's carriage made hasty and respectful way, the
men doffing broad-brimmed hats and bowing almost to the
ground, the women curtseying, the children waving their hands
and handkerchiefs—all cheering and laughing at the same time.

"If Godoy could see this," said Paco, "he'd never have sent you into exile. What a demonstration."

The carriage drew up before the *ayuntamiento*. Two liveried footmen leaped down from their seats at the rear; one opened the door and the other placed a stool on the hard-packed earth, reaching in to take María's black-gloved hand. Goya followed unassisted and stayed a respectful step behind as the great duchess ascended the short flight of steps to the portico of the town hall. They were greeted at the summit by the smiling, effusive *alcalde mayor* who happened also to be María's main provisioner.

She then turned and acknowledged with repeated waves of her hand the continued cheers of the crowd. As the tumult increased in volume and movement, she removed the black mantilla and passed it magisterially back and forth over her head. The painter remained motionless; this was *her* hour, and he begrudged her not a jot of the pleasure it gave her. After a few minutes, the welcome subsided. María took the middle of three chairs. The *alcalde* was on her right, conversing volubly; Paco sat on her left, feeling ignored, overcome (as he hadn't been for a long time) by the silent loneliness in which he was enveloped. He had, at first, objected to accompanying her. He thought it indiscreet to be seen in public with her so soon after she had been widowed. She brushed aside this consideration. "I could appear with the devil himself in Sanlúcar, Paco, and my people would still adore me." Only the prospect of a bullfight had lured him.

The parade of the *toreros* and their *cuadrilla* began with a signal from four inept horn players who were ranged in front of the *ayuntamiento*. Hands and kerchiefs raised by the crowd flashed in the bright noonday sun; banners and streamers fluttered languidly in the lazy, hot breeze that came in from the sea. María tapped Goya's wrist. "It's going to be a real gala," she said excitedly, shifting in her great chair like an eager child. "The *alcalde* says we're going to have *two toreros*."

"Can't be much more gala than that," said the painter gloom-

ily, feeling no desire to conceal his sullen turn of mind. "And
how many bulls will they fight?"

She pointed to an improvised stockade across the square.
"Don't I see four?"

"Gala indeed," he muttered dourly.

"For God's sake, Paco, this is only a village fiesta. It's not
Seville or Madrid."

"And we're not going to see any Costillares perform either."

"No," she responded, grinning, "but I might discover another Costillares in the making."

Goya grunted but refused to be baited. Two very young
toreros moved out onto the plaza at the head of the procession,
self-conscious and obviously uncomfortable in their severe, un-
adorned, tight-fitting costumes of black velvet. They carried
their *muletas* like flags, not cloths intended to annoy the bulls.
Behind them rode the *picadores* on their spavined nags. Hardened as he was by attendance at hundreds of *corridas* and by
personal experience during his youth as a minor member of one
of the *cuadrillas* in Madrid, Goya felt a wave of revulsion and
guilt when he thought of the pitiable fate that was in store for
these animals. Like the *toreros*, the *picadores* were less splen-
didly dressed than their counterparts in the great city plazas,
their principal decoration the flat-topped sombreros which they
affected at a rakish angle. The *banderilleros*, who brought up
the rear of the parade, were peasant lads of the district who
grinned and chatted with each other, waving to friends and
relatives in the crowd, thoroughly enjoying their little moment
of glory.

The *toreros* came to a stop before the duchess, whipped off
their hard little hats, and bowed from the waist. She nodded
solemnly, but smiled. The procession resumed its tour of the
square. The preliminaries were at an end. There was a sudden
hush as a gate opened at the far end of the plaza.

The first bull edged hesitantly from his stall. He trotted
efficiently forward a few yards; he paused, lifting his fine, com-
pact head slightly, sniffing the gentle wind, flicking his lank tail
like a whip. He was alerted now, if not to danger, then to the

notion that his initial impression of being freed had been
illusory. Goya saw a *banderillo* protruding from his rump; the
animal had been reluctant to emerge from his pen. A little
trickle of blood dripped slowly down the sleek, black hind-
quarter.

The crowd became animated, encouraging the bull to more
decisive movement. A *picador* shambled into the arena. His
aged, broken horse wore a blindfold over his right eye. The
rider urged him forward with flashing spurs. What a stunning
contrast between this doddering wreck of a beast, already
ridden practically to destruction over the fields and fences of
Andalucía, and the innocent young bull, shimmering in the
high summer sunlight; but it was a contrast without relevance:
Within fifteen minutes, both would be dead.

The *picador* approached. The bull, uncertain of himself,
eyed the man and his mount with suspicion. The *picador* waved
his lance in provocation, calling, "Eh, *toro.*" The bull was attracted and came nearer to investigate, but not near enough for
contact. The *picador* made his nag draw alongside the bull. He
planted his weapon securely in the creature's superb, sinuous
neck. The bull halted, pained, surprised, offended. The *picador*, delighted by the crowd's murmurings of "Allah!," put a
little distance between himself and the bull, giving the
wounded animal room for his expected charge.

The bull turned, his movement markedly stiffer now and less
confident; the embedded lance was weakening him. He pawed
the earth once and once again; then he was in motion, fear
abruptly supplanted by fury. The force seemed irresistible as he
gathered speed. The horse sensed the approach that the blindfold deliberately prevented him from seeing, and could hear the
staccato hammering of hoofs on the hard, dusty surface of the
square; perhaps he even smelled the blood flowing from the two
wounds, for he was downwind of the bull.

The horse stirred uneasily, making a tragically inept effort to
rear; and at exactly the moment when his forelegs left the
ground, the bull struck him in the side, horns puncturing the
shaggy hide. The horse fell heavily sideways, tumbling the

satisfied *picador* beneath him. The bull retreated two quick, impatient steps, and charged again, snorting loudly. The long, straight façade of his head was almost parallel with the ground, the throat bellowing his rage and pain and humiliation. The horns plunged deeply into the exposed belly of the horse, to the hilt. His head twisted sharply, first right, then left. The crowd sighed, "Allah!" Here was indeed a noble bull.

The dying horse lifted his head perhaps six inches from the earth and uttered a terrible shriek, his uncovered eye wild with agony and fear and bewilderment. Youthful *banderilleros* scudded swiftly across the plaza, their motion as precise as sandpipers', to lure the bull away from the perishing horse. They waved their red *capotes* now to this side of him, now to that. After what seemed an eternity, the impaling bull retracted his horns; as they emerged from the horse's belly, they trailed ice-pink entrails, which he attempted to throw off with angry wrenchings of his marvelous head. At last the guts dropped to the dust. Bemused, even slightly inured to the injuries in his neck and rump, the bull pirouetted grotesquely, digging his forehoofs at the soil.

An attendant dashed out and attempted to cram the spilled intestines back into the gaping hole in the flesh of the moribund horse, but they were too slippery for him. The *picador* gave the beast a savage kick in the head. The laughter and applause of the crowd were general. The horse made a pitifully gallant attempt to rise and succeeded in placing his forefeet more or less firmly on the ground, achieving for an unsteady moment an absurd sitting position, his entrails trailing obscenely beneath him. Then he collapsed with a wheezing gasp of merciful expiration, amid the hisses and jeers of the spectators. A team of donkeys was led at a floppy, irregular trot in the direction of the fallen horse. Ropes were drawn about the corpse's legs and withers and he was dragged from the plaza, leaving a wake of bright gore that quickly turned brown as the hungry earth absorbed its moisture.

Now was the turn of the *banderilleros*. Three of them, the clowns of the piece, danced about, goading the bull, taunting him, jabbing beribboned darts into the black shoulders to break down the powerful muscles. They leaped about him, their legs clumsily splayed, arms waving in mock frenzy. The bull discovered a renewal of energy and another reason for rage. Again he pawed the ground and began to careen heedlessly toward a side of the square. Screams of apprehension rose from those of the crowd who were threatened by the approach of this black juggernaut; they were protected only by the flimsiest of fencing. Just short of the barrier, the bull wheeled, his powers ebbing. He made a second dash, more desperate than determined this time. The ribbons of the *banderillos* fluttered lackadaisically in the sunlight, like the pennants of a defeated regiment. Narrow streams of blood coursed down the bull's steaming sides. The *banderilleros* moved to an edge of the plaza, their part of the entertainment over.

The *torero*, bareheaded and stripped of his jacket, entered the square armed with *muleta* and sword. Delicate, lithe little steps carried him effortlessly across the broad arena until he stood no more than five yards from the wounded enemy. It was cat and mouse now. "Eh, *toro* . . . eh, *toro.*" The *muleta* was extended; he made a spin. The bull seemed contemplative, then moved forward at a rapid but sluggish-footed trot. The *torero* made a pass with the *muleta*, then another and another, closer and closer to the points of the horns, which were still bloody from the guts of the gored horse. He made a final pass, closer still; now no daylight could be seen between the flat belly of the young man and the bull's bleeding side. The *torero* whirled, almost casually, on the ball of a foot, showing to all the spectators that his white silk blouse was stained with blood—the bull's, not his. There was no mistaking that.

The crowd expressed its approval. The *torero* made a little bow and addressed himself once more, with greater purpose, to his performance. There was a sigh from the spectators. Head down, gait teetering, drunken, the bull brushed the *muleta* aside with his horns. The *torero* spun about swiftly, sword in the air. He aimed over the bull's shoulder, then brought the blade down, glittering heartlessly in the sun, and disappearing.

The crowd gasped. The bull moved two steps onward, paused, then made a third step. It stopped, bellowed, and fell dead. The crowd was ecstatic.

María gripped the painter's arm. "You *see?* You *see?* And you dared to be scornful of a fiesta at Sanlúcar. You'd not have seen a better kill in Madrid. That boy's a wonder."

Goya said nothing. Her hand dropped to his inner thigh, where it encountered an erection of which, until that moment, he had been unaware. He flushed. "Stop it, for God's sake."

She laughed. "You swine. You were as excited as I was."

"Not in the same way."

"No?"

"Not by the same thing. I'm moved by the spectacle. You're moved by the boy."

The rest was anticlimax. The jubilant *torero,* laughing and smiling, made a ceremonial tour of the plaza, dodging flowers, waving his bloodied *muleta.* He completed his round by placing himself before the duchess, to whom he bowed, his hands trembling with pleasure and excitement. The donkeys drew the carcass of the slain bull from the square. As the young *torero* vanished from sight, the applause and cheering gradually died away. The crowd was collecting its emotional juices for the next orgy.

"Life can never be happier than this," said Goya. He said it repeatedly, aloud or to himself, during the months of his stay at Sanlúcar. Previous sojourns in the houses of the great had been, by comparison to this one, eminently unsatisfactory, marred by a sense of inferiority that had, willy-nilly, been imposed on him by his hosts. His visit to the Arenas de San Pedro had been something of a command performance; he was invited not for his company but for his services. And though Don Luis de Borbón had shown him every courtesy, there had never been a question of regarding him as a guest; he was a well-considered craftsman who was fit to associate, but at a clear remove, with the gentle infante and his charming little family.

His reception at the Alameda of the Osunas had certainly

been warmer than that of the late king's brother. Yet, in spite of Goya's physical intimacy with Doña María Teresa, there had been a patronizing undertone in their relationship which lovemaking failed to eradicate. When they were in the presence of a third person, her behavior was aloof. "You may be my lover, Paco," she told him when he had accused her of cruelty, "but you're not my equal. Sexual intercourse with María Teresa gives you no right to a social introduction to the Duchess of Osuna."

At Sanlúcar, Goya was treated by the Duchess of Alba, and therefore by her domestics, as second in importance only to herself—and this by but the narrowest of margins. They called him "Don Francisco," not "Don Paco." They bowed to him, opened doors for him, prepared his favorite dishes, and were in general solicitous of his least desires. He was *somebody* in their estimation, and he relished this consideration. In effect, he was the new duke. He basked shamelessly in the sumptuousness that was the prerogative of a great and rich man.

Chiefly, of course, he was happy because his life with María could be that of a married couple. They spent almost all their hours together. This blessing was not unmixed; she could still nettle him. She interrupted their lovemaking with a sudden burst of laughter prompted by some importunate and irrelevant thought. She criticized him for snoring. She rebuked him for his occasional flatulence and summarily rejected his excuse that it was due to the spicy Andalucian dishes that she insisted he sample. She teased him for his clumsiness. She spoke too rapidly at times and then reproached him for misunderstanding her. But the moment she suspected that his patience was about to fail him, she apologized so tenderly that all accumulated anger was vitiated.

Goya appreciated that he loved María in part for the very qualities that annoyed him most. She was often childishly headstrong and whimsical; he loved the child in her quite as much as the woman. Even in her perversity there was integrity, a characteristic that colored all she put her hand to. Her thrust was so direct, her attack so spontaneous, that he would have been churlish to condemn even her least appealing impulses.

They passed their days easily. Except for the infrequent fiestas when María felt obliged to make a public appearance, they remained on her great estate—driving in her park, visiting with her peasants, or sitting in the shade of an immense tree to watch the muddy waters of the Guadalquivir pass lazily into the bay. Their conversation, as a rule, was bantering and desultory, rarely serious. So profound was their affection that it seemed superfluous to explore it in words; occasional allusions to it were gently deprecating, a luxury they could afford because their commitment to each other was now absolute.

Nothing blemished the tranquillity of the first months. Paco dismissed with an airiness that amazed him the number of commissions he had left behind in Madrid. Word from Gómez and Julio indicated that all was in order, insofar as this was possible with the master away. Despite María's protest, he had brought no drawing materials; this was to be a true holiday—no work at all. There could be no greater luxury for one who had, save during the period of his illness in Cádiz, worked every day of his adult life. If there was a single flaw, it was that his mistress denied him permission to hunt—"There's no sport in killing the defenseless." But it was a very minor flaw indeed. Nevertheless, he became restless for reasons he was unable to determine. Though he made no mention of it, María, so attuned by now to his nature, perceived it almost as soon as did Paco himself. She too remained silent, hoping it to be transitory. But time proved this not to be the case.

One autumn morning, as they were breakfasting within the white-walled confines of a patio, Goya involuntarily gave himself up to a long, loud sigh, which embarrassed him. "I'm just relaxing," he explained defensively.

"You're bored," she responded.

"How *could* I be bored?"

"Because you're not painting."

"You know how I feel about work. That's why I left everything behind."

"Think about it."

"I've done that."

"Really?"

"No," he confessed. "As a matter of fact, it's not crossed my mind."

"I know how you *used* to feel, but it may be different now. You may actually miss work."

"If I do, it's because it's a habit."

"It's more than that, Paco. It's your life."

"Never. *You're* my life."

"Only part of it, and perhaps not the most important part, either."

"You're crazy."

"Shall I prove you wrong?"

"How?"

"Come with me."

With a murmur of skepticism he rose and followed her into the great house, through cool corridors, up the broad staircase, to the door of a room he had never seen. She turned the knob and stood aside. "Go in," she commanded with a smile.

The room was empty of furniture. In a corner were several large wicker hampers, a roll of canvas, and a dismantled easel which he at once recognized as his own. He wheeled about and confronted her with a frown that failed to hide his amusement and pleasure. "What a nerve you've got."

"You're angry?"

"I love you, but what a nerve all the same. When did this arrive?"

"A week ago. I wrote Julio to send everything you could possibly want . . . if you wanted it at all. Do you?"

"I can't wait. What an inspiration. I'm amazed you could keep it from me for so long."

"I hoped you'd see for yourself what was wrong."

"I suppose I didn't want to see," he said softly, and embraced her.

From that day on, he sketched and painted every morning with a growing delight. He felt renewed, restored in a fashion quite different from that effected by his love. He had had only to be separated from his craft, willingly rather than through necessity, to comprehend that his engagement to it was as great in its way as was his devotion to María. Everything and everyone in sight became his subjects—his mistress' adopted children, the acerbic old La Beata, Brother Basil, the servants, the peasants at their daily tasks and pleasures. He portrayed the duchess in a variety of attitudes; she happily complied with his requests that she walk for him, run, dance, dress, undress. Often he watched her without putting pen or charcoal to paper. "I think," he said, "I'd rather see you move than have my hearing restored." For like her temperament, her grace was natural and girlish. "If you'd been born poor, *amada,* you'd have been the greatest dancer in Spain."

"But what a difference *that* would have made for us."

"We might have become lovers much sooner."

"And I'd have lost you to a duchess."

His eagerness for work increased. It was sometimes difficult to induce him to stop for a meal. María pretended to deplore his obsession, but she was elated; she had accomplished the impossible. She watched him for hours at a time in silence, her pride that of a mother. This was *her* achievement, and she lost no occasion to remind him of it.

He reveled too in the charming life of her house, especially enjoying the hours when the children were about. He fondled them as lovingly as did María. He told them the harrowing folktales of Aragón, which his mother had recounted to him. The duchess was horrified, but little María de la Luz and Luis de Berganza were enchanted. He permitted them to force him to the ground and use him as a small hill for their games. He encouraged them to make pictures with his materials and expressed vast admiration for their efforts. Like María, he was charmed by their innocence and gaiety.

For the amusement of the children, at first, he made in a notebook sketches that illustrated some of the cautionary tales and fables he told them. Some were sad, some grotesquely comic, some savage. Each drawing was elucidated by a brief comment on the margin, extolling or criticizing some aspect of

the human condition. As in his tales, anthropomorphism figured significantly in the sketches. Especially plentiful were the
asses—as teachers, as priests, as physicians, as victims of their own
folly or of man's cruelty, or in turnabout situations in which the
ass victimized his human master.

It was only natural that the children should be most diverted
by the drawings in which they recognized themselves or others
of the duchess' household. La Beata also found them intriguing;
now and then she was scandalized when Goya indulged his taste
for scatology, though she was herself no less of the Spanish earth
than he. Such was her reaction to a watercolor in which he
showed a naked baby held aloft by a nude woman—unmistak-
ably María. As the woman kissed him, the baby was farting. Yet
another *putti* was doing a handstand while a bent old man,
Brother Basil, looked on with a lascivious leer. In the lower
right-hand corner was the head of the sleeping Goya.

"It's too indecent, Don Francisco," the old woman complained.

"How so, Beata? Don't babies belch and fart?"

"Just the same."

"You think it shouldn't be shown, even though it's perfectly
natural."

"Not as something amusing."

"It would be all right if I made it seem sad?"

"You twist my meaning, Don Francisco."

"No, Beata, *you* twist *mine.*"

"Would you draw a man and a woman . . . in bed together?"

Goya hastily sketched the scene he knew she had in mind. "Is
that it?"

She blushed and tried to avert her eyes, but they were held by
the drawing. "It's obscene."

"Why? Would there be babies if there were no lovemaking?
It's as natural and good as walking."

"Not the same."

"It's ugly?"

La Beata studied the drawing with relief that she need no longer appear offended. "No, it's beautiful in its way."

"Can it be beautiful in *another* way? I mean, as far as a picture is concerned. If it's beautiful, can it be obscene? *Obscenity* is the ugliness, Beata. Your *mind* is what's ugly."

María thought the sketch of the farting baby delightful; she found most of the drawings in the notebook entertaining. "But they're not serious."

"If they *were* serious, you'd not like them?"

"I'm not a serious person, Paco. I like to be amused. These amuse me."

"That's ironic, because I made them in the same way as I make what you'd call 'serious' art."

"But you enjoyed making these."

"They're instructive, all the same."

"Ah? What child could understand them?"

"A Spanish child."

"You have a very high opinion of our education."

He riffled through the pages until he came on a scene in which a donkey was portrayed as a schoolmaster. "Do I?"

"You should make copies of that and circulate them."

"For the enlightenment of the Holy Office?"

"What a coward you are, Paco. Do you imagine that picture would get you into trouble?"

"Not a single example of it, no. But if I made an etching of it and distributed prints . . . "

"And you boast of your powerful friends?"

"What would be the point?"

"Wasn't it *you* who were damning the schooling you had in Zaragoza? You said you learned nothing but Latin and church history."

"And arithmetic," he added grimly, "which is the only subject I've retained."

"Well, then, this picture says something you think important, something useful. Say it so it can be heard. I dare you. Let me see how courageous you really are, what you really dare."

"Damn you, I will."

After this explosive exchange, Goya became more systematic in the notebook sketching. The theme of inadequate education adumbrated many others in a political vein. One idea suggested another, until he had filled several volumes with drafts of images which, with refinement, could become a devastating series of comments on the contemporary situation in Spain. They could be etched on copper plates—a technique he had learned a quarter of a century earlier in Venice, while studying with Domenico Tiepolo. On only one previous occasion, however, had he done any profession etching—copies of paintings, mainly by Velázquez, which he had made at the request of Carlos III, who wished to circulate them in the provinces.

As these savage studies proliferated, Goya wondered increasingly about the possibility of publication; they were reminiscent of *Les Caprices,* a collection of etchings by the French artist Callot that his friend Moratín had brought him from Paris a few years before. Whereas Callot's intention had been to divert, to "amuse," as María put it, frivolity was scarcely the touchstone of Goya's bitter drawings. "You're a damned reformer," she accused him. "You may even be a revolutionary. You've attacked every institution in Spain, including womanhood. I double my challenge to publish these."

"Goya dares anything," he said again.

"I doubt it."

He had promised to paint another portrait of María, but it was well into the spring of 1797 before he would tear himself away from the studies for the etchings. The new portrait showed María dressed in black, standing on a beach that resembled the seascape a few miles from her house at Sanlúcar. She was disappointed with it. "You see me as the same woman I was two years ago?"

"Look again. Your expression is completely different."

She acknowledged this reluctantly. "But what am I supposed to be saying to you? I assume it's *you* I'm looking at."

"Just what you see." He pointed to the rings on the fingers of her right hand. One bore the inscription "Goya," and the other

"Alba." Her index finger drew attention to letters in the sand: "Solo Goya."

" 'Only Goya,' " she said musingly. "And what's that meant to suggest? That you painted the picture by yourself, or that I'm yours alone, or that you're *mine* alone?"

"All three."

"You needn't be so smug. I'll not let you take me for granted. I'm not your wife." She threw her hands into the air gaily. "I'm no one's wife now. I'm free as the air. And I'm nothing like the woman you've painted. Any fool can see that."

He shrugged. "It doesn't matter. This one is for me."

"But where will you hang it?"

"In my studio."

"What will Josefa say?"

"Nothing. And if she does, I'll pay no attention."

"That seems unnecessarily cruel."

"She won't mind. She certainly won't demand an explanation."

For Goya, the year of exile in Sanlúcar ended too soon—a year without responsibility, without pressure, and without any annoyance more important than an occasional argument with María over something trivial. But most surprisingly, it had been for him a year of revelation, the period in which he had discovered the need to express himself through his art. María had caused him to stumble on the secret of Michelangelo and El Greco and Rembrandt—subjectivism. From now on, Goya felt he would give to the art of the self a new and transfiguring importance.

He was both eager and unhappy about the return to Madrid. "I've been so happy here," he said mournfully to his mistress. "I know we have to go back, and I *want* to . . . but I don't want to."

"Well, I have no mixed feelings. *I'm* getting bored now."

"With me?"

"To a degree, yes."

"You should have spoken sooner."

"And have you leave me?"

"Of course."

"No self-pity, Paco. You know what I mean. I need more excitement."

"Than I could provide."

"That, certainly."

"You need a whole army of entertainers. You'll have them in Madrid."

"But we'll see each other there, *amigito*. But we'll see other people too. I wasn't intended to be a nun or a hermit, and neither were you, if you'll only admit it."

"You're enough for me," he growled.

"What about the etching project? You've talked about it so much that even though *I* suggested it, I'm sick of hearing about it."

"It depresses me *because* it was your idea and you'll not be near to share in it when it's done."

"What an ass you can be. I'll be near."

"Not near enough, not all the time. I know you, María. You'll have other men. Whom will *I* have?"

"Your friends, your work, your money, your fame, your son."

He remained gloomy. "I'll never have Javier. Josefa's seen to that."

"But it will be nice to see him."

"And when it pleases you, I'll see *you?*"

"Exactly," was her bland reply.

"And if it doesn't please *me?*"

"What foolishness. If it doesn't please *you*, Paco, how could it possibly please *me?*"

four

WHEN IT WAS KNOWN that the illustrious Goya had returned to Madrid, commissions poured in. These pressing demands simplified readjustment to his former mode of life. He was frequently fortified by sweet recollections of that leisurely year in Sanlúcar, by visits with María, by an occasional if still remote exchange of pleasantries with Javier, and by a renewal of friendships at the *taberna*. But life was mostly work of a sort, which, save for the etchings to which he gave as much time as he could, he didn't much like. Individuals who had acceded to titles and affluence under the aegis of Godoy were clamoring for portraits to commemorate their altered status. The Duchess of Osuna, greatly relieved to find her former lover in so refreshed a frame of mine, requested that he paint a series of scenes of peasant life, and her husband obtained for him a commission to make a religious painting for a provincial church.

In terms of prestige, the most significant development was a message from Godoy demanding an interview to discuss a number of pictures which he required for his palace, recently redecorated. Goya's previous encounters with the first minister had been casual, brief conversations at official gatherings, their relations marred during the past couple of years, no doubt, by the artist's connection with the Duchess of Alba.

The period of Goya's absence had been a particularly active one for the Prince of the Peace. Partially in the hope of improving his strained relations with his mistress-queen, he had accompanied her on a "triumphal" tour of the provinces—omitting Andalucía, where the popularity of the Duchess of Alba seemed unsusceptible to successful challenge, but including the most pompous of state visits to his native Badajoz, where Doña María Luisa spent two comfortless nights in the Godoy family castle, an ancient and ill-restored fortress as drafty as a public square. Another reason for the prolonged journey was to rally support for himself among the nobles who, he hoped, would aid him in his continuing struggle with the clergy. He had only recently learned that the queen's own confessor was affiliated with the church-inspired conspiracy to denounce him to the Inquisition as a blasphemer and debauchee, crimes against the faith for which evidence abounded. By ingratiating himself with the provincial aristocracy, he meant to thwart any attempt to displace him.

But the most crucial reason for the grand tour was to provide an excuse for postponing the moment when Spain must definitely announce her alliance with France against the British. Godoy took the view that since the French were admirably soldiering on by themselves, he could enjoy the fruits of victory without having to incur the terrible costs of war. The decision to sign a treaty with Paris was further delayed by the ingenious counterintrigues of Lord Bute, Britain's ambassador in Madrid, who impressed lesser government officials with his argument that war against his country might lead to unfortunate complications of which Godoy appeared ignorant. What, he tactlessly asked, did the Prince of the Peace propose to do about Portugal, whose ports remained open to the British navy? If Spain were to declare war, said Bute, surely France would insist that Godoy take immediate steps to see that these harbors were closed against the mutual enemy.

Though the British ambassador apparently never phrased it in public, there was another question that needed little mention since it had previously beclouded dealings between France and Spain: The Spanish infanta Carlotta was married to the Duke of Brazil, regent of Portugal. Did Godoy mean to take military action against his mistress' daughter? He ignored the question, certain as ever, and as mistaken, that intrigue would give him an answer when the time came. But, for all of Bute's maneuvering and Godoy's foot-dragging, Carlos IV signed a mutual assistance pact with the French Directoire in August, 1797.

This remarkable document provided for the intervention of 25,000 Spanish troops. The prince had no misgivings about acceding to this stipulation since, in the first place, Spain couldn't put more than 10,000 trained men into the field; and even if such a muster were managed, there was no danger of its being made to march against Portugal. For he had (cleverly, as he imagined) inserted a provision that Spanish forces were to be deployed only against those of the British. The ink on the treaty was not long dry before the Directoire advised him that he was obliged by its terms to take "whatever steps are necessary" to compel the closure of the Portuguese ports to British shipping. Godoy assured his new French friends that he would comply at once—but at the same time he let it be known in Lisbon that he proposed no action whatever. After all, he explained to himself, Spain had already done more than her share in the war. Had a Spanish fleet not driven the great Lord Nelson from the Mediterranean?

Godoy's rationale for maintaining a posture of inactivity was strengthened by his annoyance with France's duplicity. He knew that while Paris was urging him to commit his country to war with Britain, the Directoire had sent Talleyrand to London to negotiate secretly with Pitt to secure peace. And in Italy, where the Spanish connection was, if anything, stronger than with Lisbon, a young French general named Bonaparte had declined the offer of Spain's good offices in his dealings with Parma and Naples.

France was comparably disenchanted with Spain. General Pérignon (the French ambassador and author of the Spanish defeat two years before) learned of Godoy's bad faith in the question of Portugal and lost no time in informing his government. In addition, although Spain officially recognized the authority of the Directoire, Godoy persisted in his efforts to restore a French monarchy. He urged Cabarrús to persuade his daughter to solicit sympathy for the accession of a Spanish Borbón to the French throne. To imagine that the promiscuous Madame Tallien would dream of such an undertaking was evidence, according to Goya's friends, of Godoy's complete ignorance of the realities of the French political scene. "This is comic opera stuff," said Ceán Bermúdez. "The man is mad beyond hope of remedy."

"Ah, yes," answered the more philosophical Jovellanos, "but by pressing the Borbón cause, however futile it may seem, the sausage merchant assures himself of Doña María Luisa's affection. If he loses that, he'd be lucky to finish his life even in the pork trade."

Gradually, comic opera was translated into farce whose tragic undertones were still muted, save to those whose hearing was particularly attuned to the Spanish way of doing things. Such was not the endowment of the soldierly Pérignon, and to make matters worse, his grasp of the diplomatic niceties was imperfect as well. His social ineptitude was becoming legendary and provided the jaded Spanish court with many occasions for low hilarity. His position was made more difficult by Mangourit, his chargé d'affaires—a vehement republican who refused to deal directly with the Spanish royal family, so poor an opinion did he properly cherish of the aberrations of this monarchy. Moreover, he attracted to the embassy many liberal Spaniards whom he filled with admiration for the radical means by which France had rid herself of absolutism.

The king and queen were alarmed. To Pérignon, Godoy expressed the view that if the price of friendship with France was the infiltration of seditious ideas, he would have preferred that the war continue. Mangourit must go. He was dispatched to America, for whose beautiful young women he had already shown a lively interest that owed nothing at all to their political views. With Mangourit on his way to Washington, Pérignon believed his troubles to be at an end, but in fact they had only begun. Shortly afterwards, a lovely and ambitious young Parisienne, Jeanne Riflon, appeared in Madrid. She made her presence known to her country's embassy. What could be more natural? To diplomats longing for a breath of French air after months or years of isolation in a city where rendezvous were almost always inhibited by the attendance of a *dueña,* Mlle. Riflon's arrival was electrifying. She fought off her admirers with intelligent selectivity, accepting the protection of a young French official who was as generous with his gifts as his attentions and, as a fillip, proved very informative.

For a time the couple lived in what seemed perfect harmony—until Pérignon was drawn by La Riflon's charms. Though disillusioned by his mistress' fecklessness, the younger diplomat knew his place and yielded gracefully to his superior. But he soon learned that his sometime friend was sharing her favors with the royalist Duc du Havre. More embarrassing than that, she was sharing with him the secrets that Pérignon, in the comfort of her arms, was unwisely imparting to her. It wasn't long before all Madrid was privy to Jeanne Riflon's complicated personal life, and to the secrets she conveyed to the amorous duke. These had mainly to do with the rivalries among the five members of the Directoire, intelligence that the monarchist agents in Paris might readily exploit.

This information was soon made useless for the French royalists. For in early September, 1797, there was a dramatic upheaval, the *coup d'état* of 18 Fructidor. As a corollary of its effects on the French government, this shift of power resulted in the recall of Pérignon and the subsequent deportation of Mlle. Riflon. So ended the last laugh that Spain would have at the expense of France.

Godoy boasted to the queen that Spain's situation, after the *coup* in Paris, was stronger than ever. He had contrived to hold the French at bay in the matter of the Portuguese ports, and Spanish troops had yet to fight a battle. A new era, he asserted, was aborning. In the latter regard, at any rate, he was right. Out of the still-confused position in France was emerging the single, diminutive figure of Napoleon Bonaparte. The prospect of this Corsican as *de facto* head of the French state satisfied the Prince

of the Peace because only recently the young general had
proposed the name of Godoy to the Directoire as a possible
successor to the deceased Prince de Rohan for the post of grand
master of the Knights of Malta. After negotiations in which
Godoy had typically revealed his avarice, the suggestion came to
nothing, for the appalled Maltese hastily selected a leader for
themselves. But the futility of the plan failed to obscure the fact
that Bonaparte thought highly of Godoy—or such was Godoy's
interpretation. And the only other important leader to survive
unscathed the events of 18 Fructidor, Talleyrand, also had
endorsed the prince's candidacy—and for the same reason as
Napoleon: He distrusted Godoy absolutely; by sending him to
Malta, they would be permanently rid of him.

To make his cup run over, Godoy was on the point of
matrimony. Madrid laughed over this as it had over the Riflon
affair. There was no doubt that the idea had originated with the
queen. She was irritated with her profligate lover's prolonged
infatuation with Pepa Tudo. If she found him a suitable mate,
she might restrict his extramarital activities to herself. Such was
the common gossip. But whom would he agree to marry? And
who would marry such a monster? By now hopelessly inflated
with the sense of his own sublimity, the Prince of the Peace
straight-facedly proposed a union with Madame Royale, daughter of the dead Louis XVI. If the present French regime collapsed, as he confidently expected, he would ascend the throne
once occupied by Charlemagne and Louis XIV. The trifling
difficulty of the Salic Law, which forbade the accession of
women to the thrones of France and Spain, could easily be
overcome.

Whether this extraordinary idea tickled Doña María Luisa's
risibilities as it did those of the rest of Madrid was not announced. Understandably, she preferred him to be betrothed to
a woman she could easily dominate, one who stood in need of a
service that could be granted only by Carlos IV. About a week
before Goya's interview with Godoy, it was officially stated that
the first Princess of the Peace was to be the tiny, shy, fragile
Countess of Chinchón, daughter of Don Luis de Borbón, whom

Goya had painted in her childhood almost fifteen years before. He remembered her vividly—grave, wise, and self-possessed well beyond her five or six years.

In these terms Goya described her to his friends at the *taberna* soon after the news was made public. Jovellanos expressed a rage very rare in one normally composed. "And this is the sort of child that bitch means to put in the bed of that scoundrel?"

The startled painter was placating. "She'll be perfectly safe, Gaspar," he said with more hope than conviction. "You don't know her. No one could dream of being unkind to her."

"How unworldly you can be, Paco. That pair would be unkind to the Virgin Herself. I pity the little countess."

The young fiancée gave voice to no such fears. She felt she had no reason for complaint. She would become a princess, and her brothers thereafter would be allowed, by royal decree, to make use of the Borbón name in spite of their father's morganatic marriage. As evidence of the state's gratitude, her future husband was to receive a dowry whose value was estimated at five million reales. It seemed an auspicious beginning for any marriage. The countess publicly acknowledged to the queen that she owed everything to Godoy; she counted herself the happiest and most fortunate of women.

For all Jovellanos' reassurances, Goya was still troubled about the propriety of commercial dealings with Godoy. When the day of their meeting arrived, he felt dirty as he drove to the minister's palace; it was as if he were on the point of committing treason. But as Gasper and other friends tirelessly reiterated, it was wiser to have Godoy as an ally than an enemy, at least for the present. And there was now the Countess of Chinchón to be considered.

The Prince of the Peace received the painter in a richly over-furnished room where he entertained his many ardent feminine petitioners. As Goya tried to adjust his eyes to the rapid, slurred movements of the minister's full lips, he found it hard to reconcile his immediate impression of the man with the legend that enveloped his career. Godoy certainly hadn't the appearance of a monster. He was tall, heavily made without yet having achieved corpulence. A little stoop-shouldered, he was ruddy—a complexion he owed more to exposure to wine than to the harshness of the Spanish climate. He smiled easily with bright dark eyes that suggested an animal's alertness rather than an actively functioning intellect—the shrewdness of the fox which he so often ascribed to himself.

Yet, for God's sake, *this* was Godoy, who imagined himself to be the most accomplished statesman in Europe, the equal of Talleyrand in cunning, of Bonaparte in military genius. But to Goya he seemed just another country boy, like himself—with a little more money in his childhood, a little more education. Had Paco been a guardsman, would he have been bed partner for a queen? he wondered. There, all were equal. Poor Spain.

The prince spoke casually at first of mutual acquaintances in the arts. He was too young to have known Mengs or the Tiepolos, but he offered his condolences on the loss of Francisco Bayeu and mentioned with respect artists of whom Goya thought little. When he went on to mention the artist's patrons, his omission of the Duchess of Alba was pointed. He was solicitous of the artist's health, of Josefa's, of Javier's—thus demonstrating how well informed he was on subjects which, one might have expected, would be of no interest to a chief of state. He expressed solemn gratification that "so great an artist as yourself" was restored to normal strength and clucked sympathetically when Goya complained in a perfunctory way of the problems that deafness created.

Without warning, Godoy stood up. "Let me show you where I want these paintings of yours to be hung," he said brusquely, "and then I'll tell you what I have in mind."

He led the way through a paneled door into a spacious hall, where he paused to let Goya catch up. "You know, if the choice were mine, I'd have asked Maella or Ferro to make these paintings. I'm sure you're as good as everyone says, but your friendship with La Alba is no recommendation to me."

Paco felt his hackles rise, but controlled himself. "Ah, Highness," he said coldly, "I'm sure either of them would do very well for you."

"*They* know what I like." Godoy hesitated, to give emphasis to what he now added. "I notice that you overlooked my mention of Doña María del Pilár."

Goya maintained his composure. "Should these things be discussed, Highness?"

"Why not, since they're so well known? You don't suppose your scandalous affair is any secret."

"No, Highness, but does that mean that *I* may discuss *your* personal affairs with equal freedom?"

The prince stopped abruptly and considered the artist with interest. "I've been told you're candid, Goya, but I didn't think you were foolhardy in your courage."

"It has nothing to do with courage, Highness. I want things clear between us. If you asked me here to talk about paintings, I'm honored. If it's a question of the way I choose to live *my* life, or of how Doña María chooses to live *hers,* I'm bound to say that this has nothing to do with you and I shall bid you good-day."

"And turn down a commission from Godoy?"

"That surprises you?"

"Stuns me."

"Do I understand that you offer this commission with the stipulation that Doña María and I cease to see each other?"

"The thought occurred to me," said Godoy with a complacent smile.

"Then I *do* bid you good-day."

"You'd really reject my commission under those conditions?"

"What else would a man do?"

The minister stiffened and made a few superflous adjustments to his uniform of captain-general. "I was just testing you."

"For what purpose, Highness?"

"I test everyone. I need to know with whom I'm dealing."

Goya breathed deeply before replying. "Since you prefer the work of Maella and Ferro, Highness, I suggest that you apply to them—with respect, of course."

"Ah, but you see, Goya, my little countess insists that I offer the commission to *you* first. She remembers you happily from your visit to the Arenas de San Pedro."

"No more happily, I promise you, Highness, than *I* remember *her*. Please convey my respects to her."

The prince went on, ignoring this interruption. "Therefore, whatever my personal feelings, I bow to her whims."

They now entered an immense reception room. Godoy extended his arms and swung himself in a series of circles, as easy on his feet as a professional dancer. "I want three large paintings for each of the long walls."

Goya inspected the chamber. It was well-proportioned, with plenty of light, thank God. "You said, Highness, that you had an idea of the kind of pictures you wanted."

"Allegories."

"Allegories?"

"Peace, Justice, Truth, Poetry—you know the kind of thing. Like Rubens."

The painter laughed. "Like Rubens, Highness? But I'm Goya."

"No need to be obtuse. I meant the subjects, the things Rubens did so well, or at any rate to *my* taste."

"Loose drapery and quantities of pink flesh?"

"The very thing."

Godoy moved to the door. Paco followed, then stopped to look back at the room. "And plenty of bright colors," he murmured. "Intense blues and yellows and reds."

"The very thing," the prince repeated. "You'll accept the commission?"

"But of course, Highness. How could I refuse?"

They returned in silence to Godoy's private cabinet. When the prince had seated himself behind his superb writing table, he looked up at the standing painter. "How much time will you require?"

"A few months. If only you'd let me know sooner, I might have had them ready in time for your wedding."

Godoy nodded and grinned. "But the fact is, Goya, that I've

known my own marriage plans only for a fortnight. If they'd been other than what they are, you'd not have been summoned at all."

"You've made that perfectly clear, Highness."

"No need for you to take umbrage."

Paco shifted uneasily. "There *is* the question of my fees, Highness."

The minister regarded him fixedly, his expression amusedly quizzical. *"Is* there? Somehow, I had the idea that you'd naturally think of these paintings as a wedding gift, in view of my countess' affection for you. Or, if you prefer the harder-headed view, you might call them an investment in our future happiness—meaning *yours* too."

"I take your point, Highness."

"But you don't seem happy about it. Wasn't this more or less your arrangement with Floridablanca?"

"I made a portrait of Don José. Nothing more."

"The more fool he, then."

"Fool or not, Highness, he was kind to me."

Godoy let this observation pass. "You can imagine how expensive this wedding will be." Once again he spread wide his arms and smiled disingenuously. "And think of the possibilities that may lie before you, Goya. Only *your* paintings hanging in that splendid room. What an honor. What an opportunity. Who knows what might come of it?"

There was no way out. Goya's responding smile was wry. "I shall be satisfied, Highness, if you and the dear countess find pleasure in them."

"I'm sure we shall," said Godoy cheerfully.

The wedding of Godoy and the Countess of Chinchón in September was accounted the most magnificent since the nuptials of Carlos IV and his nymphomaniac María Luisa de Parma. However, there were disturbing rumbles of unhappiness not long after the ceremony. The queen was rumored to be not at all pleased with the living arrangements of her lover's newly augmented household. Far from rendering Godoy more attentive to

her, his marriage had divided his purportedly prodigious powers by three instead of two. For Pepa Tudo was as firmly established as ever; she dined each evening with the prince and his
bride—and with Doña María Luisa, if she were lucky enough to
be asked. As for the new princess, she had apparently resigned
herself already to the sort of life Godoy would lead her, and was
on the best of terms with both of her husband's mistresses.

Opinion in Madrid was divided about what the queen's next
move would be. For though everyone acknowledged that she
was furiously jealous and bitterly disillusioned over the failure
of her scheme, some felt that she must at last accord Godoy the
rejection he so richly merited. Others, however, believed that
since she had supported so many of his snubs, she would respond as before—by doing nothing.

She surprised some students of her concupiscent career by
openly casting about for a new lover whose role, presumably,
would be restricted to the bedchamber; leadership of the government was to remain in the hands of Godoy. For the queen's
confidence in Don Manuel as a politician had, over the years,
been reinforced by the inane Don Carlos' almost mystical conviction that not even Satan was half so nimble-footed in the
manipulation of the tiresome affairs of state as his darling
Godoy. The king proudly confessed that he would have felt
himself incapable of deciding when to move his bowels without
the prior counsel of the prince.

Doña María Luisa's new lover was Don Pedro de Saavedra. A
banker like his friend Francisco de Cabarrús, and a liberal
freemason, Saavedra was in his thirties. He deemed himself a
patriot, thinking it more useful to bore at the foundations of
Godoy's regime from within than to give himself up to the
despair that was the prevailing mood of the *acalofilos*. He
despised his mistress' ugly, flabby, used body but recognized
that prominence, of however dubious a kind, might have its
advantages to the cause of a better-governed Spain. The queen
rewarded him with the post of minister of finance, second in
importance only to Godoy. To his credit, Saavedra agreed to
accept this only on the condition that his friend Jovellanos at

last receive the appointment of minister of justice. At Doña María Luisa's urging, the king complied with the request.

These developments disturbed Godoy, who was more and more apprehensive about the stability of the jerry-built structure of government. It was based on intrigue, blackmail, terror, and corruption—the stuff of all authoritarian rule. Yet it had supported very well, so far, the charming existence which he felt he had only begun fully to savor. He managed to keep his peace, persuaded that the queen's flesh must sooner or later cry out for his, and that this minor misunderstanding would be resolved in his favor. He even thought it judicious to retreat a step or two into the background, to permit Saavedra and Jovellanos to make the move against him which he correctly anticipated.

Goya was so taken aback by his friend Gaspar's acceptance of a ministry that he was unable to keep *his* peace. "All *I* did was to make pictures for Godoy. *You* mean to work with him in double harness?"

"You think I enjoy the idea?"

"You're going to help him?"

"That's the opposite of our intention. Saavedra and I mean to break him forever."

"And are you going to break Don Carlos too, who swears by Godoy's honor?"

"Oh, Paco, are you still playing the role of Spain's common people? Don't worry. Don Carlos will come to no harm."

"I don't like it, Gaspar. I fear for *you* as much as I do for Spain. No good can come of it."

"But it's a chance we can't allow to pass. And you mistake the implication." The new minister poked a long finger into his friend's ribs. "Suppose those etchings you're going to publish were offensive to certain important people. Wouldn't you rather have *me* pass on their suitability than someone else—a bishop, for instance?"

Goya groaned. "It will be a year before all the plates can be printed. By that time, you and Saavedra will be in exile, or even in prison. Besides, whom could my pictures offend?"

"The ones you've shown me are very sharp, very political."

"Not at all."

"You're joking."

"They're political only in the sense that you could as reasonably describe the Scriptures as political—the Ten Commandments or the Sermon on the Mount."

Jovellanos laughed. "I didn't know you were a student of Holy Writ, Paco. But what about those 'fables,' as you call them?"

"Perfectly harmless. More than that, they're positive, apposite. My purpose is to edify."

"Commendable, no doubt. But more important fellows than you have been garroted at the order of the Inquisition for wanting to edify."

In December, 1797, the French were more disturbed than ever by continuing Spanish lethargy over the closing of the Portuguese ports. Their apprehensions were aggravated by the breakdown of negotiations with Britain and by the apparent fall from grace of Godoy. If he was still in authority, he must be reminded of how terrible a whip Talleyrand could wield; if not, his successors must be made aware of their obligations. Heavier pressure was applied. Initially, this took the form of ominously suave messages to the effect that General Bonaparte was much concerned about Spain's internal affairs.

Disappointed by Cabarrús' inability to keep the French at bay, the Prince of the Peace sent another friend, Izquierdo, to seek some sort of accommodation with Talleyrand; for he was all too aware that if, at this particular moment, he were compelled to take arms against his mistress' daughter and son-in-law in Lisbon, his own position, already precarious, would become intolerable. The mission was very nearly a fatal mistake. Izquierdo, whose mentality, such as it was, strikingly resembled Godoy's, was almost immediately detected in a bewildering succession of acts of bribery and blackmail. He was promptly expelled from France and, further to confound Godoy's intrigues, the angered Directoire rejected the appointment of Cabarrús as new ambassador—although Talleyrand, who was distributing his sexual favors between the banker's daughter and the wife of a French diplomat named Charles Delacroix, privately expressed his affection for Cabarrús. In public, the great minister insisted that Spain must act with dispatch.

For once, Godoy showed the faintest flicker of intelligence, albeit that of a cornered rat. Perceiving at last the dismaying dimensions of the dilemma he had himself invented, he decided, at the end of the following March, to resign—after soberly and cynically informing Don Carlos that he refused to be the minister who must, at the behest of an alien power, prescribe a desperate military adventure against his king's close relations. Although she was still displeased by Godoy's resolute attachment to Pepa Tudo, the queen was even more distressed by his decision to leave office. Saavedra was proving less tractable than she had anticipated. His ideas about the responsibilities of the crown to the people were positively alarming, and even more regrettable was his opinion that if Godoy's resignation were taken at face value, the logical consequence was the immediate and total dismantling of the alliance with France.

Since the inevitable result of such a gesture could be only a second war in which, this time, the enemy's forces would be directed by Bonaparte, the queen's fears were reasonably grounded. Nor were they assuaged by the designation of a new French ambassador, Dr. Guillemardet, whose reputation was for the iciest of blood, the clearest of sight, and the most insidiously effective means by which to attain his country's ends. What, everyone was asking, did France have in mind?

The liberals of Madrid shared none of Doña María Luisa's disappointment over the loss of Godoy. Impromptu celebrations took place all over the city, in low places as well as high, for the poor had suffered frightfully from his oppressive fiscal policies, far more than had the rich. When he heard the news, Goya naturally headed for the *taberna* and was soon joined there by Ceán Bermúdez and Moratín, neither of whom knew more of the matter than the bare fact: Godoy had resigned.

"We can't know what it means until Gaspar arrives," said the scholarly Leandro Moratín.

Delayed by a summons to the royal presence, Jovellanos entered the *taberna* an hour later. There was the purest jubilation in his eyes, but when he spoke he made a brave attempt to maintain his judicial caution. "Oh, it's fine news, but it's still too early to say that it's a permanent cure and not just an illusory remission."

"For God's sake, Gaspar," said the impatient Goya, "he *did* resign."

"But he still has his apartment in the palace, and his bedroom still connects with the queen's. It's no time to proclaim a miracle."

"So you and Saavedra are our masters now," said Ceán with warm feeling. "What's *your* part?"

"To back Don Pedro as best I can, poor devil." Jovellanos turned to Goya. "I was about to send you a message. With Godoy's help, I've got you an important commission. You must have made a good impression on him."

"Not wittingly," said the painter with a frown.

"Well, believe it or not, he was enthusiastic when I mentioned your name."

"Coming from your lips, Gaspar, I have to believe it."

"And there's an architect who was instrumental, too. You certainly are well connected for a fellow who never gets involved in politics."

"I make no enemies."

Moratín burst out laughing. "Just cuckolds."

"No more," said Goya with mock gravity. "I sleep only with widows now. I'm too old to fight duels."

"What's the commission, Gaspar?" asked Ceán. "Paco may be indifferent, but I'm not."

"You know the Hermitage of San Antonio de la Florida?" the minister asked the artist.

"Well, I drive past it whenever I go to the Palacio de Liria. Is it finished?"

"Just finished, or so I'm told. What would you say if I told you your name has been proposed to make the frescoes?"

"I'd ask you if it's safe."

"Safe?"

"You haven't forgotten the terrible row I had with poor Francho over the frescoes I did in Zaragoza."

"But that was before you were *Goya*. And it was a family squabble in any case."

"I could have a free hand?"

Jovellanos shrugged. "I know nothing about it. You'll have to talk to Ventura Rodríguez. It's his church, and it was *he* who supported you. I presume there's some definite theme you'll have to follow, but I can't imagine that you'd be restricted in any other way."

"I'll have to see it first," said Goya, his lips pursed.

"By God, you're a hard man to please. Does the fall of Godoy make you so choosy? I can remember the day . . ."

The painter raised a hand. "So can I, dear Gaspar. No, it's just that I can *afford* to be choosy now. It's a luxury, nothing more." He smiled and laid a hand on his old friend's arm. "But that doesn't mean I'm not grateful."

"You overwhelm me," said the minister. "I may tell Rodríguez that Goya will look at the church and let him know how he feels . . . before the world ends?"

"Very soon."

"Come with me," said Goya to María, his manner surprisingly stern. "I want to show you something."

"I have things to do," she complained.

"Nothing more important than this." He almost literally dragged her from her palace to his carriage.

"What is it?" she asked pettishly as they drove through the spring-scented woodland of her secluded estate.

"I'm taking you to church."

"I haven't been in a church since I buried José. My own chapels suit me perfectly well for the odd prayer now and then, thanks. So you can tell your man to turn right around and drive me home."

Goya was delighted. "Oh, I promise not to make you pray, *amada*. You won't even have to cover your head."

"It's a church, isn't it?"

"You'll see."

The Hermitage of San Antonio de la Florida was only a short distance from the duchess' mansion, for it stood in the heart of the Florida district, overlooking the Manzanares, near the Puerta de San Vicente, on the outskirts of the capital. Goya ordered the coachman to stop at the main door of the little church. María peered from the window of the carriage. "*This* is what you brought me to look at? I see the wretched thing every time I go into Madrid."

"But you've not been inside it."

"And I don't want to go inside now."

For reply, he helped her out, then restrained her so that he could look once again at the simple, classical lines of the white stone façade which, from this vantage point, all but concealed the modest dome with its lantern cupola. "Let's go in, Paco, and get this nonsense over with. I have things to do, as I told you."

After the sharp brightness of the April day, it took a few moments for their eyes to adjust to the comparative somberness of the interior—though in fact the church was well lit by the broad, tall windows that lined the high walls of the nave. They were standing in the center of the transept crossing. Goya pointed to the dome fifty feet or so above them. "There," he proclaimed with a flourish. Then his arm swung in a circle to indicate the entire interior. "And there, and there, and there. The whole damned thing. Isn't it stupendous?"

She was perplexed, inclining her lovely head upward so rapidly that the dark mantilla dropped to her shoulders. "There? Where? What are you talking about?"

"What I just said. The whole church. I'm going to make frescoes in the dome, in the apse, and between the windows. What do you think of that?"

"Do I have to have an opinion?"

"Can't you see how excited I am? You're the one who kept saying how I should enjoy my work."

"But *frescoes*, Paco? After Zaragoza?"

"This is different, *querida*. I can do what I like."

María refused to be overwhelmed. "I don't understand why anyone would ask Goya to make religious paintings. You're as much a heathen as I am."

"But they ask me, all the same, and they're always satisfied."

"God bless God," she said dryly.

"It's not the religious part that appeals to me. A completely free hand. Can you imagine what that means to me, to me as *you've* made me?"

"You'll not get around me by flattery, Paco."

"You made me see."

"But it was there, all the time."

"So is the machinery for making love, but we wait around for years before we find out that it's for more than pissing with."

"You're quite a philosopher. Kiss me. I don't think I've ever been kissed in a church."

He embraced her roughly. "Is that all you can ever think about?"

"You brought the subject up, and in a church, too."

"I wanted to share my happiness with you," he said sadly.

She pushed him away and smiled. "I know. And I want to share mine with you."

"If you were my wife, I'd strangle you."

"But I'm not your wife, so what *will* you do? Go home, I suppose and take your petulant anger out on poor Josefa."

He sighed. "No, I'll go home with you and make love." He led her out into the warm sunshine. "But aren't you even a little pleased?"

"I'm thrilled."

"Why? Because I'm coming home with you?"

The duchess refused to answer.

five

THERE WERE MANY LEGENDS of the miracles accomplished by San Antonio de Padua; Goya selected for the central subject of his fresco the one most popular among the Spanish: The saint, a Portuguese monk residing in Italy, learned that his merchant father in Lisbon, Don Martín Bulloes, had been condemned to death as a murderer. The young Antonio asked permission of his superior to depart at once for his native land and, leave granted, he was instantaneously translated to the Portuguese capital. After vainly pleading Don Martín's innocence, the holy man demanded that the corpse of the murder victim be exhumed so that he might interrogate him, thus to vindicate his father. This odd request was acceded to because, so went the tale, the young monk seemed to have strange powers, yet there was an understandable skepticism about the outcome of the questioning. A fascinated throng looked on as the saint-to-be offered fervent prayers that God would restore life to the cold body at least long enough for him to indicate whether or not Don Martín Bulloes was guilty as charged. The prayer was answered; the voice of the dead man resoundingly proclaimed the innocence of Antonio's father, naming another as his murderer. Justice was done, and was *seen* to be done. Don Martín was released. Lisbon had witnessed a miracle.

Ascensio Julio and another assistant made detailed measurements of the areas of the church to be painted—the dome, the pendentives, the intrados, and the curved ceiling of the apse. Each figure was called out in ringing tones to old Pedro Gómez, who dutifully copied them in a small notebook which he passed on to Goya. Only when all the dimensions had been established did the painter begin his drawings of the main theme. These were followed by somewhat more elaborate oil studies, though to himself alone did these suggest the scope and manner he proposed for the finished work. Not even the devoted Julio, so long accustomed to his master's methods, could infer from the hasty little canvases a reliable idea of the full-scale frescoes—for not in his long experience with Goya had such a project come along. When he timidly protested his state of ignorance, Paco snorted, "I always said you had no imagination, Ascensio. But it may be just as well this time, because you'd be horrified if you knew the terrible truth."

Nor did the artist doubt that, were they still on this earth, Mengs and Francho Bayeu would be more scandalized than Julio by the daring of the plan he had conceived for the decoration of the church. The notion had come to him in a frenzy of delight. "I'm going to create my own sort of miracle," he boasted to his assistant, "my own sort of revolution. In fact, I'm making *two* revolutions." He said no more than this. For even if he had wanted to give verbal expression to his vision, he could find no words to convey its total pictoriality or to furnish more than the sketchiest gloss on its electric nature, its divergence from fresco styles hitherto seen in Spain or, as far as he knew, anywhere else.

His impatience was the most anguishing of his life. He believed himself to be on the threshold of an artistic achievement of truly transcendent magnitude. The door had never before been opened; no one, heretofore, had suspected its existence. Not before María had shown him the direction in which he must look, had he been made to see it. Once he had opened it, he was sure no one would ever close it again.

Nothing could be done in the church until the irascible old Trápaga, an apothecary who had for years supplied his colors, was able to deliver the great quantities of dry pigments and the

dozens of special brushes he required. Another contractor would
furnish the plaster. And even when the materials were on hand,
there was a further delay to exasperate him, for the elaborate
scaffolding erected beneath the dome had to be reconstructed.
As the painter angrily observed to the carpenters, "That
damned thing is the right height for a dwarf. You expect *me* to
work up there lying flat on my back?"

Early in August, 1798, all was at last in readiness. So important did the state apparently consider this project that Goya and
Julio were provided with an official carriage in order that Josefa
not be deprived of transport during their absence. They looked
severely on as a team of workmen prepared the first batch of
plaster which was lifted by pulley to the platform atop the re-
built scaffold. When the artist and his assistant reached the
upper level, Goya drew a sleeve across his perspiring face. "My
God, I wonder if I can make that climb every day in heat like
this." He instructed Julio to apply a thin layer of white finish-
ing plaster to the rough undercoat on the curving surface of the
dome. As he watched this operation, he stripped to the waist,
and complained of the heat once again. But he knew well that
he was sweating as much from excitement as from the tem-
perature.

As soon as Ascensio had covered a couple of square yards with
plaster, Goya made a series of bold, shallow incisions in the
damp surface with a table knife. He gasped with elation.
"There, *amigo*, we've done something at last. We're finally on
our damned way."

Julio looked at the marks in apprehension. "You've forgotten
to bring the studies."

Goya laughed sharply and tapped his head. "All I need from
those I've got right here." He pointed to the lines he had just
inscribed, which were meaningless to Julio. "We don't even
have to worry about *those*. If it turns out that they're not quite
properly placed, we can hide them with color. From the floor,
no one will know the difference. And it's only from the floor,
Ascensio, that they'll see what we've done."

"You're going to paint this from memory, master?" The younger man was appalled.

"Memory?" Goya's laughter was nearly hysterical. "I'm going to paint this thing straight from my soul."

"You worry me."

"Well, stop worrying. Lower that bucket for more plaster. We have work to do."

Goya squatted on the floor of the lofty platform and, with a sharp knife, began to shorten a number of thick brushes, in order that the colors they carried, when applied to the surface, could be variously textured and thus capable of reflecting the light from the windows of the lantern or from the chandelier that would be suspended from the center of the dome. The first tones he used were of the pale blue-gray for the sky that radiated from the center of the concave form. Goya worked with a swift sureness that astounded even Julio, who knew his master's hasty technique. He was barely able to add plaster quickly enough to keep up with Paco's flying brushes. "This is the dreary stuff, Ascensio, so let's get through it as soon as we can. Then we can begin enjoying ourselves. I can hardly wait."

"I can see that," said Julio worriedly.

But wait they must, and Goya proved increasingly difficult to live with. A week passed in which he failed to call on María, and only the central portions of the ceiling, with a single, softly outlined tree and blue-green mountain landscape, were completed.

"You'll make me sorry that I ever opened my mouth if this is what you're like when you're painting something that's important to you," said the duchess when he finally put in an appearance at the Palacio de Liria.

"Ah, amigita, be patient with me. When this thing is finished, you'll want to have a hundred masses said for me."

"Me? You know what I'll want."

He leered. "You want it now?"

"You smell."

"You're talking to the greatest living painter."

"If you want to touch me, you can bathe."

"You have no respect for your own creation?"

"I hate myself for having thought of it."

But she was, of course, enchanted with his enchantment.

"You'll take me like this," he roared, "or not at all."

She whimpered. "I might as well have a swineherd."

The fresco process demanded the scrupulous masking, with tempera or dry color, of the demarcation between the work of one day and that of the next. Goya assigned this meticulous and onerous task to Julio, who accepted it with his usual gentle affability, even going so far as to express gratitude for being given a role of importance in so grandiose an undertaking.

As soon as he had inscribed the outlines of the first human figure, that of San Antonio, the painter's mood was abruptly transformed. All the fury and impatience that had marked his behavior during the previous fortnight were drained from him. For this was the instant to which he had so long looked forward. "It's the people who matter in this damned thing, Ascensio," he bawled. "And *there's* the first person."

Little Julio's earlier awe was redoubled as he watched the master sprawl on the dun shades of the saint's robe, the brushstrokes so quick that they seemed not gestures of creation, but acts of violence, brutality, as if he were flogging the ceiling; he was like one pressed on by some dark, terrible, terrifying force, a force over which he neither had nor sought control. He seemed to be acting out a dream of which poor Ascensio must remain ignorant. Because the two men were so close to the surface they were covering, it was impossible for Julio to comprehend the nature of his master's plan. And this was the more alarming because the dome was invisible from the floor, hidden by the scaffolding. With each day's progress, the assistant's anxiety increased. The images so rapidly evolving appeared to him all daubs and streaks and splashes of color hurled against the damp plaster more or less at random. Here and there, it was true, certain facial and other anatomical features could be discerned in the general confusion, but from the platform they were vague, devoid of the sharpness that normally characterized the work of Goya. The single element that was easily identified was a painted railing that encircled the base of the dome. This, the artist explained, was a device he had borrowed from the Tiepolos. "But mine is different. None of their elegant stone balustrades for me, Ascensio. Where have you seen a barrier like this before?"

"On a balcony, or at the *corrida,* master."

"Correct, and that sets the proper atmosphere, something simple but definite, and not obtrusive. It's a framework, so you can see things happening *on* it, and *behind* it. It's part of the scene."

Julio had to acknowledge that this was so. A portion of the railing was concealed by a draped white cloth. In another section, just beneath the towering figure of San Antonio, an urchin was sitting astride it, while a second was attempting to climb it. Such comprehensible fragments, however, were too few to suggest a coherent impression of the whole. Julio held his tongue, though by now he was persuaded that Goya had lost contact with reason. He attended to his tasks of concealing the boundaries between each day's work and removing the sections of unpainted plaster left over from the previous evening—for only a moist surface would absorb the pigments.

After more than a month of daily toil, the painting of the dome was finished. Julio was breathless with a fearful excitement as he and Goya stood by while workmen undertook the dismantling of the scaffold. The master appeared calm, even indifferent. "I don't understand what's upsetting you, Ascensio. I know what the damned thing's going to look like."

"But *I* don't, master."

"Oh, ye of little faith."

"It's no lack of faith," the assistant lied. "It's curiosity."

But his anxiety was not to be relieved that day. By the time the complicated staging had been fully removed, the September evening darkness prevented him from seeing enough of the ceiling to gain more than the slightest sense of its form and tonality. So great were his apprehensions that he was uncharacteristically adamant in his refusal of Goya's invitation to share a

ceremonial bottle at the *taberna.* "Thank you all the same,
master, but I'm going to spend the night here."
"Without even a bit of bread or cheese?"
"I don't think I could eat if my life depended on it."
"You're as skeptical as that?"
Julio flushed and was happy that Paco couldn't detect his
reaction in the failing light. "That *concerned,* that *involved,*
that *excited.* After all, it's the first time I've had anything to do
with a fresco."
The painter recognized the lie and understood its charitable
inspiration. He was touched. He chuckled softly and laid a
sympathetic hand on the younger man's narrow, bony shoulder.
"Well, it's done. It's not going to be changed in the night, you
know, so come along, for God's sake, and keep me company."
"But don't you understand, master? I *have* to stay."
"And you can sleep here, *amigo?*"
"As well as in my own bed, and that's not very well. I shall
dream."
"Dream reasonably then," said the departing Paco. "*I* shall
sleep like a baby." This too was a lie.
Julio's sleep was fitful. His dreams, like Goya's new etchings,
were caricatures of the physically and emotionally depleting
weeks spent on the scaffolding. He awakened with the first light,
and hastened from his improvised bed of rumpled canvas to the
center of the transept crossing. His red, weary eyes were un-
blinking as he gazed intently upward. But it was still too dark
for him to make out appreciably more than he had seen the
previous evening. He lay down on the cold tiles, waiting and
watching with damp eyes as the great circular painting gradually, tantalizingly disclosed itself in the growing light of the
rising sun. Suddenly, there was a moment when he realized that
he was seeing the fresco completely. Only then did he appreciate, with conflicting feelings of admiration and chagrin, what
Goya had contrived. His awe wasn't limited to the miracle of
brushwork that his master had accomplished with such apparent
ease. The relevance of this technical brilliance, however stun-

ning to one who so well understood the degree of its virtuosity, was all but effaced by a second discovery—the scene itself.

"I'm going to make two revolutions," Goya had told him. And it was the second which Julio had just grasped. For this was no ordinary ceiling fresco. Tiepolo's angels were not deployed in the clouds which clustered over the mountain landscape. The conventions were flouted. It was the custom, when depicting an earthly event, to show it in the hemisphere of the apse, so that the heavenly host, in a gloria, looked benignly down upon it. In Goya's rendering, the seraphic multitude would have to look up at San Antonio's miracle. Moreover, the scene differed in substance from any the studious Julio had noted in other churches. While the posture and placement of the saint were conventional, the figures surrounding him represented an extraordinary departure from the types made traditional in Spain by Italian and French fresco painters. In addition to the pair of scruffy lads on the railing, there were numerous characters drawn from the ranks of the common people—the *manolos* and *manolas,* the *majos* and *majas,* the beggars and madmen and whores who thronged through the streets and squares of Madrid.

There were other differences. The usual rendition of this legend placed it in a crypt in which the corpse of the murdered man was entombed. Goya had created a scene out of doors, a street scene. Julio apprehended further discrepancies: Although some of the onlookers appeared suitably rapt or reverent, others peered vacantly into space, absorbed in private reflections. A few spectators were plainly bored. Ascensio wondered how the Holy Office, well known for its concern over the iconographic proprieties, would react to Goya's dallying with tradition.

The manner was totally new, technically, pictorially, and spiritually. The colors were boldly bright and boldly dark; the effect was of intense drama. Only the pallid sky and remote landscape were in soft shades, so that attention was drawn to the activity taking place at the base of the dome. The setting was Madrid, not Lisbon; the occurrence of the present, not of centuries past. And it was happening in the presence of the people, not before a solemn, select group of nobles and clerics, as was the rule.

With a sigh of wonder and exhaustion, Julio fell asleep in his position beneath the dome. When the workmen entered the church to erect a platform in the apse, their ribald chatter and the noise of their hammers and saws failed to disturb him. He was awakened by the gentle pressure of Goya's boot prodding his ribs. He started and stood up, much embarrassed.

"Well," inquired the painter mildly, "will it do?"

"I'll never doubt you again, master."

Goya casually glanced up at his handiwork and nodded. "It's really not bad, is it?" He grinned. "To tell you the truth, Ascensio, *I* had a few doubts about it myself after I left you. I drank a bottle of wine and even that didn't help me sleep."

"I'm glad I wasn't alone in my doubts."

"To the devil with it now."

"*Now*," said Julio fervently. "But I'll never forget last night."

"Nor shall I. I've brought you some food. You must be starved, so get it inside you. We have to get on with this. There are other mountains to climb."

"But the dome is finished, master, and it's a miracle."

"I wonder how many others will have the intelligence to share your opinion."

"I've wondered too," said Julio.

Goya jammed his roughened hands into the pockets of his dusty smock and grimaced. "To the devil with *that* too. It doesn't matter. For once in my life, I'm satisfied simply to have done something for wanting to do it. What anyone else thinks is unimportant. *You* know and *I* know that it's the finest thing I've ever painted."

"But *do* I know that? It's the most daring—but the finest?"

"You just called it a miracle."

"Because of the way you did it, the way it seemed to spring from you."

"You *have* the point but you don't understand it. I painted my feelings."

"Very unusual," said Julio weakly.

"Unusual?" bellowed Goya. "It's goddamned well unique. That's *me* up there, that's Goya. There, at last, is a painting that expresses myself alone."

"But is that what a painter ought to do?"

"Why not? Should a painter always do the thing that's expected of him? Must he always please someone else?"

"I thought . . ."

"But that's it, *amigo*. I *didn't* think. I know what *you* thought. How else is the artist to live? Quite right. But suppose, as now, the moment presents itself. If he can get away with it, a fellow should clutch at the chance with both hands and run as if he were pursued by Satan himself. The chances are that few."

"Who has ever done such a thing before?"

Goya considered this, then responded coolly, "I can think of three artists: Michelangelo, El Greco, and Rembrandt." He laughed softly. "That's not bad company for a simple Zaragozan, is it?"

Not before the middle of November was the work in the Hermitage of San Antonio de la Florida completed. And by this time Madrid was not disposed to receive, with either approval or scorn, any work of art, however important—even one whose author was proclaiming it to be his apotheosis. When the scaffolding was finally taken down and the floors cleaned, a representative of the Madrid hierarchy viewed the frescoes for a full ten minutes, nodded, and went away to instruct his superiors that final payment for the work should be made. This was the extent of official recognition.

For while Goya and his assistants had been at their daily labors, the rest of the populace had been preoccupied with rumors and factual reports about life in the upper reaches of the government. Shortly after the painter began work on the dome, Saavedra resigned his post, pleading an illness that was more diplomatic than debilitating. He was supplanted by Don Mariano Luis de Urquijo, whose principal known virtue was a prolonged physical intimacy with the Marquesa de Branciforte,

Godoy's sister, a connection that few liberals thought promising for the future of their country. And shortly before the frescoes were completed, Jovellanos retired. His successor, Caballero, was a magistrate who had enjoyed a spectacular rise from provincial obscurity under the protection of the Prince of the Peace.

Goya's initial response of alarm gave way to relief when he learned that Jovellanos had resumed his former office of chief justice. It was deplorable that Godoy had compelled him and Saavedra to quit the government, but the men who regularly gathered at the *taberna* conceded that neither Urquijo nor Caballero was unintelligent nor a craven disciple of the detested prince.

But when the painter was thus reassured about the political situation, he found time to reflect upon his disappointment over the failure of Madrid (meaning, especially, the royal family who had commissioned it) to remark on the magnitude of his achievement in the church of San Antonio. Mariano Maella, the only artist to rival Goya in reputation (and that but feebly), paid an almost clandestine visit to the hermitage and dismissed what he saw, in his next meeting with its creator, as amateurish. "A child could have done no worse, Paco. You should have studied the Casita del Labrado in Aranjuez before you started, to see how *I* make frescoes. That's what you should paint like, and I'm not talking just about the unorthodoxy of your ideas. You paint like a madman."

"How do *you* know? The last time *you* had an idea—"

"Ideas are beside the point. Who needs ideas?"

"Spain does."

Maella moaned. "Not again, please. Spain would choke on a new idea, and before you're done, I warn you, *you'll* choke on Spain."

"Never," said Goya hotly.

The painter took Maella's scorn as high praise, so low an opinion did he have of his critic's vapid style. For the rest, such comment as there was proved indifferent but, astonishingly, never outraged. It would be a long time, Goya suspected, before his frescoes were understood and valued. The most informed and sympathetic of his friends, Ceán Bermúdez, evinced nothing more amazing than: "Curious . . . interesting . . . different." Goya must content himself with his own certainty of their brilliance and dear Julio's awe.

There was little time for him to cherish his rue. Another matter pressed for his attention. The printer Cardeña informed him that he was ready to begin producing the etchings on which Goya had been working sporadically since his return from Sanlúcar. The prospect was exciting, for here, by God, was a thing that *must* attract just the sort of attention that had been denied the San Antonio frescoes. Here was a volume that would be in the hands of many Madrileños, be in their homes, on their tables, impossible to ignore. As soon as he had completed the San Antonio commission, he began making diurnal visits to Cardeña's shop to supervise the printing of his plates.

He was thrilled as the copies accumulated. "Christ, Leandro," he said to Moratín, "it gives me such a feeling of power, to think that I'm making something that's to be reproduced three hundred times, that three hundred different people will have copies of it."

From the moment he had been informed of the project, the literary Moratín had taken a great and critical interest in it. He became his friend's informal editor, advising him that some of the pictures would be thought seditious; these Goya didn't commit to plates. "You're taking a risk by issuing these just now. People are very edgy, and the ones who are edgiest are at the top. Even Godoy is treading lightly. Why don't you wait?"

"Most of them are funny, very funny. Isn't that the prescription for a nervous period? They'll take people's minds off their worries. What could be happier?"

"You think them amusing?"

"They've amused you."

"Privately, Paco. But the amusement is malicious. If you circulated a few copies privately, among those who know you and love you and understand you, I'd not be concerned. An edition of three hundred is different."

"What would you have me do? Cardeña says I have to sell two hundred copies before I recover my expenses."

The librarian chuckled, as did most of Goya's friends when he brought up the subject of money. "But suppose a copy falls into the wrong hands."

"I've withdrawn every picture you thought too pointed. Have you other reservations?"

Moratín frowned and shuffled his feet in embarrassment. "Perhaps. It's odd. When I saw them simply as drawings, I was looking at them as individual things. *I* was looking at them for *my* eyes only. I wasn't thinking of them as pictures intended for a wide circulation. I recognized how biting they were, how bitter."

"Bitter?"

"Of course they are. *You* can see that. Especially the ones where the figures are so easily identified. How will the king and queen and Godoy feel when they see themselves as you've so ingeniously cast them? When it comes to that, I'd suppose your own Doña María might take exception to seeing her head on the body of a bird. You're so damned arrogant, Paco. You think no one will dare attack Goya."

The painter's smile was ravishing. "Oh, there may be a ruffled feather here and there, but I can't see that as a good enough reason to withdraw a volume of ninety plates. I've got sixty thousand reales tied up in this."

"Well, if you must go ahead, the only thing I can suggest is that you soften the blow. I'd publish a notice in the *Diario de Madrid* disclaiming any intention of representing real people. Say that your only aim is to condemn human folly and vice and stupidity in the most general terms, that you're not commenting on particular events."

Goya was skeptical. "Will anyone believe it after seeing the etchings?"

Moratín smiled cunningly. "Probably not. But which of the people you've so cruelly portrayed will come forward to object? Who wants to add to the publicity? The more so if you've already publicly disavowed any ulterior motive."

"Including the Holy Office?"

"Peculiarly enough," said the librarian, "it's *there* that I think you're on the safest ground. For the temper of the times is on your side. The Inquisition isn't so highly considered now, since the Archbishop of Toledo failed to get Godoy condemned. I don't think you'll have trouble with the church. No, it's the sausage merchant and his whore that I'm most worried about."

"And you think this notice in the press will help?"

"It can't do any harm."

"Will you compose it for me, Leandro? Words aren't my weapon."

Moratín carefully drafted three short paragraphs which were inserted in the *Diario de Madrid* for February 6, 1799. The painter professed a wholly moral purpose and followed this disclaimer with the information that copies of *Los Caprichos,* as he called the volume, were currently on sale in the sweetshop that occupied the ground floor of his residence in the Calle del Desengaño. The price was one ounce of gold or 320 reales. In slightly revised form, the same advertisement was reprinted in the capital's rival paper, *Gaceta de Madrid,* a fortnight later. Further to convince the public of his lofty intent, Goya persuaded Moratín to prepare brief explanatory texts for each of the plates, generalizations that tended to blur the impact of the ferocious etchings themselves.

The palliative tone of the published notices and the exegetic captions did no harm and thus may have served their purpose. For Goya was apprised of not a single wail or bellow of outrage from any of the notable persons of Madrid's society whom he had so rudely and cavalierly depicted in the fantasies, satires, and cautionary illustrations that made up the large collection— the first of its kind to appear in Spain, and the most scathing to be published anywhere.

The *acalofilos* were pleased with *Los Caprichos,* for in many of the plates Goya had shown with savage honesty the plight of the poor, especially those of Madrid. He could never drive from his memory the shock of revelation when he had stepped down from the *diligencia* that had brought him to the capital from

Zaragoza more than thirty years earlier. There, in the Plaza Mayor with its fine old buildings, he had been importuned by beggars of every description, most of them cripples—blind, limbless, bent with age or deformity, clutching at his cloak from all sides. That most of these defects had been inflicted by the beggars' parents, to make them more proficient at the only trade they could ply in the miserable economy of Spain, merely added to the horror. And after three decades, he was still unable to turn aside, to refuse a beggar in the cold manner affected by most Madrileños. "You've shown the world what Spain is really like, Paco," said Jovellanos sadly. "It's terrible, but it's true."

María, however, was understandably annoyed, for Goya had unkindly exploited her features in several of the pictures. The one to which Moratín had referred was the most striking because it seemed the most pointed. To mitigate its cruelty, the artist had incorporated a portrait of himself, also in the guise of a bird, watching with jealousy from the lower branch of a tree as his mistress flirted with a bird-*torero* on a higher branch. Elsewhere, she appeared as a whore, as a *maja*, as a dancer dressing while a monstrously caricatured La Beata leared.

"Why, Paco?" she cried after going through the copy of *Los Caprichos* which he had presented her.

"Because you tease me."

"You said I made teasing bearable."

"Not since we've been back in Madrid. You meant to hurt me."

"So cruel?"

"Wry, I think, and sad."

"Savage."

"Exact."

María then professed herself more amused than offended, more pleased to be included than to have been left out—the only alternative, Paco assured her. I've drawn only the things I've seen or felt."

She shuddered. "What a terrible soul you have, *querido*."

"Every time you say that, you make it seem a new discovery." He turned to the forty-third plate: A seated man was asleep, his head resting on a table, his slumber disturbed by a swarm of demonic creatures, the monsters of Goya's nightmares. The caption was, "The sleep of reason produces monsters."

"That," he said, "was meant to be the frontispiece. It's the real burden of all these etchings: When we stop thinking, when *Spain* stops thinking, when reason ceases to function, we give ourselves up to possession by monsters—the monsters of ignorance and greed and self-obsession, monsters like Godoy and Doña María Luisa . . . "

"Monsters like Goya and Doña María del Pilár?"

"Obviously."

"We're as terrible as that?"

"We haven't the purity and simplicity of the poor."

"You hate the condition of the poor as much as I do."

"Like all missionaries, I must know at first hand the sins I condemn . . . like vice and avarice as well as poverty."

"Hypocrite. If this picture is so important, why isn't it at the beginning? Why do you hide it?"

"Leandro thought the message too easy to understand. 'Put something harmless at the beginning,' he told me." Goya laughed uneasily. "I could think of nothing less harmful than a portrait of myself, and that's why it's the frontispiece."

"Moratín thinks this picture of the man asleep subversive?"

He nodded. "Because reason is asleep in Spain."

"Nothing new about that idea," said the duchess. "My grandfather used to say that Spain died with Felipe II, but what he really meant was that she died with his great-grandfather Alba, when Felipe lost his only good general."

"You agree with me, then."

"But I don't believe your pictures. *Such* monsters?"

"*My* monsters, María. The ones my mama told me about. But here, I mean them to be Spain's monsters."

"So irrational? Who'll believe you?"

"I'm not sure I want to be believed. If Godoy understood, I'd be in prison tomorrow."

"Why run the risk?"

"You challenged me. I told you I dared anything, and that

was a lie. I've always been a coward, or until now. But now, something has to be said, even if it's put as timidly as I put it here."

"Challenge or not," she said, dropping the heavy book to the floor, "I wish you no good fortune for this, Paco."

"But why? It has its origins in you."

"'I didn't expect anything so horrible, so bitter."

"That was Leandro's word for it, too. But it's not really bitter."

"All right, angry, enraged. The word doesn't matter. You know what I mean. Your friends may find these pictures diverting, but *I* don't. I don't recognize *you* in them. They're cruel and crude and ugly, the inventions of a diseased mind, a sick imagination."

"You'll not forgive me?"

"But I've not *condemned* you. You're not the first man to do something I don't like. I love you, but I detest your book."

"Yet you said you were happy to be included."

"I don't confuse vanity with common sense. My vanity is bruised but, on the whole, flattered. Sensibly, I'm disillusioned."

"Then I'm glad I didn't dedicate the book to you."

"I'd have refused you permission."

As he rode back to Madrid, Goya remembered María's phrase, "the inventions of a diseased mind, a sick imagination." The truth of the accusation scalded. Ever since childhood, his fantasies had been "sick," "diseased." But since the moment of recovering consciousness, after his illness in Cádiz, these qualities had been emphasized more strongly than any other. The hallucinations of his period of delirium still haunted him, and they pervaded *Los Caprichos*. The arrival of his carriage in the Calle del Desengaño interrupted this reflection. He had been living on borrowed time since 1792. Who better than he, therefore, to afford the risk of publishing these veiled attacks against authority? Were *Los Caprichos* to effect a single happy change, a purpose would have been honored. As he stepped out of the coach, he felt proud of himself, felt courageous. Goya was a sort of hero. Who would have thought it possible?

The duchess' curse was, however, prophetic. By early summer, fewer than thirty copies of *Los Caprichos* had been sold to the public. Old Tomasina, who had been proprietress of the sweetshop on the ground floor of Goya's house for years before he had purchased it, protested that the tall stacks of unsold folios were interfering with her trade. "If you don't get them out of here, Don Paco, *I'll* start charging *you* rent." With bitterness, he ordered his domestics to remove all but a sample copy from Tomasina's premises.

When he complained to Moratín that he had lost 50,000 reales on the project, the librarian laughed and told him to keep quiet. "You're lucky you weren't brought before the Inquisition. There were rumblings, according to Gaspar."

"I was told nothing."

"What was the point of telling you."

"What's the point now?"

"Your self-pity. As long as there wasn't a large sale, you were safe enough."

"What were these rumblings?"

"A bit of unhappiness in high ecclesiastical places. You portrayed the church as an ass. That's unusual."

"Why wasn't I summoned before the tribunal?"

Moratín grinned. "You're disappointed?"

"I'd prepared myself for any ordeal."

"You have Gaspar and me to thank for being spared."

"I know you meant well, Leandro, so of course I do thank you. But I did nothing I'm ashamed of."

"Goya, the *new* Goya, defender of Spain's virtue."

The court was concerned with matters it thought more important than Goya's corrosive satires on its manners and morals. The queen had chosen yet another lover, a young nobleman named Mallo; like Godoy, he was an officer in the royal bodyguard. She appointed him majordomo. The Prince of the Peace, nevertheless, was still the power behind the throne, because the king trusted no one else, and for all his attentions to Pepa Tudo, he still retained the affection of Doña María Luisa.

Mallo's intrusion disturbed him as had no other such royal liaison, for he recognized in the young officer's eyes the same glint of fathomless ambition he perceived in his own. Indeed, Mallo was almost a mirror image of Godoy—attractive, stupid, shrewd, arrogant, and without the encumbrance of a solitary scruple. The prince forced the issue with a decisiveness that would have done him credit had he chosen to apply it to matters of state.

Godoy selected wisely his moment for action. The king (whose refusal to believe his wife guilty of any imperfection was legendary) casually inquired of the prince just what sort of person this Mallo creature was. The reply was sufficiently oblique to be intriguing without leaving room for possible confusion in the vacant mind of Don Carlos. Mallo, he said, was at the moment being kept by an ugly old woman of high birth whom he was systematically plundering. Although the great lady wasn't named, the message was clear to the king, who was annoyed by this cutting reference to the woman he adored. But he was even more upset by the alleged conduct of the officer. He must discuss his doubts with someone else. Who else was there except Doña María Luisa, from whom, in any case, he could never keep a secret? He reported to her the gist of his conversation with Don Manuel. Her anger was amazing to her husband, and its increase was geometrically intensified when she learned that the king had dismissed Mallo from his service.

The young man retired in consternation to his family's estate near Madrid, there to contemplate revenge for Godoy's treachery. The prince, however, gave him no time for putting a plan into action. Within a week of his banishment, a small company of guards surrounded the Mallo residence and conducted a detailed search of its contents. They returned to the capital with a collection of fascinating trophies—some secret state papers and, of greater utility to Godoy in his scheme to regain absolute power, a number of most compromising letters in the hand of the queen. When he confronted his erstwhile mistress with this evidence, he brought her meekly to her knees. Though she didn't say so, the queen was delighted by this turn of events; Mallo wasn't nearly so skilled a lover as Godoy.

"It won't be long," said Jovellanos, staring unhappily into his manzanilla, "before the sausage merchant is in complete charge again."

"Not, I hope, before I've finished my portrait of Urquijo," said Goya.

"You'd better work quickly. Things could change at any moment."

The invitation to portray the man who bore, for however brief a period, the title of first minister had come but a few months after the appearance of *Los Caprichos*—evidence that whatever the opinion of the church, the artist's reputation had not been at all impaired by their publication. He had been tempted to decline the commission, but not because he had anything against Urquijo. The man was amiable enough. The combined disappointments of public indifference to the San Antonio frescoes and his etchings had taken away much of his enthusiasm for work, no matter how profitable or prestigious. "Portraits," he had muttered to Julio. "That's the only thing anyone really wants of me."

He agreed to paint Urquijo because his friends said it would be politic. The portrait, though faithful in Goya's unique fashion to the man, disclosed the artist's downcast state of mind. It possessed neither fire nor conviction.

"I don't seem to care about anything anymore, except you," he complained to María.

"You need a new woman."

He embraced her with a fervor that was rare these days. "You're never to say that again, do you hear? I won't forgive you."

"All right, all right." Her face became grave. "You know, Paco, you're the first man who has ever been able to intimidate me."

"I meant it."

"I promise."

"But I *do* need something new, something different, something challenging. You're right about that. But I don't need a new woman. I can't even take proper care of you."

six

GOYA WAS BREAKFASTING in bed on the morning of October 31, 1799, a customary luxury he rationalized by grim references to his "declining years," a condition in which he took perverse pleasure—though in fact he had not been in such robust health since his youth. He was emptying a cup of hot chocolate, wondering when the heat from the copper brazier would give appreciable warmth to the large room, when Javier cautiously entered.

Almost sixteen now, the painter's only child was dressed for the fashionable college "for sons of gentlemen" that he attended. But even in this severe black habit he retained the willowy elegance his father had succeeded brilliantly in capturing in a portrait he had made a few weeks after the publication of *Los Caprichos*—a painting as vital as his more recent works seemed to him lifeless and mechanical. Yet the remoteness between father and son persisted. Javier disliked his father because he loved his mother. This distaste manifested itself in small ways—a mild scorn for Goya's dress, for his affair with the Duchess of Alba, for his awkwardness. The boy respected his father's achievements and continued to mulct him of favors and gratuities; these he deemed penalties for Goya's failure as a parent. The sight of him could break Paco's heart.

Javier crossed the floor with grace, even with daintiness, qualities he had inherited from the Bayeus. He handed his father a large, sealed document and looked over his shoulder as Goya read:

"Desiring to reward your great personal merits as an artist, and desiring through you to furnish the fine arts with a testimonial of the importance in which he holds them, and to demonstrate to you in person the high esteem in which he holds your talent in the noble craft you have so long embraced, His Gracious and Most Catholic Majesty has commanded me to inform you of your appointment to the post of First Painter of the Royal Chamber, with an emolument of 50,000 reales per annum, together with an additional allowance of 5,500 reales per annum for the maintenance of the official carriage which will be placed at your disposal as a perquisite of this office." The elaborately underscored signature was that of Urquijo.

Goya let the sheet of paper fall to the floor and rested his heavy, graying head against the bolster. He sighed. His hands were trembling. He smiled wistfully. "I wonder what great scheme they have in mind for me."

Javier was much more impressed by the news than his father. "It's an honor, surely, Papa. Don Carlos can do no more for you than this."

"He could have done it when your uncle Francho died."

"He's just acknowledging, if a little late, what everyone else in Spain has known for years, that you're our greatest painter."

Paco looked hopefully into the clear, untroubled, pale features of his beloved son. He detested his suspicion of Javier's motives for this praise. They came so easily, his words. There was an odd formality about them, like something he had memorized without conviction—like his own recent portraits. "Perhaps," he murmured wearily. "But I'll bet that's not the whole explanation. Things just don't happen that way. You can't understand that yet, of course, and I'm glad of it. Keep your illusions as long as you can, Javier. They're the only source of untroubled pleasure in life. But in time you'll lose them, and you'll see that everything, every man, has a price."

"You're not going to refuse it."

The artist chuckled. "Refuse it? Of course not. Refuse fifty thousand reales, *and* a carriage, not to mention what you call the 'honor.' What would your mother say?"

Javier moved toward the door, then turned, determined to have the last word. "I didn't think you cared about what Mama thinks, one way or the other."

"I know how you feel about me, *hijo*. On the whole, I suppose I deserve it. But there are factors you don't know anything about. You'll have to learn to think for yourself one of these days. It's a much more important lesson than any you're taught in that fine school." With a tired gesture, Goya waved his son from the room.

María was delighted by the news of his elevation to the post of Pintor de Cámara and deplored his reception of it. "Sometimes I think you're secretly a Protestant, Paco. You like to deny yourself pleasure, don't you? Ever since you were stung, and so properly too, by those filthy etchings, you've been behaving just like one of those donkeys you drew, idiotic and willful and childish. You want your way, and nothing else will do."

"You think me wrong to be skeptical?"

"I think you wrong to be *only* skeptical."

"The king has no big project for me?"

"Of course he does."

"Well, then . . ."

"Well, then, *what?* Favors are given for favors received, a *quid pro quo*. It's as old as Adam. Must you be the exception in everything?" Her exasperation mounted. "I don't know whether to spank you or console you."

"I want to show that I *am* the exception."

She studied him, her eyes bright with tender amusement. "You want me to persuade you to accept this honor, don't you?"

"Of course not," he growled, and shifted his position to remove a cushion from the couch he was sitting on. He threw it, with no accuracy, at his mistress' head.

She caught it easily and stood up to drop it in his lap. "Try again."

"How you love to torment me, María." His tone belied the words.

"What a boy you are. You're excited and pleased. It's the nicest thing that's ever happened to you."

"No. *You're* that."

She waved the flattery aside. "You've written your friend Zapater about it already, haven't you?"

Goya flushed. "I mentioned it. I didn't say I was accepting, though. I wasn't boasting."

She frowned. "Was there ever any doubt about your accepting?"

"Never."

"So who, in fact, was tormenting *whom?*"

For the first time in years, Josefa accompanied her husband to an official reception. She stood beside him, smiling, as he was invested with the sash and scroll which accorded him the title and honor of Pintor de Cámara. The ceremony was brief. The king, who was asked to preside at such occasions more often than he would have liked, was in haste to be off to the chase in the great park of El Retiro, which was stocked with game for his delectation. Clearly bored, plumper and ruddier than when Goya had last seen him, Don Carlos made polite but perfunctory inquiries about Don Francisco's health, about Josefa's and Javier's. She blushed furiously when her monarch questioned her and stammered the lie that she had never felt better in her life. The king said he was delighted (but his manner was of indifference) with the frescoes in San Antonio. "So unusual," was his most perceptive comment. "But then," he added with the wisp of a smile, "the unusual in all things is what we expect from you, Don Francisco."

Don Carlos paused for a diplomatic cough, embarrassed that he must now come to the point. He turned to Urquijo, who bowed to Goya. "His Majesty would like me to suggest, I believe, that it might not be inappropriate if you were to commemorate the tenth anniversary of his coronation by painting a portrait of the royal family."

This was not the moment for laughter, though Goya had difficulty suppressing it. He bowed first to Don Carlos, then to

Urquijo, and returned his gaze to the fatuous king. "You've already made me the happiest of men, sire, by naming me Pintor de Cámara. Now you've made me the proudest, all in the one day."

Goya's appointment was marked by a ball given by the Duke and Duchess of Osuna in their great Alameda. It was only at the painter's absolute insistence that Josefa attended; even the lure of a fine new gown and a jewel-encrusted pendant was of doubtful attraction, for she well knew and feared that she would that evening be confronted by at least two of the great ladies who had robbed her of her husband's affections. He paid no heed to her protests; her absence would be unthinkable. "It's not as if either of the duchesses was going to eat you, Josefa. And you have nothing to reproach them for. They didn't take anything from you that you wanted."

"Can you be so insensitive?" she wailed. "*Can* you? I *did* want you."

"But not as I was. Not on terms acceptable to me."

"I admit my error."

"Heaven, I'm sure, will be pleased, but it's too late for me. You'll just have to put as good a face on it as you can."

"Will you dance with me?" she asked timidly.

"It's up to you. If you don't mind my stepping on your feet. I can't hear the music. Or have you forgotten that I'm deaf."

"Do you ever let me forget?"

"*I* can't forget it."

This mood prevailed throughout the day. Just before their arrival at the Alameda de Osuna, they were bickering. Josefa drew a handkerchief from her white satin sack and wiped her eyes. "I don't know why we bother to talk to each other anymore, Paco. All we do is quarrel."

The coach jerked to a stop. Goya didn't wait for the footman to open the door. He jumped out and paused with furious impatience while the servant helped his wife to step down. She took his arm and submitted in silence as he drew her angrily into the great entrance hall. By the time they had been divested of their cloaks, the painter's temper had cooled. He was even apologetic. "No point in spoiling the rest of the evening."

She heartily agreed, though she was still alarmed at the prospect of having to meet her rivals, former and present. The Duchess of Osuna partially allayed her misgivings when she took Josefa's hands in hers. "I'm so glad you were well enough to come. Don Paco has told me how ill you've been." The women conversed with superficial amiability on the subject that was of tireless interest to the painter's wife—health, and in particular her own. For a time, she forgot that Doña María Teresa de Osuna and Paco had been lovers for years.

When the dancing began, Paco tried to make amends for his churlishness. He led Josefa to the floor and sought to emulate the movements of the other couples who were performing the sarabande, guiding himself imperfectly by his sensing of the tempo through the soles of his shoes. His effort would have been calamitous were it not comical. Immeasurably stronger than his wife, he ignored her attempts to guide him. At last, unable to endure any longer the chagrin of the spectacle he was making of her, Josefa dropped her arms. "You idiot," she mouthed. "Follow me."

"I was doing my best," he replied sadly and led her to a chair. "I thought you wanted me to dance with you."

"It was as if I were a bull and you were the *torero*."

"I'm that sort of fellow. Other women like it."

This exchange was interrupted by the arrival of the Duchess of Alba, who made her appearance on the arm of a young dancer who was enjoying the praise of all Madrid. When the formalities of greeting the hostess had been warmly accomplished, the couple whirled effortlessly across the floor of the ballroom. They performed with a grace so superb that Goya, raging in silence at his mistress' effrontery, couldn't withhold his admiration—the artist at war with the lover. As soon as the music stopped, María led her latest conquest to Goya and Josefa. Her eyes brimmed with wicked pleasure as she allowed the painter to kiss her hand. Josefa rose and curtsied, by instinct, when presented to one so important, failing for the moment to recall that this was the great love of her husband's life.

The duchess blushed at this gesture of deference. "No, Doña Josefa, I beg of you. It's I who should curtsey to you."

"*I* always observe the customs, Doña María," Josefa responded with a sudden bitterness of a kind she had never dreamed herself capable of. She appraised the features and dress of Spain's greatest lady, remembering with a twinge of ironic humor that the last time she had seen her, she had wished Paco no worse a fate than to have this woman as his mistress. Now, her flesh crept at the thought.

María considered Josefa, trying to discern in the worn, weary features, the wispy reddish hair now going gray, the sad but tranquil eyes, just what it had been in her, even as a girl of sixteen, that Paco had found irresistible. It seemed doubtful that she had ever been a beauty. But delicate, fragile, and "well brought up." These qualities would have attracted a great brute of a boy, clumsy, animal, provincial, and burning with a desire to better himself.

The orchestra resumed. María's handsome partner tugged at her sleeve and seemed offended when she resisted. She slapped his hand but said nothing to him. "I'm so glad to have met you, Doña Josefa. We must see each other again to discuss our mutual interests—or should I say our mutual problems?"

"*Must* we, Doña María?" Josefa's voice was more plaintive than querulous. "I should have thought the opposite."

The duchess was undismayed. "Haven't we a great deal in common? Whatever you may think of me, I can promise you that if I thought it would be good for him, I'd never see your Paco again."

Surprisingly, especially to herself, Josefa giggled. "If I thought it would help me, Doña María, I'd do the same thing myself."

The young man attempted once more to attract his partner's attention. She turned on him, her eyes bright with fury. "You can go to the devil." She swept him off with a broad gesture of disdain, another servant banished. "Forgive that intrusion," she said to Josefa.

"I'm sure Paco would dance with you," said Goya's wife blandly.

The painter had been able to follow little of this conversation, though he comprehended its tenor. When María raised her eyes to his, he smiled and shook his head. Then, to Josefa, he murmured, "You bitch."

María smiled, then expressed reproach. "I appreciate the suggestion, Doña Josefa, but I prefer Paco in a horizontal position."

The wife bristled. "I daresay you know him best that way."

"I do," replied the duchess evenly. "Don't you agree, Paco?" Goya averted his eyes. "Leave me out of this."

The women laughed. "Isn't that just like a man," said María. "*He* causes the trouble, then demands to be left out of a conversation about the trouble he's caused." She offered her hand to Josefa. "Forgive me. I have to leave you. But let me tell you how interesting it's been to meet the woman Paco married when he was young."

Appointments to make studies of the numerous members of the royal family for the great portrait were settled immediately after Goya's investiture as Pintor de Cámara and put off within a matter of days. For news reached Madrid of a series of events in Paris on November 8, the *coup d'état* of 18 Brumaire, by means of which Sieyès, Fouché, and Talleyrand successfully effected the replacement of the five vacillating and purportedly corrupt members of the Directoire by a single head of state, the First Consul, Napoleon Bonaparte. This information was received in Madrid with relief, as a sign that the more extreme passions of the ultrarevolutionaries and the ultraroyalists, which had promised a renewal of the violence of the years 1789 through 1795, were cooling. Common sense would prevail at last because a true moderate was in power, one who would offer France the best of the rival factions. All would yet be well.

Although the Spanish government still clung officially to a

policy of restoring the legitimate Bourbons to the throne of France, it could acknowledge gracefully that Bonaparte was a more satisfactory alternative to absolutism than the Directoire.

In this atmosphere of optimism, a somewhat rejuvenated Goya undertook individual portraits of the king, the queen, and the young Prince of the Asturias, who would, presumably, succeed one day to the throne of Spain. He also made an equestrian portrait of Godoy, which prompted Moratín to inquire wickedly, "And does the horse have the features of the queen?" When the separate portraits were completed, Paco made head studies of all the other figures who were to appear in the painting of the entire family. The only significant absentee was the infanta Carlotta, wife of the Portuguese regent. His subjects differed dramatically in appearance, intelligence, and temperament, presenting him with problems of judgment and discretion that had not affected the other two family portraits he had created—those of the Osunas and the infante Don Luis. Of all the royal progeny, only Don Francisco de Paula and Doña María Isabel were more or less presentable physically; both of these children were believed to have been sired by Godoy, not Don Carlos. The crown prince, Don Fernando, was endowed with an ugliness that bordered on bestiality, and with an ignorance that even Goya, who normally admired simplicity of mind, considered frightening, given the fact that this youth might one day be king.

Even more grotesque were the features of Doña María Josefa, the king's sister. She wore an expression of perpetual bewilderment and was cursed by God with a birthmark of the dimensions and color of a ripe almond on her right temple. The king's younger brother, Don Antonio, seemed equally perplexed by life's little problems; his nephew Don Luis was a fop, and the young man's bride, posed in the portrait with her newborn son in her arms, was blessed with a prettiness that failed to disguise the absence of intelligence that characterized the Borbón family and many who married into it. Indeed, it was only in the rutted, sagging, debauched countenance of the queen, like that of an aging ape, that there appeared the minutest semblance of a functioning intellect—one so corrupted and befogged by the continuing indulgence of her insatiable appetites that it had long since ceased to operate in a rational manner. While painting her portrait, Goya exchanged perhaps ten sentences with Doña María Luisa, all quite desultory. Yet he conceived a curious sympathy for this rapacious woman. *She,* at least, understood her needs and knew how, if misguidedly, to go about satisfying them with a single-mindedness that the artist could understand, however much he might deplore them in the wife of his sovereign. He agreed that her notion of a Spain fit to be governed by Borbóns was as repugnant as the *acalofilos* maintained. But it *was* a notion; this woman had ideas, a talent she shared with no other member of her family.

With the completion of the studies Goya appreciated the dimensions of his difficulty. He arranged the collection of small canvases on the floor of his studio in an attempt to establish the posing for the final work. "What monsters," he grumbled to Julio. "If God had scoured the earth, He couldn't have brought together a less lovely group. And people have the temerity to criticize me for some of the faces I drew in *Los Caprichos.* But *this* is life. This is truth. These people exist as I've painted them. Can you believe it? And can you imagine what it will be like with these beasts together in one room?"

The occasion, however, passed off without problems. For the first time in a decade, the Spanish Borbóns could imagine that their position was strong. During the posing for the great portrait, the royal family was festive. They astonished Goya by their odd behavior. They slapped one another on shoulder or bottom, scratched themselves, roaring with laughter over the most dismal of inanities, jokes that even a peasant from his native Fuendetodos, in Aragón, would have thought simple-minded. The children played charades intended to mock the artist's deafness, imagining that because he couldn't hear their words he was unable to understand the meaning of their antics. No one thought it proper to rebuke their rudeness.

The only difficulty to develop during this session had to do with the placement of the Princess of the Asturias; there was none. A mate for Spain's crown prince had yet to be chosen, a fact that appeared extraordinary in an age when early betrothals were the rule with royalty and commoners alike. Goya had known that the queen was said to despise her eldest son and rarely missed an opportunity to show her scorn by showering gifts and affection on Don Francisco de Paula, thus serving the dual purpose of reproaching the lethargic Don Carlos and glorifying Godoy. She and the Prince of the Peace were alleged to be calculating and systematic in their attempts to brutalize the youth who must one day carry the name of Fernando VII. They had entrusted his education to an order of monks who were hardly more literate than their charge and had seen to it that whatever sensibilities he possessed were assailed by various outrages—their nature, however, undisclosed. "The boy is more of an oaf than his father," the queen was reported to have said of him in public, "and that's how he must be dealt with."

Certainly, Don Fernando wasn't very prepossessing in dress, manner, or deportment, but when Goya considered that this prince was only sixteen, Javier's age, he was filled with pity. The question of the nonexistent princess was tactfully resolved by the artist: He would paint in the figure of a young woman, dressed in the fashion of the queen and the other royal ladies in his picture. Her face was averted, so that the matter of her features didn't arise.

When this immense canvas was officially unveiled in the spring of 1800, it was accounted by all who viewed it to be a masterpiece. And so, Goya agreed, it was—a masterpiece of illumination, of color, of arrangements of bodies in space, of absolute (but not unsympathetic) honesty to the subjects. He had vindicated himself as a Spanish patriot by disclosing the full, horrible truth, and his integrity as an artist by managing to give this truth the quality of great aesthetic beauty. Delighted by the warmth of this reception, Goya feigned modesty. "But I'm an *acalofilo*. I have to love ugliness. How else should I have painted this?"

Urquijo was filled with wonder. "What a demonstration of

the power of genius over material. And I'm bound to tell you, confidentially, that the placement of your own portrait, in the background, so discreetly, was more flattering to Don Carlos than you can imagine." The minister laughed sardonically. " 'If Goya included a portrait of himself,' His Majesty told me, 'this must be a great picture.' "

"Only Velázquez has done better," Paco replied, "but *he* had more promising subjects than you gave *me*."

The euphoria generated by the 18 Brumaire of Paris was sustained in Spain through the whole of 1800. Carlos IV was pleased by the ascendancy of Bonaparte because, he believed, the French general would abrogate the revolutionary Civil Constitution of the Clergy and restore church property that had been confiscated. Only Don Carlos' devotion to his wife, to Godoy, and to the chase took precedence over his fidelity to the church and her ministers. No act of his father's more dismayed him than the banishment of the Jesuits, and he never ceased to blame the departed Count of Floridablanca for his role in this act of repression against God's soldiers.

Doña María Luisa's appreciation of the French *coup* was more hedonistic; it would now be easier for her to obtain her gowns from Paris. Her only regret was that her bloated torso made it impossible for her to wear the transparent dresses currently worn in Paris by *les merveilleuses,* the very final cry of Parisian fashion. To Godoy, a *rapprochement* with France suggested possibilities which, in his highly colored imagination, were limitless. Bonaparte had thought him the ideal candidate for the position of Grand Knight of Malta. That a number of years had elapsed since then, during which period Spain had consistently refused to keep her promises, was of no consequence in the prince's illusory appraisal.

Through Muzquiz, the Spanish ambassador in Paris, he organized a network of espionage agents whose mission was to report to Godoy personally. His plan was to be accurately informed of Bonaparte's true intentions for Spain, so that when he elected to displace Urquijo, he would know where Paris stood. The prince was pleased with himself for another reason. He was on the point of becoming a father, legitimately. Goya was put out by his friends' ribald conjecture that Godoy's little princess might have cuckolded her husband as he for so many years had been cuckolding the king. "You know nothing about her," the painter said contemptuously. "It's out of the question. Her parents were nearly saints. She wouldn't know how to be deceitful."

Officially, Spain was still at war with Britain, a state forgotten in Madrid. Since Napoleon was ordering his military operations in other directions, there seemed little reason to think about the British. Spain's commitment was not, however, forgotten in Paris. To jog the Spanish memory, Talleyrand delegated the canny General Berthier to negotiate with Urquijo a new agreement to augment Madrid's contributions to the First Consul's campaigns, especially on the sea, and to his efforts to reduce resistance in Italy. Urquijo believed he was driving a shrewd bargain by exchanging the largely unexplored American territory of Louisiana, a possession that had never been profitable to Spain, for a modest enlargement of the domain of Parma, which was still nominally ruled by a branch of the Bourbon family. Urquijo knew, moreover, that the six ships of the line he had promised France were barely seaworthy.

Napoleon soon discovered that whatever hopes he had entertained about the effectiveness of the Spanish fleet were groundless. In two sharp encounters, off Ferrol and Cádiz, a smaller British flotilla under Lord Keith inflicted severe losses. There was a small redemption of pride after the second sea battle when the garrison at Cádiz, many of its defenders suffering from yellow fever, resisted Keith's assault for weeks before surrendering. For want of even a minor victory to proclaim, the Spanish wildly celebrated a valiant defeat.

These disasters and the signing of the new treaty with France recalled to Spain that her involvement in Europe's affairs was deeper than her leaders had been leading her to think in recent years. Nor were Spanish international problems confined to the Continent. Disturbing reports were emanating from some colo-

nies in the New World. Dissident elements, a few led by
Irishmen who knew more than most about effective opposition
to an occupying power, were growing in number and violence.
Though still on a restricted scale, uprisings were frequent and
alarming—for these regions were the source of Spain's gold and
silver. Without these imports, her condition of near-bankruptcy,
which was merely disastrous, would develop into total economic and financial collapse which would be catastrophic.
Urquijo ordered the ruthless suppression of each insurrection
and the execution of its leaders in the fashion common in
Spain—by the garrote. That this policy was destined to fail was
evident only to those who had already observed its futility in
France and Ireland.

In November, 1800, Napoleon designated his brother Lucien
to be ambassador to Madrid. Ill-informed Madrileños took the
appointment as evidence of Spain's importance in Bonaparte's
grand design, for Lucien's cool-headedness on 18 Brumaire had
assured his brother's leadership of France. The royal family was
flattered. Important gifts were exchanged—or promised. The
city hooted when it was learned that Don Carlos, whose rainy-
day avocation was cobbling, had manufactured for the new
envoy a pair of boots with his own hands. Still operating from
his comfortable positions behind the king and astride the queen,
Godoy offered the suggestion that the unmarried Lucien take
the infanta Doña María Isabel as his bride. He assumed, guile-
lessly, that the Borbón name still possessed an inestimable
cachet in the royal marriage market. The proposal distressed the
queen, who thought her daughter (and Godoy's) deserved a
more illustrious mate. She wanted the infanta to replace the
childless Josephine de Beauharnais as wife of the great First
Consul himself. From Paris, Francisco de Cabarrús wrote his
friend Jovellanos that Napoleon had dismissed this offer with
scorn. "By God," the banker reported the general as saying, "if
I *do* remarry, you can be sure I won't marry into a ruined,
decadent house of fools."

Humiliating defeats, growing unrest in the New World, and
Napoleon's icy rebuff played into Godoy's hands. In the middle
of December, he saw to the dismissal of Urquijo and his exile

from the capital. His successor was Don Pedro de Ceballo, the prince's cousin—malleable, unimaginative, unintelligent, and willing to do precisely as he was told. This transaction was perplexing. Why did Godoy bother with the pretense that Ceballo ruled when no one in Spain was deceived? There were several explanations offered. The most plausible seemed Moratín's: "The sausage merchant prefers it this way. Ceballo, or whoever happens to be the puppet of the hour, takes responsibility for Godoy's errors of judgment. After all, his main concern now must be to keep what he's already stolen. He can't expect to become much richer than he is now, can he?"

Godoy himself answered this rhetorical question little more than a month later, when Ceballo was suddenly dismissed. He once again assumed the title of first minister. The reason for this decision was soon clear. Napoleon was pressing hard for action against Portugal, whose ports were still open to British shipping. The Prince of the Peace imagined that he alone was able to match wits with Lucien Bonaparte and Talleyrand. Once again, he was mistaken. When it was apparent that resistance to the French demands would be unavailing, Godoy coolly reversed himself, and now persuaded the royal family that there was no alternative to war with Portugal. Since this was the case, he argued with the cogency of a jackal, Spain might as well profit from this unhappy necessity by annexing her neighbor. He craftily reminded Don Carlos that not since the epoch of Felipe II had the Iberian peninsula been united under a single monarch.

Events moved with a rush in the first months of 1801. France and Spain signed new conventions devoted to the prosecution of the war with Portugal. The Prince of Brazil, the Portuguese regent, was presented with an ultimatum; if he rejected it, French and Spanish forces would attack forthwith. Unable to withstand such an onslaught alone, the regent appealed for aid from Britain. But the younger Pitt, ill, weary of war with France, and currently enduring a lively exacerbation of the perennial Irish question, could see no point in a further complication of circumstances already so miserably confused.

War was declared by Spain at the end of March. Mobilization

followed at once, though the quality of recruits was pitiably poor. And only those officers too impoverished to buy off their commissions rallied, sluggishly, to the colors. As leaders, they left everything to be desired. Godoy's only consolation was that the enemy's army was even more ineffectual. The promised backing of 15,000 French troops was not an unmitigated blessing; alien forces crossing Spanish soil were, per se, undesirable.

In early May, the Prince of the Peace took full command of his ragged force. He made a bit of personal political capital by leading this army through his native Estremadura, entering Portugal on the nineteenth. The following day, the Spaniards had no difficulty in capturing the fortified town of Elvas. According to the apocrypha of battle, a Spanish soldier broke off the branch of an orange tree and handed it to the brilliant captain-general who was the author of this notable victory. Hence the name of this brief conflict: the War of the Oranges.

The Prince of Brazil immediately sued for peace. Godoy was delighted. A quick end to the war meant that there would be no need for the intervention of the French; the first minister had no desire to share with Bonaparte either the glory or the spoils. But the French army was already in Spain, marching toward the Portuguese frontier. Even so slow a thinker as Godoy understood that negotiations were impossible without consulting Lucien Bonaparte, who came at top speed to the prince's family home at Badajoz. There, these thieves drafted terms for a settlement. Napoleon instructed his brother to extract from Portugal 15 million francs in reparations. Lucien, whose avarice was equal to Godoy's, proposed a figure of 30 million and offered to split the surplus with him. The Portuguese agreed to 25 million, and on June 6 a peace treaty was signed, to the delight of Lucien and Godoy, who calculated their respective profits at 5 million francs.

Less concerned about the money than the other terms of the pact, Napoleon insisted that all Portugal be occupied by his armies in order to ensure the permanent closure of the ports. He therefore refused to ratify the treaty and informed his brother that although he would continue to use Godoy as long as it seemed necessary, he neither trusted him nor respected him. The Prince of the Peace and Lucien Bonaparte returned to Madrid in some bewilderment. Close friends, partners in a most lucrative venture, they must now oppose each other across a conference table. As first minister, Godoy was further alarmed by the French forces in Portugal. Napoleon's "protective occupations" had previously shown themselves to be annexations. A Frenchified Portugal was unthinkable to the Spanish.

A compromise provided for a joint occupation, an arrangement satisfactory to neither conquerors nor conquered. Disappointed by the falsity of Godoy's promise of a united Iberia, Carlos IV allowed himself to be persuaded that the fault lay with Lucien Bonaparte, whom the Spanish minister accused of having betrayed his friendship. The king demanded his recall and expressed relief that the proposed marriage between Doña María Isabel and the departing ambassador had not been contracted.

In spite of the disillusionments with France, the royal family of Spain hailed Godoy's victory in the one-day war as the most brilliant achievement of the entire past century. "Why not?" asked the sardonic Moratín. "It *is* the first time in at least a century that we've won any battle at all. It *couldn't* have been our rotting ships that drove Nelson out of the Mediterranean. Still, there's more to be said for celebrating a one-day victory than for celebrating a five-week defeat like the siege of Cádiz." Among the additional honors to which he fell heir, Godoy accepted the queen's suggestion that the battle of Elvas be marked by a Goya portrait of him in his role of hero of the century.

It would have been folly to decline this commission, in view of his official post as Chief Court Painter, but Goya was chagrined, certain that, as on the last occasion, he would receive no payment and would probably not even be reimbursed for expenses incurred in making the journey to Aranjuez, where, in August, the court was in residence.

Godoy's apartments were in the gloomy palace that Felipe II had erected. He greeted the painter with gratifying warmth, recalling their earlier meetings. He praised more extravagantly than they merited the murals he had made for the prince's residence in Madrid and spoke enthusiastically of the equestrian portrait accomplished the previous summer. Then, with characteristic abruptness, he came to the point. "In addition to the picture of myself, which you know about, I'd be pleased if you could find time to paint one of my dear wife."

"But I should be only too happy, Highness. You know how I respect her."

"Quite," said the prince indifferently. His smile was sly. "And since I understand you have all the necessary materials with you, I have another project for you." He paused, seemingly embarrassed. "It's a matter of some delicacy. You may know—in fact, I'm sure you do—that I enjoy the . . . friendship . . . of Doña Josefina Tudo."

Goya contained his laughter. Certain that he knew what was to come, he replied with dignity, "Do I understand, Highness, that you'd like me to paint a portrait of Doña Josefina too?"

Godoy cleared his throat. "You could put it that way, I suppose . . . You see, I have this idea. I've thought of it for a long time, Goya. You may find it a little . . . unusual." The prince stood up and strolled to a large window which overlooked the magnificent palace gardens of Aranjuez. He gave the appearance of considering them for some time, then wheeled about to confront the artist, his expression strangely fierce. "To put it bluntly, I'd like you to paint Doña Josefina in the nude."

The painter made an effort to keep his face clear of smiles. "That's unusual indeed, Highness."

"You're not suggesting that you've never painted such a picture before."

This time, Goya grinned. "Not a painting, Highness, but of course I've made many drawings and watercolors. All artists do. It helps us understand anatomy. I've made studies of nude men too," he added gratuitously.

"And in these pictures you've made use only of paid models." This was phrased not as a question. Godoy's eyes narrowed menacingly as he drew nearer and peered down at the seated Paco.

"Most of the time, Highness, yes. As I said, it's the custom."

"Ah." There was another pause. "Then there *have* been exceptions. Doña María del Pilár, for example?"

Goya concealed his irritation. "You always express such an interest in her, Highness. May I ask why?"

"You don't need to ask. You know very well. She's not very highly thought of at this court, nor should she be. She makes it all too plain that she holds Don Carlos and Doña María Luisa in contempt. It's quite intolerable. She makes a mockery of them whenever it pleases her. It's most unwise of her. And it's most unwise of *you* to associate with her."

Furious, the painter compelled himself to restrict his demonstration of feelings to a shrug. "I won't try to defend the views of the duchess, Highness. She's well able to do that for herself, should the need arise. As for myself, I'm too old to be frightened by veiled threats."

Calmer now, the prince resumed his seat. "But I wasn't trying to frighten you."

"I got the impression you were."

"I was *warning* you, as a friend—an important friend, I beg you to remember. But there we are. Make what you will of it. You've not answered my question. Will you do this for me? I *am* aware that this is a particularly strange request."

For a moment, Goya was puzzled. Was there more? He waited discreetly as he studied the great man's manner. Then it struck him. "You'd prefer that the matter be secret, Highness?"

Godoy beamed gratefully. "Precisely, Goya. A complete secret. No one but yourself and me . . . and of course Doña Josefina, must know of it."

"It would be difficult to explain, Highness, why Doña Josefina was posing for me if there's no portrait to show for the time spent. I could," said Goya slyly, "make *two* paintings, one of Doña Josefina in the nude and another of her clothed. No one would be the wiser."

The first minister of Spain slapped his plump thigh. Wearing the sneaky smile that had denoted the beginning of their conversation, he said, "I think you'll be happy to know that I'll pay for both of *those* paintings."

"Naturally, Highness," Goya replied solemnly. But he had no confidence in Godoy's promise; there were no witnesses.

Socially, Godoy was an amiable, easygoing fellow, convivial and friendly. While he posed for Goya, he recounted with considerable vivacity several anecdotes about his experiences in the brief tin-soldier war against the defenseless Portuguese. His boasts were so transparently false that they were endearing to the artist, who knew from his friends in Madrid of the prince's renowned cowardice under fire.

In the portrait depicting the minister as captain-general near the scene of the skirmish at Elvas, Goya attempted to convey the man's geniality, his most attractive attribute. For an official military work, the mood was relaxed. Napoleon, for example, would never have permitted a portrait of himself in such a pose. Godoy was seen slouched in a camp chair, with a map held loosely in his right hand. The Count of Tepa, his adjutant at Elvas, looked over the general's shoulder, his face registering more bemusement than awe. The finished work provoked improbably effusive praise from the subject himself, then from the queen and king, and, less surprisingly, from the sycophants of the court. There was in this rendering of Godoy's features a gentleness that startled Goya and disappointed him (for he would have liked to despise the prince much more than personal contact with him made possible). Ever honest to his craft, the painter was unable to conceal Godoy's nature—or this aspect of it. Paradoxically, therefore, the portrait was that of an affable, complacent sensualist, a man obviously unfit to operate even a brothel, not to say a great nation or an army. A rational monarch would have laughed at the suggestion that there was greatness in Godoy. But the monarch wasn't rational, so he was in no position to agree with Goya's friends who described this painting as that of a sausage merchant dressed up as a soldier for a masked ball of the palace domestics.

Goya's portrait of the Princess of the Peace was all tenderness and remoteness, for so did she impress him during the hours of their sittings. So, indeed, had she impressed him eighteen years before, when he had portrayed her in the security of her father's house at Arenas de San Pedro. Despite the affection that pervaded their meetings, their conversations were terse. She was no more talkative today than she had been as a child, nor was the painter able to draw her out for long on any subject—even that of her infant daughter Carlotta, and never that of Godoy. It was as if her marriage to the bluff, egregious prince had caused her to withdraw into herself. She seemed to inhabit a world in which her husband figured little, if at all. She was sorrowful, but her sorrow had nothing of the wildness of grief that was the rule among the women of Spain. She reminded him of Josefa at the time of their wedding.

Endowed with the loving nature of her parents, she appeared to have suppressed it, whether consciously or not, without having found a satisfactory alternative. Perhaps she was pleased simply to wallow in the woe of her resignation to the life God intended for her, as was Josefa. Goya painted everything he saw in this tragic young woman. The effect was of joylessness and fragility and utter, doleful calm—the Virgin perplexed by the miracle that was occurring in her belly, for the princess was pregnant now. She had a grave beauty which she accepted as a gift, to be received as she greeted her husband's outrageous behavior; it was all the will of God, or of nature, to be neither approved nor disdained, but to be endured.

"Yes," she said quietly when Goya invited her to see the finished painting. "I'm afraid you've seen into my nature much too well, Don Paco. Your candor embarrasses me." A small smile crossed her features. "But I suppose what I mean is that when I see myself as *you* see me, I'm embarrassed by myself."

Goya was upset. "I've offended you, Highness?"

"You've touched me, which is worse." She took his coarse, paint-stained hand. "You've remembered me as I *was* and put that into what I *am*. That would unnerve the boldest woman."

She laid a hand on the edge of the picture. "I'll never part with it."

Godoy's reaction to the portrait of his neglected wife was of admiration for its fidelity, and disappointment. "You might have tried to make her look a little more cheerful." Before Goya could say anything, the prince resumed, in higher spirits. "And now it's the moment for you to paint my darling Pepita."

When Pepa Tudo entered the bare, bright room that Goya was using as a studio, he understood at once why Godoy had refused to dismiss her from his life. She was plainly the sausage merchant's soul mate, in a sense his alter ego—a cheerful, brainless voluptuary. Her face was coarsely made. She was too fond of rouge. And though Goya couldn't hear her voice, he was sure that her speech was in harmony with her features. In her movements and gestures, she was a true *maja,* sensuous and sensual.

He liked Pepa Tudo. He felt even more for her than that. He desired her; she was the first woman so to move him since his meeting with María de Alba eight years before. She smelled right, for she eschewed altogether the use of perfume and was thus redolent of that profoundly exciting odor that was woman's. He bowed to kiss her hand, holding it a moment too long as he inhaled its fragrance. He straightened and explained how she must enunciate so that he could catch her words. She laughed at the ceiling. "But I have nothing to say, Don Paco."

He asked her to recline on a chaise longue that he had provided for this pair of portraits. As she took her position, she placed her hands loosely over her head. "Would you like to paint me smiling?" she inquired languidly.

"No, Doña Pepa. You must be serious. Imagine that I'm a prospective lover, a brand-new possibility in your life, one whom you've not yet embraced. Imagine that this is about to occur."

She lifted her brows. "Must I simply *imagine* it, Don Paco? There's to be nothing real?"

He stared at her for a long time before finding the courage for a reply; he could scarcely give credence to the obvious, the

only interpretation of the question. It was too fantastic. Like
María, in one of her flights of fancy, she must be teasing him.
"One doesn't flirt with Paco Goya," he finally muttered.

"*Was* I flirting?" she asked calmly. "Forgive me. I thought I
recognized you."

Paco felt his common sense giving way. "I thought I recognized *you*."

She smiled. "Well, there we are, then."

"Where, exactly, are we, Doña Pepa?"

"I couldn't possibly *imagine* what you ask. I'm not an actress.
You want me to pretend something I know nothing about. I
can't do that. I can't show you what I *would* feel. But I can
show you very well what I *do* feel."

Goya gasped. "Don Manuel would be sure to know."

"Who'd be fool enough to tell him?"

He gave up any attempt to reason. Like an automaton, he
moved to the door and bolted it, then returned to his sketching
paper and gave La Pepa a glazed smile. "All right, I *am* your
new lover. As soon as I've made a few sketches, I'm going to
make love to you. I'm a savage, a peasant from the hills of Aragón. That's a fact. So you'd better prepare yourself."

Pepa's black eyes were bright with pleasurable anticipation.
Her lips were pressed firmly together, but not tightly as in
anxiety. What did she see? Excitement? Apprehension? A sense
of danger, but a danger she thought delicious? All of that, and
more. Something of María's whimsy. This mad young woman
was willing to risk everything, her whole future; yet not, Goya
was sure, because she felt more drawn to him than to Godoy,
but simply because she was a gambler. The game, the chance,
the danger were everything. The situation amused her. His
hand trembled as he made the first strokes of a drawing. He
managed to concentrate, but with a herculean effort of will.
When he completed his preliminary sketches, he snapped the
piece of milled charcoal between blunt fingers. "Now," he
murmured, "I think it's time, Doña Pepa."

With the artless ease of a cat, she rose from the couch. He
watched her in silence, marveling at her aplomb. He was at

once exultant, fearful, charmed, and strangely disgusted. It was
so effortless; her want of shyness or demureness made him
almost jealous. She disclosed her body with the disarming candor of a child, unconcerned about whether or not he thought
well of her flesh—but dead certain of the effect she was having
on him. She resumed her position on the couch. Only then did
he have the strength to undress.

But this was insanity. What could they be thinking of? They
were a pair of animals in rut, neither domesticated nor dignified, reverting to type. They responded to each other mindlessly. Her body was a full meal, a supreme celebration of the
flesh—a meal, he feared, too rich for him to digest at his age, too
delectable to turn away from. Her body was for the *gourman-
dise* of a Godoy. Goya envied the prince his appetite, for he
suspected that Pepa was insatiable, as her lover was said to be.

She clutched at his back, her nails digging deep into his skin.
She required not a moment's preparation. She would abide no
postponement. He entered her with a single thrust, and in a
flash she was gone and gone and gone again, long before Goya
was ready. He could feel her moans and murmurings in the
palm of his hand, which rested on her throat, and went himself
at last. He collapsed on her, their sweats combining. God damn
her, she was laughing. He looked into her face for a trace of
disdain, but there was none; only pleasure. She might be licking
her chops.

Goya dressed himself hastily and began to sketch her. She lay
as he had left her; her face flushed, beggaring the rouge, her
eyes calm, her smile contented. She placed a lazy, caressing hand
over her mount of Venus.

Goya lost no time completing the two portraits of Doña
Josefina Tudo as an odalisque, a *maja* clothed and unclothed.
Technically, these paintings were admirable, yet he despised
them; they were so plainly what they were meant to be, portraits of a whore who loved her work, and hence deficient in the
qualities that Pepa herself lacked—refinement, sensibility, spir-
ituality, poetry. But she was enthralled. "My Manolito must see

them right away. I'm sure they're just what he wants," she exclaimed, and rushed from the room to find the prince.

The pictures were propped against a wall facing the door. With his mistress standing just behind him, Godoy paused before entering and turned his attention first to the portrait of Pepa clothed. It was of no interest to him. His eye moved to the nude, which was the larger of the pair. To this he devoted some minutes of reflection before directing his gaze, very hostile indeed, to Goya. His voice was cold. "You bastard. You've been fucking her."

Paco slapped his hand helplessly against his leg and was bewildered to find Pepa's cloudless smile perched just above the minister's shoulder—a full moon on the verge of a mountainous horizon. He could think of no response. Godoy suddenly lurched forward and brought the flat of his large, soft hand against the side of the painter's head. Goya fell heavily, clutching his cheek. As far as he could determine, he wasn't seriously injured—and this was disappointing. He peered bleakly up into his assailant's features, still unable to speak.

"Don't bother to lie."

"I've said nothing, Highness."

"I know that look of Pepita's too well. You can't fool me."

"If I'd wanted to fool you, Highness, I'd not have painted her as I did."

"You haven't heard the end of this. If you were a nobleman, I'd challenge you. But since you're only a peasant, I'll have to find a less gentlemanly way of satisfying my honor."

seven

GOYA MADE THE JOURNEY back to Madrid in a state of emotional crisis—bitter, defensive, and reproachful. He hadn't the least ground for being angry with Godoy, but he was in no mood to be reasonable. He felt no guilt. He had *not* seduced La Pepa. If anything, the reverse had been the case, though even this evaluation fell wide of the mark. They had seduced each other. However, it would have been impossible to establish their innocence. The painter's fury against the prince was not based on his discovery; in a way, he had known from the start that discovery was inevitable. Rather was it the blow Godoy had struck. Not since Goya's boyhood had such a thing happened to him. But in those days, he had been free to strike back. To have reacted so to the prince's violence would have produced repercussions more damaging than any implicit in the minister's vague threats.

What, exactly, could Godoy do to him? Almost anything that suited him. What *would* he do? Goya felt safe in assuming that after the heat of his anger had been dissipated, the great man would do nothing. For at heart, the painter told himself once more, the man was gentle; he was a knave and a coward, a sausage merchant—not a knight errant. But Paco then remembered the fate of others who had incurred Godoy's wrath—Aranda, Floridablanca, Urquijo. Would he too be imprisoned or banished? These anxious questions were the more disturbing because Goya could discuss them with no one; the account of anything so sensational as his brief tussle with La Pepa would quickly find its way back to the court. If Godoy learned that all had been told of the nude portrait, he would have no choice but to avenge with ferocity an honor impugned in public.

Goya's detestation of the Prince of the Peace was intensified within weeks of his return to the capital. Without pretext, he ordered the dismissal of Jovellanos as chief justice and decreed his detention in the Alhambra, the prison for important figures. The *acalofilos*, though pained and angered, were less startled than was Goya. The brave Gaspar had interposed himself between Godoy and the operation of the Spanish legal machinery. In his earlier personal regime, the prince had avoided a direct clash over the administration of justice, but on resuming authority, such a confrontation had been inescapable. His friends had advised Jovellanos to find some way of fending off Godoy's assault, but he had demurred. "What you're suggesting is that I thwart Godoy by doing just what he'd have me do in his name, corrupt the system. Things are bad enough as they are. If he wants the courts to function *his* way, he'll have to drive me out. I don't believe he'll dare do that." But dear Gaspar was gone.

A pall of despairing gloom fell over conversations among the handful of politically oriented intellectuals in Madrid. Jovellanos had been their leader. With him imprisoned, the *acalofilos* floundered; such was Godoy's reason for taking him from the scene. Though Goya had no reason to imagine any connection between his friend's arrest and his own case, he passed the months of autumn and winter in anxious waiting. Would *he* be Godoy's next victim?

Nothing remarkable took place. Gradually, the painter's apprehensions subsided. He continued to draw his salary as Pintor de Cámara, though naturally he received no royal commissions. From a financial standpoint, this was a matter of indifference. Demands for portraits had never been greater; he was compelled to find another assistant, Rafaelo Estéve, a skilled draftsman and engraver, who now aided Julio in the execution of backgrounds and the copying of portraits, especially those of the king and queen.

Domestic life was comparatively tranquil. Increasingly frail, Josefa had all but withdrawn from his existence. She took most of her meals in her room, though her confinement had no effect on her control over the management of the household, which was as efficient as ever. Goya visited her each morning. Their conversations were brief, awkward, but correct. The only source of disagreement between them continued to be Javier. Josefa was resolute in her opposition to her son's becoming an artist. When the question arose at this late hour, it was endowed with little of the acrimony that had characterized their disputes of earlier years.

Paco understood the futility of his anger. What his wife decreed was what Javier would say he wanted. Nevertheless, like a fallen soldier warding off the *coup de grâce,* he plaintively observed that the boy should be allowed to decide for himself, something *he* himself had not been permitted to do, even though he knew Javier didn't like painting.

When he completed his university studies in the winter of 1802, Javier accepted a clerical post in the Treasury, a situation Ceán Bermúdez had arranged for him. Both son and mother were pleased; such a position of responsibility and respectability would make it possible for Javier to associate with the very best people, "the ones who don't soil their hands," observed Paco forlornly to his wife. "Yet I've never known you to object to the hundreds of thousands of reales these dirty hands of mine have put at your disposal."

He denied his son nothing, and with Javier's appointment to the Treasury, he cheerfully made up the difference between what the young man earned and what he spent—which was substantial, for Javier was as extravagant as he was demanding. María accused Goya of seeking to hold his son's affections by what, in her view, amounted to bribery.

"Is it bribery," he complained, "when *you* spoil your waifs as you do?"

"It's not the same, Paco. I pay attention to them too. You hardly see Javier."

"Is it *my* fault? Josefa has always kept him from me. She says I'm bad for him. He has no time for me."

"Quite right too. Any rational mother would think you a bad influence on a growing child. Besides, *you* had no time for *him*, either, not when time was needed. If you weren't painting, you were out of the house."

"With *you*."

"You can't rub the guilt off that easily, Paco. I'm not your first mistress." Her smile was wry. "And I doubt that I'll be your last, no matter how infirm you claim to feel. And you've no right to criticize Josefa. She was present when she was needed. She paid attention to Javier. I know you love him, but you love him as a symbol, not as a person, as your heir, as an object a father can be proud of. It's that kind of thinking that makes you imagine gifts as a substitute for love."

"And you think Javier doesn't love me?"

"Damn you, Goya, what a bonehead you can be. Can you think of no one but yourself? Hasn't it ever occurred to you to wonder what he feels *not* about you, but about life? You complain that he's extravagant. Whose fault is *that*? Of course he loves you, but isn't it natural that his feeling for Josefa should be stronger? If you insist on answering all his demands with a 'yes,' isn't it logical that he should have more respect for someone who says 'no' to him once in a while?"

Goya could only mumble, "But I don't think I can learn to say 'no' to him, *querida*."

She shrugged. "It doesn't matter now. He's grown up. But you're going to gain nothing more by bribes. That won't, I know, stop you from trying."

But these preoccupations, like those of every other Spaniard, were distracted by the news that the king was on his deathbed. If Don Carlos died, the Prince of the Asturias would succeed. It seemed an occasion for sober joy, for Spain would at last be definitively rid of Godoy and the strumpet queen. The infante Don Fernando hated his mother and her lover with a fervor that was boundless and reasonable—the most recent occasion for his detestation being Doña María Luisa's insistence that he compose an obsequious letter of praise to Godoy for his role in the victory over Portugal and his less decisive part in the drafting of the Treaty of Amiens, by which a truce had been arranged with Britain. The demand had been as absurd as it was vindictive. Though not very bright, the crown prince knew who his enemies were; the moment he acceded to the throne, Godoy would have to run for his life—nor would he be the first monarch to proscribe his mother.

As Carlos IV hovered between life and death, Goya learned of a further turn of events which was both ludicrous and frightening. "Only Godoy," said Ceán Bermúdez, "could have thought of anything so presumptuously preposterous. If the king dies, the sausage merchant proposes to divorce his wife and marry Doña María Luisa. The two of them will rule the country."

"The people won't stand for it," replied Goya indignantly. "The Salic Law, for one thing . . . "

Ceán grunted. "How many of your precious people know what that is?"

"*I* learned it in school."

"How many *go* to school?"

"Enough to prevent a woman taking the throne, especially when there's a legitimate male heir."

"We'll see," said Moratín. "But you have to admire Godoy's footwork. If Don Fernando succeeds, he'll lose everything. He'll be lucky to escape in his boots. You can't blame him for wanting to save his skin. It's a primordial urge. You'd do the same yourself. In fact, Paco, you've been doing it for years."

"But I don't rule the country," said Goya.

"Well, no matter how ingenious Godoy's plan, it won't come to anything," said Moratín. "Talleyrand has made it clear that France will recognize only Don Fernando. Without Napoleon's backing, regardless of what your people feel, Godoy and the whore wouldn't keep the throne for a week."

Ceán brightened. "Don't underestimate Paco's people, Leandro. The other day, in the Avenida de Alcalá, I saw some beggars and vendors and God knows who else spit at Godoy's carriage when it passed. Fortunately for them it was empty, but I don't think they knew that."

The crisis was averted. Miraculously, it seemed, Don Carlos survived his illness, but the specter of Don Fernando's succession now loomed large in the minds of Godoy and the queen. To turn his mind from reflections about how near he had been to power, they arranged for proxy marriages for him and his sister, Doña María Isabel, to cousins from the house of Naples. He would wed the Princess Marie-Antoinette, and the infanta was to be the bride of Prince Francis Javier, heir to the throne of Etruria. The people of Spain rejoiced, for in their loathing of the queen and Godoy they had conceived an adulation for the young crown prince, an emotion much enhanced by the rumors of Doña María Luisa's intention to violate the Salic Law. The announcement of the nuptials was well timed for another reason; there had been a famine the previous autumn, with resulting increases in the price of bread and wine and olive oil—the staples of the Spanish diet. Since the inflation couldn't be controlled, the people were to be offered a circus. As Moratín put it, "Godoy proposes to invite them to laugh and sing and dance as they starve to death."

Francisco Goya, however, couldn't share in the festive spirit of his compatriots. On the day, late in July, 1802, when news of the proposed marriages first circulated in Madrid, he was unexpectedly summoned to the Palacio de Liria. The Duchess of Alba had been taken gravely ill. She would see no one but him.

When Goya gained admission to María's room, so tearingly familiar, he was informed by the weeping La Beata that his mistress had lost consciousness shortly after calling his name. There was no hope. Brother Basil, also in tears, rose as the painter entered and, with a gesture of surpassing sweetness, indicated that Paco must place himself in the chair nearest his beloved's head. He remained there through the rest of the day and the whole of the night, studying her features, recalling with pangs of anguish every moment of the years they had known together.

With the daylight, a physician appeared and placed his cheek against the pale lips of the beautiful duchess, his fingers clutching her wrist in search of a pulsebeat. He straightened and sighed, shaking his head. He folded her limp arms across her breasts and drew the covers over her face, crossing himself. Everyone present began to sob helplessly, hopelessly, as old, bent, crippled Brother Basil stammered through the words of the Extreme Unction.

Goya was stunned. He felt nothing. He had been emptied, voided, gutted, destroyed, disintegrated. He was dead, or might as well be dead, because María was dead. It wasn't possible. God couldn't permit such a catastrophe, not to him, not to her, not to life. He had felt alone before, but never in this way. His loneliness would be lifelong, because he had known María, who was no more. They had been friends as well as lovers . . . friends more than lovers.

Now the sweet flesh was going ashen beneath that wretched cover. He must touch it once more. The hand that was once so warm was cold, going rigid. So soon? Her laughter would be no more. *He* would never laugh again. Her righteous anger would be no more. *He* would be forever angry. Her sharp, clear, biting presence had vanished for all time. *He* would be dull and surly forever.

Oh, María, María, María, was this a sign, a terrible sign, a punishment? If it was, then, dear God, let *him* die; punish *him,* but let her live. Oh, San Antonio must descend from that dome and perform a miracle.

He had no recollection of departing from the Palacio de Liria, nor did he remember anything of his journey back to the Calle del Desengaño. Speaking to no one, he went directly to his bedchamber. He locked the door and drew the blinds to shut out the callously cheerful sunlight of the summer's morning. Naked, he placed himself between the sheets. Sleep came almost at once, but it wasn't merciful, for it was filled with dreams of

the dreaded monsters which had not, for years, disturbed his
slumber.

María was dead. Therefore, reason slept, and would sleep
forever.

PART II

War

eight

⊠   THE SUDDEN DEATH of the Duchess of Alba, at the age of
forty, caused a sensation in Madrid. It was widely reported that
she had been poisoned; her physician could offer no alternative
cause. Until the day of her seizure, she had enjoyed good health
and had known, throughout her life, not a moment of major
illness. But who could want such a thing to happen? The names
of the queen and Godoy were frequently suggested as suspects.
And a numbed Goya discerned in this allegation a plausibility
undetectable to others—his own experience with Pepa Tudo
and the Prince of the Peace, which he kept a secret; for he felt
revelation of his knowledge could cause recriminations against
Josefa and Javier. The need to protect his own, when the
temptation to condemn the pair who were undoubtedly his
mistress' murderers, added terribly to his burden of despair.

Yet *would* Godoy go so far in his quest for vengeance? Despising María as he and the queen so notoriously did, and knowing
that her death would wound the painter immeasurably more
than anything done to him directly, *had* the prince ordered the
murder of the only lovely thing in Goya's life? The truth could
never be known, nor would suspicion ever be dispelled. But the
couple shared already so vast a debt of vice and cruelty for
which they must atone that, on the day of judgment, the assassi-
nation of a rich widow must appear minuscule in God's eyes.

María's funeral, though hastily and secretly arranged, was

observed as it passed through the sunny streets of Madrid by a larger number of ordinary, disinterested mourners than had witnessed such a procession since the death of Carlos III in 1788. This was of only the slightest comfort to Paco. It was enough that *he* mourned. It was more than enough.

When the contents of the duchess' will were made public, a second sensation erupted. With no direct heirs, she had bequeathed the whole of her enormous personal fortune to her servants, to charities, and to her friends and their progeny—naturally providing handsomely for the futures of the adopted María de la Luz and Luis de Berganza. She had left Javier an annuity of 3,500 reales. The greater Alba holdings, which had been entailed for centuries, passed automatically to the wife of the Duke of Berwick, a French descendant of the British James II. This uniquely generous testament dismayed the royal family. Doña María Luisa and her lover persuaded the king that the late duchess' capricious dispersal of her possessions was improper and that the validity of the document should be investigated. This inquiry must be headed by a figure above reproach —as, for example, Godoy himself, whose motives were unquestionable.

Legal formalities were dispensed with. A drumhead inquest disclosed that the Duchess of Alba had been mad at the time of the composition of her will. It had been drafted under duress. She had been influenced by grasping domestics and self-seeking friends. It was declared invalid and its terms summarily abrogated. Noble but politically irrelevant beneficiaries were threatened with indefinite incarceration if they dared to oppose Godoy's judgment. Her servants were menaced. To Goya, the Prince of the Peace rightly supposed, nothing at all need be said.

Though Moratín's scorn for Spain's rulers was bottomless, he was unwilling to believe that they had acted out of greed or malice. "I'm sure they're defending the interests of the Duchess of Berwick," he told Goya. "You're just annoyed that Javier will lose his inheritance."

The painter spat on the tiles of the *taberna*. "For God's sake,

Leandro, don't talk like an ass. They're just pissing on María's grave, nothing else. The Berwicks are rich in their own right. If I feel bitter about Javier's annuity, it's because María's pretty thought has been dragged through the muck and ruined. And that's just what the sausage merchant and his slut want most."

All grounds for doubt were removed a couple of months later when the marriages of Don Fernando and Doña María Isabel were celebrated. The queen made her appearance at a grand ball wearing the most precious necklace and bracelets from the Duchess of Alba's collection of jewelry. And somewhat later, Goya was informed by recent visitors to Godoy's palace in the capital that they had been shown a number of important paintings, including several by his hand, that had formerly belonged to María.

The six years that followed the death of the Duchess of Alba were dark for Goya. Though friends tried loyally to comfort him, his loneliness seemed only to deepen, his emptiness to grow so bitter that he felt only death would relieve it permanently. The realization was all the more intolerable because even temporary relief, if remotely possible, could be provided only by the presence of another woman in his life. What woman he could care for would love him—deaf, ill-tempered, stubborn, selfish, and fifty-six years old? Besides, the idea of seeking anyone to take the hallowed place of María was repugnant.

He knew that he was wallowing in this depression; it was a penance for his multiplicity of sins. His friends naturally feared a regression to the Goya they had known seven years before. He was touched by their solicitude, but assured them that he would accept his new fate without reversion to fury. He was sure that God and Godoy would find additional ways of punishing him; he would be condemned "to a long life in which to reflect on my wickedness and folly," as he phrased it. Moratín saw clearly through his defenses and tried to prod his friend into a more positive outlook. Goya seemed an automaton now, performing the vital functions of his existence with neither interest nor attention—a somnambulist.

Only the drive to safeguard the financial security of his wife and son could impel him to continue painting. A year after María's death, Josefa informed Paco that she was arranging, by correspondence with the Goicoechea family of Zaragoza, the betrothal of Javier to their daughter Gumersinda. To the degree that any news could make him happy, this intelligence succeeded. He had pleasant memories of the Goicoecheas; the girl's grandfather had been instrumental in obtaining an important commission for him twenty years before, following the quarrel with Francho Bayeu and the canons of the Zaragoza cathedral over his frescoes. This work, a painting for the new church of San Francisco el Grande in Madrid, had restored his self-confidence, and its success had led to his permanent independence of Bayeu's support. The idea of this proposed union was happy for another reason: It might produce a child who would like to paint. Javier's spurning of his father's craft still galled him.

The prospect of his son's marriage made Goya think it advisable to try to improve his much tarnished relations with the crown, especially since Javier was still in the employ of the Treasury. He consulted Ceán Bermúdez. "You could give Don Carlos a painting," said his friend.

Paco was dubious. "Paint something specifically for him?" He laughed wryly. "A hunting scene, or a view of the regal cobbler at his craft?"

"Would it be so silly?"

"Perhaps not, but it's all I can do to make myself paint even the occasional portrait these days. I'll never paint anything *I* want to look at. I might as well be dead."

"Well, give the king something you have on hand." Ceán grinned. "*Los Caprichos,* for instance. Give him the plates for the Calcografía."

"What the devil would he want with them?"

"Leandro will think of a reason. He's very inventive."

The painter grunted. "And I could give him the unsold copies too. I don't know what they'd be worth to Don Carlos, but they're worth fifty thousand reales to me. That's a full year's salary as Pinto—a damned handsome gift for the cobbler."

Moratín had no difficulty in finding what seemed a plausible excuse for the presentation. However well-intended, *Los Caprichos* had been misunderstood; in order to prevent the remaining copies from falling into the wrong hands, the artist wanted them to be under royal sequestration. The librarian offered to approach Don Miguel Cayetano de Soler, the minister in charge of the king's print collection, the Calcografía which Goya had enriched a quarter of a century before with his etchings of paintings by Velázquez. By early October, agreement between Soler and the painter had been reached. In addition to an expression of his effusive gratitude, Carlos IV authorized a pension to augment the painter's salary; Goya persuaded the minister to pay this annuity to Javier. For the rest of his life, the artist's son would receive a pension of 12,000 reales each year.

Paco was grimly satisfied with this settlement. He had, in effect, achieved a double victory. He was not himself accepting a new benefice, but he could boast that his investment in the etchings was finally reaping a reward. Moreover, as Javier glibly pointed out to his father, "That's twelve thousand a year I'll not have to ask *you* for." Goya was sure his son would remain far from self-sufficient, but he kept his doubts to himself.

After the conclusion of these negotiations, the painter once again lapsed into torpor. He went through the motions of work, but made nothing of importance. He had resigned his Academia post as director of painting; its associations with María were too poignant. And the election of the mediocre Gregorio Ferro as his successor made no impression on him. Vicente López, a painter of comparable modest distinction, was designated second Pintor de Cámara, nominally to assist Goya, though in fact López received royal commissions in a profusion Paco had never enjoyed. "It's quite natural that those idiots should prefer his painting to mine," Paco observed with unconcern. "He'll never try to jar their shallow convictions about what's suitable. I don't care a damn as long as they go on paying me. They can take on a hundred fellows like López and Maella and Ferro. I begrudge them nothing. If I'd wanted to be like them, it would have been very easy, too easy."

There were occasions when Goya thought he should resign his official post out of respect for María's memory. It seemed clear now that Godoy would do nothing to damage him directly; what worse could he do? But Ceán and Moratín dissuaded him. Resignation might terminate Javier's annuity. "And as you've said yourself," said Leandro, "since it's *our* money in the first place, it only makes sense to get some of it back. With Javier about to be married and *you* doing so little work, you may have to draw on capital." This thought chilled Goya as could no other. He kept his office, and had to satisfy himself by muttering that he was a whore. The chimerical menace of impending poverty spurred him to accept more portrait commissions, for it revived memories of his poor childhood in Aragón which had lost none of their vividness. Indeed, like his recurrent nightmares, they were more anguishing than ever.

He was surprised and somewhat mortified to discover that he was enjoying this renewal of effort. It seemed vaguely treacherous for him to find pleasure in anything, so awesome was the void left by María. His dead mistress would have been the first to illuminate his feelings of shame. "You're such a Protestant," she had said, "such a Jansenist."

Javier Goya and Gumersinda de Goicoechea were married in July, 1805, a few months before the young man's twenty-first birthday. Goya made portraits of every member of the wedding party, and settled on the couple an important sum of money and the tenancy of a fine house in the Calle de Valverde. Despite the injuries inflicted by the cruel death of María, life did go on.

In fact, the prognosis for Spain was more dire than the one for Goya's well-being. Still engaged in playing his own game at his country's expense, Godoy had acceded to Napoleon's demand for more gold and more ships, thus committing the nation to a course which any fool but the prince could perceive to be catastrophic. The economic exigencies of war, the attacks against Spanish merchantmen by British ships, the worsening famines and the resulting inflation of the two preceding years, and the conspicuous and unconscionable extravagance of the court had provoked growing opposition among the people and nobles alike to Godoy's continuance in office. He was the most detested of Spaniards since Torquemada, master of the Inquisition during the reign of Fernando and Isabel.

In the years since the ignominious War of the Oranges, Bonaparte had attempted through intrigue to separate the king from the adored Don Manuel. All efforts had been abortive, for Don Carlos continued to assert that Godoy was his right arm, by which he meant that he was his buffer against the alarming incursions of the real world, which he was incapable of comprehending. Now, Napoleon revised his tactics and urged the prince to believe that in Bonaparte, for the past year recognized as emperor of the French, he had found a friend upon whom he could unreservedly rely. Godoy was easily convinced. The French ambassador in Madrid soon found occasion to reinforce this impression. His agents intercepted a letter from Doña Marie-Antoinette, Princess of the Asturias, to her mother in Naples; she baldly stated her husband's intention, the moment he mounted the throne, to imprison the Prince of the Peace, to confiscate his ill-got fortune, and to drive his relations and adherents into exile.

This information was no surprise to Godoy, but to see it in writing gave him a nasty turn. He deemed it advisable to toe Napoleon's line. In exchange for an oath in writing of total fidelity to France, he extracted from Talleyrand what he construed to be an assurance that he would become king of a Portuguese province. The prince had yet to learn that France's perfidy was more studied and professional than his own.

The first of a series of disasters was in the making as Javier and Gumersinda were being wed. Combined Spanish and French fleets under Admiral Villeneuve were to draw the flotilla of Lord Nelson from the western approaches to Britain, thereby leaving the English Channel open for an invasion from

France. Two minor engagements led the French commander to hope, against his better judgment and previous experience, that the Spanish elements of his fleet might not be so ill-manned and ill-founded as Decrès, the French naval minister, had described them. By the end of October, however, Villeneuve and the rest of the world knew the worst—Trafalgar. Napoleon's dream of investing Britain was forever dashed.

The defeat off Cape Trafalgar deflated Godoy not a bit. He concluded, wrongly, that the poor performance of the Spanish vessels had been the fault of Villeneuve's defective command. *He* had lived up to his side of the bargain; now Bonaparte must honor his word about Portugal. The cool Talleyrand demanded a specific proposal in the prince's own hand. The naïve Don Manuel willingly agreed, submitting a scheme whereby Portugal was to be divided into four kingdoms—one for Godoy, another for his putative son Don Francisco de Paula, a third for the infante Don Carlos, and the last for the regent, the Prince of Brazil.

As soon as this memorandum was in French possession, Napoleon had the greedy Spaniard just where he wanted him. The emperor demanded, on pain of making public this sensationally self-incriminating document, that Spain at once remit the 24 million francs she owed. Sweating in fear and smarting over this unexpected humiliation, Godoy replied that so huge a sum couldn't be raised without a foreign loan. Talleyrand cheerfully made the necessary arrangements with a bank in Amsterdam and saw nothing amiss in accepting a substantial commission from both lender and borrower.

On May 21, 1806, Marie-Antoinette of Naples, Princess of the Asturias, died in circumstances reminiscent of those surrounding the death four years earlier of the Duchess of Alba. The queen and Godoy were naturally suspected of foul play, for they had made no secret of their hatred for this young woman. More than once had she opposed Napoleon's plan to incorporate the Kingdom of Etruria, still nominally governed by her brother, into his Italian system. In vilifying Bonaparte, Doña Marie-Antoinette had been thwarting Godoy as well, for the French had stipulated that only the cession of Etruria would induce Napoleon to agree to the prince's fairy-tale solution of the Portuguese question. Whatever the cause, Don Fernando's princess was dead. The people, already distressingly vocal in their opposition to Godoy, were given yet another cause for despising him and Doña María Luisa.

"First comic opera, then farce, and now tragedy," murmured Moratín. "Can't Godoy see what Napoleon is up to? He's almost swallowed Italy. He's moving toward Prussia and Poland. Then he'll turn back and gobble up Spain. We *must* be next on his list. He's just playing the sausage merchant for the fool he is. That means he's playing *us* for fools. If he bargains, it's only because he needs time. He wants us on his side until he's quite ready to turn against us." Moratín's conclusions seemed impeccable, but at this point he reversed himself, and in doing so, he perfectly reflected the ambivalence that beset so many Spanish intellectuals. "It might not be such a terrible thing if Napoleon *were* to conquer Spain, if we were given a taste of Napoleonic government. Think of what he's done in the Low Countries, what he plans for Italy. He might be the one man who could civilize this country."

Goya shook his head in vigorous dissent and pounded the sturdy table about which he and his friends were, as usual, gathered. "No, by God, you're wrong. He may do all things, but if he doesn't get approval for them from Don Carlos, he'll get nowhere in trying to 'civilize' us." He glared at Moratín. "What a word to use. The only things that count for our people, after the symbol of the king, are bread and wine and oil."

Ceán Bermúdez cocked his head wearily to one side and raised his eyes to the heavens. "Oh, God, here we are again. Goya, the voice of the true Spain."

Paco leaned back in his chair and drained his glass. "You can scoff, *amigito*. It doesn't matter a damn to me. I'm too old to be worried about anything except the fact that I'm going to be a grandfather."

"Why all that passion, then?"

"I'm a Spaniard. When I talk, I'm animated."

"Spain can go to the devil, for all you care?" Ceán inquired softly.

"You and Leandro have just been saying that it's already *gone* to the devil, or to Napoleon, and none of us can stop it."

"We *could* oppose it," said the banker.

Goya snorted. "And spend the rest of our days in the Alhambra with poor Gaspar? That may be the way you want it, but it's not for me. If the moment presented itself, I might be willing to die for Spain . . ."

"For the Spain of Don Carlos?"

"For Spain, for the *people*. But I'm damned if I'll rot in a dungeon."

Goya's grandson, Mariano, was born in July, 1806. The painter celebrated the occasion by adding appreciably to his endowment of Javier—though his previous largesse made it possible for the prodigal son to live on a scale far more lavish than any the father would have thought suitable. But in the manner of some self-made men, Paco took a wry pleasure in Javier's extravagance. "As long as I have it to give you," he confessed, "it's yours." Javier resigned his Treasury post, a decision Josefa thought shameful. "Papa will look after me," he replied. "He'll do anything I ask." The lesson he had learned as a boy remained with him. When mother opposed, father supported. He conceded to Gumersinda that the policy might not be virtuous or admirable, but it was certainly effective.

Meanwhile, a broad and comprehensive net was being drawn slowly and securely around Spain. Unwittingly and witlessly, Godoy was pulling the strings tighter. In the early autumn of 1806, he gave misguided credence to secret reports that Napoleon's star was on the decline; the emperor was meeting with reverses in his campaigns to subjugate Prussia and Poland. The Prince of the Peace concluded that this was the time for him to begin negotiations in other directions. He conceived the idea of an alliance of Spain, Britain, and Russia against France. In theory, this plan had merit both for St. Petersburg and London, suspicious though both capitals rightly were of Madrid's capacity to deliver more than a pinprick in Bonaparte's southern flank. These overtures were warmly received. Godoy was encouraged to make the proposed bond even stronger by a marriage between the Russian Grand Duchess and Don Francisco de Paula. In a strange letter to the tsar, he described this thirteen-year-old boy as possessing "much native wit and vivacity. I might even call him a genius." Whether the ruler of all the Russias divined in this eulogy the enthusiasm of a father, or simply deplored the suggestion for practical or religious reasons, he declined the offer of the infante's hand.

By October, Godoy was so certain of Napoleon's impending collapse that he induced the king to proclaim a state of general military emergency. The enemy was unnamed, but few could doubt that it was France. If Bonaparte failed in his operations in Central Europe, Spain could quickly move against his forces isolated in Portugal. The age-old dream of a reunified Iberia might yet be realized. Spain might even conquer France herself. Then the jackal would have to be reckoned a lion. The alliance with Britain and Russia failed to materialize because Napoleon won two very convincing victories at Jena and Auerstädt.

Godoy was rapidly restored to such senses as he possessed. Laughing nervously, he assured the angry French ambassador that he had never doubted the emperor's prowess in the field. The prince was Bonaparte's most constant friend in Europe. Since the great Frenchman had no friends at all, the statement had a grain of truth. For his part, Napoleon felt that, however hyperbolic, Godoy's protestations of eternal amity might be useful to one who was the most hated figure of modern times. Therefore, professing no bitterness over the prince's recent treachery, he contented himself with making it plain that he would abide no future examples of such double dealing.

Spain responded like a whipped dog. Without a whimper, she paid the arrears of her debt to France. She agreed to close her ports to Russian vessels. She joined the Continental blockade which was to bring Great Britain to her knees by starvation. She dispatched her finest 10,000 to Hanover, where they became a permanent element of the emperor's Grande Armée. In recompense for these gestures of extorted goodwill, Napoleon again dangled before the greedy Godoy the temptation of a Portuguese kingdom. The prince snapped at the bait like a ravenous trout.

Problems at home, however, prevented him from devoting his full attention to this proposition. After Don Carlos' nearly fatal illness and the revelation of Godoy's plan to take the throne as husband of the widowed queen, a group of disgruntled courtiers had banded together to give all possible aid to Don Fernando's rightful claim to the crown in the event of his father's death. They counted among their numbers many important officers of the army and navy and highly placed civil servants. When these *Fernandistos* were apprised of the possibility that Godoy planned to become king of a section of a divided Portugal, they revealed their plan to oppose him. The prince realized that this faction must be suppressed.

To achieve this end, Godoy persuaded the king to name him Commandant-Inspector of the Royal Military Establishment and Admiral-General of Spain and the Indies. Quite incidentally, with these appointments came additional revenues of something approaching 3.5 million reales per year. Godoy's purge of the *Fernandistos'* activities in all departments of the regime was systematic, ruthless, and, he believed, complete. He reported with confidence to Napoleon that his authority was once again unquestioned. The emperor agreed to resume talks about the division of Portugal—this time into two parts, one to be ruled by the Spanish infanta María Isabel (whom Bonaparte was expelling from Italy), and the other by Godoy. So delighted was the prince with this masterstroke of diplomacy that he elevated Pepa Tudo, who had by now borne him two children, to the high nobility.

As compensation for his generosity in the partition of Portugal, Napoleon made certain demands to which Godoy readily assented: French troops which were to aid in the realignment of the Portuguese borders were to be paid by France, but their maintenance would be the responsibility of Spain. In addition, these friendly forces were to be given absolute freedom to traverse the Spanish frontiers in both directions for the purpose, said Bonaparte, of gaining and leaving Portugal. Most ominous of all, French reserves might remain in Spain for unspecified periods. Only after consenting, did Godoy appreciate the implications of these terms. Moreover, though the armies of both nations were to occupy Portugal, the central portion, including Lisbon, would be held by the French. A second French reserve army of 40,000 men was to be stationed at Bayonne, just across the border, ready to move if the British decided to oppose the dismantling of Portugal.

When these preparations had been completed, Bonaparte sat back. Godoy at last understood what had been clear to more detached observers for years. Napoleon's plan to secure Portugal against British infiltration was genuine. But Spain herself was the more important target of his manipulations.

Godoy shared none of the mixed feelings that afflicted the *acalofilos*. French conquest of their land would shatter all his hopes and destroy his fortune. He cared nothing for the possible constitutional reforms that might follow such a victory. For, in any case, he would surely not be around to enjoy their blessings. In October, 1807, after a year's postponement of the execution of Napoleon's plan to occupy Spain, the Prince of the Asturias furnished Godoy with what he hoped would prove an effective weapon against the emperor. In his efforts to scourge the civil service of Don Fernando's friends, he had turned up a *Fernandisto* plot to drive himself from power. Unnerving in itself, the plan was more dismaying for its evidence of Bonaparte's complicity. Godoy reasoned that if he exposed this conspiracy, heavily underscoring Napoleon's role, he would assure himself of popular support, thus causing a further delay in French plans.

As usual in this darkening season, the court was residing within the somber confines of the Escorial. Pleading a mild indisposition, Godoy departed for Madrid. Doña María Luisa remained behind and took the odd precaution of ordering the changing of every lock in the vast royal palace that was attached to the monastery. Don José Caballero, relegated to the post of minister of justice when Godoy had resumed power, was hastily summoned from the capital. On his arrival, he placed the crown prince of Spain under arrest, confronting him with the unquestionable evidence of his treason.

No other action could have taken the country so by surprise. For precedent, one had to recall the reign of Felipe II, when a Prince of the Asturias had been accused of betraying his homeland. Don Fernando was reminded of the fate of that infante, Don Carlos, who had been murdered—if not by his father's command, then certainly with his knowledge and consent. After two days and nights of interrogation, the young prince confessed to his intimate share in the conspiracy and went on to denounce other plotters about whom there had been no information at all. The role of the French emperor was explained in detail, as was that of his ambassador in Madrid, Beauharnais. His confession duly signed and witnessed, the heir to the throne threw himself upon the mercy of his father, his mother, and Godoy.

Though these disclosures were as electrifying as the Prince of the Peace had meant them to be, in Spain and elsewhere, their effect was at complete odds with his estimate. Instead of joining with the king in condemning Don Fernando's treason, the people demonstrated wildly in the infante's favor. Even the urbane Talleyrand was bemused by this response, but he recovered rapidly and urged Bonaparte to let it be known that, as always everywhere, he sided with the plain people in their struggles against the oppression of the stupid absolutists. He described himself the most ardent supporter of the right of the Prince of the Asturias to take his place on the throne at once.

Stupefied by this incredible turn of the screw, Godoy did his urgent best to hush the affair up. Don Fernando was granted an unconditional pardon; there had been a misunderstanding. The other conspirators were released from custody, their titles and estates restored. But by the time these reparations had been made, the obtuse Prince of the Peace realized that he had no further cards to play; the game was lost.

Napoleon ordered two large forces to cross the frontier from

Bayonne. One was to proceed to Portugal, the other to remain "in reserve" in Navarre. Panic reigned in Lisbon. After a second vain appeal for aid from London, the Prince of Brazil decided to move his court to Rio de Janeiro. In this plan, at least, the British offered assistance: Under the protection of a large flotilla, the Portuguese royal family evacuated the capital on November 29, 1807, a day before the French marshal Junot's first divisions entered.

Godoy was assured by Talleyrand that Napoleon intended to honor his plan for the partition of Portugal, but the Prince of the Peace remained uneasy about the presence of French troops in Navarre. It portended ill, and he was the more dismayed because of his helplessness. Nor were these "reserves" his only cause for grief. Throughout the brief Portuguese campaign, the emperor had been occupied in Italy, where, among other actions, he had informed Queen María Isabel of Etruria that she must renounce her throne and return to her parents in Madrid. The young woman offered no protest. Her arrival in the Spanish capital, accompanied by sixty wagonloads of possessions, did nothing to lift the sinking spirits of her father and mother.

When Napoleon returned to Paris just before Christmas, he was told that the time was ripe for him to rid himself of Godoy once and for all. His agents informed him, accurately, that the prince's popularity had never been at so low a point, that the *Fernandisto* scandal had damaged him irreparably, and that the people would welcome any French action that would appear to bring nearer Don Fernando's accession. The emperor acted with typical vigor and deception. He ordered the reinforcement of his troops in Navarre and allowed word to be circulated that he would himself lead a crusade to drive Don Carlos, Doña María Luisa, and Godoy from power—and replace them with the Prince of the Asturias, who had become, in the popular view, a god.

By mid-February, 1808, a French army had easily overrun the fortress of Pamplona. A fortnight later, Barcelona and Montjuich fell virtually without a struggle. Rumors in Madrid during these weeks had it that French soldiers, especially the fearsome Mamelukes, were committing countless atrocities, but such reports did nothing to dampen public enthusiasm for this march that would end with the liberation of Spain from the toils of the hated Prince of the Peace and his regal whore. At long last, the people were to be delivered. Crowds in the Spanish capital were in a festive mood when they learned that a French force was nearing Madrid, under the command of the great Murat.

Contrary to custom for this season of spring, the court was at Aranjuez. Godoy was doing his best to persuade the king and queen to follow the example of the Prince of Brazil and emigrate to Buenos Aires in the Spanish New World—for by now even he could no longer remain ignorant of Bonaparte's intentions. Don Fernando, under the impression that *his* hour was at hand, refused to leave and ordered his adherents to make the cowardly plan of flight known to the people. With Murat's columns on the outskirts of Madrid, barely thirty miles from Aranjuez, Godoy yielded up whatever courage and sangfroid were left him. He commanded the palace servants to load the royal belongings; the Borbón family was to depart at once for the nearest unblockaded port. If Don Fernando elected to remain and sample Bonaparte's rigorous hospitality, the Prince of the Peace could assume no responsibility for his safety. For himself, he had no desire to languish in a French equivalent of the Alhambra.

When the citizens of Madrid learned that the royal family was planning to leave the country, there was a spontaneous and violent reaction. Angry little groups formed in all quarters of the city and shambled off irregularly in the direction of Aranjuez—most of them motivated by the mistaken but inspired allegation that their darling Don Fernando was to be borne away by force. "Save the *infantido!*" many shouted as they passed out into open country. Before dawn of the next day, a sizable mob presented itself in front of the palace in Aranjuez. Their spokesman demanded the immediate release of the Prince of the Asturias and the head of Godoy. This constantly growing crowd of the poor was augmented by soldiers whose officers were eager to show themselves as supporters of Don Fernando.

The bewildered and rather pitiable Don Carlos was torn by doubts and fears. For the first time in his career as king, he realized that Godoy had been lying to him. The people, a factor he had hitherto been told to ignore in all his political considerations, were about to drive him from his throne and would succeed unless he gave them Don Manuel, who had deceived him. What a dilemma. For though he was disillusioned to learn that his minister had told him an untruth, he still thought himself incapable of exercising his authority without Godoy at his side. For the first time in his life, he must make a decision for himself. Doña María Luisa could be of no assistance; he still refused to believe that she had cuckolded him, but there was no doubt that she would resist the prince's dismissal. He consulted her, nevertheless, and to add to her husband's conclusive confusion, she gave a display of histrionics whose range was, even for her, exceptionally wide. She swore she would kill herself. She promised to . . . There seemed nothing to which she wouldn't resort if her precious Manolito were taken from her. If this great servant of Spain were delivered into the hands of this bloodthirsty mob, he would be torn to pieces.

In a blinding flash of comprehension, Don Carlos recognized that the issue of Godoy's fate had become academic. The mob must be propitiated; Don Manuel had to go. On the morning of March 18, as the queen sobbed piteously, Don Carlos ordered Godoy's dismissal and commanded his majordomo to make this fact known to the crowds that encircled the palace. This announcement came too late by hours to pacify the throngs. "Give us Godoy," they cried. "The garrote for Godoy." "Death to Godoy." These violent imprecations resounded throughout the afternoon and evening.

Most semblances of order had already vanished because of Don Carlos' indecision. When Godoy learned of his dismissal, he sought skulking refuge in the capacious attics of the palace where, until that morning, he had been Spain's ruler for fifteen years. Now a portly forty-one, he passed a sleepless, terrified night, aware that at any moment a band of *Fernandistos* might come upon him. His fright-stained imagination boggled at what must inevitably and swiftly follow such a capture. Hardly less alarmed were the king and queen. By dawn of the nineteenth, Don José Caballero (who had been renamed first minister) had convinced his master that the only hope, dim though it was, of restoring domestic tranquillity lay in his abdication in favor of the Prince of the Asturias. Doña María Luisa refused to believe that the situation was that dire, but her husband, exhausted and totally befuddled without Godoy to advise him (and a reluctant monarch in the best of seasons), agreed with Caballero.

His abdication was announced to the people in the patio of the palace gardens at nine in the morning. It was received with roars of ecstatic approval. *"Viva Don Fernando! Viva el infantido! Viva el rey idolatrado!"* The smirking Don Fernando presented himself to his worshipers from a balcony, his face adorned with a most vindictive smile. He waved a fleshy hand and withdrew. Now that he was king, by public acclamation, there were things to which he must give his attention, old scores to settle.

By noon, the crowds had mostly dispersed. Godoy, still cringing in the attic, believed it safe to creep downstairs. He was cold, hungry, and not much less frightened than before, but he thought that if he were arrested, the officers of the guard (to which he had once belonged) would treat him kindly, protect him from the wrath of the new king. However, when this pathetic, bedraggled figure was recognized by the soldiers on duty, he was seized and dragged by his epaulets, protesting his innocence of all offense, into the presence of Don Fernando, his archenemy, at whose feet Godoy cravenly flung his bloated form at full length, vowing utter allegiance to the young man whom he had done everything to corrupt and pervert.

Whatever his shortcomings, the new king had his mother's highly developed instinct for melodrama. He permitted Godoy to continue to humiliate himself for several minutes, and then let another few moments pass in silence, his lip curled with a malevolence that filled him with joy, as he contemplated the

prostrate figure of the man for whom he had so long harbored
the most terrible hatred. At last, he gave composed voice to his
promised revenge. "So now you're my prisoner, Manolito.
Everything that was yours is mine. You're just Manuel Godoy,
criminal. You're to be taken to my most unhealthy dungeon
and there it's my hope that your rot will be slow. And when you
finally die, it's my faith that God will continue your punishment in hell—in the arms, no doubt, of the cadaver of my slut of
a mother."

These developments at Aranjuez had occurred so quickly that
Murat, encamped with his troops outside Madrid, was ignorant
of them until the following day. By this time, everyone else in
the capital was as well informed as he. Godoy's palace was
sacked by rioters in the best of holiday spirits. Purportedly to
restore order, French forces took up strategic positions in all
sections of Madrid. Some Madrileños were skeptical of Murat's
alleged reasons for thus deploying his soldiers—none more so
than Moratín. "I can't believe that Bonaparte really means to
give his support to Don Fernando. He's no more likely to trust
him than he did Godoy and Don Carlos." He shrugged. "And if
I were in his position, *I* certainly wouldn't."

Moratín's suspicions were wisely founded. The emperor
offered the crown of Spain to his brother Louis, currently
puppet ruler in the Netherlands, who rejected the proposal out
of hand. Joseph Bonaparte, king of Naples, readily accepted,
imagining it to be a promotion. But of these negotiations,
Madrid was temporarily ignorant. While Napoleon was making
arrangements for Joseph's change of residence, Murat was instructed to remain obdurate in his refusal to have official dealings with Don Fernando. This created embarrassments for both
sides, for Fernando VII, unheralded, had ridden into the capital
only four days after his informal accession. As word of his
arrival passed from mouth to mouth, he was accorded a welcome whose tumultuous proportions were without precedent.
The crowds needed to know nothing better of their new monarch than that he had imprisoned Godoy and replaced his
apathetic father and revolting mother. Their only regret was

that the former royal couple had found refuge with the French.

To commemorate these great events, the Academia commissioned Goya to paint an equestrian portrait of the idolized king which would occupy the traditional place of honor in its great hall. So preoccupied was he with affairs of the state he thought he was ruling, however, that Fernando VII had no time to pose for this work. Paco drew on his earlier pictures of the young man, adding the standard horse (an animal of whose conformation he was not invariably the most formidable of masters) and the uniform of commander in chief.

During the fortnight after the king's entry, Madrid was the scene of continuous celebrations whose degree of frenzy increased rather than diminished. French troops, under Murat's strictest orders to be on their most decorous behavior, were everywhere feted as heroes and liberators. Napoleon was toasted at all gatherings as the savior of Spain. Even so hardened an observer as Ceán was inclined to question Moratín's doleful prediction that Don Fernando's reign was temporary. He joined his compatriots in the wave of euphoric optimism that swept the nation. "I *know* Don Fernando is a dolt, but that's only because his mother and Godoy kept him in ignorance," he exhorted his friends at the *taberna*. "I don't think he's fundamentally stupid. He'll learn if he's given a chance. He takes the advice of his confessor, Canon Escoiquez, who's a brilliant fellow. I don't like the man's politics, but at least he's got brains, which is more than anyone could say for the sausage merchant. And no matter what his convictions are, any bright man *has* to see that Spain has to have a constitution."

Ceán's sanguine opinions received substantiation only days later with the news that after seven years of imprisonment, Jovellanos had been freed. Much aged, but apparently in the best of health, he reappeared in Madrid, where his reception was at once uproarious and tearful. He too agreed that a constitutional monarchy was the only hope for the establishment of a stable regime, but he was much less optimistic than Ceán of its likelihood. "I've had plenty of time to consider it, and I'm convinced that Paco has been right all along. We need a constitution, agreed, but the people don't know it yet. I talked by the hour to my jailers because they were the only people I *could* talk to. I tried to reason with them, but they were just as sure on the day I left as when I arrived that the king is Spain and Spain is the king—what Paco's been telling us. It's got to be changed, of course, but that's the way it is. If France had had the crazy government *we've* had for the past twenty years, her people would have rebelled twenty times over. What have *our* people done?"

On April 9, a shadow of doubt fell—but it was so pale that no one at the moment understood its implication. Don Carlos and Doña María Luisa were whisked from the palace at night under a heavy French guard—their destination Bayonne, where Napoleon awaited them. Under identical circumstances, Don Fernando vanished from Madrid the next morning; he too was bound for Bayonne. In his absence, his uncle, Don Antonio, would preside over a junta that was to govern.

Popular jubilation ceased as abruptly as it had begun. Everyone was in a suspension of mingled incredulity and despair. The people would not yet accept the idea that so soon after his accession, their new idol had been snatched from them. When the *infantido's* carriage reached the Spanish border town of Irún a few days later, anxious crowds gathered round it and detached the horses, attempting to prevent the French from taking their beloved Don Fernando across the frontier. They were rightly convinced that, once gone, he wouldn't soon return. These efforts were abortive—but descriptions of Spaniards placing themselves between the traces of the royal coach and trying to draw it off were almost immediately adopted into the folklore of every province.

In Bayonne, the former and present kings of Spain were cordially received by Bonaparte, who was anxious quickly to resolve a problem that to him appeared elementary. He explained that all he wanted was the very best for the Spanish people; this blameless purpose could be best implemented by the replacement of Don Fernando by his own brother Joseph. He insisted that the transfer of power be accomplished in an open, orderly, and unquestionably legal manner. To this end, therefore, Fernando VII must first abdicate in favor of his father, for it was obvious to many, said the emperor, that the son had acceded under objectionable conditions. Don Carlos must then in his turn abdicate in favor of Joseph Bonaparte.

Overawed, a priori, by the legend of Napoleon, Fernando VII offered no resistance to this high-handed demand. To the slow dictation of Canon Escoiquez, he wrote out the fateful document and tremulously signed it. Surprisingly, it was Don Carlos who proved the more difficult to persuade. He described himself as incapable of making so grave a decision without consulting Godoy, whom he still called Prince of the Peace. An exasperated Bonaparte immediately ordered that Don Manuel be released from prison and brought, posthaste, to Bayonne. The clouds of consternation that had been gathering over Madrid since the departure of Don Fernando turned instantly into a storm of frustrated rage when Godoy's flight from Spain became public knowledge. The people yielded to furious despair. They had lost their king; now they were losing the possibility of scourging, with their own hands, the monster who was, in their supportable view, the principal author of the wrongs that beset their country.

Murat was a soldier, not a policeman. He placed more troops at each important intersection and in every plaza of the city. Uneasy order was maintained through the last days of April. He was perplexed by the change in popular emotion. For no discernible reason, the open-armed welcome that had greeted his troops little more than a month before had turned abruptly to a hatred that, while still merely sullen and furtive, threatened to become violent at any instant. He recognized that the merest flicker of a spark was all that would be needed to ignite the flames of insurrection.

The spark was struck early in the morning of May 2. There was a rumor that the French were planning to extradite the regent, Don Antonio, to Bayonne. The purpose was evident: to replace the direction of the ruling junta with French officials. Spain would no longer be governed by her own. That there wasn't a bit of truth in this report was of no importance. A crowd began to gather in the Puerta del Sol, before the gates of the Palacio del Prado, where Don Antonio was in residence. In the courtyard, a carriage was being loaded for what seemed to be a long journey. The barrier was easily forced. The horses were unharnessed. *"Muerta a Bonaparte!"* was the first cry to ring out over the paving blocks. *"Viva Don Antonio! Viva el rey idolatrado!"*

The proportions of the mob increased rapidly. A young aide-de-camp from Murat's headquarters arrived alone on horseback and was set upon with hands and sticks. He was loudly jeered. Managing to escape this unexpected assault, he rode off, to the derisive laughter of the crowd, and reappeared within a half hour at the head of a column of perhaps fifty magnificent Mamelukes who charged directly into the center of the densely packed throng. There was a single shot, followed by the screams of women and children. Both sides were confused. The crowd was hemmed in on one flank by walls and railings and by horsemen on the other. Scimitars flashed in the spring sunshine and descended blindly and blindingly, chunking hideously as they slashed into defenseless flesh. More shots were fired from various positions on the square.

It was still not clear who had the advantage. A few of the Mamelukes were unhorsed, their gored mounts shrieking like the horses of the *picadores* in the *corrida,* rearing dangerously, their hooves coming down to trample indiscriminately soldier and civilian alike. The crowd's numbers grew. Reinforcements were brought up amid bursts of musket fire. Armed only with pikestaffs, Spaniards attacked the cavalry and fell, to be crushed underfoot. Light artillery was summoned, but as had been the case during the siege of the Bastille in Paris twenty years earlier, it was of no utility; it was impossible to fire into this scene of chaos without risking the injury of as many French as Spanish combatants.

It was some time before a higher degree of military intelligence took command. A French officer ordered his troops to withdraw to the edges of the Puerta del Sol. There they regrouped and made a concerted charge, driving the confused mob off in all directions, scurrying down avenues and streets, seeking cover. Clusters of insurrectionists were pursued by horsemen, who cut them down. Others were shot. The wounded insurgents who lay where they had fallen were dispatched without ceremony. Others who managed temporarily to escape were rounded up and manacled, to be held for more leisurely execution.

Within three hours of its beginning, the riot was suppressed. The Puerta del Sol was deserted, save for the corpses of horses and humans alike, French and Spanish, which were strewn in their sun-caked gore on the worn cobbles. The droning of insects was the only sound, but just for a little time. From the next morning onward there was more musket fire, these volleys well drilled. All over Madrid and in the hilly outskirts, the captured insurrectionists and many innocents were systematically put to death by infuriated French troops. So great were their numbers that these firing squads worked through the day of May 3 and all through the night until the last pitiful victim, his black eyes bulging with fear, fell to the blood-soaked Spanish earth.

Francisco Goya heard not a sound. But what he saw . . . He saw these terrible things, the weeping Julio at his side, and would never forget, never forgive. The silence in which he lived only added to his rage and his horror and his feeling of futility. He compelled himself to witness what was unendurable. He smelled the smoke of the musketry, the odor of fresh-flowing blood, of dying flesh, of dead flesh. Through the soles of his boots, he felt the rumble of caissons and tumbrils reeling through the rutted streets. He remained motionless, transfixed; it was probably only this, and his gentleman's dress, that prevented him and Julio from becoming victims of the terrible French retribution.

He looked up at the blue innocence of the cloudless sky and noted, as the vast plaza lay empty of life except for himself and the nauseated Julio, that predatory birds, like those of his nightmares, were circling with graceful intensity, drawn so far from their normal hunting grounds by a stench that grew more revolting as the hot hours of this May afternoon progressed.

He felt that he had just seen his country die. It was *his* agony as well, yet he felt renewed. Why was this so? To what purpose was he to put this energy? There must be a reason, somewhere, in someone's soul, for this senseless passion and death, for the crucifixion of Spain.

"God knows," he muttered to himself. He thought of God. Was it only death, or its proximity, that could bring him close to God? Had God placed him here, now, for a reason other than to torture him? Here, truly, he had witnessed an ugliness that he would cherish as a friend of his soul, would remember forever.

He was engaged at last, committed at last, purposeful at last. Out of his soul he would paint this war. No one would be permitted to forget that on the second day of May, 1808, Spain died . . . and Paco Goya was again reborn.

nine

🦅 "THE FOOLS, the fools, the fools," roared Jovellanos. "Oh, Paco, those goddamned fools. The French could have had every Spaniard worshiping them. All they had to do was show a flicker of the intelligence they boast of. If they'd left Don Fernando on the throne, they could have controlled everything in his name, made the reforms we all agree are needed, taxed us as harshly as they pleased. But look what they've got now, what *we've* got—war." The deposed chief justice pounded the table in a remarkable demonstration of frustration and anger.

"If it's war," chimed in the unhappy Moratín, "I wish our people could wage it in a cause a little more worthy than that of Don Fernando's right to the throne."

Goya heatedly demurred. "We're not fighting only for *him*, Leandro. We're fighting for Spain. What nobler cause than that?"

"But what *kind* of Spain, Paco? Isn't it grotesque? Isn't it monstrous? What we *acalofilos* want is a government very much in the French style, but administered by our own officials. What Borbón would give us that?"

For a few minutes the three men consulted their manzanilla in silent thought. Moratín emptied the bottle and said, "We're right back where we were twenty years ago." He suddenly fell silent and turned to Goya, grinning and shaking his head. "No, I'm wrong. For now, Paco is completely on our side."

"I damned well am," the artist bellowed. "But what can *I* do?"

"There's a great deal you can do," replied Jovellanos. "Consider your position. It's unique among the *acalofilos*. For one thing, you have no reputation for subversive political beliefs. If you can keep your mouth shut, Joseph Bonaparte will probably want you to keep your post as Pintor de Cámara, where you might prove useful. Even more important, they'll probably allow you to travel. You can go where Leandro and Ceán and I would never be permitted. You can be the most important eyes in Spain."

Moratín joined in this encouragement. "There's no more highly trained observer in the whole country. Look for us, watch for us, observe for us, and then make drawings of the things you see. They can be more helpful than reports of conversation that might be contrived to deceive us."

Goya frowned. "But where will *you* two be, and Ceán?"

"Who knows?" said Jovellanos. "In Andalucía, perhaps, or in the Estremadura. But right now, I don't know."

"And what will you do?"

"Form a junta of our own, find ways of harassing the French. We'll write our own laws. We'll make the bastards sorry they ever started with us. Since, whether we will it or not, the people are going to resist, *we* might as well lead them."

During the late spring of 1808, French forces moved without encountering serious opposition in areas north and south of Madrid. By the end of June, approximately two-thirds of the country was in their control, and there seemed no reason to suppose that soon the remaining regions, Aragón and Catalonia in the north, Valencia and Andalucía in the south, wouldn't fall as a matter of course.

Of Goya's *acalofilo* friends, all but Moratín had left the capital in ones and twos, their destinations secret. Of the Spaniards who remained, those who admired the French, the *afrancesados*, were the most conspicuous in society. Mostly intellectuals or nobles, many were members of the high civil service

increasing difficulties in the regular supply of staples for even a diminishing population. Food and drink were scarcer and dearer, but not calamitously so. And if stocks of fuel were growing low, that presented no cause for immediate concern in this warm season.

Did he detect any mounting tension in the atmosphere of the quarters he visited? If anything, he sadly wrote Jovellanos, it was the opposite. Their resources of deepest, blackest emotion depleted, perhaps permanently exhausted, by the atrocities of the second and third of May, the *Madrileños* were lethargic, as if they had yet to come to solid grips with the essential new reality of their lives—that they were captives of the French.

Paco and Julio watched in angry silence as a gaudy procession of French hussars preceded the gilded carriage in which sat the figure of Spain's new alien monarch, Joseph Bonaparte. Though his arrival had been widely heralded, it provoked no coordinated demonstrations of enthusiasm or disdain. Though hardly overjoyed to inherit this middle-aged Corsican as their king, *Madrileños*, without effective means of resistance, chose to turn their backs as the royal vehicle passed. A few wheeled about to spit, as they had done when Godoy's coach had clattered along the Avenida de Alcalá. A single daring youth calmly unbuttoned his shoddy breeches and urinated into the street as the puppet king's carriage drew abreast of him. Guards averted their eyes.

Wise enough to take good advice when it was available, Joseph Bonaparte chose not to insist on any trumped-up evidence of popular acclaim; he asked no more than the maintenance of civic order. This much he had learned from his experience in Naples. There too he had entered as an enemy, but departed as someone very like a hero. This bracing thought seemed to him grounds for his conviction that he would enjoy a similar success in Spain.

King Joseph's initial occupancy of the Prado was of exceptional brevity, however. For at virtually the instant when his carriage drew into the Puerta del Sol, a few minor miracles were occurring, and a major one was in the making. In Gerona, in

Zaragoza, in Valencia, and in Seville, Spaniards were offering successful resistance to repeated attacks by French infantry and artillery. At Bailén, in a high, narrow valley of the Andalucian Sierra de Moreña, a force of 13,000 well-trained and admirably armed enemy soldiers under General Dupont, an officer who had hitherto proved daring and competent, found itself engulfed by a ludicrously irregular army of desperadoes led by a guerrilla chief who called himself Il Incognito. The astonished French fought back with commendable professional courage, but they were no match for the enraged, inspired, reckless peasants. Given the extraordinary conditions, the battle was brief. Dupont had no choice but to surrender. Spanish casualties were high, but the cost could be regretfully justified by the effect on morale of this incredible victory and by the amounts of arms and ammunition thus acquired—which would render much more dangerous further dissident operations. So elated was Il Incognito's ragged army that he felt it only proper that he should march on Madrid.

News of the battle of Bailén galvanized the torpid capital. The apathy of recent months was dispelled in a flash. Crowds lined the avenues and hooted at the coach of the departing Joseph Bonaparte and his entourage. *Afrancesados* fled the city by every gate. Everyone was saying that soon Don Fernando would return. Il Incognito was toasted as had been Napoleon only the year before. There was dancing in the streets. The second of May in Madrid had been avenged by the tenth of July at Bailén. Goya joined fellow *Madrileños* in tears of relief and joy.

From his refuge in Bayonne, Joseph Bonaparte warned his imperial brother that it was now his judgment that Spain could not be conquered or, if conquered, couldn't be controlled by force of arms alone. Napoleon paid him no heed. In his view, Joseph was a nice enough man and an intelligent administrator, but he knew nothing of warfare. Moreover, the emperor was in no mood to listen to counsel, good or bad. The fiasco at Bailén wasn't his only cause for disquiet in Spain. It was beginning to cross his mind that he had not a single good commander in the entire country, so persistent were reports of repulse, stalemate, and even retreat in the face of constant harrassment by the *guerrilleros*. There seemed only one solution. He must himself go to Spain and direct operations. So dramatic a conclusion was made all the more urgent by intelligence he now received that two sizable British forces, one led by Sir John Moore, the other by Sir Arthur Wellesley, were making serious incursions into northwestern Spain and Portugal.

The emperor's supervision of the campaign had the desired effect both on his own troops and on those of the enemies, British and Spanish. Resistance seemed to wither at the very prospect of having to do battle with forces under the personal direction of Napoleon. His physical presence gave tangibility to the awesome legend.

In the north, Goya's home city of Zaragoza finally surrendered. In this region, only the Catalonian fortress of Gerona continued to hold out against siege—and in the emperor's opinion this town was of no strategic importance. In the south, Valencia yielded, and although Seville and the rest of Andalucía maintained a stout defense, Bonaparte knew that it could be only a matter of time before the whole of that province was his. The two British armies made advances, but he was certain that his superior numbers and less precarious supply routes must eventually prevail against them.

His brother Joseph was reinstalled on his throne in the Prado only days after Il Incognito acknowledged the futility of trying to defend a city that had no fortifications. The guerrilla bands retreated southward. Napoleon, believing his task accomplished, returned to Paris. His judgment in leaving the reduction of Seville to his generals was probably correct. What he was unable or unwilling to understand was the potential significance of the junta that had been established there. For it was in Seville that Jovellanos and his friends and numerous delegates were now congregating for the opening of the first democratically elected Cortes in the history of Spain.

Only after Joseph's restoration showed every sign of permanence did Moratín return to Madrid from a visit in Seville. He

lost no time in seeking out Goya at his usual table in the
taberna. "Gaspar tells me," he reported gloomily, "that I must
at all costs find a post in this damnable government. Since it
seems we're *both* to be spies, I've allowed myself to be reappointed royal librarian." He hesitated, then grinned sheepishly.
"Besides, even though I hate the French as much as you do, I
can't think of a single one of their ideas which we couldn't put
to good use."

"You'll never get it through your head, will you, Leandro,
that French ideas, no matter how brilliant, just can't be made to
work in Spain?"

"But they do know so much better than we what government
is about. We need them. We need their guidance. There's so
much they could and would do for us if only we'd let them."
Moratín sighed. "But we won't. You're right about that. I hate
it, but I know it." He abruptly changed the subject. "Now tell
me, what's been happening since I left?"

"Nothing of importance. I continue to receive my salary. My
bank accounts are intact, but taxes are higher. I'm well
treated." He smiled wryly. "But no one has asked me to paint
the portrait of Don José Bonaparte."

"I thought you were to travel in the provinces."

"You've only to tell me where."

"To Zaragoza, I should think. You have good connections
there. Since the French moved in, we've had very sketchy
reports. Would you be willing to go?"

"What a question. I'd do almost anything to escape the
boredom of Madrid. You've no idea, Leandro. The French may
be as marvelous as you say, but they have a soporific effect on
this place. The *tabernas* are filled with soldiers and *afrancesados.* The *corrida* has been forbidden as too uncivilized a
sport. The theater, I'm told, is devoted to Spanish translations
of French plays." The painter checked himself and laid a stubby
finger on a nostril. "There's a new actress, Antonia Zárate. I
painted her. She's very handsome."

"And *had* her?"

Paco bowed his head, his expression morose. "I didn't bother to ask. I'm too old for that. Even if I *had* asked, it wouldn't have done me any good. Not for the finest portrait in the world would that bitch have shown me an inch of her thigh."

Moratín threw his small, wiry body against the back of his chair and cackled. "You liar. You did ask her."

Goya flushed and nodded glumly. "She called me a dirty old man."

"Then it's certainly time for you to go out into the provinces. Maybe there you'll find a pretty girl who doesn't mind dirty old men."

Javier objected vehemently to his father's proposed journey to the north. "You mustn't consider it, Papa. It can bring only trouble for all of us."

"*Us?* How can it possibly affect *you?*"

"You're my father. If *you* get into trouble, *I'll* be in trouble . . . *and* Gumersinda, *and* Mariano, *and* Mama."

"Don't be an ass. I'll have a paper giving me the right to travel. As Moratín says, for all their brutality, the French don't behave like monsters."

"I still say it's much too risky."

Goya had never felt more contemptuous of his son. "I suppose I ought to be pleased that you're concerned for my safety, but I'm scandalized. Don't you understand that I have friends there, and relations? Poor Martín Zapater, for instance, if he's lucky enough to have lived through a hell you won't even trouble to imagine. It hasn't passed through that mind of yours, has it? You think of no one but yourself. What about Gumersinda's papa? What about your uncle Tomás? Why in the name of God should I fear for myself? I'm almost sixty-three. I've seen the best of my life. From here on, it's going to be down hill and no turning back, no matter what I wish. But for Spain, Javier, it must one day be different. And Spain is in hell now. I'm of no importance at all."

"I still don't see why Don Gaspar should send *you*."

"Why *not* me? I'm a Spaniard. My country is in agony. I have to see. I have to weep. And I have to memorize everything I see and weep over and make pictures. I *need* it. I need it for myself. And if I happen to learn something useful, so much the better."

Goya left for Zaragoza in early October, 1808, accompanied by an excited Julio who had resolutely insisted that he be taken along. Normally the most timorous of men, he had dared on this occasion to assert himself with astounding passion. He threatened his master. "I'll leave you, Don Paco, if you don't let me come." Though unable to hear his assistant's voice, he had descried in his manner a determination so remarkable that he was impressed, and even a little intimidated. Man had bitten dog.

They traveled only a short distance beyond the gates of Madrid before they began to see sickening vestiges of the violence that was afflicting all Spain. On the branches of a leafless tree was suspended the nude torso of a man—without arms or legs, decapitated; the only evidence of sex was the flatness of the scrawny chest. This gruesome corpse couldn't have been hanging thus for long; decay had yet to show itself, nor had the scavengers detected its presence. "Who?" groaned Goya. He felt the need to retch. "Why?"

Farther along, they came upon the soot-blackened ruin of a peasant dwelling. Lifeless bodies, stripped of their clothing, were heaped obscenely before the burned-out doorway. As in the Puerta del Sol in May, the stench was frightful. The two men wept. "The bastards," howled the old man. "Oh, the filthy bastards."

Just as the carriage reached the crest of a small rise, there were evidences that the Spanish had got back a bit of their own. Torn remnants of red tunics were scattered over a wide area of the frosty ground. But there were no bodies. There had been survivors of this skirmish who had buried their dead.

And so it continued, an unutterably tragic reiteration of murder and torture, rape and the torch, throughout the whole of their long journey. They were importuned on several occasions by groups of suspicious, hot-eyed *guerrilleros* rudely demanding identification. Though not a one of them was literate, all were almost embarrassingly respectful when they recognized the great seal of Carlos IV on the painter's original warrant from the Spanish king, a document he thanked God he had had the foresight to bring along. After he or Julio had explained their mission, the leader of each band was eager to describe in caressing, colorful, and bitter detail some exploit recently accomplished against the French, and with equal enthusiasm to recount the atrocities perpetrated by the enemy—lingering, as if haunted, over the more sanguinary moments of the slaughter of innocents, of multiple rapes, or the firing of houses, public buildings, monasteries, and churches.

One leader described the literal crucifixion of a village priest on a cross, improvised of green timber, which had been erected before the altar of the victim's own small church. After the man's hands had been nailed to the crude bit of carpentry, the building was set ablaze. His cries of anguish had been hideous, and even now, it was solemnly sworn, his ultimate scream of horror as he gave up the ghost still echoed through the hamlet every day, at precisely the moment of his death. There was no doubt that this priest was already a saint in the hearts of his parishioners.

At other points along the route, and especially when the coach approached a major town, the travelers were stopped by French patrols. Though few of the soldiers they met were masters of more than a rough-and-ready Spanish, they were able to decipher the seal of Joseph Bonaparte on Goya's *laissez-passer*, which entitled him and Julio to journey where they wished. The French treated them with courtesy and waved them on their way. This hospitality annoyed Goya, who thought he would have enjoyed a little rough handling.

A trip that in normal times required four or five days took a fortnight in the autumn of 1808. When they reached the hill that loomed over Zaragoza Goya told the driver to pause. From the heights, the city appeared surprisingly unscathed by the long siege. Here and there, they could see important breaches in the mighty, ancient walls and a few sections were leveled, but

the two great cathedrals were intact, as were the mercantile
exchange and the archiepiscopal palace.

The carriage moved down the slope. A relaxed squad of
French guards delayed its passage only briefly at the gate. When
they drove into the city, many more troops were in evidence
than they had seen in any other town through which they had
journeyed. And they apprehended at once how sadly deceptive
had been the impression of their view from above. House after
house, prticularly those near the fortifications, were simply
shells of crumbling masonry. The windows of many others,
more distant from the walls, were boarded up to keep out the
worst of the biting north wind that roared down from the
Pyrenees at this season.

Goya directed his coachman to his boyhood home, where
Tomás had continued to operate their father's gilding shop. His
heart sank as the carriage turned into the familiar, narrow
street, for every structure on the side where the Goya family had
lived was demolished. He insisted, in spite of Julio's protest that
it was too cold for his health, on dismounting to examine the
ruins more carefully. To Ascensio, who followed him, there
seemed nothing to distinguish one gutted building from another, but the anguished painter marched without hesitation a
few yards ahead of the carriage, then stopped and pointed at the
rubble-strewn ground. "Here," he said hoarsely. At his feet lay
the charred remains of a wooden sign; faint traces of gilt could
be discerned on the frame. JOSÉ GOYA Y HIJO, it once had read,
but the elaborate script (he recalled bitterly the day when his
father had suspended it from an iron bracket) was totally
effaced.

He covered his eyes with gloved hands and listlessly permitted his assistant to lead him, stumbling, back to the waiting
coach. By the time they were reinstalled in their seats, he had
regained some of his composure. "To Zapater's," he told the
driver. "I'll show you the way."

Martín Zapater was Goya's oldest friend. As children, they
had sat side by side during morning lessons; as pubescent boys,

their paths had separated slightly—Martín intensifying his education with afternoons of private tutelage that led to university, Paco becoming a pupil of José de Luzán, at the time one of the province's most distinguished painters. But continuing matutinal association had preserved their intimacy.

Today one of Zaragoza's most prosperous merchants, Martín had, in addition to being the person who reconciled Goya to a career in art, two other distinctions where Paco was concerned. He was the only boyhood acquaintance with whom the painter had never engaged in physical combat nor even seriously quarreled. And throughout their long separations, he had remained the only friend with whom Paco had maintained a fairly regular correspondence.

Their love for each other had always appeared paradoxical to those professing to know both of them well. Martín was fastidious, orderly, systematic, rational, self-disciplined, eventempered, and deeply religious—though, because he was an intellectual of sorts, he was also anticlerical. He cared nothing for art, yet confessed to an admiration for Goya's portraits because of their fidelity. He opposed the *corrida* for its violence. He was dismayed and mortified by Paco's frank acknowledgment of his sexual promiscuity. Their differences, however, were those of the faces of the same coin. For each was endowed with the two qualities that made true friendship—utter selflessness where the other was concerned, and absolute, unshakable tolerance for what in each was incomprehensible to the other.

The carriage drew to a stop in the small courtyard before Zapater's mansion, which was undamaged. Goya and Julio descended. The old man walked rapidly to the door and knocked with all the force of his powerful knuckles. A young servant girl poked an alarmed face through a narrow opening and didn't appear relieved by the figure she beheld. He managed to force a smile. "Would you have the goodness to tell Don Martín that Goya is here with a friend?"

The girl studied his face anxiously. *"Goya, señor?"* she inquired tremulously.

"Just tell him 'Goya.' He'll understand. I take it he's at home."

She barely nodded and hastily closed the door. Only seconds later, Julio heard great shouts and commotion in the house. The door was flung violently wide as Martín rushed into the windy court. He bobbed his head politely at Ascensio, remembering him from infrequent meetings in Madrid, then threw his long arms about Goya. Only when he released his friend did the taller Zapater consider the painter's sad expression. His own elation collapsed.

"Tomás," said Paco, his voice caught between a whisper of agony and a croak of despair. His eyes glistened. "We've just come from there. What happened, Martín? When?"

The friend stared at him sadly. "But I sent you a letter, weeks ago."

"It never came, *amigo*. So tell me."

"We're not sure. I think he was trying to save his gilt."

Goya returned Zapater's gaze—their faces revealing the harrowing despair of their understanding that each, in this painful fraction of time, was helpless to come to the other's relief. "Do you think he suffered much?" Paco finally asked, his tone steadier.

Martín shook his fine, narrow head. "I can't swear he didn't, *mi amigito*. Nobody knew he'd gone to the house. It was during the last days of the siege. Everyone was underground, you understand, for what safety could be found there. He was dead when they discovered him."

"And Antonia and his children?"

"She hasn't written you?"

"Perhaps, but I've not had a letter."

"They went to stay with her father in Barcelona a month or so before."

They fell silent again. Goya wiped his eyes with the sleeve of his heavy cloak and sniffed loudly. "Poor, gentle, foolish Tomás. God help us all."

Zapater came abruptly back to life. He briskly directed his timid little domestic to help Goya's coachman with the baggage and took each of his guests by an elbow and propelled them into the house. The drawing room wasn't a great deal warmer than the courtyard. The host helped Julio divest the painter of his outer garment and apologized for the chill. "Fuel is hard to come by these days. People have taken to making charcoal from the timbers of the wrecked houses. But with hard winter coming, those won't last us long."

Goya was indignant. "The French won't let you bring wood in from the hills?"

"For once it's not their fault, Paco. There just aren't many men around who are fit enough to cut down the trees and burn the charcoal and carry it down to the city. Most of the stronger fellows have gone off to join the *guerrilleros*."

"Well, there's consolation in that. If we have to endure the cold, it's in a good cause," said the artist.

When the three men were settled in chairs before the copper brazier, wrapped in rugs, Goya gave Martín a brief but highly colored account of their journey from Madrid. "You know," he concluded, "I'm exhausted, and of course I'm devastated about poor Tomás, but I'm exhilarated too. I know it's perverse. We may not be winning this damnable war, but when I saw those brave men . . . and the boys, Martín, hardly more than children, perfectly willing to die, maybe even *hoping* to die, in that curious Spanish way, my God, I felt we were seeing something wonderful."

"You're right, Paco. The trouble is we need leaders for the *guerrilleros*, real military leaders. What we have now is a crowd of fellows who are reckless lunatics. Most of them are tobacco smugglers or bandits turned honest for the duration of the war, with little idea of how to use surprise and ambush to their best advantage. And then, of course, we have the other kind, the ones who are seeking a death by martyrdom, like María Agustina. She led a fantastic, brainless, absolutely hopeless charge. I suppose she had it in her head that God had destined her to be Zaragoza's Jeanne d'Arc. What a country." Zapater paused for breath. "But we have one fellow, thank God, Palafox. He's another breed altogether. If we hadn't had him to lead us during the siege, Zaragoza would have fallen in days. What an organizer. What a leader. What a strategist. You should have seen him, Paco. He gave the impression that he could be everywhere at the same moment—directing, criticizing, encouraging, laughing, singing, cursing. An authentic hero, I tell you. You can't go back to Madrid without painting his portrait."

Zapater had aged little in the five or six years since the friends had seen each other last in the capital. His body was still slender and erect, his face remarkably unlined, his hair a bit whiter and less profuse, but in dress he was as elegant as ever. He gave Goya news of Gumersinda's parents, the Goicoecheas. They were well and safe and, he believed, would almost certainly decline the painter's suggestion that they return with him to Madrid—as, indeed, did Martín himself, who offered not a syllable of complaint. If his trade had dwindled to nothing, he had sufficient reserves of gold to see himself and his family through the crisis. He did promise to inform Paco at once were there anything, no matter how trifling, that he required.

Zapater's single regret was that there was so little he could do in the interest of the Spanish cause. "Oh, I give Palafox gold for the things he can buy. But he gets his most important supplies by stealing from the French." He grinned toothily. "That's cheaper and more amusing."

He listened attentively as Paco told him of the activities and intentions of Jovellanos and his associates of the junta in Seville, and took solemn joy from the report that resistance in the south continued. When the painter finished, Martín extended his arms above his head, clasped his hands, and brought them sharply down to his lap. "Well, damn it, we're still resisting too. Not so successfully, perhaps, but you needn't worry. We're going to throw the scum out again. Palafox is making plans."

Goya leaned forward in his chair so that he might, in the failing light, see his friend's lips more clearly. "Tell me, Martín. How is it that he hasn't been caught yet?"

Zapater chuckled. "He's a genius. He's in hiding right here in Zaragoza. One of the most extraordinary and gratifying things to come out of this war is that it's made friends of people who used to be sworn enemies. Everyone, *everyone,* is united by it. If I didn't see it every day with my own eyes, I'd never believe it. Do you know the name of Don Juan Antonio Llorente?"

Goya scratched an ear reflectively. "The priest who wrote an honest history of the Spanish Inquisition and was defrocked for his pains?"

"The same. Well, Llorente has come here several times since the siege. He's given himself the task of instructing the nuns and monks in the ways of concealing fugitives, storing and transporting weapons and gunpowder, that sort of thing. In his way, *he's* a genius too. But the point I want to make is that, defrocked or not, he's welcome in every convent and monastery he goes to. Can you imagine such a thing happening a year ago?"

Goya nodded. "It's the same everywhere we've been since we left Madrid. When Ascensio and I were standing in the Puerta del Sol on the evening of the second of May, I told myself that I had just seen Spain die. I was wrong, Martín. I was watching a birth, not a funeral."

Goya and Julio spent several wintry months as Zapater's guests, making brief but frequent sorties from Zaragoza into the wild, hazardous hinterlands. They encountered the same evidences of violence that they had found during the journey from Madrid, all committed in the name of subjugation at the order of Napoleon. Heartening, though no less savage, were traces of *guerrillero* retribution. When they returned to the provincial capital from each excursion, Goya described to Martín what he and Ascensio had seen and provided quick but detailed sketches to accompany these accounts which were spirited at once to the hiding General Palafox, who praised them. "He says you're the perfect spy," said Zapater proudly. " 'Who,' he says, 'would ever suspect a deaf artist?' "

The painter shook his head and inclined it toward Julio. "But I'm *not* deaf, Martín. Ascensio is my ears, *and* my right arm."

The gentle assistant beamed. "No, Don Paco, I'm just your dry nurse."

"You're his *friend*, Ascensio," said Zapater reprovingly.

Julio seemed to recoil from this comment as though pained by its implications. His eyes widened. Could such a thing be possible? Could he be friend to one he idolized? He stiffened abruptly and threw back his little head with such force that his lank black hair flew in all directions. He made no effort to restore its order. "*Yes*, Don Martín, it's true. I am Don Paco's friend." It was the most sublime moment of Julio's life.

Whatever vices Goya possessed, snobbery wasn't one of them. He wordlessly cursed himself for not having made so obvious an observation to Ascensio long before. He had taken the man for granted. He stood up and walked the two steps that separated him from Julio and embraced him, weeping, as was more and more his inclination in moments of great emotion. But he could find no words that would serve this instant. That was all right, for Julio needed none. His modest cup of joy was running over.

Unable to abide the intensity of this interchange of affection so long but so innocently suppressed, Goya released Ascensio and turned to Zapater. "When am I to meet this paragon of yours, this legendary Palafox. I can't make a portrait of him without seeing him."

"Don't fret, Paco," said his host calmly. "It will be arranged."

But it was March before the promised meeting took place. The snow had been falling heavily all day. The painter and Julio, grateful that the blizzard had not caught them on one of their expeditions, huddled by the poor charcoal fire, wrapped in their rugs. Zapater was absent, but there was nothing unusual about this; he vanished from the house, destination undisclosed, at least once each week and sometimes more often. As the sky darkened into evening, Julio heard a great knocking at the door. The anxious servant girl scurried to respond and was all but swept off her feet by a great blast of wind and the swift entrance of a tall, bulky figure whose face was concealed by a heavy woolen muffler. It was Palafox. "I want to see the painter," he reported to the girl, his baritone echoing in the corridor like a musket shot.

She scampered obediently ahead and opened the drawing room door, leaping back in fear of being trampled underfoot by the man. Palafox strode to the corner where Paco and Ascensio were toasting their hands over the bleak coals in the brazier. Julio leaped to his feet and tapped his master on the shoulder, pointing to the general. The soldier eyed the artist. There was in his bold, candid expression something of natural hostility, something of mild astonishment, and not a little suspicion. "You're Goya?" he barked.

The painter slowly rose and approached the general at a leisurely pace. "I am. And who may you be?"

"I am Palafox."

"And you would like me to make a portrait of you."

"That's why I'm here. Can you show me on a horse?"

"I can."

"How long will it take you?"

"How much of *your* time? Very little, an hour at the most. I'll make some studies of your face. The rest I can manage without you."

Palafox almost smiled. "At last," he snapped, "I've met a man who says he can accomplish something without me. If you were younger, I'd put you on my staff."

"If I were younger," said the painter with a laugh, "I'd have volunteered already."

By the time the portrait had been completed, as the last snows of the bitter winter were melting, the heroic general had escaped into the hills. He was planning a second effort, based in part on information furnished by Goya and Julio, to relieve Zaragoza. Zapater was daily urging the painter to leave the city before hostilities recommenced. "Go home, Paco. Tell your friend Jovellanos and his people in Seville all you know. Tell them we may fail, but even in failing, we'll tie down at least two French regiments and a lot of artillery."

Goya was most reluctant. "I want to see this wonder for myself."

"You don't know what you're talking about. What good can you do here? You'd be a liability, both of you—just two more mouths to feed when, God knows, supplies will be stretched beyond their limits. Don't you understand, *hombre?* A deaf man in the middle of a battle, for God's sake. You wouldn't even know you were being shot at. You'd just be in the way."

"Don Martín is right, Don Paco," said Julio cautiously. "But *I* can stay."

Zapater rejected this proposal with an asperity that shocked Goya. "God in heaven, Ascensio. *Think,* will you? Just think. The trip back to Madrid isn't going to be easier than the journey here was. The French or our own people are as likely as not to shoot this mad, stubborn fool if you're not with him. He needs you more than we do."

Paco absorbed this injunction with open mouth. Never had he seen this side of Martín; he was both astounded and delighted. With an unwonted show of meekness he agreed to leave as soon as possible, protesting only against the unfairness of it all.

On their return to Madrid in the spring of 1809, Goya and Julio found the atmosphere much changed. The *afrancesados,* who had flocked back with the restoration of Joseph Bonaparte, were confident that his generous behavior, and the intelligent, desperately needed reforms being implemented in government and the courts, must soon win over all but the most obstinate *guerrilleros* and *Fernandistos.* And if, in the provinces, French troops had as yet failed to eliminate all resistance, the prospects of eventual success seemed bright. For the cities still withstanding siege could cherish no rational hope for relief from foreign sources.

The British army of Sir John Moore, which at one point had nearly delivered the capital from the enemy, had been beaten back. At La Coruña, in the northwest corner of Spain, that brave officer had fallen in a frenzied battle whose sole purpose had been to allow his battered forces to be evacuated through the nearby port of Ferrol. And in Portugal, it was all that the remaining British army on the peninsula, led by Sir Arthur Wellesley, could do to keep a foothold in the hills north of Lisbon.

After the longest of the war's sieges, in which thousands perished, the bastion of Gerona was finally captured by the French. General Palafox was successful in his campaign to retake Zaragoza. The painter's elation, however, was short-lived. Within weeks, the city was again in enemy hands. He learned that Martín Zapater had died, but was not informed of the nature of his death. Gumersinda Goya's father, who had written her of Zapater's demise, also noted with regret that all of Paco's paintings made during his stay in Zaragoza had been vandalized by the returning French.

If Moratín had harbored any private convictions that the French would succeed in "domesticating our people," as he put it now, he was firmly disabused of his illusions. He had never been so baleful. "With Gerona and Zaragoza captured, the French can concentrate all their energies on Seville. Poor Gaspar. Poor Spain."

In January, 1810, Seville surrendered. But members of the junta and delegates to the Cortes, all with enormous bounties on their heads, found refuge in Cádiz. Determined that the *guerrillero* activity should continue, the rump Cortes proclaimed that "all inhabitants of this country are hereby empowered by their rightful interim government to bear arms for the purpose of attacking and despoiling the soldiery of France." The chief of the French military staff in Spain responded in kind: "Any persons captured while in possession of weapons of any sort will be executed without formality of trial."

As Moratín noted scathingly, "There's nothing new in *that* message. They've been doing it right along, even if the people they captured were armed with nothing more dangerous than a kerchief."

"There's no remedy," murmured Goya, "except death and death and still more death."

At Cádiz, members of the Cortes occupied themselves in long, abstruse, and often acrimonious debates over the clauses of a constitution which, they insisted with more faith than certainty, would one day form the basis of a new Spanish regime. Now wholly won over to Paco's pessimism, Moratín could only moan over sporadic reports of these bitter arguments. "From what Gaspar says, it will take those fools twenty years to get their work done, unless Cádiz falls in the meantime, in which case they'll be dead men."

"But at least dead heroes," said Goya.

"Dead heroes are useful only to the French."

The survival of Wellesley's hard-pressed army, the courageous resistance of Cádiz, the optimistic planning of the Cortes, and the constant *guerrillero* harassment of enemy transport were the only rays of light in a scene that seemed to grow darker with each passing month. The country's communications were constipated. Shipment of food and fuel was hazardous and unpredictable—a factor that added to the misery of the population, especially in the cities, and most particularly in landlocked Madrid. The plight of the poor was appalling. For if one had useful connections with the French or the *afrancesados* and the required gold, it was possible to obtain the essentials, though at prices several times higher than a couple of years before. The poor were left to the mercy of God.

Through Moratín and because of his official attachment to the alien court, Goya and his family managed comfortably, though in nothing like the luxury they had enjoyed in better days. The painter accepted this spartan existence with a resignation that had no undertones of bitterness. In fact, he welcomed it; it was the only kind of penance he could share with his compatriots. But Javier was incessant in his complaints about the inferior bread and wine; he deplored the virtual disappearance of fresh fruit and vegetables. "We're living like swine," he said.

"But we're *living*," answered his father warmly, resentful that he had to depend on the detested French for his rations of food and charcoal, that it must be through their largesse that he received canvas and paints so that he might make portraits of the officers and high officials.

Moratín reminded Paco that Jovellanos still regarded him as a spy. The painter snorted. "But I'm of no use as a spy in a place like this, Leandro. In Aragón, where things were happening, I may have been a bit helpful. But these men who pose for me here . . . What is a general or a judge likely to say in my presence that Gaspar doesn't know already?"

"Just the fact that a man is in *your* presence instead of being somewhere else might be of enormous importance. You can't know in advance, Paco."

With increasing unease and anger, Goya continued to make routine portraits of the enemy's commanders and civic leaders. He was again almost as busy as he had been before the outbreak of war, for a portrait by Goya remained a symbol of the sitter's distinction. One of the principal *afrancesados* of the capital was Don Tadeo Bravo del Ribero, a sycophantic Castilian who served as the city's *alcalde mayor*. Ravished by Goya's vapid rendering of his unremarkable features, Don Tadeo invited the chief court painter to make a mural with an allegorical theme based on the evolution of Madrid. The central portion would feature a portrait of King Joseph. This canvas was to hang in the great hall of the *ayuntamiento*.

Though he offered no objection to the commission, Goya was disturbed to think that Joseph Bonaparte must pose for his portrait. What caused his anxiety was the idea that confrontation with this man might result in his being attracted to him. For Paco remembered too vividly how he had, against his will and better judgment, been seduced by Godoy's charm. The painter's reluctance stemmed from the fact that Joseph was reputedly difficult to dislike for any reason except that he was French. He was leaning over backwards to ingratiate himself with his subjects, especially the Madrileños. During the famines, he ordered that bread baked in the ovens of the Prado be distributed freely among the poor. On more than one occasion, he had driven to the more blighted sectors, where, with his own hands, he passed out loaves to the pathetic women and children who surrounded his carriage. He remarked percipiently to an aide on the absence of young or middle-aged men in these crowds. Were they too proud to accept alms? "No, sire. They're off in the hills, killing our soldiers."

From his personal funds, Joseph gave gold to relieve (insofar as gold *could* relieve) the direst suffering of cold and hunger. But he was among the first to recognize that this charity was inadequate and appreciated only to the degree that it kept a Spaniard alive long enough to murder another Frenchman. Nor were his praiseworthy reforms proving effective either. To one of his generals he sadly noted, "They're *all* against us, every single one of them, even those in whom we place such trust. And I understand it. When we had *our* revolution, it was made by our people. Without them, it would never have succeeded. Here, the revolution we're attempting pleases no one, not even the intellectuals who know that some kind of reform is required. They hate what we propose because we're foreigners, the enemy."

It turned out that pressures of public and private obligations made it impossible for Joseph Bonaparte to sit for his portrait. Instead, he dispatched an etching of his features of which he was particularly fond, expressing the wish that Goya base his picture on this. Now that the issue had been resolved, Paco was uncertain of his feelings. As a loyal Spaniard, he was relieved; for no one, in that nirvana of a restored Borbón monarchy, would be able to accuse him of having dealt with the usurper face to face. As a curious human being, however, he was let down. And as a professional, he was angry; this was the first king of Spain in Goya's working lifetime to decline an opportunity to sit for him.

The painting for the *ayuntamiento* was made, as the *alcalde* had requested, in the French manner that had for so long seemed to Paco insipid and innocuous. "They should have asked that whore, Maella, instead of me. The damned thing lies on my soul like a lump of lead." Goya thought it ironic that for this enormous, vacuous canvas he should be awarded by Bravo del Ribero the Red Cravat of the Order of Spain, the highest decoration the French bestowed. It was called by the Spanish the *berenjena,* the eggplant, and it was only after Moratín's severest stricture that refusal might be more compromising to the resistance cause than acceptance that he bowed his head and allowed the *alcalde* to drape the scarlet ribbon over his shoulders. He never wore it again.

This lacklustre painting had a second consequence. The Academia was informed that Joseph Bonaparte had decided to establish a museum of fine arts in Madrid—a gallery accessible not only to artists and connoisseurs, but to the general public. It would incorporate the most important treasures of the royal collections and be enriched by paintings and other objects of art confiscated from monasteries and convents that had been dissolved by the anticlerical French.

Joseph couldn't claim this salutary conception as his own, nor could his brother. Indeed, the idea had been in the final stages of realization under Louis XVI, who had been converting the Louvre into just such a museum in 1789. Though postponed by the events of the Revolution, the opening of the immense palace in Paris took place in 1793 and became that city's most popular attraction. When he could keep his head clear of self-deluding dreams, Napoleon was a man who noted well. He ordained that similar museums be established in many of the major cities in his hands—Venice, Amsterdam, Naples, and now Madrid. Goya was invited to join his fellow academicians Maella and Ferro in making a selection of paintings for the new institution. In particular, the three judges were asked to choose from the works by Spanish artists of the previous two centuries the fifty that they collectively thought represented the highest expression of their antecedents. This special group was to hang in the principal room of the new gallery.

Goya was complimented by the request that he participate in the selection and addressed himself to the work with zeal. The artists grew especially heated in their disputes over the fifty most important Spanish paintings. As their own work disclosed, Maella and Ferro inclined to the harmless, slick, nonresistant styles made fashionable by Mengs and the Tiepolos. Thus, Goya

was outnumbered, though he knew very well that since the
death of Velázquez there had been only one Spanish painter of
real distinction—himself. Not a single work of his was included.

It was all quite hopeless. When it came to making a choice of
the finest pictures of the seventeenth century, the favorites of
Maella and Ferro were equally predictable—Murillo, Ribera,
and Zurburán. They literally threw up their hands in horror
when Goya described them as "the most disgraceful pimps in
the history of Spanish art." And it was only after the most
savage argument that he prevailed on them to include three
works by Velázquez, whom he called "a perfect painter. There
was nothing he couldn't do, nothing he *didn't* do."

When the selection of the fifty most beautiful pictures had
been completed, Goya reported sourly to Moratín his resolve
never again to take part in committee work. "But I did get
those two imbeciles to include the Velázquez pictures, and
when they see them hanging beside the ones they chose, they
may be just bright enough to realize that old Diego has stolen
the show. He'll stand out like the morning sun among all the
rubbish they insisted on."

The librarian listened with amused patience to Paco's dia-
tribe. "You're quite finished? I don't want to cut you off in the
middle of a thought."

"Oh, no, Leandro. I've got plenty more to say."

Moratín raised a hand. "No, please. Because it's time for *me*
to tell *you* something I just found out today. Those pictures
were never meant to hang in Madrid."

Goya stared. "You're mad. All that argument for nothing?"

"Not for nothing, Paco. They're to be sent to Paris. They're
going to hang in the Louvre."

The painter demanded a repetition, his black eyes wide with
disbelief. But there was no mistaking his friend's words. "You're
certain?"

Leandro nodded. "Bravo del Ribero was under strict instructions to deceive you. The emperor wanted to be sure of getting
only the very best."

As if by command, the men rose from their chairs in the

taberna and fell into each other's arms, laughing helplessly. "So, by God, there *is* some justice after all," said Paco when he had recovered his breath. Then he frowned. "Now, of course, I shall curse myself for having made those two fools agree to the paintings by Velázquez. If I'd kept my mouth shut, I could have saved them for Spain."

ten

⚜ THE IDEA ORIGINATED with Moratín, who visited Goya's studio on an afternoon in June, a few weeks after the painter and Julio had returned from Zaragoza. When he entered, Moratín found his friend seated before a large table, slowly going through a pile of sketches he had made during his stay in Aragón. Most of these vignettes depicted the incidents of horror that he and Ascensio had witnessed or been told of. As Goya looked up, there were tears in his eyes, tears of frustrated rage and the feeling of helplessness in the face of the terrible memories these pictures evoked.

He rose and took the librarian's hand, excusing his distress as that of an old man who couldn't help yielding to the temptation of reviewing those agonizing months. "I do it at least once a week, just to remind myself that what we saw was real."

"May I see them, *amigo?* You've talked of them so often."

The painter waved him to a chair. "They're very hasty, I'm afraid, and you needn't pay attention to my captions, but there's a kind of order in their arrangement."

Moratín eyed him questioningly. "You're so defensive about them, Paco. What's the matter?"

"I'm not defending them. I'm attacking them. They're not good enough, not savage enough. They should be drawn in blood, not ink or charcoal."

"Be silent. Since when has a picture by Goya required apology?"

Moratín addressed himself to the drawings. The first, of a threadbare, starving man who knelt in supplication, hands outstretched in a gesture of loneliness and despair, was, to Leandro, incongruously religious in feeling—out of keeping with the direct and emphatically irreverent Goya style he knew. Only when he read the caption, which Paco had told him to disregard, did he understand the reason for its position as frontispiece: "Doleful presentiment of what lies ahead."

The contrast between the first and the second caused him to shiver, to sense what did lie ahead. Two ragged Spaniards were being executed by a French firing squad. "With reason or without," Paco had scribbled in the margin. In the third, the situation was reversed. A wild-eyed *guerrillero*, straddling an enemy soldier whom he had just killed, wielded an ax over another fallen Frenchman whose hand was lifted in unavailing protest. To the left, a second Spaniard sat astride a soldier's back and pummeled him with his fists. The laconic comment: "The same."

In a few succeeding sketches, Goya portrayed the valor of his countrywomen, picking up the swords of their fallen men, lancing the enemy with pikestaffs, or hurling stones. A woman touched off the fuse of a cannon, for all the male resistants had been slain or wounded. Perishing horses writhed in agony. A young woman fiercely fought off an attempted rape while an older one was about to stab the assailant ("They want none of it"). "Nor do they" was the caption of the next two sketches whose themes were similar.

By the time he had reached the thirteenth, Moratín was so distraught that it required an enormous effort of will for him to continue. Horror was joined by terror and then revulsion as he proceeded, with the deliberate care that typified all he did, to study every detail of every page—his mind reeled, but his reason compelled acceptance, for Goya wouldn't lie. There it all was, vision after grisly vision: decapitations, hangings, mutilations, mass burials, garrotings, pillage, torture, senseless laughter, hideous reprisal, scenes of starvation and of the famished dead being hefted onto carts for interment in nameless communal graves.

The first sixty-five of the eighty drawings seemed to Moratín to be all of a piece, straightforward expositions of fact. With the sixty-sixth was introduced a new note—anticlericalism. Pedestrians devoutly knelt as the relics of a saint were borne through the street on muleback ("Extraordinary devotion!"). The next showed a procession of penitents carrying on their shoulders a hallowed statue ("No less strange."). In the sixty-ninth drawing, a scene of sprawling, decaying corpses, the central figure held a pencil between eroded fingers. Before expiring he had written the single word *"Nada."* Paco's caption was, "Nothing. It speaks for itself."

But the end was not yet. Snaking along a shadowy, circuitous, rocky footpath was a gloomy straggle of captives—gentlemen and peasants linked to one another by a length of rope wound around each neck ("They know not their way.").

A second pronounced change of mood was detectable in the seventy-first, which vividly reminded Moratín of Paco's abortive edition of *Los Caprichos*. For here the artist introduced some of the ingredients of his private fantasies. As if wholly depleted by his efforts to convey through reality the hideousness of war, he had resorted to the satanic symbols of his own demonology, that terrifying subworld of his nightmares to which he had so often referred. Here was an *afrancesado* justice with hollow features and a pursed mouth, writing in a large volume a judgment he had just pronounced against one of his compatriots. In place of ears, Goya had given the judge the widespread wings of a bat ("Contrary to the general welfare.").

This drawing adumbrated the next four, each more atrocious and lurid than its predecessor. The seventy-sixth and seventy-seventh were meant to be juxtaposed. In the first, one of Goya's most alarming creatures (a bird with short, useless wings, several times taller than the man who fended it off with a pitchfork) danced an ungainly fandango before a huddled mass of Spaniards ("Carnivorous vulture."). In its counterpart, a high cleric, dressed for celebrating mass, teetered precariously on a fraying rope that was loosely suspended above an awed crowd. To this ironic picture Paco posited a subjunctive caption: "May the cord break." The identification of the church with the vulture was plain. So also was the reason for this libel: During the two years of war, the high clergy had been equivocal in its attitude toward an enemy whose anticlericalism it hoped, by obsequiousness, to propitiate. This groveling was an old story with the French; their own bishops and cardinals had played a double game during the revolution. In Spain, they cynically exploited the church's cowardice, knowing that the great clerics would ride the fence, or walk a swaying rope, until certain which side it would be safer to choose for a soft landing, heedless of the interests of the people whose souls were its only ostensible concern.

Now Goya's spleen had been drained. In the next drawing he sought solace in a happier symbolism. A white horse lashed out with powerful hind legs at a pack of dogs. "He defends himself well," Paco proudly wrote, in clear allusion to the heroic efforts of the *guerrilleros*. The two final pictures were also to be seen together. In the penultimate drawing, a silent, solemn, tenebrous throng wept at a graveside watching the brilliantly illuminated body of a young woman clad in the white gown of virginity. "Truth is dead," was his comment. The concluding sketch was the same in atmosphere and theme—the same crowd, the same virginal body that had been laid in the grave. She appeared, however, to be trying to raise herself. From her breast and face emanated the dazzling light of hope. Moratín was elated; truth would revive. Paco hadn't given way utterly to despair. Then his eye fell to the caption: "Will she rise?" Not an expression of hope, but a question—the supreme question.

Moratín seemed to shrivel as he fell against the back of the chair. His features were gray. He turned to find Goya standing beside him, a glass of manzanilla in his hand. He grasped it and emptied it at once, gasping in relief as the fortified wine made its comfort felt in his belly. The painter replenished it from a carafe. This time, Leandro consumed the contents less hurriedly. Then he rose, but there remained a wildness in his eyes as he finally discovered his voice. "You've just given me the most terrible hour of my life, Paco."

Goya pointed to a clock on the wall. "*Two* hours, *amigo,*" he said with satisfaction.

"It's not possible."

"They shocked you?"

"Much more, I think, than the things I've seen with my own eyes."

"You're probably right. The eye loses focus when a number of things are happening at the same time. It sees too many things at once and the vision becomes diffuse. With a picture, you concentrate on what the artist has compressed—what, I mean, he's given focus to."

"Perhaps," said the librarian reflectively, "but it's more than that. In two hours you've exposed me to all you and Ascensio saw in months."

"Not all."

"You know what I mean, Paco."

"And I invented nothing of the horror, you know. I've drawn what we saw."

"What will you do with these?"

"Nothing."

"You should engrave them."

Goya's laughter was hollow. "So I can lose another fifty thousand reales?"

"They needn't be published."

"You know damned well they *couldn't* be published, not now."

"They'd be part of your—what shall I call it? Your witness. They belong in your collected work. People have a right to know what you felt, where you stood, what your faith and hope were during these terrible times." Moratín sighed profoundly as the manzanilla calmed him. "If the people of the world believed what you've shown in these drawings, they'd never be tempted to make another war."

The painter's smile was sardonic. "If I thought there was a

chance of that, I'd etch them and publish them tomorrow and
scatter copies from the spire of the cathedral, or hand them out
as Don José Bonaparte distributes his bread, and be damned to
whatever might happen to me or my family. It would be worth
any risk. But no one *will* believe, Leandro. No one *wants* to
believe."

"But they must be engraved."

"To add to Javier's legacy?"

"To add to man's wisdom."

"No one will ever be interested in the moral of these things,
amigo. It's the perversity of our world. And I thought *you* so
well-versed in history and myself so ignorant. The world wor-
ships war. Our greatest heroes are generals or admirals. No one
dares to think of war in the terms I show here." He flipped his
hand toward the sketches on the table. "But God damn it, that's
what war is really like. It has nothing to do with the chivalry
other painters glorify. You know what I mean . . . where
generals are compassionate, where soldiers are magnanimous in
victory and proud even in defeat. That kind of image is revolting because it's a lie. I've known of not a single example of
chivalry or even of common humanity during this war. It's all
blood and greed and cruelty for their own sakes, on both sides.
And the worst thing of all is the indifference, the shrug of the
shoulders, the looking away. It's monstrous. Do you remember
the caption of the fifteenth drawing, where the blindfolded men
are tied to stakes and shot? 'There is no remedy.' *That's* the
problem, Leandro. The sense, if there ever was any, has gone
out of the war now, the intelligence, the reason. The French
and Spanish are killing each other today not for cause, but out
of a reflex they can't control, because of an instinct they can't
even give a name to, least of all the name of total victory. Even
if we *do* eventually win—and I suppose I *have* to believe we
shall—we'll have lost much more than we can possibly gain. We
can't restore the lives of the thousands killed already."

"What a misanthrope."

"My hatred isn't for *man*, Leandro, but for *men*, for the

institutions that compel us to commit such atrocities, the state and the church."

After several months of Moratín's intermittent hounding, Goya agreed to engrave the eighty drawings depicting the horrors of the continuing war, though both men were certain that publication even under a restored Borbón monarchy was out of the question; Paco's indictment of the church and of Spanish cruelties was too sharp. He gave this series the title *Los Desastres de la Guerra*. He pulled about a dozen proofs of each etching and distributed them to discreet friends. He stored the copper plates in the fastnesses of his remotest closet.

The most telling of Moratín's arguments in favor of committing these sketches to plates was the assertion that however disparaging some were of Spanish institutions, the overwhelming responsibility for the horrors he had shown fell clearly on the French. Posterity, through Goya's engravings, would be made to understand this fact far more readily than could be learned from a reading of history; seeing was believing.

The engraving took two years, a period in which Goya made many small paintings of subjects closely related to the etchings. Quite different in apparent theme (though its connection, subconsciously, was intimate) was a large canvas that he called "Colossus." Standing in a valley, arms akimbo, was the hard-muscled figure of a nude man, his back to the viewer; his manner and posture suggested menace. A side of the giant's face and his left biceps were dramatized by the light of a setting sun. On a flatland beneath him, in the descending darkness, was a scene of panic. Humans and beasts were dashing off in all directions, seeking refuge from the threat of this looming symbol of war—of France. But there was no escape, so great was the giant's stride, so voracious his appetite. It was the most emotionally charged painting he had ever attempted. "*My* allegory, this time," he observed to Moratín. "It's not the kind of picture Tadeo Bravo would want to hang in the *ayuntamiento*."

Leandro was disturbed by this painting, and not merely because of its forceful effect on him. It seemed to augur dire things for his friend. He was alarmed because Goya, after years of having suppressed his deepest emotions, appeared now to have lost control of them. "You need a change, Paco. You're much too obsessed with these visions of the war."

"Aren't *you, amigo?* Isn't everyone? Am I the exception?" He inclined his head toward the picture of the giant. "That's just the meaning of this. We're all of us involved with it to the point of madness. *You* need a change as much as I do. *Spain* needs a change. But who's going to bring it about, and when?"

"Do more portraits. Get your mind off this morbid business."

"I *make* portraits, whenever I'm asked. But I'm not especially proud of them." He paused and grinned. "No, I mean that I'm proud that I'm *not* proud of them. It *pleases* me to portray the *afrancesados* and the French in a dull way. But there *is* one portrait I'm happy with, a good painting, of Don Juan Antonio Llorente. He was a friend of Martín Zapater's, and he's a most admirable man." He sighed. "But portraiture on the whole bores me. I've done too many of them—hundreds, perhaps even a thousand." Paco pressed his fingers to his temples and studied Moratín's features. "I've been looking back a lot recently, not at my life but at my work. I suppose that's a sign I'm ready to die, running back into my past because the present is unendurable and the future looks even worse. I'm not physically weak, thank God. But at sixty-five, I'm conscious of death much more than I used to be."

"We're all conscious of it," said Moratín. "Man is the only animal that is."

"What a fine distinction."

"But it's no good brooding about it, as you do. You've still not dealt with my original complaint. Can't you get this damned war out of your mind? Can't you find something else, something more amiable to paint? There must be plenty of pleasant little scenes to choose from, even today.

"No doubt. But when I'm painting what I *feel* like painting, it's not easy to keep that obsession from intruding, to the exclusion of everything else. It's my cancer. It's *Spain's* cancer, and it's not to be cured simply because we wish it would be."

"All I ask, Paco, is that you consider what I've said. You do
need a change. I worry about you."

When Goya saw Moratín a few days later, he expected to be
subjected again to the librarian's views about his need for a new
outlook. But from the moment Leandro entered the *taberna*
and settled himself in a chair, Paco knew there was something of
much greater importance troubling him; his features were those
of a man in deepest mourning. Hoping to cheer him, the
painter was gay. "I'm still thinking of what you said, *amigo*.
You don't need to be so worried."

"Gaspar is dead," murmured Moratín. There was as much
astonishment in his tone as sorrow. "Jovellanos is dead."

Paco placed his elbows on the table and held his head between his palms, sobbing. "Did the bastards kill him?"

"No. He was delivering a speech to the Cortes, and he
suddenly dropped to the floor and was dead. Like *that.*" Moratín snapped his fingers.

Goya straightened and summoned the tavern-keeper. "Bring
coñac," he shouted. Then, to Leandro, he said, "We must drink
to the soul of dear Gaspar, which is surely in paradise. He'd
have no objection, except that he's not with us."

When their glasses were filled, the two men solemnly raised
them, brought them together, and drained the contents in a
single, scalding, antiseptic gulp. "More," commanded Moratín
with passion. "It's the vilest stuff I've ever drunk, but bring us
more."

"Just the thing," said Goya. "Brandy has saved more souls
than all the bishops put together." He laughed, and found it
impossible to stop. Moratín joined in his hysteria. While others
in the *taberna* looked on amusedly, both yielded to this uncon-
trollable emotion.

"What you said was blasphemy," Leandro observed, when he
had mastered his feelings.

"To laugh was blasphemous too, I suppose."

"It was."

"Well, I don't give a damn about the bishops. But you should know that neither of us knows how to blaspheme the memory of Gaspar. We laugh to keep from crying."

"You're always catching me off balance, Paco, always saying something I don't expect."

"You do the same to me, but I never shocked Gaspar. I never knew a man so unlikely to lose his balance."

"There is one thing," said Moratín, less miserable now, "to be happy about. Gaspar had nearly finished his work. The constitution will be completed soon, in draft form. Only *he* could have accomplished that. He was the hardest-minded political thinker in Spain."

As ever when this topic was raised, Goya became gloomy. "I'm not mocking Gaspar, Leandro, but of what use to us is a constitution if we don't have our own king to put it into practice?"

"The intention of the Cortes is to have a constitution ready for Don Fernando when he comes back. If Don Fernando is willing to agree to the terms of the constitution, we can finally have peace . . . and justice."

"And if he's not willing?"

"There's no question of that. He'll have to deal with the realities. He'll have to deal directly with the Cortes. If he refuses to accept the constitution, the Cortes will deny his authority."

Goya considered his friend; he was a man he didn't know, a creature from another universe. "And add *more* deaths with a civil war? You're as foolish as the people you condemn. You won't see the facts because they don't correspond to your wishes. They don't correspond to mine, either, but I yield to them. And the central fact is, as I've said so often, that as far as our people are concerned, no matter what the damned Cortes says or hopes or believes or does or tries, Don Fernando can come back to Spain and take back his throne on any terms he pleases. The people care nothing for a constitution."

"All this agony?"

"Do you dream that the agony is over a just, constitutional monarchy? The people resist for just one reason—*one, one, one.*

They want Don Fernando, not Don José. It's got nothing to do with justice. If *that* were the issue, or even *an* issue, wouldn't they be happier now than they were under Godoy? Wouldn't they have accepted your precious French Enlightenment? They want *el rey idolatrado*—nothing less, but absolutely nothing more."

PART III

Leocadia

eleven

❧ ONE AFTERNOON in the summer of 1811, Goya was seated at the polished table in Javier's dining room in the Calle de Valverde. He was sketching with a stick of charcoal and recounting anecdotes to accompany his drawings for the diversion of his grandson. Mariano was ravished by these attentions; he looked forward to the old man's visits because he found him so amusing, so affectionate, so good-humored, so generous. He saw nothing exceptional about his grandfather's patience with his antics and incessant questions and was surprised that his parents repeatedly remarked about it. The painter's love for the boy was the only cloudless feature of his existence. He knew it was wrong of him to be secretly pleased that Josefa, wholly bedridden and wasting slowly but inexorably toward her demise, saw so little of the child now. Paco went out of his way, however, not to take advantage of this circumstance. He avoided any word or sign that might imply his wish that the boy follow in his footsteps, though he didn't doubt that Josefa, were she to look in on them at this moment, would accuse him of doing just that.

He was completing a vividly illustrated account of a *corrida* years before in which the great *torero* Pepe Hillo had lost his life. Mariano hung on every word, delighted by his grandfather's tales of gore and glory. As the narrative was coming to a close, Gumersinda appeared in the doorway. Mariano leaped to

his feet and ran to his mother's side. She laughed and lifted his
easy weight, embracing him quickly before restoring him to his
feet. It was only as she performed this maneuver that Goya
noticed the presence of a second woman, who stood behind his
daughter-in-law. She held the hand of a small boy of about his
grandson's age.

Gumersinda stood aside to allow the guest to enter. She was
young and slender, her figure poignantly reminiscent of María's.
Her movements, too, reminded him of his dead mistress, though
she was much more simply dressed than the duchess. She wasn't
beautiful—not, at any rate, to the same degree that María had
been lovely. In her regular features there were traces of sullen-
ness and discontent, nor did she seem concerned to hide these
feelings. Goya was intrigued because he thought he detected
in her the qualities of difficulty, of restless temperament and
willful dissatisfaction that had simultaneously delighted and
infuriated him in the Duchess of Alba. What he knew intu-
itively about this young woman was that she was a bitch.
Bitches had always interested him, and he doubted not, when he
reflected (which was rare) on the essential failure of his marriage, that a measure of its incompatability lay in the simple but
fatal reality that Josefa wasn't a bitch but a martyr.

"Papa," said Gumersinda, leading the newcomer by the arm,
"this is Doña Leocadia Weiss. She's a cousin of mine from
Aragón."

Paco had risen when the two women entered. He bowed and
took the visitor's small, moist hand, pressing it lightly to his lips.
She wore no perfume; she smelled of humanity, of woman. She
smelled of Pepa Tudo eleven years before. She possessed the
distressingly attractive aura of venery. "What a pity, Doña
Leocadia, that you should come to Madrid at this unhappy
time."

"Oh, I've not just arrived, Don Francisco. I've been living
here for seven years. My husband is in commerce here." The
well-modulated voice was lost on Paco, but the voluptuousness
of the mouth was not.

"Ah? And this is your son?"

The small boy appeared startled by this reference to him. He retreated behind his mother's skirt. "Guillermo," she said severely. "That's not the way to behave." She turned abruptly and gave him a smart slap across his meager right cheek.

This intemperate gesture caught Goya between emotions. It was something he could never, no matter how great his fury, bring himself to do. He was offended, yet he was admiring too. There was something appealing in the directness of the woman's response. The blow caused Guillermo to emerge hesitantly from his hiding place. He eyed the painter, then devoted a more suspicious attention to Mariano. It was evident that the children had not previously met. Doña Leocadia shook her son's shoulders with both hands. "Offer Don Francisco your hand, *idioto,* and say good-day," she commanded.

Goya interceded, laying his coarse fingers on the boy's flushed face. "It's all right, Guillermo. I know how it is. I don't like meeting people either."

"Please, *señor,*" the mother protested. "You mustn't indulge him." Her sharpness pleased him. She was afraid of no one. "He has to learn these things."

"Oh, if he *has* to learn them, *señora,* then he *shall* learn them. Life will see to that."

Doña Leocadia perceived that she was boxed in, torn between an urgent desire to have another go at the refractory child and a comparably strong impulse not to make too great a show of it. She glared at the famous artist for several seconds. At last she sighed and wordlessly conceded a setback, but it would be temporary. Paco knew that once they were out of his sight, poor little Guillermo would be made to atone for his intractability. But now she placed a hand in the small of his back and pushed him toward Mariano. "Go and play, but play nicely, do you hear?"

The children edged cautiously toward each other, like a pair of strange dogs in the street. Goya laughed. "Why don't you go and play in another room?" he asked genially. They were relieved and grateful when Gumersinda nodded her assent and led them into the adjoining salon—a room so elaborately furnished (at her father-in-law's expense) that Goya was always uncomfortable in it. It was a room exclusively for woman, he thought, and what he thought, he gave utterance to.

When Paco and Doña Leocadia were seated, Gumersinda excused herself to arrange for refreshments. He leaned forward eagerly and smiled at the young woman across the table. "If you're so long in Madrid, *señora,* how is it that I haven't seen you before? I thought I'd seen every beautiful lady in town."

He watched her face carefully for a reaction to this fulsome compliment. She accepted it with total composure, as if nothing could be less remarkable. "But I know all about *you,* Don Francisco."

Paco grinned wickedly and, he hoped, engagingly. "So? And may I ask you the source of this great knowledge?"

"Mostly Gumersinda, though of course your name comes up in other places very often."

"I hope it's pronounced with the affection it deserves."

"Short names present no problems," she said, aware of the ambiguity of her reply.

"Those who know me call me Paco."

"So I'm told, Don Paco."

"But you've not answered me, Doña Leocadia. How is it that I've not laid eyes on you until today?"

"I've been warned against you."

He laughed. "I suppose I should be flattered that anyone thinks me a menace." He instructed his features to register astonishment. "But I can't imagine who would say such a thing."

"My husband, for one."

"Extraordinary."

"He compares you to the plague."

"A plague to *you?*"

"To all women, but especially to me, I daresay, because I'm his wife. He thinks your reputation . . . unsavory." Her voice trailed off. He noted, however, that her speech seemed not equated with any look of apprehension.

"Ah, yes, my reputation. Well, as you see, I've left my fangs on my bedside table. A man's reputation is usually exaggerated, for good or bad. For example, the Duchess of Alba, whom I had the pleasure of knowing, has acquired since her death the reputation of being mad. But that's a lie."

She regarded him with amusement and mild curiosity. "You're suggesting that your reputation as a . . . as an admirer of women . . . is a lie?"

Goya threw up his hands in mock horror. "Good God, no. The very opposite. An admirer, by all means. But that's not what you meant, is it?"

She acknowledged this with a pretty sideways and downward inclination of her face. "One seeks a phrase that's suitable."

"I'm moved to know that someone in Spain is still concerned with the proprieties. But Goya is not, nor has he ever tried to conceal his feelings behind that dehumanizing construction, 'one.' "

"I can see that, Don Paco." She closed her eyes. "I'm also able to see what my husband means about you."

"Then you're both deluded." He sighed histrionically. "There was a time, Doña Leocadia, when husbands were well-advised to lock up their wives and daughters against me, but no more. Now I'm a menace only to myself."

"How old *are* you?"

He flushed but answered with only the slightest remorse. "Sixty-five. How old are *you?*"

"Twenty-five."

"You see?" he said wistfully. "No danger at all."

"Because you're too old, Don Paco? What nonsense. You're just asking for sympathy. You should be ashamed of yourself."

Goya felt as if he had been stabbed. Dear God in heaven, María had said the same thing to him, lives before. Tearfully, he raised his eyes and found her distressed. "I've hurt your feelings. Please forgive me. I had no idea . . ."

"No, no, of course you've not hurt my feelings. It's just that you said something that reminded me of a woman I loved very much."

Leocadia studied her hands. He sensed that she felt herself on hazardous terrain. Her face was set more firmly as she looked at him again. "I was just going to say that your eyes aren't the eyes of an old man, nor are your hands."

"Thank you for the compliment, Doña Leocadia, but it's my head that's too old, too sensible to be turned by pretty words."

She resolved herself. "You're mistaken, Don Paco. They're not just pretty words. In the most important way, I suspect you're younger than my husband, and he's only thirty."

He fixed her brutally, skewering her with his most pointed glance. "Indeed? How unfortunate for you."

"Indeed," she murmured bitterly.

Gumersinda returned, followed by a domestic who bore a tray of delicacies, the poor best the troubled times afforded. "I'm so sorry Don Isidoro couldn't come with you, Leocadia. I'm sure Papa would have liked to meet him."

Goya grinned. "There's nothing I'd have enjoyed more. Perhaps another time."

"I was just explaining to Don Paco," said the young woman with an airy smile, "that Isidoro thinks him a threat to every husband."

His daughter-in-law wagged an admonishing finger. "You see, Papa? It takes a long time to live down your old days."

"Yes, and it mortifies me. Rest assured of that, my child, but not for the reason you suppose. As I was explaining to your charming cousin, I'm dismayed because I'm guilty of so small a fraction of the exploits people ascribe to me. I was never such a dreadful fellow."

Gumersinda served him with a piece of sugarless pastry and a glass of dismal manzanilla. "There's no use denying that you were very wicked."

"You pay too much attention to what Josefa says." He turned to Leocadia. "Josefa has the misfortune of being my wife."

"Misfortune, Don Paco?"

"So she and the rest of the world seem to think."

"Papa." Gumersinda's expression told him she was going to be severe unless he behaved himself.

"Whose damned appearances are you keeping up *now?*" he

asked irritably, then regretted the outburst. "I'm sorry," he said, but more to Leocadia than to his daughter-in-law. "My wife is an invalid. What were we saying?"

"Your reputation, Don Paco."

"As a womanizer, yes. Well, I don't care a damn about it. All that interests me is painting. And my reputation as a painter has the advantage of being well-founded. My only complaint is that it's based on the wrong pictures, but that doesn't matter either."

"You see, Leocadia?" said Gumersinda despairingly. "He's quite incorrigible. To hear him tell it, you'd think he'd been no worse than a naughty altar boy."

Doña Leocadia arched her thick black brows. "Isidoro says that vice is easier to find in Madrid than virtue."

"Virtue is difficult to find anywhere, *señora*, because one of its most important attributes is secrecy."

"My husband doesn't agree with you."

"He seems to have an obsession on the subject. If he's correct, then the vice in Madrid is the delight of the young. For myself, I've been compelled by age to realize that my capacity for vice, if that's what it was, has diminished in direct proportion to the increase in my appetite for it."

The young woman's pout was mocking. "The poor old gentleman."

Goya responded with icy negation. "I'm neither poor, Doña Leocadia, nor a gentleman, but I'm certainly old."

Her smile was small and secret and tantalizing. "I wonder, Don Paco. I wonder."

For a week after this encounter, Goya's thoughts were exclusively for the piquant, sharp-tongued, strong-minded Leocadia. Through Moratín's informants he gleaned a few facts to mull over in his agitated state. Her maiden name was Zorrilla; her parents were impecunious relations of the wealthy Goicoecheas. The little Guillermo was her only child. The merchant husband, Isidoro Weiss, was descended from one of the Bohemian families who had settled in the uplands of the Sierra de Moreña during the reign of Carlos III. He was said to be enterprising but unlucky. In fact, if his intelligence was accurate, Goya surmised that Weiss' principal asset was his young wife whom he was known to hover over with a maniacal jealousy.

These fragments of knowledge, while intriguing because they related to Leocadia, were hardly a meal that could satisfy Goya. But what, exactly, did he want to know? What was in his mind? Like Socrates, in *The Symposium,* he posed these questions to himself because he knew the answers. Yet he dared not give voice, except in imagination, to the thoughts that spun there like nebulae—so preposterous were they, so vain (in both senses), so arrogant. He was, for the love of God, lapsing into senility. Could he rationally believe that he could seduce a woman young enough to be his granddaughter? How could such a dream be reconciled with common sense?

He made numerous hysterically pornographic drawings to which, in moments of excruciating desire, he yielded himself in onanistic contemplation, experiences that left him restless and revolted. He persisted in this practice for want of an alternative. He had to admit darkly that at sixty-five he was nearly as febrile sexually as he had been at twelve, when the fleeting sight of his sister's bared breasts could excite him unendurably. The beautiful actress Antonia Zárate had been only too apposite in calling him a dirty old man. Recognition of his hopeless passion for Leocadia, however, only served to fan its delicious and disquieting flame.

In spite of the despair of his desire, Goya refused to risk the humiliation he was sure would result from asking Gumersinda when, if ever, he could expect to see Leocadia again. But his daughter-in-law divined the degree of his interest. For since the day of their meeting, the old man had religiously called at her house at the same hour each day, and though he never mentioned the name of Leocadia, he alluded to her in what he thought more subtle ways. He asked Mariano how he had liked Guillermo Weiss and was inordinately delighted by his grandson's tepid words of approval.

Gumersinda was disturbed and perplexed. She wasn't at all

fond of Leocadia. Only strong family feeling had induced her to
maintain contact with her cousin. She acknowledged that the
young woman's marriage was something of a catastrophe but
was unconvinced by Leocadia's assertion that the fault lay with
her husband—with his false pride, his jealousy, his commercial
failure and their resulting penury. Leocadia was too ambitious
socially, too greedy, and outrageously outspoken; she was un-
ladylike, the severest epithet Gumersinda could apply to another woman of her own class. She shuddered to recall the
blinding glint of avarice in Leocadia's eyes when she had been
taken on a tour of the younger Goyas' apartments. Such nakedness of envy was unnerving to one who had never endured
privation.

Even before Leocadia's arrival in Madrid, the cousins had not
been close. They had seen each other often as children, but at
family gatherings in Zaragoza where intimacy was unlikely to
develop. Since her marriage to Weiss, they had met rarely,
despite the fact that the two couples resided in the same parish.
For the circles in which the Goyas moved were not those of the
Weisses. Isidoro discouraged his wife from making friends with
people whose tastes and manner of living he couldn't possibly
afford. The invitation to call with Guillermo had been casually
extended, at a meeting after mass. Leocadia's eagerness had
surprised the innocent Gumersinda; the cousin had insisted that
a date and hour be set at once.

Most distressing was Leocadia's litany of obloquy about her
husband, a disrespect she was at pains, even during the briefest
of conversations, to communicate. Raised in a world where the
man of the household was above open criticism, Gumersinda
found her cousin's vitriolic abuse of Weiss scandalous. A wife
was entitled to doubts and reservations, as she herself felt
toward Javier's indifference to his faith, his refusal to live
within his considerable means, and his scornful exploitation of
his father's generosity. But it would never have occurred to her
to set herself against him in public. And however much she
quarreled with him in private, the thought of disobeying his
order was repellent. Javier was her lord. That was that.

Goya's son was neither able nor inclined to offer moral comfort when Gumersinda confronted him with what seemed to her a dilemma of enormous dimensions. His attitude was typically cynical. "If we *don't* invite her, Papa will manage some other way."

"You don't *care* what he does?"

"What's the harm of his seeing her?"

"You know what he has in mind."

"Of course, and who's to blame him?"

"You want her *too?*"

"No, for God's sake. I mean Papa. He's never pretended to be a saint. He's never pretended to be anything, except the greatest painter in Spain, and there's no pretense in that."

Gumersinda brooded, seeking a phrase sharp enough to puncture the balloon of complacency that enveloped her husband's indifference. "But your *mama,*" she said plaintively.

"But he still *loves* Mama, what there's left of her to love, poor dear Mama. He's very tender with her. He visits her every day, tries to make things bright for her. Sometimes I've seen him weep for her. There's nothing left for him to do."

"He can be faithful. At his age, that's not asking much."

Javier's laughter was cold. "At *his* age, perhaps fidelity is all he has to offer, even to himself."

"Don't be a beast."

"What's beastly in my saying that it's been an abysmal marriage? That's the truth. But he loves her just the same, out of loyalty, out of decency."

Gumersinda sank into a chair and looked up at her husband, her expression bleak. "But *Leocadia, querido?* Leocadia? The thought of her makes my flesh creep."

"She must make Papa's flesh creep too."

"Be serious."

"I'm *being* serious. You don't like her; *I* don't know her, but from what you've said, I wouldn't like her either. But it doesn't matter, because *Papa* likes her. It has nothing to do with us."

"And if they . . ."

"Wouldn't it be a blessing?"

"It would be a scandal."

He sat down before her, placing his hands on her knees, his passionless eyes holding hers. "Now listen to me very carefully. Mama isn't going to be with us much longer. You know that. A year at most. You've heard the doctor yourself. What's to happen then? Isn't it almost certain that Papa will want to move in with us, or ask us to move in with *him?*"

"What could be more logical or more natural, when you consider, *if* you consider, all he's done for us?"

"I've considered it. I agree with everything you say. But what could be more ghastly and embarrassing than to have that old ruffian underfoot day in and day out? Have *you* considered that?"

"How thoughtless and how cruel."

"And how *true*. Think about it, having to care for him for the rest of his life. And he's a tough old rooster, is Papa. Look at him. If he could survive that illness in Cádiz twenty years ago, he can probably survive anything. His deafness and his rheumatism and his bad eyes haven't slowed him down very much, in spite of his complaints."

"Please God you're right," said Gumersinda, crossing herself.

"Please God I'm right too, but not under our roof. But let's suppose that your cousin Leocadia, or some other woman, comes into his life, and is willing to be his . . ."

"Mistress?"

"No, at his age, the idea of a mistress is absurd. But she could be his housekeeper."

"It *would* be a fine thing for him to have some sort of companion . . . in a way."

"And in *all* ways it would be fine for us."

"For once I insist that you think only of Papa."

"I'm *thinking* of him, of his happiness. That doesn't mean I mustn't think of ours at the same time, does it? Especially when the two are so clearly in harmony. The thing to do is for you to invite Leocadia and to be sure Papa is here when she comes."

Gumersinda laughed nervously. "There'll be no trouble in seeing to *that*."

"And then all we'll have to do is sit back and watch what happens."

"And if something *does* happen?"

"I'll be relieved and delighted."

"And *I'll* cry myself to sleep."

"No, *amada,* just hurry to church and confess your sins. Then your conscience will be clear. No need for tears."

"In your fashion, Javier, you're a much wickeder man than your father."

"I only wonder that it's taken you so long to find that out. But really, I'm not wicked, just practical."

"*Practical?* To turn an honest, God-fearing woman into a procuress."

"Don't dramatize it. You've agreed that it's the sensible thing."

"It still disgusts me."

"Put it down to the tragedies of war. The sensible thing, Gumersinda, is the *right* thing in the eyes of man, even if it doesn't look that way when seen through the eyes of your God."

twelve

"DOÑA LEOCADIA is having lunch with us, Papa," said Gumersinda, her face a mask of innocence. "I hope you don't mind."

Poised in the doorway between dining room and entry hall, Goya staggered. He trembled and stared at his daughter-in-law. "*Mind?*" he snapped. "Why should I mind? It's your house."

"We wouldn't want to cheat you of your time for playing with Mariano," responded Javier, smiling maliciously.

"If I feel like playing with him, I shall."

The painter's son left it at that, watching with amusement as his father gave distracted attention to his grandson. Mariano sensed that the old man's heart wasn't in it today. "What's the matter, *abuelo?* Aren't you feeling well?"

Goya pounded his chest. "I've never felt better."

Javier couldn't suppress his laughter. Gumersinda blushed.

"What's so damned funny?" Paco demanded.

"Nothing, Papa," said the son, but his smile was sly. "You just seem a little . . . tense?"

The artist marched to a mirror that hung over the formal little hearth. He studied his features. They were remarkably firm and unlined, he thought, remarkably. He smoothed his thick, graying hair with an affectionate hand, then turned to Gumersinda and asked petulantly, "When is that little bitch supposed to be here? I'm starved."

"Soon, Papa. Just be a little patient."

"*Patient?* I'm always patient. Isn't that so, Mariano?"

There was no time for an answer, for at this moment a domestic announced the arrival of the second guest. Goya brushed past Gumersinda to greet Leocadia, taking her hand and kissing it with fervor. "You're the most welcome sight in Madrid, *señora,* in the whole of Spain. These two have been laughing at me. *You'll* not laugh at me, will you?"

The young woman was startled by his ardent manner. She smiled hesitantly, seeking an appropriate reply. She decided to affect seriousness. "Of course not, Don Paco."

"That's a relief, anyhow," he proclaimed, releasing her hand. He addressed the servant with a military sharpness. "What are you standing there for? Bring us some of that dreadful manzanilla. We have to celebrate this occasion." The woman scuttled off in a flurry of consternation, for Goya had never raised his voice to her before.

"You want manzanilla, Papa?" said Javier uncharitably. "But I thought you were dying of hunger."

"I've changed my mind," the painter replied without looking at his son, for his eyes now were only for Leocadia.

She had taken special pains with her appearance for this moment which she thought likely to prove her life's principal turning point. Her gleaming black hair was carefully ordered and fixed in place with a pair of ivory combs. Her pale gray gown, probably and pitiably her best, was cut lower across the bosom than the one she had worn on her first visit. It was all Goya could do to prevent his hands from plunging into the inviting bodice. He knew precisely how those young breasts would feel, and began to tremble again. This was more an annoyance than a temptation. For him, anticipation of pleasure had never been tantamount to pleasure itself; his joys were unsubtle. Patience? What idiocy. There was no time for patience.

Four glasses of the golden fortified wine of Andalucía calmed him somewhat, and throughout the meal he acted with more decorum than the urgencies of his flesh were trying to dictate.

He hardly touched his food and looked at no one but Leocadia
—the only nourishment he craved. When the others had finished
eating, he all but leaped from his chair. "Is your carriage
waiting for you, Doña Leocadia?" he asked eagerly.

"Oh, no, Don Paco. We don't have one. I came on foot."

"What a pity. My coach is at the door. I'd be delighted to
drive you home."

"You're leaving so soon, Papa?" Gumersinda thoughtlessly
protested.

He looked at her scornfully. "You imagine I have nothing to
do. You think I support you in all this"—he swept the room
with a hand—"by spending my afternoons sitting about and
prattling about society? There's nothing that need detain us
here, don't you agree, Doña Leocadia?"

The young woman was floundering in embarrassment. "Well,
I . . ."

"No need for politeness." He beamed at her. "And on our
way to your house, I can have the pleasure of showing you my
studio, if that would be of interest to you."

"Oh, it would interest me very much. I only hope my
husband doesn't hear of it. You know his opinion of you. So you
see, Don Paco," she murmured demurely, "my reputation is in
your hands."

The studio was empty of assistants, for Goya habitually released them on summer afternoons when the pressure of commissions wasn't excessive. He bolted the door, then turned and
leaned his back against it, breathing heavily from the exertion
of mounting the steep, long staircase—and from excitement. He
watched in overwrought silence as Leocadia moved about the
room. She looked at everything—at his easels and brushes and
paints and drawing tables, at the pictures hanging on the walls.
Some were in progress, others completed. Leocadia gave a
moment of full attention to his portrait of María. She made
nothing of his portraits of Josefa and Francho Bayeu. She
peered into the racks where his oil studies and the paintings he
had made for his own pleasure were stored. She thumbed

casually through a copy of *Los Caprichos* and, to his delight, gave a little shudder of distaste as she closed it. She glanced at a few of the proofs of *Los Desastres* and disappointed him by showing no reaction at all. She gave an idle turn to the wheel of his etching press, and frowned when she noticed stains of ink on her immaculate fingers.

Goya hastened to a bin beside the press and extracted a clean rag which he doused with turpentine. He took her soiled hand and gently wiped away the offending spots, afterwards cherishing the pungent cloth as if it were a sacred relic. Leocadia smiled her gratitude and continued her investigation of his premises. She paused at the hearth and lifted the small ceramic statue of Nuestra Señora del Pilár. She cradled it in her arms as she turned to Paco. "From Zaragoza?"

"I've had her ever since I first came to Madrid, fifty years ago."

"How strange."

"Why?"

"People say you're against the church."

"I'm against the clergy, but that doesn't mean I'm against the church."

"Is there a difference?"

"Do you believe everything our bishops say?"

"Shouldn't I?"

"Not if you have a mind of your own."

She smiled radiantly. "Oh, I have *that*, Don Paco."

She spun about and replaced the statuette on the mantel. As she faced him again, there was a question in her eyes. Then her face cleared. She took the smelly rag from his hands and turned again toward the fireplace. He was unable to see her enigmatic smile as she draped the cloth over the figure of Zaragoza's patron saint. Goya was paralyzed with astonishment. His old heart pounded violently. "What made you do that?"

The feline smile was still in place as she looked at him. "I thought it was your custom," she said evenly. "I'm afraid you're going to have to help with the buttons."

The time for words had passed. His fingers were awkward as

they fumbled with the buttons. He trembled. His breath was short. The dress tumbled about her ankles. He had trouble with the laces of her camisole. Her arms were long and flexible, like the wings of a swan, like the branches of a willow. She stepped out of her shoes. She removed her stockings with the grace of María, but she was much more careful about her clothes than María would have been, laying them gently on the back of a chair. Christ, what a fine line there was in her bending back. The camisole was gone at last, but she was wearing a chemise. The pantaloons descended unhurriedly, her back still turned to him. Perhaps he'd catch a fleeting glimpse of her bottom. The bitch was deliberately prolonging this affair, to torment him.

She stepped out of her pantaloons. His palms were sweating. The chemise was about to come off. Her fingers grasped the lacy hem. Her legs tapered upward from the slim ankles to precisely fashioned calves to thighs that were full and promising—but not too full. And then he saw her bottom, a pair of perfectly matched oblates. Soon would he make his oblations to them. Should he venture a touch? No, by God, he'd wait, though the waiting was the most terrible of tortures, his martyrdom—San Francisco Goya de Zaragoza.

Her back was fully disclosed. Along the valley indentation of her spine, from neck to narrow waist, was a faint shadow of fine black down. Her skin was white with the minutest trace of yellow ochre in it, or perhaps of raw umber. She placed the chemise on the chair, still turned away from him, and removed the combs from her hair. It tumbled free, a silken black cataract reaching just to the reversed parentheses where bottom joined her thighs. She began to turn, her head revolving first, held briefly in silhouette against the bright window. The chin was strong, determined, the lips voluptuous, the nose pronounced but of soft construction. Her brow was high above shallow-set eyes.

The turn was complete. He wouldn't touch her, not yet. San Francisco Goya would study her, commit her to memory, every detail, for he might never see her so again. He must mesmerize himself. Her neck was narrow, the veins showing aquamarine through translucent skin, the tendons taut. She placed her hands behind her head—the motion and gesture like Pepa Tudo's. The tufts of her armpits, moist and glittering, were pure charcoal and clear lacquer. The pose made her breasts protrude unnaturally. They were edible, the nipples contracted, the size of hazelnuts—burnt umber with a touch of chrome yellow, rising and falling evenly. The rib cage was distinct but not cadaverous, the bones small, concentric parabolas meeting at the sternum, which was ingeniously concealed between her breasts.

Her belly was genius, the vertical muscles tensed. The navel was deeply recessed and shadowy in this chiaroscuro light. Beneath it began the hair, each strand as distinct as a thread of a spider's web, sharply defined against the undulating flesh, becoming more profuse and clustered downward to the Circean, floccose grove of her groin where the whorls glittered blue-black and ominous.

He moved forward two steps and embraced her softly. He lifted her. Dear God, how light she was. Her skin was moistened velvet. His hand ran slowly from the back of her neck to the tight, narrow cleft between her hams. He seized her bottom and pressed her with all his strength against his pelvis. Leocadia gave a little cry of pain and pulled herself free. He looked at her in wounded surprise. "What's the matter?"

She pointed angrily at the silver buckle of his belt. "*That's* what's the matter. Besides, you've had enough looking. Get undressed. I have to go home soon. Isidoro is expecting me."

He nodded contritely and began to remove his clothing, his fingers maladroit. "Here," she said in exasperation, and came deftly to his assistance, her long hair falling recklessly about her shoulders as she bent to unclasp the buckle. He let his hands drop to his sides and offered no further effort. She quickly completed the operation, her actions efficient, utterly detached. She might as well be undressing her little son.

When the last of his clothing had been removed, Leocadia stood back and coolly appraised his body. He was embarrassed by her objectivity. The painful erection of a moment before subsided pathetically beneath her icy scrutiny. He felt impotent. Her wooden indifference frightened him. He made himself look into her eyes. "I'm too old for you, as I predicted."

"I don't know that yet, do I?"

"I revolt you."

"You're no god, if that's what you mean."

"I never was."

She moved toward the couch where so many women had casually given their bodies to him in the years before the advent of María. She turned back and stared at him in hostility. "Are you coming or not?" She lay back on the coarse upholstery and laughed sarcastically. "You don't believe in giving your conquests many of the creature comforts, do you? Do you have a fire burning in winter, or do you freeze them to death too?"

He stretched out beside her. "I'll see that there's something softer next time."

"Don't jump to conclusions," she said to the ceiling. "There may not *be* a next time." But Goya missed this. His attention was directed elsewhere. And she chose not to repeat herself.

Puffing heavily, the old man was arousing in her the pure animal desire she had divined on their first meeting. His rough, calloused hands were as assured as he had himself, a moment before, been diffident. She was caught up in the rhythm he was setting for her, enjoying sensations she had never known, responding with instinctive utterances hitherto foreign to her, with movements over which she had no control. She gave herself to this strange, forceful, evil-tempered old man as she had never given herself to Isidoro. This aging, sagging flesh of his, she acknowledged with a whimper of excruciating pleasure, sheltered a special sort of genius.

Panting, perspiring, his joints aching, his muscles tremulous, Goya collapsed at her side—but his weariness was sublime. "Thank you," he mumbled in her ear, then tongued it affectionately.

"You're welcome." Her eyes were again on the ceiling. He looked at her and was pleased to discover an expression of tranquillity.

"If I'm to see you again, you'll have to learn how to speak to me. You forget that I'm deaf."

"*Am* I to see you again?"

"Not if you don't want to."

"I'll have to think about it."

"What is there to think about? Bodies that are harmonious have no use for thought. They just feel. They act. Either you want to see me again or you don't."

"There are other considerations. I have to think of my position . . . about Guillermo . . . about Isidoro."

"Liar. You'd never have come here if those things mattered to you. That's hypocrisy. I can't abide it."

"To you, perhaps, Don Paco, but not to me. One experience is merely chancy. A second is an invitation to disgrace."

He looked at her suspiciously. "You mean something quite different from what you're saying. Why don't you just say what's on your mind?"

"I have to protect myself."

Goya chuckled and shook his disheveled head. "No, *amigita* . . ."

"I'm not your little friend yet."

He ignored the interruption. "You've given me a little taste, a sample, and what you're wondering now is how high a price you dare to set on the entire lot. You don't mean that you have to protect *yourself*. You want me to protect you."

As she shrugged, her little breasts shuddered gelatinously. "It comes to the same thing, doesn't it? I must be protected. That's the principle involved."

" 'Principle' is a good word, very elegant. If I'm to see you again, I must make the necessary arrangements."

"Something of that sort."

"What arrangements, speaking generally, do you think suitable?"

She again offered her catlike smile. "How would *I* know about such things, Don Paco? This is the first time I've ever betrayed Isidoro. You've got much more experience than I."

His eyes clouded over with displeasure. Her smile disappeared. "I'll tell you something, *mujer*, which may come as a surprise. I've had perhaps more than my share of mistresses. But I've never kept a woman in my life."

"You forget that you were younger then," she said with easy malice.

He was not fazed by her animus. "You didn't mind the difference in our ages a little while ago. I may not be lovely, but I'm skillful."

"You miss my point. I admit your skill. I enjoyed our little interlude. I even confess that I *want* to see you again and again. But do *you* want *me?*"

"You know the answer to that, Doña Leocadia."

"I'm just a toy for you. But it's different for me. You know I can't see you every day or even every week without Isidoro finding out. He may even suspect already."

"So you say."

"It's true. You're too well known. You have enemies who'd love nothing better than to cause you trouble by causing *me* trouble. Isidoro himself would be delighted. 'What right has an uneducated man to be worth a million reales,' he asks me. 'when someone like me is so near privation?' "

"I'm worth a lot more than that. But what do you answer him?"

"That you have a genius and all he has is a talent for failure."

"Very nice encouragement for one's husband."

"I was defending *you*."

"I'm touched. But I suspect you'd not be very miserable if your husband found out. That would give him a reason for leaving you, and you're not above using me to suit your purpose."

"Haven't you already used *me* to suit *yours?*"

He fell thoughtfully silent, and when he spoke again his tone was musing. "Leocadia, my dear child, I admire you in a perverse way. I'm not speaking of your body now. You know how I feel about that." He stroked her damp belly with avuncular fondness. "I'm speaking about *you*. You know what you want, and you don't give a solitary damn what means you use to get it. I'd bet my life that you haven't a scruple to your name."

"And you admire *that* in me?" she asked with charming bewilderment.

"Because when I was your age, I was the same as you. All that nonsense about Guillermo and the husband you despise. You're not thinking of either of them. You're not thinking of your reputation. You're certainly not thinking of me. You're thinking only of yourself. What attracts you is that I can give you money to buy the *things* you've wanted all your life—the clothes, the good food and wine, a softer bed, servants, and the important people you'd meet if you were my official mistress. That's what you mean by protection. That, and money of your own."

"Yes," she replied, her face expressionless.

"I'm not interested."

"Are you sure?"

"I'm positive."

"You can say that now, when your energies for love have been spent inside me. But wait till tonight, or tomorrow, when you want me again . . . "

It was in this instant that Paco knew he loved Leocadia. He couldn't decide whether to strike her, embrace her, or laugh at her, whether to weep or tear his hair. But he did know, as only a man seasoned in the rough and tumble of seven years with María could know, that he must for a little while conceal his feeling. First he must prove himself her master. "What a spectacular bitch you are, Leocadia, but no."

"You're a fool, Don Paco. How many respectable young married women do you know who'd dream of making you so generous and dignified an offer—a straightforward and honest exchange: my flesh for your protection? How can you reject it so casually?"

"For one thing, because you're so cold-blooded about it. It's as if you were bargaining over a cask of manzanilla. And for another, what you're proposing is neither honest nor straightforward. When you meet a younger, more attractive man, you'll leave me without a qualm. Don't try to deny it. Respectable married woman indeed. You make a street whore seem as pure as Nuestra Señora del Pilár."

She was unperturbed by these accusations. "Even assuming that I do leave you one day, Don Paco, you'll have me for a time. Wouldn't that be better than nothing?"

He wanted to laugh with delight, but he controlled himself. "No, by God. I'd rather be lonely than deceived. I'm used to loneliness. All the other women I've loved *have* been honest and straightforward. I have no wish to make friends with deception, even at your lovely hands."

"Well, we'll just see about that." She rose and began to dress.

He was still nude as she made the final adjustments to her coiffure and neatly fixed it with her combs. She draped a beige mantilla over her head and shoulders, then looked down at him inquiringly. "You're not going to see me home, Don Paco?"

"My coachman can do that just as well as I," was his studiedly surly reply. "And there's less danger of compromising your honest name."

"Will you see me to the door?"

The old man rose with a groan and was pleasantly surprised to remark the ease with which he could move. No more aching joints. He felt a century younger. *She* had mastered *him,* and the most annoying thing was that she had already read this in his eyes. He approached her timidly. She offered no help as he lifted her hand to his lips. "When shall I see you again?"

She took a step back, withdrawing her hand. "You've made it clear that you really don't want to see me again, Don Paco."

"Call me *Paco*, for Christ's sake."

"What I call you hardly matters anymore, does it?" Rapid little steps carried her to the door. The naked Goya followed her at a dog trot. He drew back the bolt and placed his hand on the knob.

"Must you leave me like this?"

"I don't see that I have any choice."

"But I *have* to see you again, and soon."

Her smile was evil—the triumph of vice over virtue. "So your forces have returned to you more quickly than I imagined. But no, Don Paco . . . Paco. As you said, the arrangement I have in mind wouldn't be satisfactory to you. And to discomfit you in any way would be the last thing I'd want."

"Let *me* be the judge of that."

"You'd compel me to make you unhappy? How could I live with myself?"

"What a woman," he roared. His passion for her was demented. "You cloak your iniquity so beguilingly that it has the appearance of a confirmation gown."

"Well, that seems an appropriate note for us to part on . . . Paco."

His entreaties grew frantic. *"Please,* Leocadia, I beg of you."

"Doña Leocadia, Don Paco. You forget yourself. I'm a respectable married woman and mother. Don't overstep the bounds of propriety."

"Please." His old voice cracked.

Adamantine, she shook her head solemnly, her eyes hard and cold, certain of her power. "Will you please open the door?"

His sigh of despair was grating. With tears in his weakening eyes, he turned the handle, drawing the door back. She took a single step forward, then recoiled in horror as a small figure hurtled into the room. The man's eyes were red with weeping and anger, the crabbed features pinched, the little fingers flying to Leocadia's throat. She gasped. Goya was dumbfounded. But he galvanized himself without delay and threw his strong arms about her assailant. The man's struggles were unavailing. The painter threw him easily to the floor and stood over him menacingly. "Who the devil are you?"

The enraged but helpless intruder offered no explanation. His eyes were focused obsessively on Goya's pendulous nudity, his thin lips curled in revulsion.

"As if you hadn't guessed," said Leocadia with rasping disdain, "this is my incomparable Isidoro."

The recumbent Weiss found his voice and aimed it at her. "Whore."

"Charming," she said with a smug half-smile. She turned to Goya. "On *that*, it seems, the two of you agree."

"You meant for me to find out," wailed Weiss. "That's why you made such a point of telling me where you were going and whom you were lunching with." He began cautiously to raise himself.

"Why should I want that?"

"You wanted to hurt me. You've always enjoyed doing that. But until now, you've confined your injuries to your filthy tongue." He vigorously massaged his meager arms and suddenly sniffed the air. "You smell like a fish market," he said to Goya.

"No one asked you to come," said his wife with a scornful twist of the head. "What of it?"

"What *of* it? You're mad. You think you can come back to my house after lying with this scum? You think you're fit to touch our child after this? You think I'd let you spend another night in my bed?"

As he spoke, the little man's fury increased and he made menacing gestures at his wife. He drew nearer and seemed about to strangle her again. Goya stepped between them and looked down into his rival's anguished face. "For the love of God, Don Isidoro, be reasonable."

"*Reasonable?* Are *both* of you, then, completely mad?" The suggestion that he be reasonable found Weiss between disbelief and rage. "Reasonable? Am I being *un*reasonable? My wife is seduced by a man twice her age—"

"Nearly three times her age," said the painter complacently. "And *I'm* the one who was seduced."

"*That*," said Weiss flatly, "is a lie."

"It's the truth, *idioto*," said Leocadia in precisely the tone she had used with Guillermo.

Don Isidoro tried to outflank Goya, who spread his arms. "Would you prefer to finish this tiresome conversation on the floor, *señor?*" The man shook his head. "Then, perhaps, we can return to the subject of reason. What's been done can't be undone. That's the central point. What do you propose?"

"As far as I'm concerned, this slut is dead."

"In that case, you'd have no objection to a legal separation."

Weiss regarded his adversary with suspicion. Then his little face assumed a grin of cunning. "Why should I agree to that? Do you want me to renounce her dowry? Though God knows it's small enough, considering the agony she's brought me."

"Her dowry is of no interest to me."

The husband grunted. "That's not much of a concession."

"My jewels too?" wailed Leocadia, for the first time revealing a feeling that Goya saw came straight from the heart.

"Everything," he told her firmly. "I'll buy you all the jewels you want."

She wasn't mollified, but wisely chose to vent her fury on Weiss. "You're willing to give me to this old man without a struggle? Don't you want to preserve your honor by fighting a duel with him?"

Don Isidoro sneered. "No, *mujer*. You've taught me well. When I lose you, I may *find* my honor again. And I'm not *giving* you to him. I'm *selling* you for what you are, a *putana*. I hope he makes you as miserable as you've made me these seven years. Hell would seem healthy by comparison with the bed of nettles you've made for me."

"What about Guillermo?" she demanded.

Goya put a hand to his mouth to conceal his delights. Jewels before son. That was Leocadia. Weiss bristled. "He's *mine*. You don't care about him. You never have."

She was about to reply when Paco raised a finger. "She *is* the boy's mother. She should have the right to see him now and then."

"Why? So she can humiliate him as she's done *me?*"

"Because the child has the right to see his mother."

When the offended husband had no rejoinder, Leocadia seemed disinclined to press the matter and returned to the more important question of her possessions. "What about my clothes? Will you at least send *those* on to me? They're of no use to you, unless you give them to the poor, which isn't quite your style."

"I'm not that unreasonable," was the defensive answer. "I'll send them to you when you tell me where you plan to live."

Leocadia looked inquiringly at Goya. He scratched his head. "You might as well send them here, I suppose."

Weiss was beside himself with scandalized disbelief. "You plan to keep her under your own roof?"

"Does the fact that you're ashamed of her mean that I must be too?" the painter asked amiably.

"You ought to be."

"You say that because you've lost her. You believe in 'discretion.' I don't. Besides, who in Madrid would be fooled if I found her lodgings somewhere else? No one."

Weiss moved reluctantly toward the door. As he opened it, he paused and peered once again with maniacal anger at this ill-assorted couple—his superbly handsome wife and her naked, antique, antic lover. "God damn you both," he shrieked and fled.

Goya rushed at the door and slammed it shut, almost catching the fingers of the departing Weiss. Out of breath, he whirled to discover Leocadia grinning broadly. He laughed. "That's the first time I've ever had to use force against a husband."

"You think I should be flattered?"

"You're everything he says you are. But of course I didn't need him to tell me that."

"And you don't care, do you? You must like bitches a lot to go through a scene like that."

He approached her. "You know nothing about the scenes I've lived through in my own head. They make this little charade seem like a minuet."

He was about to embrace her. She moved back a step. "Get your clothes on, Goya. I want Doña Josefa to meet her new housekeeper."

The first encounter between Leocadia and the invalid Josefa was accomplished with a minimum of embarrassment. The younger woman was so relieved to find herself free of the financial and emotional shackles that had bound her to Weiss that any temptation to flout her superiority to Goya's wife was perfectly resistible. If the comfort and security offered by a

doting lover had a rather ramshackle appearance, it was preferable to the atmosphere of house arrest that she had endured as
Isidoro's wife. Therefore, she strictly obeyed Paco's single but
heavily underscored injunction—that she say or do nothing that
might perturb Josefa, "whom I love and cherish, Cadia, not in
spite of her infirmities, but because of them."

As he promised, the perquisites of her new life were many
and delicious. She had lovely clothes. She was given jewels that
made her little inheritance from her mother negligible. The
members of Paco's circle whom she met accepted her status with
a reproach apparent only to him. Most of all, she enjoyed the
feeling of liberty. He sought to attach no cords to her, never
asked her where she went or whom she saw when she left the
house. He made no fetish of her fidelity to him, though she
knew his refusal to hem her in reflected no trust in her. Yet the
very fact that he held her on so loose a rein had the effect of
discouraging her exploration of other areas of experience.

Josefa looked on the presence of a "housekeeper" as a god-
send—though she well knew the true role of this lovely, imperi-
ous creature. Infirm she might be, but Josefa remained perfectly
lucid. And it was gratifying to remark that from her first day of
residence, Leocadia caused her authority to be felt in the house;
she made it plain that she took seriously a title that others
thought a mere euphemism. Not since Goya's wife had taken
definitively to her bed had the domestics attended to their
responsibilities so sedulously, goaded by the terrible lash of
Leocadia's savage tongue.

Moreover, Josefa looked with the resignation of a martyr on
the woman's other function. For Javier, out of what he considered enlightened self-interest, had thought it judicious to
intercede on his father's behalf, a gesture that so startled Josefa
that she succumbed to the clumsy logic of his persuasions
without protest. His case was the same as the one he had offered
Gumersinda, though he tactfully omitted reference to her de-
teriorating condition or to the desirability of Goya's having,
after her death, a companion and a well-run house.

There was little need for Javier to remind her of her failing health. She was depressingly conscious that her degenerative illness, which Dr. Arrieta was able to diagnose imprecisely as "melancolia," was pushing her slowly toward her grave. Happily, she suffered little pain. Her symptoms were characterized by an ever increasing weariness. She could sit up with difficulty for no more than a few minutes each day and was exhausted by the slightest contretemps. More than a single visitor at a time left her in tears of exhaustion. She slept a little longer every morning, ate a little less of every meal, grew more indifferent to what was taking place around her. "My life is being eaten away," she said without remorse, "bit by bit. All I ask is that the good God let me die peacefully in my sleep."

It wasn't callousness to his wife's condition that made it possible for Goya to rejoice in his dramatically altered circumstances. Rather was it that he had for so long lived in the lengthening shadows of Josefa's years of dying that they had assumed the blurred form of custom. Only now and again, as when he had anxiously urged Leocadia to do nothing to upset her, did Josefa's state reimpose itself more sharply on his consciousness, and then only for a little time. To have permitted himself the luxury of despair would have been to join her in the ineluctable grasp of death. But Paco wanted to live, and the sudden interjection of Leocadia made the desire more imperative than it had been since the death of María.

Pleased though she was by her own changed way of living, Leocadia made few concessions to Goya. From the beginning, she made it obvious that in every aspect of his life, except his work and his hours at the *taberna*, Paco was her creature. That he accepted this position with model submissiveness was testimony enough of his happiness. But his altered ego was a source of astonishment to Moratín, who communicated his surprise to their mutual friends in Cádiz as "Paco's climacteric transfiguration."

Isidoro Weiss, still as revolted as ever by his wife's and Goya's flouting of the conventions, failed initially to take action with regard to the legal separation he had promised. He was certain that the painter, after a few hectic and erotic weeks with

Leocadia, would tire of her and seek an excuse for casting her aside. Not that he would be willing to take her back. Indeed, he longed for nothing so much as to witness her expulsion from this demimondain paradise. But he was too proud to confess his humiliation until her state as Goya's mistress proved permanent—or as permanent as loose, illicit bonds could make it. In the meantime, he discussed their perfidy only with Javier because (so he imagined) only the artist's son knew everything.

"You'll see," he said confidently. "Your papa will throw her out as soon as he's had his fill of her body. I know her, Don Javier. She's the worst virago God ever made. It can't last much longer." He rubbed his hands together with malevolent glee. "And then she'll have nothing, you see? *Nothing.* She'll be destitute, and there'll be no choice but for her to take to the streets, to become in fact what she already is in her soul, a *putana.* How I look forward to that day." His cackle was high-pitched and tense. "I might even pay a few reales for a bout with her myself. What a fine joke that would be."

Javier was uneasy to find himself Weiss' confidant. The man was unspeakably dull and wholly despicable. More dismaying was the secret that he and Gumersinda had deliberately thrown his father and Leocadia together and were, therefore, the principal authors of the man's present misery. Javier treated Weiss with a detached politeness that suggested no hope. "This affair is much more serious than you imagine, Don Isidoro."

Weiss' refusal to accept this conclusion in no way altered Javier's convictions, which were based on several brief but conclusive exchanges with his father. "I know everything about Cadia, bad and good. I have no illusions."

"No illusions, Papa? You have the greatest illusion of all. You're in love with her. So for you, even her vices are virtues, as they were for Doña María."

Mention of the Duchess of Alba sobered the old man for a moment. "Oh, God knows that Cadia hasn't a patch on María, except for a streak of perversity that amuses me."

"And infuriates you."

"It comes to the same thing, Javier. I suppose you can't

understand that. But living with Cadia is like living on the edge of a volcano. I never know when she's going to erupt."

"You enjoy that? I'd hate it."

"I admit it's an acquired taste. You like things to be just as they appear, don't you? And when they're not, you try to make reality conform to your wishes. I'm the reverse. Danger is good for me. It stimulates me. It keeps me on my toes."

"And ages you more quickly, I should think."

"No, it makes me feel younger. María had the same effect. But as I say, Cadia is nothing like *her*. She's an old man's darling, nothing more. María couldn't be matched in a century of looking. But I *am* an old man, and now I need an old man's darling. I even enjoy the hazard that she could leave me tomorrow."

"You can face it so calmly?"

"Because I have to, because I enjoy the sight of her *now* . . . and all the rest of her, of course. That's enough because it has to be enough. I'll take her day by day and thank God each night for the fearful joy she's brought into my life."

By the end of summer, Weiss was convinced. He instructed his lawyer to draft a document of legal separation. The wording was less than generous. The advocate cited her infidelity, her bad temper, her arrogance, her disrespect for her husband, and her disgraceful neglect as the mother of a Christian son—all tendencies, the document insisted, which had been more than amply demonstrated. Weiss retained custody of Guillermo and only after a particularly vituperative Leocadian scene did he grudgingly consent to occasional visits with the boy.

By the time these papers were presented, Goya was confident that he had explored the full range of his mistress' emotions. He was, therefore, surprised by the total want of compunction she evinced in signing an agreement that released her husband from all further responsibilities for her well-being and deprived her of any hand in the raising of her child. "I'm damned grateful that God didn't choose you for *my* mother."

"So am I."

"I wonder how I'd feel if you became pregnant. I don't think I'd wish a child of mine so beastly a fate."

Her laughter was sharp. "Well, you can relax about *that*, Paco. There's not much danger at your age."

So the matter rested. Their violent relationship showed few signs of mellowing with the passage of months, for Leocadia understood that her abrasiveness served a purpose in Goya's life. "When I was a child," he told her after a particularly bitter argument, "my mother used to tell me frightening stories about terrible monsters. I've dreamed of them, off and on, ever since. *You're* their incarnation, Cadia. Perhaps you're intended to be my last earthly penance—but I have to have you. There are times when you're all that matters to me."

thirteen

GOYA CONTINUED WORKING, despite his obsession with Leocadia when she was near him and his vivid remembrance of her splendid carnality when she was briefly absent. His commissions at this time were mostly for official portraits, whose boredom made his preoccupation with her all the more rewarding. His routine included habitual visits to the *taberna,* where Moratín gave him word of events taking shape along the border with Portugal.

British and Portuguese forces under Sir Arthur Wellesley had for three years been operating without appreciable support from London, where hopes were deemed slim that Spain could be reconquered from this direction. These ill-equipped troops had long seemed dormant behind the mountain redoubts that protected the coastal region of Torres Verdas, north of Lisbon. Now, however, there were stirrings, indications of intense activity that revived in Moratín and other informed Spaniards the aspiration, so long suspended, that liberation from the yoke of Bonaparte might yet be realized in their lifetime.

In November, 1811, the "last British army" captured the frontier town of Fuentes de Oñoro. Late in January, it successfully attacked the first of a pair of key bastions that had for two years prevented a full-scale invasion of Spain—Ciudad Rodrigo. And in April, Godoy's home city of Badajoz, the second vital fortress, was bloodily stormed and conquered. After regrouping, Wellesley's forces turned north, taking Almarez in May. All that stood between them and Madrid were the imposing fortifications of Salamanca.

"Soon, Paco, soon," said Moratín joyfully, "we're going to breathe free air again. The French will leave Madrid like rats deserting a ship, and the *afrancesados* are pissing in their breeches and packing already. I've never seen such craven fear."

"The French won't defend Madrid?"

"It can't be defended. Without walls, there's no chance of standing off a siege."

"I'll make my will, just in case," said Goya skeptically.

Leandro laughed. "You've gone through four years of war without making a will?"

"Oh, it didn't make much difference before. But now I want to provide something for Leocadia."

Early in June, Goya and Javier completed a comprehensive inventory of all the artist's possessions, and in the process they realized how very rich he was. Even the greedy son couldn't object to his father's setting aside for his mistress a sum to which she could have access only after his death, for in the same way he made over a far larger amount to Javier, in trust for Mariano, and gave him title to the house in the Calle de Valverde and many pictures, among them two paintings by Velázquez and many by his own hand—the portraits of Josefa and Francho Bayeu and a number of still-life paintings he had been recently making to divert himself.

To Leocadia's unfeigned dismay and annoyance, he retained the portrait of María de Alba. "You'll never love me as much as you should until you've forgotten her completely," she protested.

"*That,*" said Goya with an asperity that shocked her, "is the last time you'll ever speak of María that way. I don't *want* to forget her. That would seem treasonous to me, like wanting to forget my mother. If she were alive, there'd be no room in my life for you."

Leocadia was wise enough not to press this quarrel. She must resign herself, however sullenly, to the fact that Paco's memory of this woman was a sort of shrine which she could attempt to desecrate only at her direst peril. It was galling, nevertheless, and she couldn't resist occasionally snipping at her invulnerable rival.

Thus did their intimacy maintain its precarious balance between affection and hatred. Goya put it pungently to Moratín one afternoon: "Cadia and I are lovers, but we're certainly not friends."

It was barely dawn on the morning of June 20, 1812. Goya was aroused from deepest sleep by the violent shaking of a distressed servant. "Doña Josefa, Doña Josefa, Don Francisco," the woman shrieked, her face streaked with tears. "She's gone from us." Paco's instinctive gesture of crossing himself both annoyed and pleased him; he detested such habits, which were rooted in his childhood, but was relieved that he had so responded on this occasion. He groaned as he rose and permitted the weeping woman to help him on with his dressing gown. He inveighed bitterly against the earliness of the hour and the chill of the floor as he stumbled in bare feet to his wife's bedchamber.

When he entered, he immediately remarked that no one had covered her gray features. He slowly approached the inert form and tried to remember Josefa as she had been when they first met, in the winter of 1763, when he was sixteen, she only thirteen. But too much had happened for the memory to be more than a hollow echo, too much anguish and bitterness and recrimination and sorrow.

As Goya began to weep, he was aware of Leocadia beside him at the deathbed. She took his arm with surprising force and attempted to pull him away. "That's enough, Paco. You'll catch cold. There's nothing more you can do."

He twisted himself free. "Leave me *alone*," he bellowed. He bent over and, before drawing the light blanket over Josefa's face, he planted a kiss on the lifeless forehead. "*Adiós*, my virginal wife," he murmured thickly. "You didn't deserve the life I led you. *I* didn't deserve the love you gave me."

He slowly covered her features and allowed Leocadia to lead him from the room.

Wellesley was successful in reducing Salamanca in late July. This victory was attributable as much to the fact that Napoleon had drained his best regiments from Spain to take part in his Russian campaign as to the skill of the British general and his troops. Wellesley was a uniquely unlovable figure, a xenophobic reactionary whose three years on the Iberian peninsula had done nothing to ameliorate his poor regard for the soldiers under his command. It was perhaps understandable that he should hold the Portuguese in disesteem simply because they were "foreigners," but he felt much the same for his own cavalry, and if pressed only a little, he would launch into a prolonged and voluble condemnation of his entire army, officers and men alike. He reserved a special degree of opprobrium, however, for the tattered remnants of the Spanish army that had joined him. That these troops had played an important role in the defense of Seville impressed him not a bit. Seville and all of Andalucía had fallen, save for the enclave of Cádiz; therefore, these ragged soldiers had been defeated, and they certainly looked it. Wellesley was unsparing of the Spanish army, which he was widely quoted as having described as a pure bane, endowed with a single talent—that of entering a battle fully clothed and armed, of running off at first sight of the enemy, and of reappearing after the firing had stopped, without their weapons and stark naked.

He was scarcely more charitably disposed toward the heroic Spanish *guerrilleros,* whose accomplishments had been of crucial importance to his own successes. His army occupied Madrid a few weeks after the fall of Salamanca. As Wellesley reviewed these ferocious irregulars on parade in the capital, he could say only, "I don't know what effect those devils have on Boney, but by God, they frighten *me.*"

The bedraggled if triumphant entrance of Wellesley's scratch army was hailed by the Madrileños as the finest moment of their lives. Joseph Bonaparte had fled from his throne only the day before, accompanied by something like 70,000 French soldiers and a comparable number of civil servants, *afrancesados,* and camp followers. The usurper, whose brother alone was confident that this displacement was only temporary, had moved to Toledo, where he attempted to continue his already tenuous rule.

Wellesley's appearance was a disappointment to Goya, who watched the parade from a balcony of the Academia. The great man was neatly enough turned out, but where were the panache and gingerbread of might and conquest and authority? The general wore none of his decorations. He gave the old artist the impression of being just what he was—an arrogant Anglo-Irishman, the younger son of a Protestant family who found anything smacking even remotely of Popishness extremely distasteful.

Sir Arthur rode with a few comparably inelegant officers at the head of a long, straggling column of troops whom he was pleased to call the sum of the earth. He cast a regard of boundless disdain on the masses of Roman Catholics who lined the Avenida de Alcalá, cheering him as their liberator, the man whose victories would soon, they prayed in every church and before every street-corner and roadside shrine, restore their beloved Don Fernando to his rightful place in the Prado.

Goya's disillusionment over the general's simplicity of dress and austerity of manner in no way diminished his admiration for the man's achievements. He demanded at once that Moratín try to arrange for "Velsy," as the chanting Madrileños pronounced his impossible name, to sit for a portrait. "The least I can do is record the features of the fellow who's responsible for our deliverance." He was consequently pleased, only two days after Wellesley's arrival in Madrid, to be informed that the great man had accorded Goya a half hour of his time.

He hastened to the Prado on the appointed day, for it was here that the general had thought it appropriate to establish his headquarters. He was dismayed to learn that his subject had not a single word of Spanish or even Portuguese. "After three years?" he inquired irritably of the aide who was to serve as interpreter.

This young officer, whose Spanish wasn't the purest Castilian, seemed not a bit embarrassed. "Sir Arthur has found that he can make himself understood well enough if he speaks English loudly and distinctly."

"Well, *señor,*" said Goya with a dark little chuckle, "you must tell him that in my case it would be a waste of time, since I neither speak English nor hear Spanish."

Unperturbed and emotionless in the strange British fashion, the aide responded, "Sir Arthur has also discovered that a well-aimed boot can be equally effective, especially if his foot happens to be in it."

The old man nodded. "I know a woman who has the same idea. It doesn't make friendship any easier for her."

"Sir Arthur isn't here to make friends, Don Francisco. He's here to win battles."

That much Paco could respect unreservedly. When he was ushered into the throne room, he found the general seated at a camp table. He looked up in annoyance as the presence of intruders was borne in on his concentration. He offered the painter a brusque nod and turned to the officer. "Well, what the hell have you got in tow this time? Does he have a daughter for my bed or some valuable information he's only too eager to part with, for a price?"

Goya looked on in mute perplexity as the aide explained his mission. Wellesley grunted. "Oh, this is the one Lady Holland told me about. The Gainsborough of Spain, she called him." He chortled at this preposterous suggestion, for every Englishman knew that in portraiture Gainsborough was peerless; even Sir Joshua Reynolds was a hog butcher by comparison. "Like everyone else in this filthy, heathen country, he'll probably make a botch of it, but at least the swine will have something to remember me by besides ten thousand bastards born nine months after we leave." He considered the painter coldly. "Well, well, let's get this damned business over with."

"If the general would be good enough to seat himself by the

window," said Goya to the aide, "I'll make studies of him now and paint the portrait in my studio."

Wellesley complied, his movements graceless but efficient. "Tell this so-called artist that I want an equestrian portrait."

When the demand was translated, Goya nodded. "No decorations?" he asked, drawing a hand across his breast. "Don Arturo wishes to be portrayed without his decorations?"

Wellesley took a deep, impatient breath. "Go get them," he told the aide. "I suppose that's the damned drill, isn't it? A fellow doesn't look like a general to these children unless he's dressed up like a bloody Maypole."

While the medals and ribbons were being brought, Goya sketched his subject from several angles. Though he had made little sense of the man's speech, he had no trouble making out his complacency and arrogance, qualities he descried in the puffy eyes, the strong, angular jaw, the long, fleshy nose, the high-arched brows, and the narrow, cruel slit of a mouth, all of which bespoke a marked lack of common humanity. Paco thought the general more dogged than brilliant—in sum, a person he wouldn't really want to know.

In spite of this unfavorable impression, Goya tried as he worked to keep in mind that this was the liberator of Spain, a man who had been away from home for three years and who would probably not see it again for months, perhaps years—for there would be much more fighting before the last of Napoleon's forces were driven out. He kept reminding himself that Wellesley was a hero, though he neither looked nor acted the part. Only in his bluntness did this general resemble the man who Paco thought the model of the fighting leader, Palafox. But he lacked the legendary Zaragozan's dash and verve and humor. More bewildering was Moratín's information. The general was born in Ireland, a country enslaved by Britain, yet he commanded a British army and seemed satisfied with this post. Though well aware, recalling London's perfidious desertion of Portugal four years before, that things were ordered differently in that boorish nation, the painter found incomprehensible Wellesley's apparent treason against the land of his birth. He rejected as incredible Leandro's assertion that the explanation was simply that Ireland was predominantly Catholic, a religion thought inappropriate for an English-speaking country ruled by the British.

After the decorations were affixed to the general's tunic, Goya completed a detailed study. His incapacity to understand the nature of this man was disclosed (to himself, at any rate) in the work itself. It was disappointing, but he felt that no amount of repetition would eliminate the fundamental flaw. He knew there would be orders for countless copies of the finished portrait—and all would be afflicted with the fatal defect, his antipathy to the subject.

It came, however, as no surprise to learn of the general's grudging praise for the final drawing, and such would be the world's reaction. Virtually by definition, a portrait by Paco couldn't be inferior, because it was a portrait by Goya. A portrait of Wellesley by Goya was doubly blessed—or doubly cursed. It was improbable that such a combination of artistic and military genius would result in a masterpiece. But Paco had to face the fact: It was one of the worst pictures he had ever made, and Wellesley's grunted admiration of the sketch was disheartening. "For a painter," said the general condescendingly, "I suppose he's not terrible. Considering that he's Spanish, I daresay I have to think him a genius." A moment later, he bobbed his dark head and summarily dismissed Goya and the aide from his sight.

In mid-September, Wellesley undertook direction of the siege of Burgos, an operation that continued unsuccessfully for more than a month. The French inflicted frightful losses on his troops. Without adequate artillery, he could make no impression on the imposing fortifications. With winter at hand, he renounced until spring all hope of pursuing his campaign northward. So he led his weary, diseased, drunken forces back across the Portuguese frontier for yet another season of waiting.

When the British withdrew from Madrid, Joseph Bonaparte returned, but without illusions about the permanence of his stay. A year before Wellesley's occupation of the capital he had told a friend that although he was only his brother's puppet, history would hold him responsible for every disaster that had befallen Spain since he took the throne. The Spanish thought him a greedy monster. He felt he must evacuate the country to forestall a further exacerbation of the military situation which would result, he believed, in the French being expelled by force. Napoleon treated these opinions with the scorn he felt they merited. The end of the French occupation, therefore, was not yet, but the factors making its termination inevitable were in process of development.

By November, 1812, Madrid knew that the emperor's adventure into Russia had proved catastrophic. Of the 500,000 men he had sent across the Neman River in the spring, fewer than 100,000 had survived. Napoleon was back in Paris attempting to measure the implications of this defeat and the prospects for advancing his grand design for Europe—the plan that had been his consuming ambition for twenty years, and which his brother Joseph, as early as 1808, had told him would founder because of his invasion of Spain. Throughout France, there was scarcely a single rustic or urban blacksmith not engaged in feverish efforts to replace the guns and cannons that had been lost during the appalling retreat from Moscow.

A new army had to be raised within a few months. The conscription age was lowered to seventeen and the recruits were a sorry lot—youths whose bodies were pathetically underdeveloped because of the poor diet imposed by constant war. Bonaparte's obsession to establish his hegemony over Europe, to be Charlemagne or Luis XIV reincarnate, had deprived a generation of Frenchmen of more than a subsistence regime. These malnourished children suffered the additional and quite gratuitous humiliation of the nickname *"Les Marie-Louise"*—in token of disrespect for the Hapsburg empress whom Napoleon had married in hopes of producing an heir and of pacifying the Austrians.

The wishful-thinking emperor must at last recognize that his star was descending, and no less in Spain than elsewhere. From

Cádiz, which had miraculously resisted siege, the Cortes promulgated the constitution it had labored so long to produce. A handful of inspired liberals like Jovellanos had prevailed against a conservative majority to formulate a document whose terms were hardly revolutionary. It provided for freedom of speech and press, separation of church and state, and a monarchy subordinated to the control of a freely elected Cortes. To Spaniards, such provisions were staggering.

Goya remained as skeptical as ever about the feasibility of this constitution, though he professed great admiration for its proposals. Moratín, encouraged by the British victories of 1812, had rediscovered his optimism. "When Wellesley has driven the last of the bastards out, I promise you, Paco, that you're going to have your gloomy old eyes opened for you. You're going to see a new Spain."

"And I'll tell you again, Leandro, that what the people want is the old Spain."

Wellesley's campaign was promising from its beginnings in the spring of 1813. The French forces in Spain, totalling about 300,000, outnumbered his own by a margin of four to one. They had, however, been shriven of their best officers—including Marshal Soult, whom Bonaparte thought his finest tactician—who were to lead the new imperial army on the eastern fronts, which the emperor considered more important than developments likely to threaten him from the south. Better than this, from Wellesley's standpoint, Joseph Bonaparte had been named commander of the French armies. The puppet king protested to his brother that he wasn't a general and had no intention of learning that craft at his age. The position was made more problematical by the obsequiously deferential attitude of Marshal Jourdan, Joseph's chief of staff, who refused to issue orders without first clearing them with the king. To confusion was thus added inanity.

On this campaign, the British general bypassed Madrid, for he realized that if he could master the northern Spanish provinces, Joseph's supplies would be cut off and he must retreat from the capital. He concentrated his attack against Burgos for the second time. Acting on his brother's instructions, Joseph did precisely what Wellesley hoped. By June, all the French armies were at Valladolid. The evacuation of Madrid was more chaotic than the one of the previous year. As Moratín expressed it to Goya, "It's a masterpiece of panic mitigated only by avarice— like your 'Colossus' painting." Every vehicle was commandeered and loaded with the booty the French had accumulated during their five-year occupation. The *afrancesados* and their families joined the flight, rightly terrified at the prospect of the righteous wrath of a restored Don Fernando. So vast were the quantities of loot that there was insufficient transport for the essentials of war—guns and ammunition. King Joseph's baggage alone filled more than a hundred wagons.

When this fantastic caravan reached Valladolid, the French learned that Wellesley had severed their lines of further retreat. A confrontation was inevitable. It occurred on June 21 at Vitoria, north of the Ebro. Retreat was transformed into rout. The looted Spanish treasure was abandoned; it was every man for himself. In groups of three and four, the French soldiers crawled toward the frontier of the Pyrenees. "This isn't an army anymore," said a rueful French officer as he watched this humiliating pilgrimage. "It's a perambulating brothel."

Leaving a detachment of his forces to reduce the fortress of San Sebastián, Wellesley pursued the few remaining coherent elements of the French, which he caught up with at Savrorén, on the Spanish slopes of the Pyrenees; he cut them ruthlessly but joylessly to pieces. Before Christmas of 1813, Spain was free of the French, and Sir Arthur had been named Marquis of Wellington.

Had Lord Wellington, proclaimed by the British to be their greatest field commander since Marlborough, been able to accept the invitation of the Spanish junta (which was provisionally governing the country) to return to Madrid, he would have been received even more enthusiastically during the festivities of Christmas, 1813, than had been the case sixteen months before. To Spain, Wellington was the new messiah—a description he would have found as distasteful as he thought superfluous his elevation to the peerage. In the repeated retelling, his feats were translated into miracles; he became an improbable Anglo-Saxon El Cid.

During Advent, Madrileños had been expressing their relief and gratitude in every way. Despite the bitterness of the winter, there had been dancing in the streets each night. As a contrapuntal diversion, the former dwellings of the *afrancesados* and the French were sacked. To Goya, there seemed an unearthly strangeness in this atmosphere of ungovernable euphoria. He was as pleased as Moratín and Ceán Bermúdez (just returned from Cádiz) by Wellington's victories. He acknowledged that at least until Don Fernando was freed by Napoleon and returned to his throne, all their hopes must be thought susceptible of realization. A new Spain would undoubtedly emerge, but what sort of nation would it be? He remembered his casual meetings with the young Borbón to whose restoration everyone looked forward so eagerly. *Would* he, as Ceán and Moratín predicted, abide by the terms of the new constitution? *Would* he follow intelligent advice? Who would his advisers *be?* He had appeared so dull-witted to Paco that the old man quavered for the future of his country—for his recollection was of a God-struck bigot who had inherited the parental faith in the divine right of kings.

Work provided a distraction from such dark thoughts. While others gave themselves up to celebrations of liberty, Paco and his assistants reproduced portraits of Wellington to replace those of the unlamented Joseph Bonaparte. The allegorical painting in the *ayuntamiento* was altered; the representation of the alien monarch was replaced by the city's heraldic shield. With none of these commissions was Goya satisfied, but business was still business, interregnum or no.

The year expired amid rumors that Don Fernando would soon be coming back to Madrid. But as January gave way to February, they were still unconfirmed. Popular joy over the liberation was subsiding, to be supplanted by a mood of disillusionment. The people were beginning at last to comprehend, with growing shock, the extent of the depredations of war and occupation. There was privation everywhere. Starvation was a universal danger, and death from cold was prevalent from Castile northward. During the celebrations of the autumn, the harvests had been neglected. To add an unnecessary complication, there was inadequate transport for the few provisions available. Throughout the mounting crisis, the junta deliberated, the Cortes fulminated, both helpless to cope with the enormous problems. A surly silence, like the one following the outrages of the second and third of May, 1808, descended over the capital.

To add a poignant, personal note to the general distress, Leocadia became ill in February. Dr. Arrieta ascribed her malady to overexcitement and malnutrition. An alarmed Goya paid scandalously inflated prices for inferior cuts of meat and deplorable fruit, which, he had been assured, would soon see his mistress up and about again. He permitted no one else to nurse her, night and day. If Leocadia was touched by his tender ministrations, she concealed it. If anything, she was more demanding than usual. Her bolster and pillows must be arranged just so. Her blankets imposed an intolerable burden and must be more carefully deployed. The books and periodicals he read aloud to her were no diversion. His voice was too flat, without inflection. When one came right down to it, he was a very dull man. Most disturbing of all, the precious nutriments made her retch more violently than ever. For nearly three weeks of self-indulgent complaint, she perplexed her physician and made life hell for Goya. After an especially harrowing fit of nausea, the doctor gave her a more thorough examination and was still unable to make a firm diagnosis. Then he tactfully inquired about the regularity of her menstrual cycle.

Leocadia laughingly admitted that her period was delayed. "But surely . . ." she protested. "No, it's out of the question."

"That's what *I* thought too," said Dr. Arrieta, looking wonderingly at Goya, "but it seems otherwise. You should have recognized the signs for yourself."

"But I never dreamed—" She glared at Goya. "Now, damn you, see what you've done to me."

The painter beamed. "I certainly hope so."

"You're *pleased?*"

"Ravished, Cadia. You know how I feel about children."

"Other people's."

"You know how I love Javier. You can imagine how I'll feel about a child of yours."

"Very pretty. But you deceived me."

He laughed. "Not intentionally."

"For the next eight months I'm going to get fatter and more awkward and more uncomfortable, all because you thought you were too old to become a father."

"I hope it's a girl."

"*I* hope it's stillborn."

His retort was ominously menacing in its softness. "If you weren't carrying my child, I think I could kill you for saying that. Never say such a thing again."

She was cowed by the suddenness of his anger. "All right," she murmured. "I'm sorry, Paco. I was only joking."

"It's nothing to joke about. It's the final joy the wise God could have given me, at my age, because it's the one I least expected."

"In that, I agree."

"And you should be pleased too. From now on, you'll be treated as well as a queen."

"And after the baby comes? You'll not forget me?"

"You know I'm chained to you forever, Cadia."

"Yes," she responded regretfully, "and now *I'm* chained to you, too."

fourteen

   NAPOLEON'S DEFEAT AT LEIPZIG in early 1814 fore-
shadowed his doom. Nor was this disaster the only bellwether.
In southwestern France, Wellington was eliminating all resistance. Bayonne and Orthez had fallen. The marquis was
marching against Toulouse. With that city in his hands, only
the Massif Central (a less imposing obstacle than the Pyrenees)
stood between his armies and Paris. The end of the Napoleonic
era was in sight. At Talleyrand's persuasion, Bonaparte announced his intention to release Don Fernando from comfortable imprisonment in the Château de Valençay, taking the
odd precaution of holding the Spanish king's uncle, Don Antonio, as hostage against an unnamed hazard.

   When this news reached Madrid, the junta drew up a peti-
tion, a model of deference but forthright in implications: Fernando VII would be allowed to return to the throne only on
condition that he accept the terms of the Cádiz constitution of
1812. To this ultimatum, unique in Spanish history, the king
affected humble submission. All he wanted, he averred, was
what was best for his people. As soon as this affirmation of the
rights of the Cortes was made public, Moratín rushed to Goya's
studio, tremulous in his glee. "You *see,* old Paco? You see? *I* was
right and *you* were wrong. We're going to have a constitutional
Spain."

   The painter rejoicingly retracted his skepticism. "My God,
Leandro, it's magnificent, nothing less."

"Oh, I'm not letting you off so easily as that, *amigo*. You'll have to paint something superb to mark this great occasion."

The same idea had crossed Goya's mind when Moratín was telling him the wonderful news. He thought, moreover, that he knew the perfect note to strike. "The second and third of May, don't you think? We must never forget the horror and grandeur of those two days."

Leandro enthusiastically concurred, and he offered to obtain official blessing for this project from the junta. Paco urged him to stress that he proposed to make these two historical paintings a gift to the nation. "That's very important. I don't give my pictures away very often."

With a company of French guards and a small party of aides, Don Fernando reached the frontier at the end of March. From this point he proceeded without the enemy's protection to the northern Spanish town of Figueras, where he paused for a few days while news of his arrival was circulated. The whole junta and the principal figures of the Cortes hastened to Figueras to welcome the king and pledge their allegiance to him. Don Fernando received them with polite expressions of gratitude for their labors during his exile. He invited them to accompany the royal cortege in a triumphant progress toward Madrid.

Delirious Madrileños thronged the processional route from the Atocha gates to the Prado. As soon as the coach entered the city, a crowd of men and women surged forward, detaching the horses (as others had done at Irún six years before). Though the intention this day was different, the underlying motivation was identical. Forty or fifty people placed themselves between the traces and towed the carriage toward the royal palace. As this extraordinary parade moved slowly through the masses of ecstatic citizens, an occasional phrase could be distinguished above the general clamor of joy. There was one whose implications chilled the few who understood it: *"Viva los grillos!"*— "Long live fetters!"

At the age of thirty, Fernando VII was no brighter nor better educated than he had been seven years before when he had permitted the dull Godoy to outwit him and his followers. His equipment to govern was unimpaired by intelligence, wisdom, compassion, or more than a conveniently warped sense of history; this ignorance made it possible for him to believe that he alone knew best how his country should be ruled. In a single, vital respect, however, he was canny: Like Goya, he was endowed with a primordial comprehension of the popular will, the climate of opinion, which was much sounder than that of the sanguine but ill-judged notions of the junta and the Cortes, which had extorted his promise to adhere to the terms of the Cádiz constitution. He had acceded to this demand in order to avoid any possible impediment to his return.

Back on the throne in early April, he lost no time in making his real policy clear. He intended to rule absolutely, without let or hindrance, and meant to have revenge for the humiliation of being compelled to accept, however cynically, the dictates of his own subjects. He declared the constitution null and void. He decreed the death penalty for everyone involved in its drafting and in seeking to impose it upon him. The *liberales* were to be exiled or jailed. He ordered a reinstatement of the Inquisitional courts, which were to function, as had their antecedents, as political more than religious tribunals. All edicts handed down by the junta and the Cortes were abrogated. Thus, with a few strokes of his pen, Fernando VII restored the *status quo ante* of the Middle Ages.

News of these royal decrees fell like a shroud over the lives of the intellectuals and patriots who had dared so much for the dream of an enlightened Spain. Moratín, despite his vacillations in the past, was no less devastated than those for whom there had never been room for doubt. The reaction of the Madrileños staggered him. "Do you know what those idiots are shouting in the Puerta del Sol, on the very spot where their brothers and fathers were slaughtered?" he asked Paco. " 'Death to the *liberales!* Death to the constitution! Long live fetters!' Can you imagine it, *amigito?* 'Long live fetters!' It makes me want to kill myself."

"Don't bother, Leandro. You know I can imagine such a

thing very easily. I've said it to you so often. The *new* Spain is to be the *old* Spain. The people have their *rey idolatrado*. That's all they care to know about government. For the rest, they want only food and shelter—and no more war."

"And you'll be the king's man, just as you were before?"

Goya shrugged and nodded. "If he'll have me."

"How *can* you?"

"I'm Spanish. I want to go on being Spanish. I don't want to go into exile. I can't imagine living anywhere else. I was about to say it would kill me, but I know better. I just hope it's not forced on me."

Within days of the publication of Fernando's edicts, thousands of suspected *liberales* and *afrancesados* were imprisoned and tortured. Thousands more fled the country, most of them finding a hospitable refuge in Bordeaux. Among these exiles were Ceán Bermúdez and Moratín. Before his nocturnal departure, Leandro urged Goya to follow his example. "The king is bound to persecute you, even if he doesn't have you thrown into prison."

"Why should he want to harm me? I'm an artist, not a politician."

Moratín laughed bitterly. "You can certainly put on or take off your robe of politics with ease, can't you? But this time it may do you no good. They've already jailed poor Isidoro Maiquez for doing nothing more subversive than acting in plays that the French found amusing. *You* painted pictures for them. Your turn will come, believe me."

Goya wouldn't consider leaving so long as Leocadia was pregnant. "We'll just have to take our chances."

The friends parted tearfully at the *taberna*. The painter was certain he would see neither Leandro nor Ceán again, certain too that the librarian's warning was justified. The king's scourge was proving an exhaustively thorough one. It was only a question of time before he was arrested. But of this conviction he thought it better to say nothing to Leocadia, in view of her condition. He did mention it to Javier, and realized afterwards that he ought not to have been offended by his son's cold reaction. "There's nothing for us to worry about, Papa, so long as they don't touch our property or bank accounts."

"Nothing to worry about if I go to prison?"

"Oh," said his son offhandedly, "there'll surely be an amnesty one of these days. You wouldn't be in jail for very long."

"And you and Gumersinda will pray for my deliverance, I daresay, and throw me crusts of bread through the bars," said the old man bitterly.

"Don't exaggerate, Papa. The guards are easily bribed. You'll be very comfortable."

"It doesn't disturb you that I might be condemned as a traitor?"

"It disturbs me, but what do you expect me to do about it? You *insisted* on involving yourself. I told you not to. I only hope they don't come after me because I have the misfortune of being your son."

"Ah, that's the note I was waiting for. That has the ring of truth about it, the part about misfortune. That you have any fortune at all is *my* doing, and it would be more decorous, Javier, if you could find a single tear for me. No extravagance, you understand—just one small tear."

In June, 1814, Goya presented to the directors of the Academia the two large paintings in which he had depicted scenes of the second and third of May, 1808—dramatic, brilliant, stirring, and faithful renderings of incidents that had occurred in Madrid, evocative of the mood and the madness that had provoked the first resistance to French occupation. For once, the response of the stuffy academicians to his work was swift and sensible. They had only applause for these superb canvases— though their approval wasn't so emphatic as Paco's own. He told Julio and Estéve that no other Spanish painter could have so successfully compressed the essences of violence, pathos, and cruelty that had typified the period of 1808–1813.

The directors of the Academia commissioned him to make a portrait of Don Fernando which was to be installed in the great hall of that institution the next month, to celebrate *il rey idolatrado's* return to Madrid. This picture was based on the equestrian portrait Goya had painted six years earlier—for the monarch, in spite of the artist's repeated requests, had declared himself unable to afford him any time to pose for the new work. It was a triumph of Paco's passion for truth. Apprehensive for his personal safety, as he certainly was, he declined to stoop to flattery even if it could save his skin. He made no effort to conceal the king's bestiality, his obesity, or his odd physique. The portrait sang of Don Fernando's psychological and physical monstrosity, his arrogant stupidity.

The young monarch was in attendance for the unveiling of the painting, a ceremony marked by the presence of all of fashionable Madrid. When presented to Don Fernando, Goya detected in the royal glance no malevolence that he could reasonably think personal; the king viewed everyone and everything about him with the same prodigality of condescension and dislike.

With autumn well along, Goya felt increasingly confident that he would escape judgment for his modest part in the events of the occupation. Leocadia was approaching the term of her pregnancy. If all went well, they would be able to go into exile early in the new year, should this distressing course prove necessary. In a specially furnished room, the child was born on the morning of October 2. To Leocadia, the old man's pleasure was annoying and bewildering. The next day, they had a quarrel over the child's name. His mistress wanted to call her Rosaria, after her mother. Paco insisted on María, "after the Virgin, of course." The ensuing storm was, in itself, not at all unusual, but there was a remarkable outcome. The argument was settled by a compromise that favored Paco's option, not Leocadia's. The baby was christened María del Rosario Weiss.

Leocadia wore her concession less than graciously. As she nursed her daughter, she sniffed disdainfully and muttered, "Just another mouth to feed. Just another bottom to clean."

"I enjoy that smell, Cadia."

"You're mad."

"It must be my peasant blood. I like all sorts of odd sensations, the odors and gestures that seem to spring from the earth."

"You don't know any better. I'm no peasant, and I hate the stench."

Goya's joy over the birth of the child he called Rosarita was turned rudely to ashes when he received a summons, little more than a week afterwards, to appear before a tribunal at the *ayuntamiento.* He must defend himself against the charge of serving the French and of having close associations with *liberales* and *afrancesados.*

The court convened in the great reception room of the town hall, with Don Fernando in attendance—seated on a throne, flanked by a dozen high clerics and the new *alcalde mayor,* a Castilian unknown to the painter. After bowing to the king and his henchmen, the old man obeyed the *alcalde's* command that he take his place in a balustered witness box, where he stood as a clerk droned out a lengthy bill of particulars. He had difficulty reading the man's thin, fast-moving lips and interrupted respectfully to ask that he begin the recital again, speaking more slowly and distinctly. Though the request was granted, the accused painter wasn't much enlightened by the result, so complex was the phraseology, so highly seasoned with dates and names and places which seemed irrelevant to events occurring during the occupation.

When the reading of the charges was concluded, a bishop rose to question him. "You have heard the accusations, Don Francisco. How do you plead?"

"I plead ignorance, *señor.* I didn't understand much of what was said, but if, as I gather, the claim is that I was a traitor, I must naturally plead innocent."

"You have a long history of opposition to authority."

"Have I, *señor?* I'm not aware of it."

"Well, let me refresh your memory. In seventeen-ninety-nine, did you not engrave and cause to be published a volume of etchings entitled *Los Caprichos?*"

"That's so, *señor.*"

"And in this volume did you not hold the royal family and the Holy Mother Church up to ridicule?"

"Forgive me, *señor,* but how does *Los Caprichos* affect my conduct while the French were in Spain?"

"There *is* a point, Don Francisco. Just answer the question."

"Ridicule, *señor?* It wasn't my intention. As I wrote in the advertisements at the time, I had *no* particular persons in mind. The pictures were generalizations on the human condition as I saw it, fables and parables, if you like."

"But you'll not deny that these 'fables' and 'parables' were directed against the sacred institutions of the crown and the church."

What was the point of quibbling? The caricatures were there to be seen. A copy of *Los Caprichos* lay on a table before the prosecutor. "I drew attention to *other* abuses, *señor.* They're against human foibles." He paused and smiled. "And against Don Manuel Godoy."

"A good doesn't excuse an evil, Don Francisco. You'll not disagree that at the time of their publication, it was the general belief that your caricatures depicted persons in high places, royal and clerical."

"If so, *señor,* it was pure coincidence. I wasn't attempting to attack any individual *or* institution." Goya could have cut out his tongue for this lie, but it was plain that the tribunal was building a case for his having been a rebel for far longer than had been so.

"A coincidence? Indeed." The bishop sneered and consulted his notes. "Well, well, we'll let that pass for the moment. Here's another indication that your attitude toward accepted modes of conduct has long been questionable. In eighteen-eight, when the properties of the ex-Prince of the Peace were confiscated by the state—"

Goya broke in. "An action I applauded, *señor.*"

His interrogator smiled sardonically. "I'm sure that His Majesty will be heartened to know that his actions had your approval. As I was saying, among Godoy's possessions was a painting of a nude woman. It is the most objectionable work I have ever seen. This picture has been attributed to your hand. Do you deny it?"

The old man flushed. "No, *señor*. It's my work. Don Manuel requested that I make such a portrait of his mistress, Doña Pepa Tudo."

The bishop's grin suggested he had scored an important point. "And you assented willingly?"

"Don Manuel's request was a command, *señor*. It would have been impossible to refuse. I had no choice."

The questioner frowned. "Yet as a painter steeped in the traditions of the church in Spain, you were certainly aware of the strictures of the Council of Trent against the showing of nakedness in art."

"The prohibition applies only to religious art, *señor*. I know, because my master, Don José de Luzán, was employed by the Holy Office of Zaragoza to overpaint 'indecencies' in frescoes and other pictures in the churches of Aragón."

"You're evading the question, Don Francisco."

"*Is* there a stricture against nudity in paintings for private residences? Don Manuel assured me that this picture would never be displayed in public." He smiled wryly. "He wanted it for his bedchamber, which may not have been so private a place as one might hope."

The bishop was not amused. "For public or private display makes no difference. You wittingly, if not willingly, pandered to the man's debauched tastes. You knew that what you were doing was corrupt, evil, and indecent."

"You evade *my* question, *señor*. Is there a stricture?"

"There is certainly a law against indecency. And you knew you were violating that law."

Though now perspiring despite the chill of the hall, Goya refused to concede the point without a struggle. "You suggest, *señor*, that nakedness is in itself corrupt, evil, and indecent?"

"You dare to doubt it?"

"I dare to believe the obvious. Are we not born naked?"

"We're not speaking of infants," the bishop replied impatiently. "The woman you call Doña Pepa was little better than a common prostitute. The pose is lascivious."

"Santa María Madalena . . ." Goya began.

The cleric interrupted with a raised hand. "I hardly think we need detain the court with your views on fallen women. Your own way of life speaks eloquently on the subject of personal sin. Nor shall I introduce this aspect of your career, since our Heavenly Father will dispose of your immortal soul as He sees fit."

"Then perhaps you'll pardon me for asking, *señor*, why you brought up the subject of the painting."

"To demonstrate that you're not only corrupt yourself, but that you're capable of corrupting others."

"Not deliberately."

"That is a distinction without a difference."

"Ah," murmured Paco.

"You concede, Don Francisco, that it was an act of corruption, even of collaboration with the enemy, to paint a portrait of the usurper, Joseph Bonaparte."

The painter reached into a pocket and produced several sheets of foolscap. "I did anticipate *that* question, *señor*. Here's a list of every painting I made during the occupation. I should point out," he continued as he handed the pages to the bishop, "that they weren't all portraits, nor were all the portraits of the French or the *afrancesados*."

"But a substantial portion of them were."

"The bakers supplied the French with bread. The tavern keepers served them drink. The fuel merchants sold them charcoal, and what's more, all of them raised their prices for everyone. They profited wonderfully from our general misery. Are you going to bring all of *them* before this bar?"

"*There* is a distinction *with* a difference."

"I perceive none, *señor*. The baker's trade is baking. Mine is painting. *I* didn't raise *my* prices. If any man had the gold for a picture of mine, I painted what he asked for."

"No matter what sort of picture he requested?"

"Does the confessor deny absolution because a particular sin is repugnant to him personally?" Goya held up his hands. "These are all I possess. They're my entire stock-in-trade. I began life as a poor child in Aragón . . ."

"We're aware of your rise in the world, Don Francisco. It has nothing to do with the accusations."

But Paco wasn't to be interrupted; his eyes were now on the king, not the bishop. "With my bare hands, I made a decent life for myself and my family. This tribunal is trying to make me out a politician, or at least a man with profound political convictions, a thinker. But I'm not a thinker, except about my craft. I'm just a Spaniard who did no more than he had to do in order to survive. That's what I've done all my life. That doesn't make me very courageous, I know, but there have been a few occasions when I've done something I'm proud of. I was a spy for Spain for six months, and so was my assistant Ascensio Julio."

Don Fernando's face remained expressionless. He signaled with a turn of the head that Goya should look back at his interrogator, who broke in. "You mean, do you not, that you were a spy for the illegal junta?"

"Was it illegal at the time in *your* eyes, *señor?* If so, its position in history will be very strange, for the French held it to be illegal too. To apply present standards to actions that were commendable in the past is very odd reasoning. The least favorable thing you can say of the junta's role during the occupation is that the enemy of your enemy was your friend."

"You're condemning yourself out of your own mouth, Don Francisco."

Paco was too outraged to heed this warning. "Did thousands of *guerrilleros* die as traitors because, as you look at their actions today, they were unlawful? I have a trunkful of engravings that prove what atrocities the French committed. It was men like Jovellanos, who was my dearest friend, who helped to guide the *guerrilleros*. And what thanks do you offer their memory? What do you propose for the heroes who survived? The garrote or prison or exile. Do you dare to suggest, *señor,* that I have ever been disloyal to Spain?"

"That is precisely the charge, Don Francisco."

"And what were *you* doing? Where were you and these illustrious men who presume to be judging me, while our people were starving and being butchered by the French? Were most of you not right here in Spain, keeping your peace, embracing the French *and* the *afrancesados,* in hopes that they'd not dissolve all the monasteries and convents and preempt all your authority? Where was God when Spain so badly needed God?"

The bishop listened to the outburst with growing chagrin. When Goya paused for breath, he interjected uneasily, "The church, Don Francisco, is not on trial here."

"It ought to be."

"When the Spanish laity calls upon the Holy Mother Church to defend herself against the heinous crime of upholding the teachings of Our Lord, you may be sure, Don Francisco, that I shall be happy to answer your question in full. But I will say *this* much: We have no reason to be ashamed of our record. If it hadn't been for the church, there would be no Christian Spain at all. We would still be under the heel of the infidels. It would profit you to keep that in mind."

The old man couldn't repress his contempt. "Because of something the church did centuries ago, you demand that we go on applauding everything you do until the day of judgment. There were brave priests and monks and nuns who died for Spain during the occupation, but I've yet to be told the name of a brave bishop."

"The most flagrant heresy I've ever heard."

"That may be so, but it's a heresy that's on the lips of every Spanish peasant, *señor.* In accusing *me* of heresy and treason, you're accusing every *guerrillero* and every soul who wished nothing more than the return of Don Fernando."

Goya's fury staggered his interrogator. He tried to recover his aplomb. When he spoke, his tone was irritable. "You raise these points to confuse the issue. The facts we're concerned with are that you willingly portrayed the false king and his followers, French and Spanish alike. You gave aid and comfort to those who betrayed and ravaged our country."

"If 'willingly' is truly the operative word, *señor*, then I can absolve myself completely. I made them because I'm a painter and had to earn my living by painting. Besides, I could see nothing traitorous about depicting the features of persons who paraded their faces daily for all to see. As for the portrait of Bonaparte, my situation was the same as for the picture of Pepa Tudo. I had no choice."

"Nevertheless, Don Francisco," said the bishop smoothly, "you did accept the Frenchman's highest decoration."

"And refused to wear it."

"You *accepted* it. Why do you persist in making distinctions where none exists?"

"The distinction here is significant, *señor*. My friends advised me that I might jeopardize my task as informal spy in the Prado if I declined it."

"And who were your advisers? Let *me* tell *you*," the bishop went on before Goya could respond. "They were enemies of the state."

"None of my friends could be disloyal to Spain."

"You say that in the light of the documented evidence that they have been disloyal to His Majesty?"

"You've judged them so for their support of the junta during the occupation."

"*And* for supporting it afterwards, *and* for their role in the formation of an unlawful Cortes, and for presuming to draft a so-called constitution."

"But didn't His Majesty accept the terms of that constitution?" Goya turned to find the king listening with complete absorption. His gaze returned to the bishop.

"His Majesty isn't on trial here any more than is the church, Don Francisco. Keep to the point."

"But it's *I* who am on trial. My friends are on trial. The whole of Spain is on trial. And I think we've been miserably treated. If we occasionally accommodated the French, it was with the idea of obtaining a favor that would gain us more than remaining aloof would do. We hurt them badly. Joseph Bonaparte admitted that again and again. Is this the gratitude we

deserve? I'm not asking for clemency for myself *or* my friends.
I'm asking for justice. We all genuinely believed that a new
kind of government, with a constitution, would help our people. I confess freely and willingly that what's happening in this
room proves we were right. But I must confess too that I believed my friends were mistaken in their understanding of our
people's temper. This doesn't mean that I now recant. I'm not a
bit better, nor a bit worse, than any of the people you've
murdered or jailed for nothing more terrible than their love of
Spain."

"Your eloquence astonishes me, Don Francisco. My information is that you are an ill-educated man."

"That's true, *señor*, because the teachers the church gave me
were ignorant. If I'm eloquent, it's because of long association
with men whose families could afford private tutelage."

The bishop smiled complacently. "At last we seem to be
reaching the central point of your creed, Don Francisco. You
despise the church."

"But I love God."

"And do you also love His Majesty?"

Goya looked once again at Don Fernando and made a little
bow. "I've *always* been the king's man, sire. I've said so all my
life. I was your grandfather's man and your father's man. And
for the same reason, I am your man today. As I've said, I've not
always agreed with you or your officials, but I've never consciously done anything that *I* construed to be against your
interest. I may have been misguided at times, but I've never
been disloyal."

The pudgy, pig-faced king leaned forward and, with a limp
gesture of his plump hand, indicated to the bishop that he
wished to speak. His eyes returned to Goya's. "I believe I
understand your dilemma during the troubled times. I don't
condone your actions, of course. You're quite rightly on trial.
Nor do I agree that the church is in any way responsible for the
ignorance of our people, nor is she guilty of collaborating with
the French. *I* cannot be blamed for conditions while I was in
exile. So it seems to me that there's only one relevant fact in all
that you've so rashly stated. And that is that you're certainly not

a political being as we understand the term. If you *were*, Goya, you would never have spoken as you did. A politician would have been cleverer. If you'd been evasive, you'd deserve the garrote, or at least banishment, along with your disgraced friends. However, since you are reputed to be our greatest living painter and are, in consequence, an important cultural ornament, I shall, on this occasion, pardon your transgressions."

Goya wiped his eyes—though, in fact, there were no tears to be brushed away. "I'm grateful, sire."

The king's little smile was menacing and humorless. "I'm sure you are. But I beg you to remember that I shan't deal with you so leniently if you're unwise another time. And I'm bound to tell you that you'll receive no commissions from me, though I agree with my knowledgeable friends that your paintings of the events of the second and third of May are masterful."

"I'm pleased you find them so, sire, but naturally I'm distressed—"

Don Fernando interrupted. "You may continue in your office."

Goya heaved a sigh. "That's very good news, sire. I hope this decision not to commission me hasn't been influenced by these charges."

The monarch's lip curled into a sneer, his most familiar expression. "Of *course* I'm influenced by them. I've no doubt that you trafficked with my enemies and no doubt that you'd do the same again if I freed them or allowed them to return to Spain. But there's something else too. You'll probably think me ignorant, Don Francisco, but I happen to prefer the painting of Vicente López."

Goya chuckled ruefully. "I'm not sure, sire, that I wouldn't prefer the garrote to being thought inferior to that painter of fairy tales."

"*If* you're garroted, Goya, it will be for your folly, not your art."

He was a free man; the impossible had happened. Goya rode home in his official carriage, his feelings divided evenly between relief and remorse. He was elated over his pardon and dismayed to think of men like Ceán and Moratín who had enjoyed no such clemency. Had Don Fernando not fortuitously been present that day, he would not have got off so easily. Still, he was pleased for having spoken out and for having done so in total awareness of the risks he ran. Death would not have been too high a price for the privilege of saying to the faces of the king and the clergy the things he and his friends had for so long been saying behind their backs.

When he attempted to make his satisfaction intelligible to Leocadia, she responded angrily. "You were an idiot to go so far. What do *I* care how much good it did your soul? What do I care about the others? *You're* safe, Paco. That's all that matters to me."

Javier's reaction was dismally similar. "You've been lucky, Papa, but the ice is going to be very thin. So, for God's sake—for *our* sakes—be careful of what you say and whom you say it to."

Javier's cold-blooded cynicism enraged Goya the more because such had been his own policy during the years before his illness at Cádiz. Julio alone congratulated him for his forthright denunciation of king and church. "I only wish I'd been there to hear you, Don Paco."

Goya found an outlet for his anger once again in his art. He made sketches which in spirit were an extension of *Los Caprichos,* and he reworked some of the later plates of the unpublished *Desastres,* making more pointed their pertinence to the calamities inflicted on Spain by the king and the church. As he wrote to the exiled Moratín, this was probably the most futile and empty of gestures. "If there was ever a chance of publishing these in my lifetime, the changes have made it impossible." He added, more wistfully, "I miss you and Ceán more than these poor words can prove. I have Cadia and our little Rosarita, and I have my work, and dear Ascensio attends me well. But the *taberna* is a tomb. In fact the whole of Madrid is a tomb. Is it the same for you in France?"

There was little exaggeration in Paco's lament. With Don Fernando's bloody purge still in effect, only the common people and the most unassailable of the aristocracy felt safe to circulate at will. The rest had ample, if various, reasons for uncertainty. If they left their houses, they couldn't assure their loved ones that they would return when expected. The poison of fear that permeated the capital caused Goya more and more to question the virtue of his conviction that, come what might, he would always be the king's man. He couldn't deny the pleasure of being permitted to keep his official post; he still set great store by financial security, especially now when prices were outrageous and, more particularly, when he was beginning seriously to feel his years. But for how much longer could he so flatly assert that, if offered the choice of opting for the king or real reform, he would side with Don Fernando?

Recalling his last conversation with Moratín, he wondered for how much longer all of Spain would passively accept the king's harsh policies when they could be seen in juxtaposition with his casual efforts to restore the economy to something like health. The year before, he had assured Leandro that Spaniards would endure any privation if Fernando VII were restored to the throne. Was this so? *He* was of those Spaniards and had resented the French invasion as much as anyone, but in the wake of the enemy's departure, conditions had continued to deteriorate. Famine, pestilence, unemployment, coupled with political oppression, existed on a scale hitherto unknown in Spain. There was, moreover, no question that each of these calamities could in fairness be laid at the king's door. If Goya was having second thoughts about his loyalty, might not millions of his compatriots be reconsidering their opinions too?

Don Fernando was having his own second thoughts. As the first year of his new reign closed, he dissolved the special tribunals and proclaimed an amnesty for all but a handful of the exiles and those in prison. He declared that he was satisfied that the draconian measures had achieved their purpose—that he be universally and unquestioningly accepted as sole ruler of Spain. His appetite for vengeance had been sated, even glutted, for the time being. It pleased him now to play a different role, that of the magnanimous, Christian Don Fernando, willing to forgive the wretches who had presumed to challenge his divine right to exercise power as he chose. He had no doubt, he said, that his erstwhile foes had learned their lesson.

Unrepentant, Moratín and Ceán returned from their year of exile in Bordeaux in June, 1815; their bitterness against the king was more deeply embedded than before, their resolve to change the regime, by revolution if necessary, far stiffer. To the painter's relief and pleasure, both friends expressed at last a willingness to accept Leocadia as a permanent fixture in his life. He assumed that Rosarita's birth and ensuing prosperity had persuaded them that the mistress would not soon be dislodged. Therefore, they modulated their expressions of distaste for her. What couldn't be transformed had to be endured.

And Leocadia reacted to this alteration with intelligence. She treated Goya's friends with perfect correctness. She performed her tasks of hostess with a taste that delighted him. Never miserly where *she* was concerned, he was now even more lavish —insisting that she buy whatever pleased her in clothes or furnishings for the house. The moral wasn't lost on her. She redoubled her efforts to make Paco happy and discovered an unexpected gratification in the gaiety around her when guests were on hand. Her occasional fits of laughter took her, and everyone else, by surprise. This little glow of happiness helped to suppress her growing jealousy over Goya's tedious devotion to their little daughter.

The bright flame of his faith in a Spain which would eventually be reformed didn't prevent Moratín from advising Paco, in much the same terms as had Leocadia and Javier, to be cautious in all he said and did. "Our time is bound to come, but until it does, we'll have to be patient. None of us must do anything to arouse suspicion. We must pretend to be good, happy, reliable, God-fearing, wholly reconstructed *Fernandistos.*"

This admonition gave Goya a chance to repeat, word for word, his defense when called before the tribunal the previous October. "So you see, *amigo,*" he concluded, "painters don't cause alarm by what they paint. *I* have nothing to fear."

"That's so negative," Leandro protested. "You should be

positive. You should give them the impression that from now on you're an active supporter of Don Fernando."

Goya eyed his friend suspiciously. "You have something specific in mind?"

"I have an idea, the *corrida*. Don Fernando has restored it to us because he's such an *aficionado* himself. And it just happens that my father wrote a treatise on its history. I've always meant to publish it. Its chance of success would be improved if you made illustrations for it. It's harmless enough as a theme, God knows. There are no undertones that could possibly be called political, and it might help to put us back in Don Fernando's good graces. That's the most important thing. Besides, I'd like to honor my father's memory. And we might earn a little money, too."

The painter welcomed the idea, chiefly because it might help his dear friend. He hastened to a cupboard of his studio and returned to the seated Moratín with an armful of drawings. "You don't have to go through them all, but they'll give you an idea of what my bullfighting experience has been. Some of them go back years, things I did when I was a student, working with a *cuadrilla*. And I'm sure I've sketched every great *torero* in the last forty years."

Moratín worked his way respectfully through the small mountain of drawings. "Yes, yes," he said at last. "But if you're going to follow my papa's narrative, you'll have to make some illustrations of the old-fashioned ways too, when the Moors brought what they called bullbaiting to Spain. And you have to show what things were like when it was the privilege only of the nobles to kill the bull." He laughed. "What I mean, Paco, is that you're going to have to *read* what my father has written."

Ceán was equally enthusiastic and insisted on being allowed to compose the captions. Goya engraved forty plates, but as he and Rafaelo Estéve readied them for the final printing, the painter withdrew seven as superfluous. *La Tauromaquia*, as this volume was called, made its public appearance just eighteen months after Moratín had proposed it. By the spring of 1817, however, it was plain that it wasn't destined to be any more profitable a venture than *Los Caprichos,* nor did the companion edition by Moratín's father enjoy a greater reception. "It seems," said Goya sadly, "that Madrid isn't interested in anything, positive or negative."

The appearance of the book did, however, result in Leandro's rehabilitation. He was reappointed to his position as royal librarian, "mostly because," he averred, "the man who took my place turned out to be an ass."

The failure of *La Tauromaquia* in no way reflected unhappily on Goya's career as a painter. He was undertaking fewer portraits now, preferring to devote a greater proportion of his flagging energies to religious art. This change of emphasis perplexed and amused his two friends because, if possible, his views were more anticlerical than they had ever been. But as he aged and as his sight grew weaker, his faith grew stronger; he accepted the concept of the Trinity, of salvation, of a hereafter in which the soul survived. In a codicil to his will, he made specific bequests to several convents and hospitals. He even provided a sum for the liberation of the Holy Places still in Moslem hands. Another clause provided for masses to be offered in his name.

The quality of the religious paintings he made during the five years after Fernando VII's restoration was a reflection of his altered outlook and his growing sense of the nearness of death. In many, he evoked a degree of emotional intensity absent in his earlier efforts in this genre. He could discern no inconsistency in the fact that while he was composing intensely religious paintings, he was once again toying with sketches for a new series of engravings whose pessimism was much darker than any that had found expression in *Los Caprichos* or *Los Desastres.* Though he had made trial etchings of only a few of the numerous drawings, he had found a title, *Disparates*—his own eccentric illumination of proverbs and fables. Except in the blackest sense, they were humorless. Like their precursors, their publication would be impossible. But they served the purpose of mitigating his impotent rage against the king and clergy.

Though he admired the proofs, Moratín chastised Paco for

squandering his talent on work that the world was unlikely to see. "What's the use of these if no one wants them?"

"You say *you* want them. Ceán wants them. And most of all, *I* want them. I *need* to do these things. Besides, Leandro, wasn't it you who urged me to engrave *Los Desastres?* You said I must leave a record. Perhaps only the three of us will care, but that's enough."

"*Los Desastres* was a record of the war, Paco. These are like *Los Caprichos.*"

"My private art. This is what I see in my private world."

"It's a very dark world, *amigo.*"

"María used to say that. It's true. But I was born into a very dark world. So were you."

fifteen

"WHAT'S BEEN HAPPENING TO YOU, *abuelo?*" Mariano asked in complete innocence, not long after the Christmas of 1818. "You're grumpy all the time now, except when you have Rosarita on your knee."

The old man touched the boy's warm forehead with apologetic tenderness. *"Have* I been so nasty, *nieto?* It must be my rheumatism. And I've been having these headaches. You have no idea. And my eyes are getting weaker and more watery. It's a terrible thing for a painter." He extended his hands, the joints contorted. "See how they tremble?"

"Papa says you do too much. He says you should leave more of your work for Ascensio and Rafaelo."

"Your papa says a lot of things, and a lot of the time he doesn't know what he's talking about. However, I'm touched to know he's so concerned."

"He says that Dr. Arrieta tells you the same thing."

Goya sighed. "Doctors aren't much wiser than anyone else, Mariano. When I was ill in Cádiz, the doctors gave me up for dead. But here I am."

"Mama says you work too hard too, *abuelo.*"

"Your mama is a fine woman, so I'm sorry to tell you that she's mistaken too."

The child's eyes were wide with interest. "How can so many people be wrong in the same way?"

"Very easily. Isn't the whole of Spain wrong about Don Fernando?"

"Then why," the boy persisted, "are you so grumpy with everyone but Rosarita? Is *she* the only one you love?"

This question hit a nerve. He took his grandson's hand and kissed it. "You know better."

"Why, *abuelo?* That's how it seems."

"But I love you too. Haven't I always shown you that?"

"Until a few months ago. Now you're only nice to her."

It was embarrassing to be forced onto the defensive, and Goya's maneuvers in such cases were rarely adroit. "Little girls need more love than boys. She's only four. What are you? Twelve, isn't it?" He interrupted himself. Everyone needed love. "I'm sorry. I love you too, *nieto.*"

"I believe you, *abuelo.* But just the same, maybe you ought to rest more."

"What would I do with my time?"

"Rest."

"And what should I do with my mind while my body's resting? Do you think my brain will relax just because I ask it to? When you go to bed and you're not sleepy, doesn't your mind stay awake?"

"Yes."

"And what do you do?"

The boy grinned. "I light my candle and read."

"But *I* can't do that, not with *my* eyes."

"*I'll* read to you. Cadia will read to you. Mama would read to you."

"I'm too impatient. It's bad enough trying to follow lips in a conversation, but to follow someone reading . . . "

"You could travel."

"At my age? Travel would be no pleasure. When my carriage rattles, my old bones rattle along with it. And to see what, for God's sake? I've already seen more of this terrible world than I want to. No, *nieto,* the time for me to rest is in the grave."

"Are you so bored, then?"

"Not when I'm working."

Goya was more moved by Mariano's concern than by that of anyone else. He might exaggerate, for dramatic purposes, the depth of his current depression, but it was a verity he couldn't wish away; not since María's death had his spirits been so low. What *was* happening to him? Dr. Arrieta had no explanation. "You need a change, Don Paco," he had said repeatedly. But did he really need a change? And what kind of change? He was depressed, but who in Spain wouldn't be depressed? It wasn't *he* who required change, as he had told Moratín years before; it was Spain.

Nevertheless, Mariano's gentle accusation stuck in Goya's mind and, a few days later, he put the question to Rosarita. "What kind of change would *you* like in me, my little charmer?"

At four, the child was physically the image of Leocadia, but her temperament couldn't have been more different. She adored her elderly father with a single-mindedness that was daily a source of irritation to her volatile mother, who read into Rosarita's affection (especially into her inept but constant efforts to copy sketches he made to amuse her) the self-seeking motives of which she herself would have been culpable under similar circumstances. It was impossible for Leocadia to give credence to the purity of her daughter's love for Paco and for art.

The child was bemused by the question. "Why would you change? If you changed, you'd be different. I don't want you different. I don't want you to be somebody else."

He smiled at this magical logic. "*You're* going to change. You're going to grow up. What kind of change would you like for yourself?"

"To make pictures as nice as yours."

"You will, you will. I'll teach you. It takes time, but you improve every day. What else would you like?"

She reflected for an instant—the full length of her normal attention span, then her face exploded into a smile that wrenched his sentimental old heart with pleasure. "I want to watch the flowers grow. I don't like them in vases, the way

Mama does. They die so quickly. I don't like to see the flowers die."

"I don't like to see anything die," he murmured, more to himself than her. Then he brightened. "You're right. Would you like to live in the country, where the flowers grow?"

"Could we?"

"I was born in the country, *angelita.*"

"You were lucky."

"And I couldn't wait to move to the city."

"You were silly."

"Perhaps. But the place where *my* mama and papa lived wasn't very pleasant, not warm and comfortable, the way we are here. So I wasn't completely silly, was I?"

"No, Papa."

"And *you* were born in the city, so you think you'd like to live in the country." He chuckled. "Do you know what people call that? They call it perversity."

"Is it bad?"

"It's human."

"Is *that* bad?"

"Not always. It's not idiotic, you know, your desire to live in the country."

"Can we do it, then?"

"Why not? We'll find a house in the country, just for you."

Leocadia entertained the idea with some hostility at first. "Pigs and goats and hens in the living rooms? No, thank you, not for me. If I'd wanted that kind of life, Paco, I could have stayed in Aragón."

"Not that kind of place, *amada,* but a *quinta,* a real country house, with gardens and perhaps a dog. Ever since I was a little boy in Fuendetodos, I've wanted a dog."

"But your work, Paco. People won't go to the country to have their portraits painted."

"That's just what they'll have to do. And I don't much care if they don't."

"There's enough money?"

"Do you think I'd consider a move if there weren't?"

Her face cleared, then clouded as another thought occurred to her. "How far away from Madrid? How would I manage the marketing?"

He shrugged. "I can't answer that, can I? For the marketing, you have a carriage. You have servants. What are they for?"

"To rob us, as servants do."

"I don't believe they rob *you* twice."

She shifted tack again. "How large a house?"

"Any size you like, *querida*."

She looked about the salon, which was hopelessly jammed with furniture, the walls overcrowded with pictures. She had long protested that there was space for nothing more, but this hadn't prevented her from continuing her acquisitions, and she was unable to discard anything—not even articles that Josefa had chosen. "Well, it would have to be a lot larger than this house."

"Why not? It can be as large as the Palacio de Liria, if you want."

"Don't be ridiculous, Paco. Do you think I want to spend my life looking after something that size?"

"Well, let's not worry about it until we see what's to be had."

Leocadia couldn't resist a final sally. "If it had been *I* who put the idea into your head, you'd never have agreed."

"You don't believe that. If you'd thought of it, you'd have nagged me until I gave in. What difference does it make? The thing appeals to you, doesn't it?"

"I'm not sure."

"If it doesn't," he said shrewdly, "then we can forget it. I have better ways to spend my time."

Under the guidance of Don Miguel Valco García, whom Ceán's banking intimates called the most reliable notary in Madrid, Goya, Leocadia, and Rosarita spent many wintry afternoons exploring properties near the capital. The painter dismissed his friends' suggestion that he rent at first, until he was certain that country life would agree with him. For there still lingered in his memory Martín Zapater's injunction about the security of investment in real estate.

Most of the houses they saw impressed Leocadia as either too pretentious or too cramped. Only at the end of February did García show them through a villa which both she and Paco thought attractive and serviceable. It stood in a small, well-kept park of twenty-five acres that overlooked the Manzanares, the Segovia Bridge, and, in the distance, the spires of Madrid. An airy, spacious mansion with large, well-proportioned rooms, it had been built for the Madrileño merchant Don Marcelino Blanco during the reign of Carlos III, and was offered for sale by his son Don Pedro. "Those were the last years when decent craft counted for something in this country," said the notary.

"I suppose it will do, if it's the best we can find," said Leocadia, though in fact she was delighted. "But, of course, we'd have to make all sorts of alterations before we could move in."

"Anything you want, *querida*," Goya responded, then turned to his daughter. "And is the garden to your liking, *angelita?*"

The child danced across the flagstones of a small terrace and dipped her fingers in the icy water of a fountain. She came back more slowly, frowning. "But I don't see any flowers."

"They'll come in the spring."

"Many of them?"

"Thousands, I promise you."

She clapped her hands with pleasure. "Oh, yes, Papa, yes. I like it very much."

"I'll buy it," said Goya to the notary.

"But, Don Francisco, you don't know the price," García responded, but he recognized that this was purely a formality. He knew an eager client when he saw one.

The painter waved his arm in a gesture of grand indifference. "I don't care about the price, Don Miguel. If Doña Leocadia and my little *pequeña* like it, I mean to have it."

His mistress was indignant. "What a vain fool you are, Paco. Whom do you mean to impress?"

"You and Rosarita. You like the house, so you're going to have it. Goya never bargains."

"Ah," sighed García, "if all my patrons were as easy to deal with."

"If they were," said Leocadia contemptuously, "you could be sure they'd have opened up all the madhouses and let the maniacs go free."

"What *is* the price, Don Miguel."

"Sixty thousand reales."

"Banditry," screamed Leocadia, feeling in her element. She loved nothing so much as haggling over purchases. "Where is Don Pedro Blanco's gun? *I* wouldn't give him more than *fifty* thousand and I'd still feel cheated. Just think of all the work that has to be done before it's habitable."

Goya paid no attention. "I'm as deaf to her as to everyone else," he told the notary. "Besides, she hasn't got fifty thousand reales. You may tell Don Pedro that I'll meet his price. It's the perfect place, for all of us. There's plenty of space and light, and it's far enough from Madrid to discourage casual callers, but not so far to keep friends away."

"You have excellent neighbors too, Don Francisco," the notary added, quite superfluously. "Very respectable people."

Leocadia held her tongue, though she would have dearly loved to show Paco how skilled a negotiater she was. Her happiness over the prospect of being mistress of so fine a house overrode all other considerations. As their carriage was about to enter the main road, Goya ordered Pablo, his coachman, to stop. He looked back at the handsome, solid *quinta* to which he had just committed himself. "I think it will be just right," he muttered amiably, "the perfect place for me to die."

When they drove on, Leocadia discarded all pretense of reservation. "What shall we call it, Paco? La Quinta de Goya?"

"La Quinta del Sordo would be more to the point," he replied morosely.

"I don't think the House of the Deaf Man is a very nice name," said Rosarita plaintively.

"But appropriate, *angelita,* and true. Haven't Mama and I always told you to speak the truth?"

While details for the transfer of ownership were being completed, Goya and Leocadia made plans for the renovation of

their country house. Their deliberations were less than harmonious, for each had a particular conception of the changes
required. An arbiter was called for, a suggestion his mistress
received with icy approval, for her willingness to compromise,
never extraordinary, was in this case remarkably minuscule.
Since it was likely that she would outlive Paco, she thought it
only proper that her preferences be given priority. But assent
she did in the face of Goya's threat to cancel the purchase.

By promising (in addition to his normal fees) to make a
magnificent portrait of him, Paco elicited the advice and supervision of Madrid's most illustrious architect, Tiburcio Pérez, an
acquaintance of the *taberna*. After listening to the requirements
of both clients, Pérez made detailed plans which Leocadia was
compelled to accept without complaint, so ingeniously had he
combined their wishes. For her grudging praise, the architect
proclaimed himself her wondering admirer. "You're the first
lady who has ever accepted my plans without change."

The reconstruction proceeded slowly through the spring and
summer of 1819. But for once, Goya wasn't impatient. He had
just been introduced to "a new toy," as he described it—a
revolutionary printing process called lithography, which had
been developed in Germany at the end of the previous century
and had only recently been brought to Spain by the printer
Cardeña, who had helped him with the production of *Los
Caprichos* and *La Tauromaquia*. The idea that one could make
prints from blocks of polished stone at first struck the painter as
improbable. But when Cardeña demonstrated, albeit with little
talent for art, the exceptional effects of shading that were
obtainable, the variety of techniques by which the surface could
be worked, and, above all, the ease and flexibility of the process,
he undertook with boyish eagerness experiments of his own. It
was, moreover, satisfying to learn that he was the first artist in
Spain to make use of the new medium.

Leocadia was less than enchanted to find that in the weeks
when she thought he should be preoccupied with the alteration
of their new house, he was engrossed in his "play." She charged
him with wasting his time. "You're too old to be trying new

things. Stick to what you know. Be sensible. Besides," she added
bluntly, "aren't you the first to complain that you've never
earned a real from print making?"

Because in her view the rebuke had been routine, a matter of
reflex, she was startled by the vehemence of his retort. "In the
first place, *mujer,* it's none of your affair what I do in my studio.
I've told you that before, and you've respected it until now. In
the second place, I'm *not* too old to learn a new technique.
When I *am,* you'll be praying over my corpse. In the third
place, I make prints because I want to. In the fourth place,
lithography interests me because it strains my eyes less than
engraving does, and it gives me a new feeling of freedom in my
drawing. And finally, none of the rest matters, because I know
you're complaining only because you enjoy it. If your brain
were half as sharp as your tongue, you'd be the most brilliant
woman in Spain." Leocadia retired to nurse her wounds, tacitly
acknowledging that on this occasion Paco had bested her.

By the end of September, the builders had completed the
renovation of the *quinta.* With Pérez, Goya and Leocadia and
Rosarita inspected the results. The cold, empty ground-floor
room in which they stood was redolent of drying plaster. The
painter considered the brilliant walls. "I won't hang any pictures
here, by God. I'm going to make new paintings right on the
plaster."

"And if they don't please me?" his mistress asked bellig-
erently?

"They *won't* please you, Cadia. I promise you that. The only
things you like are portraits of yourself."

"And your painting of the two *majas* on the balcony with the
men in the background."

"Because one of the women resembles *you.*"

"And one of the men resembles *you.*"

"All right, all right, God damn it. I'll include a picture of
you on one of these panels, if that will keep you happy."

"It might."

Goya turned to the architect. "What did I ever do to deserve
such a woman, Pérez? She hates the best of my painting."

"And don't forget the etchings, and those new lithographs," she said, anxious to add fuel to the fires of his indignation. "They're so ugly."

Before Pérez could comment, Rosarita wailed, "Won't you *please* stop arguing."

Goya looked down at her. As he did, he felt giddy. He lost consciousness and crumpled to the floor, striking his head against the hard tiled floor.

From her room, which adjoined Goya's, Leocadia heard a faint, moaning cry and hastened to his bedside. "Well," she demanded peremptorily, "what fool's errand is it this time?"

His eyes were wide and watery as he stared up at her. "*This* time?" The voice was tremulous. "Then I've called you before?"

"You don't remember? I suppose I shouldn't be surprised." She sat in a straight chair near his head and clasped her hands irritably. "You've been calling me constantly. It seems to me that for weeks I've done nothing but rush in here, and always for nothing. You were unconscious."

"I must have been. I'm sorry to have been such a trouble to you."

"Well, you're conscious now." She sat on the edge of the bed, taking his feverish hand, her touch cool and unexpectedly gentle. He burst into tears. "There," she murmured, and bent over to kiss his damp forehead, then straightened herself so that he could read her lips. "You've come back to us, *querido*. We were afraid we'd lost you. Dr. Arrieta didn't think you'd survive."

"It mattered to you?" he croaked.

Now *she* was weeping, an event of such magnitude that he sobbed with happiness. She rubbed her eyes with the back of a wrist. "But of course it mattered. Whom would I quarrel with if you were gone?"

This moment of intense emotion passed too rapidly for Paco's taste, but he was grateful for those tears. "What happened to me?"

"You fainted at the *quinta*."

"The last thing I remember is looking down at Rosarita. Is she well? I didn't hurt her when I fell?"

"She's fine, but very upset. We've all been upset."

"You too, really, *amigita?*"

She placed her hand on his. "Very upset, Paco, especially because we'd been arguing just before you were taken."

He made an ineffectual little effort to shrug. "But we're always arguing, Cadia. That's the way we live. You've said so yourself."

"I know, but I was afraid it was *that* that made you faint."

"It takes a lot more than a minor difference of opinion between us to kill me. What happened afterward?"

"We sent Rosarita to fetch Pablo and then he and Don Tiburcio and I carried you to the carriage. My God, but you're a heavy lump of clay."

He reached for his ribs. "Not so heavy anymore."

"And no wonder. All we've been able to get into you is warm gruel."

"And then?"

"And then we brought you home and sent for Dr. Arrieta. He said the sickness was in your chest and all we could do was keep you very warm, make you perspire."

"You've certainly done that."

"I don't see how you stood it. It's been like Andalucía in August in this room."

"How long?"

"Seven weeks."

"It's November already?" he gasped.

"Almost December."

"My God."

"We sent for a priest. But that wasn't the worst of it, Paco."

"The possibility of my dying, you mean?"

"I'll not let you goad me today. You were raving like a lunatic. It was terrible, frightening."

"Tell me."

"I can't bear to think about it."

"You said I was calling for you. That's not very frightening."

"You were calling me to save you. 'They're coming for me,' you kept shrieking. 'They're going to kill me, Cadia. They're coming after me with knives. They're coming after me with their fangs. Their eyes. Jesus, their eyes! Save me, Cadia, save me.' It was hideous, Paco. I don't dare imagine what dreams you were having."

He squeezed her hand and managed a wan smile. "Mama's monsters again . . . and *you* were in my dreams too, Cadia. *You* were coming after me, too."

"But you were calling for me to *save* you."

"Maybe it's not a contradiction. You're part of my disease, in your special way, and part of my cure at the same time. Like a glass of wine with breakfast to cure me of the aftereffects of a long night spent in the company of the same wine."

Goya's slow recuperation was made somewhat less boring by a succession of visitors whose solicitude touched him deeply. To each he said, "You've come to see an old fellow who's no one anymore, the remains of a man who's melting away with years and sickness. The foolish God is either too cruel or too stupid to let me die." Few were deceived. Moratín put it best. "When Paco has the energy to feel sorry for himself, it's a sure sign of recovery." His most welcome companion was Rosarita, who spent hours of each day with him, making crude copies of drawings he had sketched for her before his illness or of illustrations she found in books. He praised her efforts more lavishly than they deserved, as he did everything she attempted.

It was well into February before he was able to leave his bed and, with the aid of a cane, make his own way about the house. He told Dr. Arrieta and Leocadia (and anyone else who would listen) that his rheumatism had worsened, his eyesight so much poorer that he must obtain more powerful spectacles. But he was improving, all the same. He would live a bit longer.

It was in February too that Moratín excitedly told him that an armed revolt had broken out in Cádiz. The insurrection was spontaneous. A colonel, Rafaelo Riego, was the leader. With a regiment, he and his junior officers were about to embark for

the New World; they had not received their pay for months.
Their equipment was inadequate. Riego complained to his
superiors, then to government officials. When these legitimate
demands were refused, he ordered his men to take possession of
the Cádiz garrison. Other regiments quickly associated themselves with this cause.

"But surely," Goya exclaimed, "Don Fernando has had them
all arrested by now."

"That's the incredible thing," replied Moratín. "The whole
army is sympathetic. Don Fernando has been forced to leave
Madrid. He's gone into hiding, but they'll catch him."

"When they do catch him, Leandro, then what?"

"He's to be made to ratify the Cádiz constitution."

"It's fine news, but I'm damned glad that no one can accuse
me of taking part, because if you can't impose your precious
constitution on him and make him abide by it permanently,
Don Fernando's vengeance will be even bloodier than it was six
years ago."

Within weeks of the Cádiz uprising, Fernando VII was
flushed out by a battalion of his own bodyguards and returned
in disgrace to the capital. The procession, bitterly reminiscent
of his humiliation at Godoy's hands in 1807, was watched in
silent awe by the Madrileños. He consented to issue a proclama-
tion undertaking to govern Spain according to the provisions of
the constitution of 1812, with a cabinet composed of members
of a democratically elected Cortes. He warned Riego that in
spite of their present inertia the people were on his side, "just as
they've always been. I'll live to see you garroted, you and every
liberale who dares to support you."

Along with a majority of intellectuals, Moratín regarded the
king's menace as empty, royal bombast. "When our people
understand what a blessing it is to be ruled justly by Spaniards,
they'll never allow Don Fernando to go back to his bad old
ways."

"I hope to God you're right," said Goya fervently, "because
whether I choose it or not, I've been drawn into this web you
liberales are weaving. The Academia has convened a meeting

where all members are to swear allegiance to this new regime."

"There's no turning back," said Moratín gruffly. "I've told you that."

"And *I* can argue, as I've done before, that Don Fernando has got the people on his side. You can argue that *they're* helpless because the army is with *you*. But wasn't the French army with Bonaparte? Did that stop the people?"

"The people will fight *our* army as they did the French?"

"I don't know, and I'm too old and too sick and too tired to worry about it."

"So," was Moratín's scornful rejoiner, "at the very moment of Spain's first real revolution, her most revolutionary painter decides he's going to desert the cause."

"No," said Goya wearily. "I'm *not* deserting. I'll sign my name to the oath, but nothing more. I'm just going to enjoy my old age, Leandro. I'll amuse myself with Mariano and Rosarita. And I'm going to start daubing away at the walls of my *quinta*."

The paintings which were to adorn the walls of the dining room and salon of his country house would be, as he had so often described his etchings and drawings, "my private art"—yet he gave to them the same sort of planning he devoted to a major commission. Who, he rhetorically inquired, could be a more demanding patron than he himself? After elaborate preparations, he began to apply oil colors directly to the plaster, a method he selected because he could do it by himself.

Leocadia was somewhat mollified by his promise to incorporate a portrait of her in his murals. But when he insisted that she stay out of the rooms until the whole conception was completed, her infuriated curiosity compensated her for this expression of grudging satisfaction. "You're going to commit some atrocity," she muttered. "That's why you're keeping this a secret."

"Secret is the right word, *amada*. I'm going to paint out my secret life, and Spain's secret life. In the house where I'll surely die, I want to be surrounded by all the images that have been burned into my soul in seventy-four years, and the images that have been burned into the Spanish soul over centuries." Wincing with the pain of his rheumatism, he crossed two trembling fingers. "Because Spain and I are just like this. I'm not the patriot Leandro and Ceán wish I were, but I'm more Spanish than either of them, than any of the intellectuals, these so-called *liberales.*"

She shivered. "I don't like the sound of it."

"I told you you wouldn't like it. But it will stir you, move you, frighten you, and that's more important."

The murals of La Quinta del Sordo were two full years in the completion. And during this time, Goya repeatedly refused his mistress access to the rooms in which he spent the two or three hours of every day in which he had the strength to work. His answer was invariable: "I want you to get the full impact of the finished thing, Cadia."

Nothing he had ever before attempted was so "secret," so "private" as these extraordinary paintings. At the end of his life, he was creating something exclusively for himself, for his own delectation; "pleasure" was the wrong word. He was now doing what María had wished him to do almost a quarter of a century before. Not, God knew, that she would have appreciated the finished work any more than she had liked *Los Caprichos.* But here, on the walls of these two rooms, he was depicting his terrifying private world.

On the first panel of the ground-floor, he portrayed Cadia, the gilded whore, ruler of his pornocracy, his sorceress.

Then he created a witches' sabbath, evoking at once his own nightmares and the Spanish obsession with the supernatural, with a demure Cadia looking on.

Judith followed, about to sever the head of Holofernes, with his own scimitar—the triumph of virtue, but bitterly ironic in its savagery.

After this came Saturn, the god of absolute license, of pillage and rapine, devouring his son, consuming the universe.

Next was a savage caricature of a festival of San Isidro, patron of Madrid, its central figure a mad-eyed singer bellowing a

protest of outrage against his country's fate, against the intermi-
nable nightmare night of Spain.

The last panel of this room showed an aged monk and a
wizened, demonic seer—premonitions of death.

In the other room, he painted first a panel in which an old
hag was spooning thin gruel into her toothless mouth, while the
white-shrouded death's head of Famine looked fiercely on.

Next came the Fates—Clotho, Lachesis, and Atropos—deter-
mining Goya's life from infancy to the grave, floating in the air
above a landscape of Aragón.

Two men knee-deep in an upland bog were having at each
other with heavy clubs in a senseless battle to the death—the two
Spains determined to destroy Spain herself.

Six men huddled together in shadows, while one read official
lies from a newspaper. Yet they had only to look up, at the men
killing each other, to see the truth. The lies were more satisfying.

A man sat cross-legged, masturbating, while two old crones
looked on gleefully. Spiritually, all Spain was committing
Onan's sin.

Pilgrims paused on a journey between the boundless aspiration that seemed possible at birth and the empty darkness that
was death's only assurance.

The penultimate panel related to himself. He was plucked
from a lofty citadel and borne off through the air by a rose-
cloaked kidnapper—Cadia, thief of his tranquillity.

And finally catharsis—purity. The black head of a dog, alert,
eager, inquiring, tranquil, whose features were apparent just
behind the edge of a rise that led . . . to what? Nothing?
Everything?

"Now you can look," he told Leocadia, and stood aside to let
her pass through the doorway of the ground-floor dining room
from which he had barred her for so long. She entered with
diffidence, for the decoration of this and the room above had
taken on in her consciousness, as in his, an element of mystery,
of a sacred rite like self-immolation, whose recesses of subtlety

and symbolism she knew she could never fathom. How had it been possible for the gregarious Paco to work for so long alone and with such a fever of intensity, sharing his secret life only with these walls and with his pillow?

The murals of the two rooms struck her with a force she disbelieved; the effect was palpable. There were no words to add to her gasp of distress, her wondering dismay. "I *told* you you wouldn't like them," he said at last.

"Is this what lives in your mind?"

"It's what lives in Spain's mind too."

"God help us," she murmured. Then she collected herself. "What fine surroundings for Rosarita to grow up in."

"Don't you want her to learn all about life?"

"*I* can tell her all she needs to know about that. These things are just grisly."

Ceán was the first of his friends to see the murals, and he wasted no time in pronouncing judgment. "These are the painted rantings of a madman."

"You may be right," said Goya calmly.

"You agree with me?"

"It doesn't matter, Ceán. I've found something in myself that would make ten seasons in a madhouse perfectly endurable. I've discovered pure painting."

The country's most distinguished historian of art could only guffaw at this pompous remark. "Pure? This is like so much *gazpacho* hurled against your walls. It's all ugliness. What's *pure, amigo,* is the ugliness."

"But pure," said Goya obdurately. "I *thought* I knew what purity meant when I was making the San Antonio frescoes, the ones you had such mixed feelings about. But now I see that I'd taken only the first step of the journey toward real purity, absolute purity."

"It's disgusting, and disturbing."

"Good. Is that all?"

"These messes can't give you pleasure, Paco, I mean aesthetic pleasure."

"But they *do,* because they're unique. No one has ever tried to do what I've done. You should be paying attention, Ceán, as our historian. It's as close as I can come to a faithful transcription of what's in my soul—*my* soul made graphic, *Spain's* soul made graphic."

"If that's so, there's only one thing to do: to pray for your soul."

Goya laughed. "Why are you historians so often reactionaries? Are you so obsessed with the past that you can't make yourselves look ahead? There's no need to worry about the future of art, Ceán. Think of it. Here I am, a product of the Spanish darkness, our first really good painter since Velázquez, and yet I've found a way, all by myself, of saying something absolutely new. Just imagine what the French will do when they learn to explore the areas of the soul which are revealed by their Enlightenment."

"But painting has to have grace, beauty, poetry, order."

"Rational painting, you mean, painting that pays, painting you approve of because it doesn't tax your imagination, doesn't tear you apart emotionally. Yes, you're right. That kind of painting demands the qualities you speak of. But I've released art from the shackles of mere prettiness."

"You just want to offend convention, to spit in the eye of the society that has supported you for so long and so generously."

"I've created a new direction, a new dimension." Goya roared with laughter. "I'm the greatest *acalofilo* of all, Ceán. I've made my two rooms the chapter houses of hell."

sixteen

⅀ DURING THE TWO YEARS of his obsessive preoccupation
with the murals of his *quinta,* Goya learned only now and then
(with little interest) of events occurring beyond the confines of
his country house. It seemed at first that the future was likely
to develop as Moratín had so sanguinely predicted. The king
apparently had resigned himself to the new order he found so
odious, though his official performance was less than ardent.
Needed reforms were commenced. The *liberales* were optimistic; their fondest hopes were, if still too slowly for their tastes,
being realized; the day of a new Spain had dawned.

From the outset, however, there were developments which
perceptive observers had viewed with alarm. For by no means
the entire intelligentsia was pleased with the changes imposed
on the king. Protest took various forms, and its intensity varied
from province to province. The most dangerous was the creation of a loose-knit organization which called itself the Army
of the Faith, a widely distributed collection of *guerrillero*
counterrevolutionaries who preyed on government convoys as
had their predecessors during the French occupation. These
raids were financially very profitable; that they could be made
in the name of Don Fernando was so much the better.

The king instituted a quasi-secret regency to function in his
personal interest for the duration of what he privately called his
"captivity." For public consumption, he maintained the fiction

that this body had evolved spontaneously as an expression of the popular will to free him from his enslavement by the army and the *liberales*. Acute students of the Spanish scene noted gloomily that the new organization operated along much the same lines as had the Cádiz junta of occupation times, directing the activities of the Army of the Faith and contriving to keep pressure on the men who now wielded power in the name of the people.

Since early 1821, Don Fernando had been dispatching abroad a stream of emissaries to the rulers of the new Holy Alliance, signatories to the Treaty of Vienna of 1815. He pleaded for their intercession. The main object of these entreaties was Louis XVIII, a Bourbon cousin who had acceded to the throne of France after Napoleon's downfall. The Spanish king hoped the French monarch would want to suppress a movement on his frontiers that might inspire a reiteration of the revolution that had doomed the *ancien régime* of his forebears.

The question of a military intervention in Spain was discussed at a meeting of the Alliance members in Verona. Louis XVIII was the most forceful advocate of such action, Britain its most vehement opponent. The government of George IV feared that such an adventure (which must of necessity be largely French) might augur a recrudescence of Gallic territorial ambitions. The matter dropped. Louis XVIII was disappointed. His new foreign minister, Chateaubriand, feared this failure to try to arrest the cancer of liberalism which, in his view, would soon attack the precarious monarchical structure of all Europe. Early in 1823, the French king announced that if other members of the Holy Alliance refused to be decisive, he would himself take steps to "preserve the crown of Spain for a descendant of Henri IV." A couple of months later, the Alliance sanctioned what it couldn't prevent. On April 7, a French army of 100,000 men, under the command of a royal brother, the Duc d'Angoulême, crossed the Spanish border from St.-Jean-de-Luz. On being apprised of this alarming news, Don Fernando's custodians whisked him from Madrid to Cádiz, where, they wrongly believed, they could resist any French siege.

What Napoleon and his brilliant marshals had been unable to accomplish in nearly six years of war, Angoulême unhurriedly achieved in less than five months. Fernando's appraisal of the popular will was once again vindicated. Whatever the convictions of the officers, they were plainly not shared by most of the rank and file of the army, who displayed the want of zeal that Wellington had so unkindly ascribed to them a decade before. Each encounter became a rout. The French army was greeted everywhere with delight. Veterans of the Bonapartist years rubbed their incredulous eyes and kept looking toward the hills, expecting a repetition of the humiliating defeat of Bailén. None occurred. As Goya had feared, the people had no interest in a constitutional government; they *wanted* fetters.

By the end of August, Angoulême's forces stood before Cádiz. On the night of the thirtieth, at nearby Trocadero, the duke eliminated the last elements of the demoralized Spanish army. Spain was not conquered by the French, but by her own people. The soldiers in the fortress compelled their officers to surrender. The war was over.

The French general took custody of Don Fernando and returned him to a Madrid that welcomed his restoration as if, observed a startled Angoulême to an aide, "he were the reincarnation of Our Lord." Immediately after his deliverance, the Spanish king had readily agreed with Louis XVIII's compassionate admonition that from this moment on, he must rule his country more intelligently—by which he meant more leniently, avoiding the promulgation of any decree that might revive opposition to his authority and, above all, eschewing any acts of reprisal against those who had preempted power. The message was clear: French intercession had been provoked by Chateaubriand's desire to stem the tide of liberalism that was rising to menace every western continental throne, not by a wish to fan its flames by creating more martyrs to its cause. Liberals everywhere would look for example to Spain. If Fernando tried to resume his former style of rule, the ultraconservative aims of France and Austria would be ill served.

Scarcely had he taken his place on the throne, however, than the king renounced his promise to Angoulême. To the wildly approving cheers of the multitudes gathered in the Puerta del Sol, he asserted that this agreement had been extorted—as had his earlier concession to the Cortes in 1814. The French commander was invited to look on helplessly as Fernando VII initiated yet another orgy of vengeance, even more savage than that of a decade earlier.

Angoulême protested in terms he was loath to employ with a reigning monarch. "It is with regret," he confided to the Spanish king, "that I am obliged to tell Your Majesty that France's efforts to liberate you will have been for naught if you persist in maintaining the pernicious system of government which led to the misfortunes that befell you in 1820. In the fortnight since Your Majesty regained the throne, we have heard of nothing but arrests and arbitrary decrees. As a result, anxiety, terror, and discontent are beginning to spread everywhere in your domain."

Don Fernando knew better than to heed these warnings. His security lay not with French support but with his own people. And vengeance would be his. "If the bull is wounded," he said, "we kill him, to put him out of his misery. I say this," he added unnecessarily, "from the standpoint of the *torero,* not the bull." If it served any purpose at all, Angoulême's denunciation spurred Don Fernando to even greater excesses of vindictive rage. The purge of the autumn of 1823 became known as *"el terror blanco"*—though its victims failed to comprehend the adjective "white," for its processes were very bloody.

Angoulême wrote to his brother in Versailles that there was no further reason for his remaining in Spain. "This country will go on tearing itself to pieces for years to come." To that extent at least, Chateaubriand's goal had been achieved. The menace of Spanish liberalism, timid at its most aggressive, was suppressed for almost a century.

As a gesture of mercy, Angoulême promised a safe-conduct to any of Fernando's enemies who could reach one of his encampments around the capital—an act of magnanimity that enraged the hate-crazed king who screamed for more and more victims, more and more blood. No one, this time, must be allowed to escape his revenge. Nevertheless, hundreds of Madrileños, including Ceán Bermúdez and Moratín, took advantage of the Frenchman's offer. They urged Goya to do the same. He refused. "No, I want to die in Spain," he told his friends who stood with him in his dining room, confronted on all sides by the nightmare paintings he had completed the year before. "This is my Pantheon," he declaimed pontifically. "I'll never be made to desert it. Besides, I've had no hand in these things. There's no price on *my* head."

"Perhaps not, Paco," responded Moratín, "but there's a warrant for the arrest of Guillermo Weiss for serving in the militia against Don Fernando."

"That has nothing to do with me."

"But Leocadia may be in danger. If *she's* in danger, how can *you* escape condemnation? And you *did* sign the Academia's oath of allegiance to the constitution."

Javier made the same point, but in far different terms. "They may confiscate our property because of your association with that woman."

"What a low, greedy dog you are. How can you speak of Cadia that way? You and Gumersinda did everything but put her bodily into my bed. Have you no loyalty at all?"

"It has nothing to do with loyalty, Papa, *or* Cadia. But you'd not want your house and everything in it taken from you, would you? In view of what Guillermo has done, you can't expect that Cadia could take possession of it."

"Well, if you think I'm going to give it to *you,* you're out of your mind. But I'll transfer title to Mariano. Cadia and Rosarita are taken care of in my will."

To this plan, the painter's son understandably offered no objection. The next day, Goya shifted ownership of the Quinta del Sordo and all its furnishings to Mariano. However, in spite of the increasing fury of the king's scourge, he remained for some months convinced that neither he nor his mistress was in danger of falling victim of the royal wrath.

Young Guillermo Weiss dramatically altered the position one

black December night, when he flung his ragged, haggard person into the presence of the old man and his mother, his eyes aglow with fear, breathless and exhausted. "They nearly caught me this time," he gasped.

Leocadia showed no sympathy for the plight of her eighteen-year-old son. In fact, she hadn't recognized him at first, and found his sweaty embrace repulsive. She stamped her little foot in displeasure. "So what did you decide to do, *idioto?* You led them right to our door."

"I don't think I was followed," he answered apologetically. "They weren't in sight when I came in. I came down the hillside behind the house."

She grunted skeptically. "Even if they didn't see you enter, this is certainly the logical place for them to look." She clasped her hands together and began to sob. "Oh, God, why did you have to get involved? You sacrificed everything, your education, your social position, your whole future, everything."

Still trying to catch his breath and recover his calm, the boy looked at his mother scornfully. "Because I thought it was the right thing to do at the time, and I *still* think so."

"And when they catch you, and garrote you or shoot you down, will you think so still?"

"I shall, Mama," he replied evenly.

She looked at Goya, her alarm giving way once more to irritation. "*You* don't seem upset. You don't understand how desperate things are for us. Something's got to be done."

"It's very simple," he replied without dismay. "We'll have to hide ourselves for a while."

"Where? Where is it safe? Who'll dare to take us in, with this . . . this fugitive on our hands?"

"I'll look into it in the morning." He looked at Guillermo. "Stay away from the windows. Don't worry about the servants. They'll not betray you. Now go and get something to eat. Have a bit of *coñac*. You're pale as death. Get some sleep and don't worry. We'll see this thing through together, Guillermo. I couldn't be prouder of you if you were my own son. But of course," he added bitterly, "my own son would never have done what *you* did."

The youth wept and kissed the painter's hand. "Thank you, Don Paco."

Leocadia snorted. "Why didn't you go to your father's house?"

"I did. He wouldn't say a word to me. He just looked at me and slammed the door in my face." He turned back to Paco. "You were my last hope. I didn't *want* to get you into this trouble."

"It's all right, Guillermo."

His mistress laughed harshly. "Isidoro isn't so stupid as I thought."

Goya sprang from his chair with an energy inspired by rage and slapped her face. She soberly placed a hand over her wounded cheek and eyed him wonderingly, at once pleased and offended. No words came to her mind before Rosarita intruded with her tears and demanded that they stop quarreling.

Goya was too old to be frightened by the menace introduced by Guillermo's appearance in his life. A man of seventy-seven, so highly reputed, was an unlikely candidate for the worst of the king's wrath. But he *was* alarmed for the safety of Leocadia and Rosarita. He nevertheless remained steadfast in his reassurances to his mistress' son. He was touched by the boy's gratitude and flattered that he had come to him for help.

Moreover, despite protestations of his innocence of complicity in the revolution and the "captivity" of the king, Paco would, in retrospect, have loved to lay claim to a significant role in those events, however futile they had eventually proved. He supposed it was what Moratín called the Spanish death wish. But these were his stairway thoughts, useless yearnings revealed to him only after the opportunity to give them purpose had passed forever.

In canvassing for possible hiding places, he was painfully surprised to discover among acquaintances, who had less cause than he to fear royal anger, such looks of naked panic when he proposed that they give shelter to him and his family. As a last resort, he called on the architect Tiburcio Pérez, whose first question was, "Why the devil didn't you come to me right away?"

Goya laughed. "Everyone else asks why I came at all."

Paco and Pérez agreed that it might be wiser if the artist himself found shelter elsewhere, though Leocadia accused him of trying to avoid arrest in the company of the hunted Guillermo. "It's just the opposite, *querida*. If they find me with him, it would be worse for *him*. They'd suspect him of being mixed up with more important things than just carrying a musket in the hills, because so many of my friends are what Don Fernando calls traitors."

"Where will you go?"

"Tiburcio has arranged something for me. Don't worry. I'll stay in close touch with you. As soon as it's safe, the three of you will go to Bordeaux. Moratín and Ceán will look after you if you leave before I do. But I'll *be* there, sooner or later."

She refused to be comforted. "I'll never see you again. What will become of us? If they catch you, they'll kill you, just as they killed Colonel Riego only the other day."

"*If* they catch me . . . But they won't. That's the point of all this hugger-mugger—to take as few chances as possible."

They parted tearfully in the winter's night. Leocadia and her two children went to the house of Pérez, Goya to the residence of Don José Duaso y Latro. Duaso was a canon of Madrid's cathedral, a conservative so resolute in his creed that the restored despot had confided to him the post of official press censor. The paradox, however, was that this intelligent cleric had long entertained a Christian sympathy for the plight of those whose opinions he opposed. He offered them the protection of his name and the hospitality of his dwelling. Like Goya, Duaso was from Aragón, a coincidence that figured in the invitation he had extended through Pérez. This refuge was made doubly secure, and doubly paradoxical, by the frequent presence of his nephew, Don Ramón Satue, an *alcalde*.

Given the distressing times, Duaso's reception was movingly generous. Long an admirer of the artist's work, he lavished his guest with praise, quartered him in the finest room, and regaled him with amusing accounts of the king's petulance while in the hands of the men he was now persecuting. Don José diffidently asked Paco to paint a portrait of his nephew—a substantial, sprawling, bibulous, perpetually disheveled man of charm and wit. The canvas, Don Ramón to the life, was the most unbuttoned, natural portrait Goya had ever made. But when it came to making a picture of his host, a project which the modest Don José repeatedly postponed, the old painter found himself possessed by an unaccountable lassitude. After four abortive beginnings, the canon begged him to give up. Paco was as embarrassed as he was baffled, for he wanted nothing better than to express, as only he could, his gratitude for the handsome and hazardous hospitality so genially offered. "After sixty-odd years of work," he complained, "you'd think I could paint a portrait automatically. But I've never done a good one that way."

"Then," said the tactful Duaso, "I'll treasure these unfinished ones more than I would a completed picture."

The cause of this lapse was not apparent to Paco. As the weeks passed, he attributed it variously—to the absence of Leocadia, for instance. It was their first separation. Her frequent notes to him were terse and only rarely affectionate, the tenor identical: The three of them were as well as could be expected, but they were anxious to leave Spain. What was he doing about this? He came gradually to perceive that the roots of his gloom were deeper than he had first thought. He read into his despair an exacerbation of the emotions that had produced the murals of the *quinta*—his sense of identification with Spain; and its converse, his alienation from Spain.

No matter what he had said to the contrary, he had cherished a secret hope for a brighter future for his country, a hope against hope. But now his reservoir of ingenuous faith was dried up. There was no hope; there was no remedy. The most ardent patriot must finally comprehend, as had the Duc d'Angoulême, that Spain (like the embattled men on the wall of Goya's *quinta*) would always be at war with herself.

His creative energies were spent as well. Never again would

he find the strength of inspiration for anything so grandiose as
the murals. That being so, what of value remained for him in
the sorry half-life he was now leading? To survive? But in itself,
survival was unthinkable without Cadia and Rosarita.

Months passed. The king's rage showed few signs of diminu-
tion, and Goya took only the smallest comfort from the knowledge that Guillermo was still safe. He supposed there was
consolation too in Duaso's assurance that as yet no warrant had
been issued for the arrest of Spain's greatest painter. But this
protracted period of waiting deepened his depression. He might
die here, like a trapped animal. He'd not be the first to suffer
such a fate—but he was repeatedly struck by the perversity of his
circumstance: He was avoiding prosecution for offenses he
merely *wished* he had committed, for crimes he hadn't had
either the courage or inclination to perpetrate—save that of
harboring Guillermo.

Anxieties for Leocadia and Rosarita added a counterpoint of
alarm to the pulsations of intensifying gloom. And, worst of all,
perhaps, he was bored, oppressed by the silence that often
inspired him to wild, redundant, hapless rages. Thirty years of
deafness had failed to inure him to his condition. He yearned
for the conviviality of his old life, for the gatherings at the
taberna, and was forced to settle for the attentive solicitude of
the good Duaso.

Death must certainly be approaching quickly now. Well, why
not? God had permitted him to complete the *quinta* murals.
What was left? Suicide? This idea, so repugnant to a good
Catholic, slowly but easily insinuated itself into his mind and
was resisted with increasing difficulty. He kept hoping that
tomorrow would prove happier or more interesting or more
dangerous—more *anything* than today. And each morning, he
knew more bitterly than ever that the hope had been vain. Yet
he clung to life because, in the end, he was curious, and because
he believed in survival for its own sake.

It was as well that Goya didn't lose hope.

Thrice a widower, Don Fernando took a fourth wife, who
influenced him to declare an amnesty on May 1, 1824. The next

day, the old painter petitioned the grand majordomo of the
court for permission to leave Spain, purportedly to seek treat-
ment for his rheumatism at the baths of Plombières, in France.
Leocadia, with whom he was joyfully reunited, was perplexed
by this move. "Since there's an amnesty, what's the point of
leaving the country?"

"I don't trust Don Fernando. He's contradicted himself before. Why shouldn't he do it again?"

"Why bother with a leave of absence, if you don't mean to
return?"

He grinned. "I thought *you'd* understand right away. If they
give me a leave, my salary as Pintor de Cámara will continue.
Fifty thousand reales a year is a lot of money. If I went into
exile, the king would stop the payments."

It was an argument whose logic seemed immaculate to his
mistress. "What about me and the children?"

"If we all went together, the authorities might suspect I
wasn't planning to come back, so Don José is arranging separate
passage for the three of you."

"Will they allow Guillermo to go?"

"We can only hope so."

"I'll not leave without him."

Goya smiled uncertainly. "You suddenly find," he inquired
sarcastically, "that after all these years of indifference to him,
you have an abiding love? You astonish me, Cadia. Mother love,
from you?"

"That shows how little you know me."

"You love Guillermo?"

"Now that I've got to know him again, of course. I love
Rosarita too. Didn't I give birth to them?"

"But you weren't very happy about it."

"And didn't Guillermo come to me for help?"

"To you or to me? And what was your reaction? Or have you
forgotten? Or do you *choose* to forget?"

"I was upset."

"You certainly were."

"Well, he's safe now," she said impatiently. "That's all that matters. And he's got to get out of the country."

Goya agreed abstractedly, but remained puzzled. There was an underlying fact to which she wasn't referring. "We'll do the best we can."

"I'd not feel safe traveling all the way to Bordeaux with no one but Rosarita for company."

He laughed. "Mother love, indeed. Why didn't you say that in the first place?"

Goya had to wait until the end of May for permission to absent himself and was disappointed to note that the leave had been granted for only six months. Still, it was preferable to no leave at all, though it meant that he must depart at once, before passage for Leocadia, Rosarita, and Guillermo had been provided. According to Duaso, the safe-conduct for his stepson was proving difficult to obtain. Amnesty or no, Fernando VII was ill disposed toward anyone, however youthful, who had borne arms against his interest. But the canon was confident that in the end his negotiations would be fruitful, and he urged Goya to hold to his plan to leave Madrid immediately.

Javier promised to see to the details that he left undone. He would see that the bank paid Julio and Estéve their monthly pensions, which were to continue until the artist's death, would see to the proper storage of his work, and, when the time came, would attend to provision for the journey of his mistress and her children to Bordeaux. Elimination of these trifling impediments made parting no less painful. To contemplate leaving Madrid forever, unexpectedly weakened the old man's will.

Madrid now seemed a cipher to him. The *taberna* was an empty cell, a prison for the memories of friends who were in the exile he was seeking. The palaces of the Albas and Osunas could compel his excitement no longer. Only two structures retained their power for him—San Antonio de la Florida, and his own *quinta,* but those holds were strong. The day before he left for France, Goya made a solitary, sentimental pilgrimage to the little church on the outskirts of the city and stared up at the frescoes he had, with little Julio, created twenty-five years before. They astonished him, so much were they of another life, another kind of life, accomplished when he was another man, happy, ebullient, outgoing; in the time of María. Now she was dead. Spain was dying. But here, thank God, he once was happy.

His farewell to the Quinta del Sordo invoked a quite different order of emotion. He looked at the murals to which he had given two years of his waning life, the final flames of his anger. He had to shudder, just as Leocadia had done when she saw them for the first time. He stood in silence beside the weeping Julio. The coach, packed for the journey to France, was at the door, awaiting his pleasure. But for a moment longer he gave himself utterly to the walls within which he had fully expected, and hoped, to die.

As he was no longer the man who had created the frescoes of San Antonio, he was no longer the painter of these ferocious murals. He understood them no more. When they were done, *that* Goya had died. What Goya remained? An old man seeking shelter and tranquillity in an alien land—doing the very thing he'd sworn he'd never do, leaving home, because home was hell, the hell he had transcribed on these walls. Would Spain always be the Spain of his walls?

He wiped his eyes and turned his back, concentrating his attention on the door. He touched Ascensio's sleeve. There could be no words between them. They had lost their voices in their tears. He limped beside him toward the door and waited as his friend, sobbing helplessly, opened it and, as ever, stood aside, silently insisting that his master precede him. Goya passed through, waited for Julio to follow, and then closed the door firmly behind him. His trembling old hand lingered on the knob, for when he released it he knew he would have left Spain forever.